A MORTAL SONG

MEGAN CREWE

Printed in the United States of America

First Printing, 2016

ISBN 13: 978-0-9939806-9-5

Cover design by Carlos Quevedo
Photo credit: David Mackenzie
Interior Design by Write Dream Repeat Book Design LLC

Another World Press
PO Box 98034 Carlaw
Toronto, ON M4M 1J0
CANADA

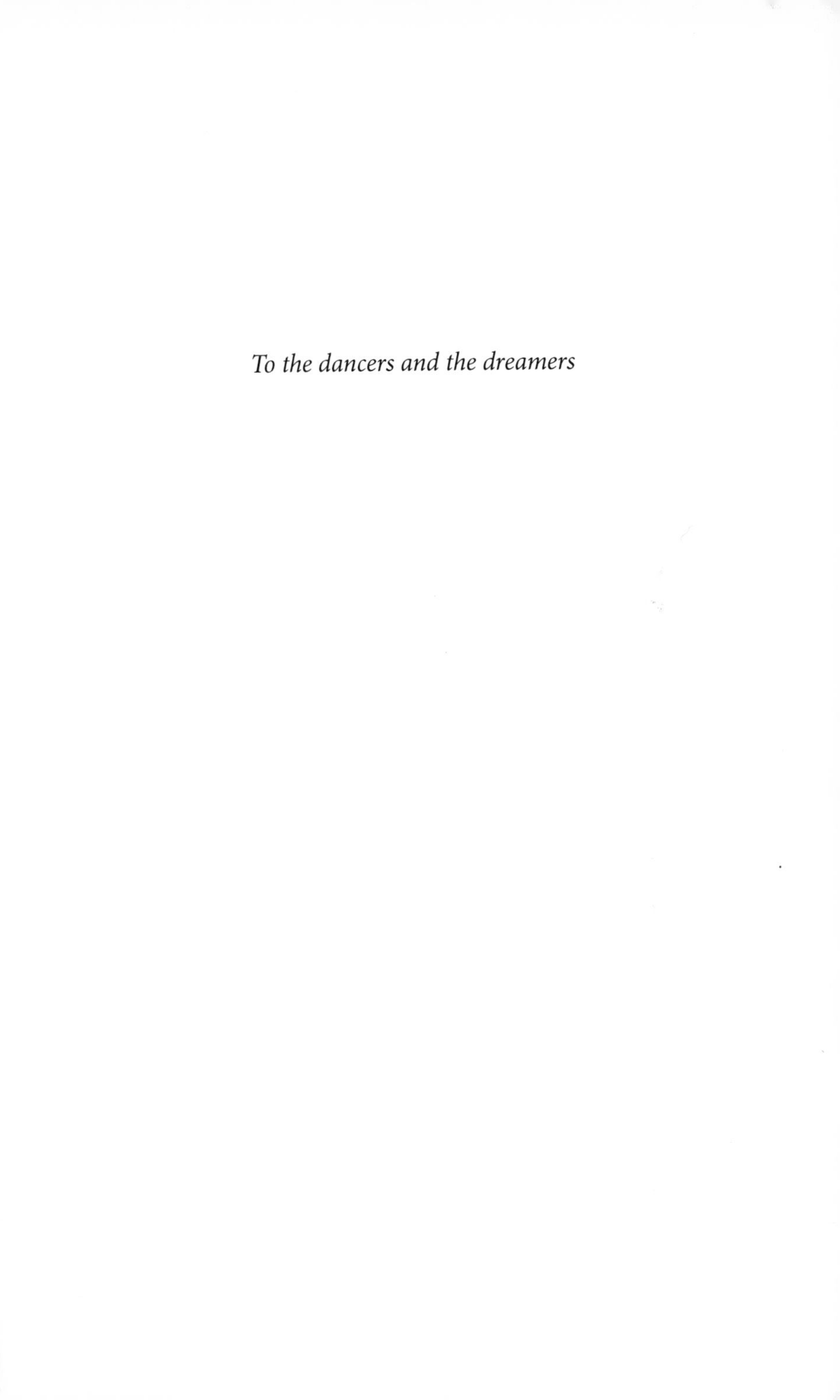

To the dancers and the dreamers

ONE

ON THE afternoon of my seventeenth birthday, I came down the mountain to visit a dying man.

The affliction had revealed itself slowly. I'd first noticed the tremor of discord in Mr. Nagamoto's ki—the life energy that glowed inside him—three months ago. Over the weeks, that tremor had swollen into a cloud, dimming the ki at the side of his abdomen. Today I arrived to find the cloud twisting and churning while he typed at his computer in the living room. It was draining his already inconceivably short human life away, but neither he nor his wife knew it was there.

They didn't know *I* was there either. I kept myself invisible as I watched from beside the narrow sofa, as I always did when I visited the households in the town at Mt. Fuji's foot. The people living in those homes looked much like myself and many of the other kami, but it was their differences that fascinated me. They shifted from one mood to another in patterns too complex to predict, and their bodies changed quickly too, for better or for ill.

As I'd drifted through the beige walls of this house over the years, Mr. and Mrs. Nagamoto had grown plumper and their hair grayer. I'd joined their children's games unseen and silently shared their laughter before the son and then the daughter had transformed into adults leaving for college. And now this sickness had come.

I stepped closer to Mr. Nagamoto. Seeing how his disease had spread made me feel sick myself, but that was why I'd come. My resolve solidified inside me, overshadowing the worries that had driven me from the palace. If I really wanted to consider myself a part of this family's lives, I should help them—help *him*.

I'd have healed him if I could, but the cloud of decay was so large and fierce I doubted even the most practiced healers of my kind would have been able to defeat it. We kami had other skills, though. I knew a few in the palace whose focus was tending to the dying. When a worthy person or creature passed away, they let it hold on to life a little longer by transferring its spirit into something it had loved. I thought Mr. Nagamoto might like to linger in the cypress tree in the yard or one of the koi in the pond beneath it, where he could continue watching over his family.

Any kami was capable of doing that. Any kami but me. Mother and Father hadn't let me learn the sacred practices yet.

I had so much more power than anyone in this town—more ki in my little toe than Mr. Nagamoto had in his whole fragile human body. It wasn't *right* for me to stand by and let his life slip away unrecognized. My parents would just have to accept that it was time I started serving the purpose I was meant to.

I bowed my farewell to Mr. Nagamoto and slipped outside. The summer sun was dipping low in the stark blue sky. Midori, my dragonfly kami friend who always accompanied me on my ventures off the mountain, flitted around me with a mischievous tickle of ki that dared me to try to reach the palace faster than her.

I took off down the street. Midori darted past me, but in a moment I'd matched her pace, sending ki to my feet to speed them on. The houses streaked by, clay walls and red-and-gray tiled roofs standing behind low fences of concrete or metal. It was strange to think most of these people barely believed my kind existed, spoke and prayed to us only out of habit, with no more faith than they had in the characters they watched on their TVs. But as long as kami lived on Mt. Fuji and elsewhere, we'd continue to act as guardians of the natural world, doing all we could to keep the crops growing, to fend off the worst storms, and to calm the fire that lurked deep inside the mountain.

Or, at least, the others did, and I hoped soon I'd find my focus too.

Midori pulled a little ahead of me, and I pushed my feet faster. I was the only one to have been born in the palace in as long as my honorary auntie Ayame could remember. She loved sharing tales of my birth even more than she did those of heroes and sages. "It was a blessing for our chosen rulers," she'd told me. "When your mother and father announced they were expecting, the celebrations lasted for weeks." The parties commemorating my birthday weren't anywhere near as extensive, but kami still traveled from far abroad to pay their respects. Surely while my parents were thinking of how much I meant to them, they'd recognize how much this request meant to me?

In a few minutes, Midori and I had left the town behind and

started up the forested slope. An odd quiet filled the pine woods we dashed through. No animals stirred, except for a couple of squirrels that rushed this way and that as if in alarm before scurrying away. I slowed, forgetting the race as I peered amid the branches for the owl kami who normally maintained the harmony in this part of the forest. "Daichi?" I called. There was no sign of him.

He must have already headed up to join the party. I'd mention my observations when I saw him in the palace.

I directed a fresh rush of ki through my legs. As I ran on, my feet hardly touched the ground. Farther up the mountain, the rustling of moving bodies and the lilt of birdsong reached my ears. Nothing was terribly wrong, then.

"Sora!"

The voice brought me to a halt. Midori settled on my hair. A tall figure was striding toward us through the trees. My heart skipped a beat.

"Takeo," I said, trying not to sound as breathless as I felt after that run.

Takeo stopped a few paces away and dipped into a low bow. He was wearing his fancier uniform with the silver embroidery along the jacket's billowing sleeves. In contrast with the deep green of the fabric, his mahogany-brown eyes gleamed as brightly as if they were made of polished wood. With his shoulder-length hair pulled back in a formal knot, the lacquered sheath of his sword at his hip, and the arc of his bow at his shoulder, he looked every inch the palace guard. But he smiled at me, warm and open, as a friend.

If I'd had a camera like the ones the tourists carried, I'd have captured the look he was giving me for keeps. Although then I'd have to explain why I wanted to, and I hadn't worked up enough courage to confess these new feelings yet. He might see me as a friend, but before that I was the daughter of his rulers, a child he'd been assigned to watch over and teach since I was seven years old, when he'd arrived at the mountain barely out of childhood himself, seeking to serve.

What if he couldn't think of me as more? Just imagining him telling me as much, struggling to let me down gently, made my stomach tie itself into knots.

I pushed those thoughts aside. I had another goal tonight. Takeo was the only kami close to my age I knew, and *he* had been training in all the skills of the kami since he was much younger than me.

"I was a little worried when I couldn't find you in the palace," Takeo said. "But then I remembered your favorite place to visit. You were in town?"

"Yes," I said. "Is something wrong?"

"Only that Ayame is looking for you. She's fretting that she won't have enough time to get you ready. You know how she is."

With a wisp of amusement, Midori cast an image into my head of Ayame calling in her usual frantic voice, "Where is that girl?" I wasn't late, but unlike humans, who might be panicking one moment and easygoing a few minutes later, kami were much more strict in their natures. It was Ayame's nature to fret over absolutely everything.

"Hush," I said to the dragonfly with a suppressed groan. *She* wasn't the one Ayame would be fussing over when we got back.

"I'm sorry," I added to Takeo.

"It's no problem at all," he said, his smile widening. "I'm pleased to escort you home.

"Is everything all right with *you*?" he asked as we continued up the mountain. "On your birthday, I'd have thought you'd be too busy to leave the palace."

The question reminded me of the niggle of doubt that had drawn me to the Nagamotos' house so I could steel myself to challenge Mother and Father's judgment tonight. "I just needed to get away from the busy-ness for a bit," I said, and bit my lip. "Takeo, do you think if I ask my parents to let me start learning the sacred practices, they'll say yes?"

"Of course," he said. "Why wouldn't they?"

"I don't know," I said. "They've avoided giving me *any* responsibility—haven't you noticed? Last year Kaito offered to teach me the way of the rain, and the year before that Manami suggested I accompany her to her shrine, and both times Mother and Father said that I shouldn't have that sort of pressure on me before I'm fully of age. But I've been able to best you with ki since I was twelve—I nearly beat you with a *sword* last week. I know every inch of this mountain. Isn't it time I learned our actual duties?"

"You should tell them that's what you want," Takeo said, ducking under a branch. "I've never known your parents to be anything less than understanding. They'll find the right answer."

The worries I'd squashed down in Mr. Nagamoto's house surged back up. What if the answer was that they had good reason not to trust me with responsibility? Grandfather always said, "The one truth I know is, we can't help but be the way we are." Which meant if I were capable, it should be as clear as Ayame's fretting, as Mother's cool collectedness, as Father's indomitable compassion.

So much of the time, nothing inside me felt clear at all. I could believe with every fiber of my being that I was ready, and a moment later be completely uncertain again. Maybe that was the problem. Maybe my parents had seen that strangeness in me and decided I was... inadequate. I'd never heard anyone else in the palace mention feeling so jumbled up, so I'd tried not to show it, but it had only gotten worse in the last few years.

I glanced sideways at Takeo. "Did you ever..." I said, and hesitated. "Have you ever felt you needed to do something, but at the same time you weren't sure you *could* do it, and—"

My voice broke when he turned his head toward me. His handsome face was puzzled.

"If there's something I can't do, I leave it to those who can," he said. "None of us can do everything." His smile returned, softer this time. "But I think you're strong enough to accomplish just about anything you decide to attempt, Sora."

Even though he hadn't understood what I'd been getting at, his smile steadied me. Was it really so unexpected that Mother and Father might want their only child to relish her youthful years before turning toward duty? "If you give enough to the Earth, it gives you joy in return," Ayame liked to say. "You are the joy it gave your parents." Every time my parents called me their "gift," every time the other kami bowed to me, every time I stood on the mountainside with its power echoing through me, I remembered those words. The Earth itself had brought me into being to do its work. I was meant to be here, to fulfill that promise. I needed to keep my mind on that and not these ridiculous fears.

For a few dazzling seconds, I let the full force of my ki rush through me in a hum of light. The landscape blurred around me. Midori's grip on my hair tightened as she sent me a glimmering thrill of exhilaration.

Then I reined myself back. At my fastest, I'd leave Takeo behind. I dodged the pale trunk of a birch—and nearly darted right through a ghost.

"Oh!" I said, jerking to a halt. "Excuse me, Miss Sakai. I didn't see you."

The filmy young woman bobbed her head to me. Wan and wide-eyed, Miss Sakai had been floating around this part of the mountain for several months. I'd gotten it out of a maple kami that her boyfriend had been walking with her along the paths and pushed her over one of the sharper inclines. She'd broken her neck. "I imagine she's stuck around to give him a piece of her mind," the maple had added, but Miss Sakai always seemed calm when I saw her.

Not today, though. I schooled my gaze away from the space partway down her legs where, as with all ghosts, her translucent body dissolved completely, leaving no knees, calves, or feet beneath her. Her ki was jittering. She stretched her mouth into an over-wide grin.

"I wasn't watching either," she said, too brightly. "So sorry." Her eyes darted from me to Takeo and back. "I should be wishing you a happy birthday, shouldn't I! The big party is about to start?"

"Thank you," I said. "Yes."

I wondered if I should invite her to join us, but she spun

around before I could say anything else. "Have a wonderful time!" she said, and shot off down the slope. In a few seconds, she'd disappeared amid the trees.

"That was strange," I said.

"It's unusual for the spirits of the dead to cling to this world at all," Takeo pointed out. "I suppose that can't help but affect their minds."

We crossed the spring that babbled just below the palace's entrance and stepped through the grove of cherry trees to the shallow cave on the far side. Any human who happened upon this spot would see nothing more than a small hollow. But when we walked through the cool stone, which tingled over my skin as if I'd passed under a waterfall, we emerged into the main hall of the great palace that housed most of Mt. Fuji's kami.

Inside, I released the energy that had held me invisible and settled back into my more comfortable corporeal form. At once, my surroundings felt more solid too: the wooden floor smooth beneath my feet, the muted sunlight that gleamed through the ceiling panels warming my long black hair. On either side of us, sliding doors painted with images of flowers and sweeping branches broke the dark wood of the walls. The thrum of the mountain's ki washed over me in welcome.

Farther down the main hall, two palace attendants were leading a group of guests toward the large public rooms. The smell of the grand dinner being prepared filled the air—kami could take all our nourishment directly from the Earth when we needed to, but that didn't stop us from enjoying good food. Frolicking music filtered through the walls. My mouth watered and my feet itched to dance, but as Midori flitted over to join the early merrymaking, I turned in the other direction, where the private apartments lay.

I'd only taken one step around the corner toward my parents' chambers when a high, nasal voice stopped me in my tracks.

"Sora!" Ayame cried, tearing across the hall with her spindly arms waving and her hair billowing around her petite frame. "Look at you, child. Bare-faced, dirt on your clothes... Augh, I can't have you seen like this, not on your birthday."

"I need to speak to Mother and Father first," I said as she tugged me toward my rooms.

"You can go when you're properly prepared."

Well, it might be wise to look my best when I made my appeal. I relented.

When we reached my inner rooms, Takeo hung back. "Wait for me?" I said. Takeo's protection was merely a formality at my age, but I'd feel more confident approaching my parents with his steady presence at my side.

"Of course," he said.

Ayame shoved the sliding door shut between us. Her assistants—one human-shaped like Ayame and me and the other three kami in the forms of a robin, a crane, and a monkey—were waiting in the bathing room. I was scrubbed and rinsed with water scented with cherry blossoms, then powdered and combed and lotioned and powdered again. Finally I was allowed to get dressed, in a silky robe more flowing than any humans ever wore. The pale blue fabric danced with golden butterflies.

"Ah!" Ayame said, clapping her hands together. "Magnificent."

"Am I done, then?" I asked as the monkey tied the sash around my waist.

Ayame made a dismissive sound and launched into a tirade about my hair. I stared longingly at the door. If I didn't distract myself, I was going to burst.

As the robin started coiling my hair and Ayame brought out her make-up palette, I exhaled, sending out a stream of ki shaped into a kite. At my mental nudge, it drifted through the door. Takeo and I had played this game since I was first learning how to use the energy inside me, but these days I offered it as a challenge.

The kite was caught by an impression that was purely Takeo, gallant as one of the mountain's young pines. I drew it back. His ki resisted, dragging the kite toward him, and the corners of my mouth twitched upward.

"Hold still!" Ayame said.

Quieting my expression, I reeled the kite in against Takeo's pull. At the last instant, Takeo whipped it away. It took all my self control not to lunge after it physically. I clung on with sharpened focus and yanked. The kite shot straight to me, Takeo's connection snapping. In the room outside, he laughed at his defeat. Ayame shook her head.

"So strong, my Sora," she murmured. "All right, you'll do. Walk carefully—and keep your hands away from your face!"

I hurried with Takeo down the narrow hall that separated my rooms from my parents'. The lamps along the wall were starting to flare on with the fading of the sun. Around us, an anxious tremor rippled through the mountain's ki. I glanced at Takeo, startled, but he showed no sign of concern. That must have been *my* anxiety, trembling out of me.

My pulse beat faster as we came to a stop at the door to my parents' private chambers. Takeo tapped on the frame and announced our presence, and Mother's voice answered.

"Come in."

She and Father were sitting on crimson cushions by their low ebony table. A light sandalwood scent wafted from the incense burner set in an alcove. Takeo eased the door shut, staying on the other side. I padded across the finely woven rush of the tatami mats to the other side of the table.

Because kami age so slowly once they reach adulthood, Mother and Father both looked as young as humans of about twenty, but otherwise they were each other's opposites. Mother was thin and lithe with ivory skin, while Father was broad and bulky and ruddy complexioned. The way they smiled at me matched their temperaments perfectly: Mother soft and bright, Father wide and warm.

"We were about to send for you," Mother said. "You look beautiful, Sora."

I blushed, lowering my eyes. Strong, I reminded myself. Strong and capable.

"I can't believe you're already seventeen," Father said in his rumbling voice. "Three more years and you'll be all grown up." He sounded strangely sad.

"It isn't so short a time," Mother said gently, as if *I* might someday leave for college or other far away places like the Nagamotos' children.

A distant shout reached my ears. Mother frowned, glancing toward the hall. Kami usually got along, but occasionally there were disputes between the guests.

The faint silhouette of Takeo's form moved away from the door's translucent panel. He must have gone to see what was the matter. I drew my mind back to my goal.

"I've been doing everything I can to prepare," I said.

"Let's not worry about that," Mother said before I could go on. "Tonight is one of the few occasions we can think of celebration instead of duty. Your father and I wanted to give you your birthday present."

She nodded to Father, who lifted a long rectangular object from the floor behind him and set it on the table. It was a lacquered case with a leather strap and a gold clasp. "Open it," he said, grinning.

I leaned forward and pushed up the clasp. As I raised the lid, my breath caught. "Thank you!" I said, staring at the instrument inside. "It's wonderful."

It was a flute made of polished bamboo, so carefully crafted I could feel how pure its sounds would be just by running my fingertips over the wood. I picked it up and brought it to my lips. The scale hummed through me as if I were as much an instrument as the flute. Each note expanded into the quiet like a flower bud unfurling. It was one of the most beautiful things I'd ever heard—and it was mine.

I set the flute back in its case, closed the lid, and hugged it to me. "Thank you," I said again. "I'll play it tonight." I'd meant to use my old flute, the one they'd given me when I'd started lessons years ago. But this was a true musician's instrument. One for a woman, not a girl. Maybe they knew I was ready to finally find my place among the kami.

I slid the case's strap over my shoulder. As I opened my mouth, another shout carried through the wall, followed by a heavy crash that shocked the words from my throat. Footsteps thumped down the hall outside. Takeo pulled open the door, and one of his fellow guards stumbled to a halt on the threshold, his breath rasping.

"Your Highnesses," he said, "forgive my intrusion. We're under attack."

TWO

THE MOUNTAIN'S *ki* shivered through me, and I realized I hadn't imagined the distress I'd felt in it before.

"Attack?" Mother said faintly. "Now?"

Father sprang to his feet. "By whom? Tell us everything."

"It's a demon," the guard said with a shudder, "with a terrible fury of power, leading an army of ghosts. They swarmed us at the entrance—they're carrying ropes and nets so vile we can't cast them off—and the demon burns with his touch alone. I barely managed to escape to warn you. Already some are heading this way. We're fighting as well as we can, but..."

Ghosts. I scrambled up, remembering Miss Sakai's odd demeanor, the way she'd hurried away from Takeo and me. Had she known an attack was coming and not warned us? My stomach turned. Was she out there joining in the assault right now?

"Our defenses?" Father asked.

The guard swiped his arm through the air. "Nothing could withstand them."

Mother stood. "We must do everything we can to stop them and protect the mountain," she said, her voice now firm. "There's still a chance. We..." She hesitated, and then turned to slip her arms around me. I only had a moment to squeeze her back before she'd let me go. Behind her, an inhuman roar thundered through the palace. Goosebumps rose on my arms. Screams echoed down the hall, and Mother blanched even whiter.

"Takeo," she said, "you must stay here with Sora. If our enemies reach this end of the palace... You remember the instructions I gave you when you were assigned?"

Takeo blinked at her and then nodded with a jerk. "Mother," I said, "what—"

"I'm sorry," she said. "If I'd known... But there isn't time."

Father squashed me in a hug as brief as hers. "Be safe, daughter," he said roughly. He and Mother swept out of the room.

"No!" I said, moving to run after them, but Takeo caught my arm. He closed the door as he held me away from it. The screams and shouts of the battle rose, louder, closer, and my heart thudded louder too. The way Mother and Father had embraced me—it was almost as if they never expected to see me again.

I wrenched against Takeo's grasp, but he refused to let go. "They ordered us to stay here," he said, his expression strained.

"So what?" I said. "We have to help!"

"Your mother gave specific orders."

I gritted my teeth. While I was "strong" and Ayame "frantic," the word that best described Takeo's nature was "steadfast." He wouldn't have been chosen as a palace guard otherwise. But there were times when unwavering loyalty was a pain in the neck.

He'd tie me up and throw me in a closet before he'd disobey my parents' word.

Another cry rang out. A paper screen ripped. My hands clenched. I needed my sword—in my rooms down the hall. Takeo drew his, taking a defensive stance I'd seen him fall into so many times when we'd sparred, but never to meet a real enemy. Our martial training served mostly to focus the mind and keep our traditions alive. The sorts of creatures kami might have fought against once rarely traveled close to Mt. Fuji, especially now that so many humans lived nearby. I'd never witnessed even a minor skirmish. How could this be happening? Nothing made sense.

Takeo's grasp on my wrist had loosened. I lunged forward, snapping his hold, and shoved open the door.

"Sora!" Takeo said, but I was already scrambling out into the hall. The sight of the scene at the far end made my heart stop. Three palace guards and a group of other kami were caught in a wave of shadowy figures that blotted out what remained of the sunlight. The onslaught of ghosts moved like a tsunami, crashing through the hall. One ghost snapped a rope tight around a bear kami's neck. Another swung a curved blade at a guard and split the billowing sleeve of her uniform. Dozens more swarmed past them, toppling some kami with the sheer mass of their momentum and heaving darkly knotted nets into their midst. The ghosts' cackles and the kami's grunts of pain ricocheted off the walls.

A cold sweat had broken over my skin, but I dashed forward all the same, gathering ki in my hands. "Catch them all!" a voice was shouting. "Push them into the rooms! We can hold them there." More ghosts charged through the panels along the hall. One burst out just a few feet ahead of me and flung a mottled net my way. I dodged backward, my feet stumbling as a sickly, rotten smell filled my nose. Then Takeo's solid hands caught my shoulders. He yanked me back into my parents' chambers with a surge of ki.

"They're almost on us," he said. "We have to go."

I struggled against him, even though my body was trembling. A shriek pierced the air from just outside. "We can't abandon everyone!" I said.

"Your mother thinks this is best." Takeo pulled me around to face him. He met my gaze, his eyes dark. "You trust her, don't you?"

Before I could answer, a body smashed through the door beside us.

It was one of the guards. As he groped through the shreds of paper for the sword he must have lost, four ghosts leapt in after him, driving their knives into his chest and sides. The ethereal weapons left no damage on his corporeal body, but they'd be raking at his ki, bringing a different sort of agony. His limbs spasmed.

The ghost at the back of the pack, a young man in a slim gray suit whose hair was streaked as red as the stain on his own knife, grinned as he watched the guard's torment. Then his gaze flicked to Takeo and me.

"Them too," he said with a jab of his hand.

I'd already shifted into a fighting stance, my legs braced and arms ready. My pulse pounded in my ears. Takeo's hand tightened on my shoulder. His ki washed over me. "Meet me below," he said into my ear and dragged both our now-ethereal bodies away from the ghosts, into the wall.

We slid through the wood and into the mountain's rock. Darkness closed in on me, so thick I could no longer see or feel Takeo beside me. I spun around, disoriented. I had to go back. The guards, Mother and Father, Ayame, Midori...

I reached to my sash instinctively, though I was carrying no blade. My flute case, still at my back, would make a poor weapon. The image of those stabbing knives flashed through my mind. I wanted to fly at all those translucent legless figures with their vicious smirks, to drive them out of here and over the horizon.

But I didn't have the slightest idea how to do it.

I drew in a shaky breath. Tears had sprung into my eyes, but the mountain's ki wore away my urge to fight even as it shuddered with displeasure.

There must be hundreds of ghosts in the palace, and there was only one of me. Throwing myself into the fray now wouldn't be strong—it'd be foolish. Mother was known for her wisdom. I *did* trust her. Whatever instructions she'd given Takeo, maybe they'd allow us to come back and recover our home.

I eased toward the mountainside and poked my ethereal head through the layer of soil that covered the slope. Immediately, I jerked back down. Ghosts were prowling all through that glade. The mountain was choked with them.

Had they seen me? I needed to move. I needed to find Takeo.

He'd told me to meet him "below," so I began to stride downward as if on unseen stairs, following the slope. The dark rock rippled past me, its pressure tugging at the edges of my body. Simply holding myself in this ethereal state took energy—moving through solid matter was draining my ki even faster. I listened in the stillness for any sign of pursuit, but all I could hear was the uneven beat of my heart.

As I neared the base of the mountain, the rock squeezed against me so tightly my chest ached. I couldn't go much farther like this. Surely by now I'd left the ghosts behind?

I peeked into the outside world and, finding myself alone, leapt up through the soil into the humid evening air, in the midst of the forest that stretched around the base of the mountain. Only the breeze stirred as I caught my balance. I turned, hugging the strap of the flute case across my chest. The mountain's peak was hidden by the trees.

"Takeo?" I called. "Takeo!"

No one answered. What if the ghosts had caught him? What if they'd—

I closed my eyes, shoving away the memory of bloody knives. Then I reached for the nearest tree, a towering pine. Pulling myself with both my muscles and my ki, I scaled it in a matter of seconds.

The mountain rose above the green sprawl of the forest, looking perfectly normal at first glance. Then, in the ruddy light of the sunset, movement glimmered between the trees that cloaked most of its lower half. Farther up, my ki-sharpened eyes made out hazy bodies swarming the rocky peak around the more solid living figures of the tourists hiking the paths to the summit, oblivious. The ghosts would be as invisible to them as I was in my ethereal form.

My fingers tightened around the branch I was clutching. Our enemies were everywhere.

A sparrow hopped onto a tuft of needles beside me and chirped. "Don't go up there," I said tightly. "Not now."

I half jumped, half glided down to the lower branches. From there, I peered into the depths of the forest, hoping my position would keep me hidden if the ghosts ventured this far. A more tender memory tickled up: playing hide and seek among the mountain's trees with Takeo as a child. Once he'd hidden so well that after a half hour of searching I'd burst into tears. And then he'd been there at my side in an instant, hugging me and promising he would never truly disappear.

A lump filled my throat. I set my jaw and gave all my senses over to the forest. After several long minutes, the crackle of pine needles reached my ears. I twisted and caught a flash of silver embroidery amid the trees.

"Takeo!" I dropped to the ground and raced to him. At my voice, he swiveled toward me. He met me halfway, catching me by the arms. A few strands of his hair had slipped from its knot, softening the severe style, but his expression was determined.

"Thank the heavens," he said. "You're all right?"

"They have the mountain," I said as I nodded. "All of it. Everyone there..." Not just the palace kami, but all the guests who had gathered. Was that why the demon had chosen tonight to attack—had it wanted to capture as many of us as possible? Or had it simply hoped the party would leave us distracted?

"They'll be alive," Takeo said. "The demon and his ghosts might have been powerful enough to overcome us, but every kami on the mountain has enough ki to live through ten more battles like that."

It was true that while kami could die, it took a long time to wear down the ki that sustained us. The people we'd left behind could still be saved. But the stabbed guard hadn't looked as if he had much more battle left in him. And even now the ghosts could be torturing my family, my friends. Hurting us had seemed to amuse them.

"I don't understand," I said. "What could they want? Why would they attack us?"

"I don't know," Takeo said. "I've seen ghosts hurt humans before, but never kami."

"How is it even possible? I wouldn't have thought there were that many ghosts in the entire world."

"Neither would I," Takeo agreed. "And normally the few of the dead who remain in the world of the living are tied to the places of their deaths. For them to travel this far, to gather so many together... Perhaps the demon has lent them power somehow. But I've never heard of a demon working with ghosts either."

"What does *it* want? Where did it come from?" I hadn't been aware of a demon existing near the mountain in the entire time I'd been alive. They were rare enough that I knew of them only from old stories, in which they were monstrous creatures, full of malevolent energy and eager to destroy. I wouldn't have expected any to be powerful enough to subdue the entire palace, though. No enemy had ever even attempted that. My gut twisted. "Did you have any idea we might be in danger?"

Takeo shook his head. "But we may have someone else we can turn to for answers."

"Mother's instructions." I stared at him. He'd been keeping

a secret from me—for how long? "What did she tell you, and when?"

He lowered his head, abruptly awkward. "It was so long ago, I'd put it out of my mind. When I was named your principal guard when you were eleven years old, your mother gave me orders she told me I must keep to myself. She said that if the mountain ever faced so great a threat that our survival was uncertain, I was to go to the valley of the doves to speak to the kami sage Rin, and if possible bring you with me. I'm supposed to tell Sage Rin that the time of the prophecy has come, and she should tell us what to do."

"Prophecy?" I repeated. "Then they knew...? But Mother and Father didn't seem prepared. They hadn't expected the attack."

"Whatever your mother anticipated, I don't think she believed it would happen soon," Takeo said. "She said she was telling me merely as a precaution, but it was likely I'd never need to act on it. She seemed to think it was best I didn't know more."

Best for her then maybe, but not for us now. "Rin." The name sounded familiar. "Rin the Obtuse! Oh, no. Ayame's told me tales about her. In all of them she gives advice no one can figure out until it's too late to use it. *She's* supposed to help us?"

"According to your mother," Takeo said. "Perhaps the stories exaggerated."

I glanced back toward the mountain. We'd have to hope so. We had no other path to follow. And we couldn't know how long the kami trapped in the palace would be able to withstand the ghosts' torment.

"Let's hurry to this valley of the doves then," I said.

Takeo crouched down and detached a sheath from his boot,

half the length of the one that hung by his hip. "My short sword," he said. "We should make our way as quickly as possible, but you'll need to be armed in case we have no choice but to fight."

I tucked the sheath into the sash of my robe. "Thank you."

Takeo grasped my hand. We had only run past the first few stands of trees when we came upon a ghostly patrol: five young men in suits that disappeared below their thighs. We were racing forward too quickly to avoid them. Instead, Takeo squeezed my fingers, and we dashed straight through the middle of the group. The touch of their filmy bodies left my skin crawling, as if I'd bitten into a peach and found it rotten.

"Hey!" one of the ghosts hollered. "Stop where you are!"

"Faster," Takeo whispered.

I sent all the energy I could summon to my feet. We darted around trees and through bushes, the ghosts' furious shouts trailing after us. My lungs burned, but I kept running, on and on, past the houses of the town and the farmlands beyond it, long after the voices behind us faded away.

Finally, after we'd slipped into another patch of forest, Takeo slowed beside me. The sky had gone dark. As soon as I let my pace falter, my legs buckled. I caught myself against a tree at the edge of a clearing. My body shifted back into its corporeal state, the humidity of the air congealing against my skin.

"I think we've lost any that might have tried to follow us," Takeo said. "You're worn out. We should rest and regain our energy."

"How far is the valley?" I asked.

"At our fastest, I think we could reach it tomorrow afternoon."

Tomorrow. And then there would be another day coming back. I couldn't see Mt. Fuji at all through these trees, couldn't feel the faintest hum of its ki. I'd never really left the mountain before, never gone farther than the town at its foot. But Takeo was right—my descent and our dash here had left me exhausted. I wasn't sure how much farther I could even walk.

I slid the flute case around my body, cradling it. The memory of my parents' beaming faces swam in my head. What was happening to them right now? What had the demon intended to do to them and the others once it had control of the mountain?

Takeo circled the clearing, scanning the forest. "We'll still have to be careful as we're traveling, but I may know a way we can fight the ghosts if we encounter more."

"What?" I said, raising my head.

"Your grandmother, Hoshi, showed me once." He brushed the fallen leaves from a spot in the middle of the clearing and arranged a handful of sticks on the dirt. "There was a ghost, not long after I came to the mountain, who was... stuck to a spot by one of the roads."

"Like Miss Sakai," I said.

"Miss Sakai keeps to herself," Takeo said, and hesitated. "At least, she did. But this ghost, he would jump out in front of the cars, startling the drivers. There were several accidents. Hoshi asked me to help her send his spirit into the afterworld. She showed me using a slip of paper, but I think bark or cloth would do as well. It's the characters you write that matter. They're like the ones on the ofuda charms humans hang by their doorways and windows to keep out evil spirits. You place the charm on the forehead of a lingering spirit—maybe other parts work too, but Hoshi seemed to think the forehead was most effective—and the ghost vanishes back to the afterworld where it belongs."

I thought of my glimpse of the mountainside. Not just hundreds, but thousands of ghosts. We were going to need a lot of ofuda.

"I'm not sure I remember the characters perfectly," Takeo went on, "but I'll try. We just need something to write with."

"Charcoal," I said, understanding. I knelt down by the pile of sticks and held out my hands. Closing my eyes, I reached for the ki within me. Heat, light, burning. The sharp twang of the energy flashed behind my eyelids and flooded my chest with warmth. I shoved it through my palms.

Nothing happened.

My arms quivered. I inhaled, exhaled, and thrust my hands forward. Not a single thread of ki leapt from them. What was wrong with me? I dragged in another breath and found myself trembling.

"Sora!" Takeo bent down beside me. I turned my head away.

"It's not working," I said, as calmly as I could manage. "I can't make the fire start—I don't know why I'm not—"

The familiar weight of Takeo's arm slid around my back.

"You're tired, and upset," he said quietly. "Your thoughts are scattered—you can't focus. It's not surprising. Here, I'll do it."

Wasn't it surprising? Had he gotten any less steadfast since this afternoon? Why should I be any less strong?

Takeo stretched his other arm toward the sticks. A flame shot up amidst them. I pressed my hands against the solid ground. I had bigger things to worry about. The life of every kami on Mt. Fuji might depend on Takeo and me.

"I'll go find some smooth bark we can write on," I said, standing up. "Then I want you to teach me those characters."

But as I walked away, my failure gnawed at me. I'd seen my abilities weaken when I was tired before, but they'd never left me completely.

THREE

I SLEPT FIRST while Takeo kept watch, both of us holding several birch bark ofuda in our sleeves. Or at least, I tried to sleep. When I closed my eyes I saw the mass of ghosts surging down the hallway and the guard I'd watched falling under their knives in my parents' room. His form shifted into Mother's, Father's, their lips pressed tight to keep from crying out as the blades stabbed them again and again.

They would be that stoic. They wouldn't want to give their captors the slightest bit of satisfaction while they bled and healed, bled and healed, feeling their energy ebbing, waiting for rescue.

When it was my watch, I stalked the edges of the clearing, fingering the rough edges of my ofuda. The scattered stars cast too faint a light to penetrate the forest's shadows, but a ghost's ki should glow brightly enough that I'd be able to spot it in the darkness if one came near.

Dawn was just touching the horizon when thin wings whirred by my ear. I glanced up, and my heart leapt. A metallic green dragonfly was hovering in front of me, her multifaceted eyes fixed on mine.

"Midori!" I said. "You got away! Did anyone escape with you? How did you find us?"

Midori extended a tendril of ki to me, and images flitted through my mind. I got the impression she had darted beneath the swing of a sword and through a gap in a net, and then bolted down the mountain. In one flash I glimpsed two figures racing ahead in the distance, the shimmer of ki making them briefly visible through the trees. Takeo and me. That particular image came with a trickle of relief at finding she wasn't alone.

She'd followed us—only her.

Was every other kami who'd been in the palace for the celebration still trapped there?

I reached out to give Midori's head a gentle stroke of welcome, but she circled me and dropped onto my hair. She tugged me as if urging me downward with an urgency that held none of her usual playfulness. "What?" I whispered as I crouched behind a cluster of bamboo plants. Her wings buzzed anxiously.

A moment later, twigs cracked under stomping feet. Several paces from our clearing, a group of hunched figures stalked through the forest in the faint dawn light. I squinted, trying to make out their faces. My hand jerked to the sword I'd borrowed from Takeo.

The nearest creature was easily eight feet tall, with bristly gray hair sprouting down its neck and across its hulking shoulders. Two immense fangs jutted from its upper jaw over its chin. The one just behind it was shorter and squat. Wide horns protruded from its shaggy mane and five scarlet eyes scattered its forehead. Their companions were similarly monstrous.

Ogres. I'd never seen them before—they were too wary of Mt. Fuji's power to set foot there—but I'd heard enough tales. They might not be as powerful in their maliciousness as demons, but they enjoyed causing what harm they could. They were certainly no friends to the kami.

As I watched them pass, my spirits sank. They were heading in the direction Takeo and I had come from, toward the mountain. Maybe it was a coincidence. Or maybe they meant to join the demon and his ghosts while the mountain's guardians were incapacitated.

When the last of the ogres had vanished from sight and hearing, I scrambled to Takeo's side and grasped his shoulder to wake him. As I described what I'd seen, he leapt up, hefting his bow.

"They're gone," I said. "But I don't know if more will come."

"They might," he agreed. "We should move now. I've rested enough."

A smudge of dirt marked his cheek and stray pine needles clung to his uniform, but he looked as dauntless as ever. I squared my shoulders. At least I still had him.

Midori, my equally faithful companion, settled onto her usual spot on the back of my head. As we ran, my hair tumbled over my back. In the rising heat of the day, it stuck to the sweat dampening my neck. My ceremonial robe dragged at my arms and legs. The strap of my flute case dug into my shoulder, which had started to radiate a dull ache.

None of that would have affected me if I had slipped into the ethereal state, but except to avoid human eyes when crossing the highways, train tracks, and villages that broke the stretches of wooded land, I was using all the energy I had for speed. If we encountered more ogres or ghosts, I didn't want to be as drained as I'd been last night. Even now, after sleeping, the flow of ki through my body felt muted, like a stream shrunk by dry weather. I thought of the mountain, of the warm thrum of its embrace, and had to blink hard to keep tears from forming.

If Takeo noticed, he didn't let on. When he spoke, it was about Rin.

"What exactly have you heard about this sage?"

"Mainly that her advice is always difficult to follow," I said, grateful for the distraction. "She used to let humans know about her, and they would go looking to get her advice. But she would just confuse them. She told a commander that the best time to strike was when darkness fell, so that night he sent his army into battle—and they were slaughtered. Because it turned out Sage Rin had meant they should take advantage of the eclipse two days later."

Takeo grimaced. "I remember that story. We'll have to hope she's mellowed in her old age."

Just after the sun had reached its peak, we crossed the ridge of a low mountain and looked down into a narrow valley. Below us, a waterfall burbled over pinkish-gray rock into a series of egg-shaped pools, shaded by stands of bright green bamboo. A delicate floral scent mixed with the crisp smell of cypress in the breeze. No roads cut through the forest below us, and no roofs showed through the trees.

"The valley of the doves," Takeo said. "I don't think we should draw too much attention to ourselves. We don't know what else might be lurking."

I eyed the forest. "I suppose it would make the most sense for Sage Rin to live near the bottom of the valley—close to the water and sheltered from the weather."

We hurried down the steep incline into the thicker vegetation, grasping saplings and bushes to keep our balance. Leaves hissed against my robe. When we reached the waterfall, we walked along the slick stone around the pools. Seeing no sign of Rin or her home, we pushed deeper into the valley. The mountains rising on either side blocked the harshest of the sun's rays, but the summer heat still hung over us. I was wiping my forehead with my sleeve when a tiny object flew through the air and pattered at my feet. Midori let out a spark of bemused consternation as a small face with a shock of red hair disappeared amid the branches of a nearby beech tree.

"A nut," I said, nudging the object at my feet with my toes.

Takeo nodded. "Tree fairies like to play, but they don't mean any harm. They're simple, friendly creatures."

I was about to ask Takeo whether the fairy might direct us to the sage when the ground beneath us shuddered. I stumbled backward into a cedar. Takeo grabbed its trunk as the earth swayed, shivered, and stilled.

"Just a small tremor," he said.

A throat cleared behind us. "Small or not, the cause is what tells," said a rusty voice.

I flinched and spun around, my hand dipping into my sleeve for my ofuda. My arm stilled when I saw the kami standing on the log beside us.

The short, pot-bellied woman studying us was so old that old hardly began to describe her. The sunlight seemed to shine right through her colorless hair, and the lines on her face ran so deep it was hard to make out which were wrinkles and which her mouth and nose. Her shoulders were stooped within the thin robe she wore, which, though scuffed, looked like silk. Shriveled toes clung to her leather sandals. She must have been thousands of years old., but her dark eyes glittered with a vitality completely at odds with her appearance, and the air around her rippled with ki. I didn't have to ask her name.

"Sage Rin," I said, and bowed. "It's an honor." The hem of my robe was splotched with dirt. I bowed lower, suddenly wishing I'd at least been able to wash before meeting with this most respected sage, obtuse or not. I couldn't tell anymore, but I probably smelled. And not of cherry blossoms.

Takeo bowed too, his tanned face forming an expression of grave deference. When we straightened up, I knew which line was Rin's mouth. It was curved into a smirk.

"I can see your purpose well enough," she said, "though I hadn't anticipated you arriving so soon." She hopped down from the log and started to shuffle away from us.

We followed her along a path we'd missed, which wound tightly through the trees at the base of the slope. "Do you know what's happened?" I asked when I couldn't take the silence any longer. "My mother—Kasumi of Mt. Fuji—she told Takeo something about a prophecy and that you would be able to help."

"I know very much and very little," Rin said.

"But you know what we have to do to save the mountain?" I said. "To rescue my parents, and everyone else?"

"Hmmm," she replied. "Possibly you have to do nothing at all."

"But—" I caught myself, swallowing my impatience. This was Rin the Obtuse. We'd be lucky to get a clear answer out of her on her own terms.

She stopped at a huge cypress that looked as though it might have been as old as she was, and tapped her knuckles against the gnarled bark. A door swung open in the trunk.

Inside, the sage's house looked like a pavilion, round-walled and high-ceilinged, with winding wooden steps leading up between its levels. Takeo and I padded after Rin to the second floor. There, she motioned for us to sit. A ceramic teapot was already set on the low table beside a single cup. The pot started to steam as she took another cup off a shelf and squatted down across from us.

"First, it is you who must talk," she said. She poured the golden liquid into both cups, passing one to Takeo and keeping one for herself. Takeo frowned. I didn't understand why she'd neglected me, but it was hard to be very bothered when we were so close to getting answers.

"We've come from the palace on Mt. Fuji," I said. As I explained about the ghosts' attack, the demon who apparently led them, and the ogres that had passed us in the morning, Rin sipped her tea.

"Ghosts and a demon," she said when I'd finished. "Not what I would have guessed. But my guesses are far less accurate than my prophecies. And even a prophecy is far from fact."

"Then the prophecy Her Highness mentioned, it was yours?" Takeo said. "You foresaw this attack?"

"I will share with you the same words I said to Kasumi and Hotaka years ago, after the vision came," Rin said. "*I have seen a darkness that rises up over the mountain, engulfing it and nearly devouring it.*"

"The ghosts," I murmured, remembering the dark wave of them in the hall.

"So it would seem," Rin said. "I knew nothing other than it would be a force terrible enough to overwhelm even the sacred mountain as never before. But that is only the beginning." She fell back into her reciting voice. "*I have seen a powerful kami striking back against that darkness and driving it away. A young woman, bearing the three kami-blessed treasures of human imperial rule: the sword, the mirror, and the jewel. And the girl herself was a marvel, with more power than I've ever seen, air lifting her hair and fire in her eyes and water flowing through her movements and earth holding her firm. A kami born of the elements combined.*"

"Like Mother and Father." My grandparents on my mother's side had affinities to air and water, and on my father's side to earth and fire. Which would have passed from my parents on to me. Which meant that—

"*So it is clear that a daughter of Mt. Fuji's current rulers will save it in its time of greatest need,*" Rin finished, folding her hands in her lap.

That had to be the reason they'd tried so hard for a child. Why Mother had sent Takeo here with me. So that I could make Rin's vision come true.

"And that's me," I said, looking up at her. I really was going to save them. It had already been decided.

"You think you speak the truth," Rin said, "when you know none of it?"

"What do you mean?" I said. "If there's more, please tell me."

"*You* have no place in this at all," Rin replied, her wizened face implacable.

For a second, I could only blink at her. "But... everything you mentioned," I said. "Those are my parents. I am their only child. How can the prophecy not be about me?"

"She *is* the daughter of Their Highnesses Kasumi and Hotaka," Takeo said. "I can attest to that. I've known her since she was a child."

"Yes," Rin said. Her smirk returned. "You've known *this* girl. But this girl is not a child of Mt. Fuji. She is not even kami."

FOUR

As RIN'S DECLARATION faded in the air, I gripped the edge of the table. "What?" I said. How could she say that— Couldn't she see me right here in front of her, as kami as I'd always been?

The sage's low voice carried on, as evenly as before. "What if others learned of my vision, beings who wished to harm the kami, and tried to undo what was foreseen by attacking the one who could save us before she gained her full power with adulthood? It would not do. I believed—wrongly, I will now admit—that the young woman in my vision must have been of age to wield such power, and so the larger threat would not appear until after she'd reached twenty. There was no need for her to be on the mountain, in such a prominent position, until then."

"You're not making any sense," I said. "I've lived on the mountain my entire life. I know who my parents are. I know what *I* am."

Rin continued, calm and certain. "So we placed her where one seeking to hurt the kami would never look. Where a different sort of energy would mask any hint of her heritage. One child was exchanged for another in a secret trade. The true daughter has lived among humans, away from notice, ignorant of her unawakened powers—safe. Her human counterpart was raised on the mountain." She finally cast her gaze toward me.

"This is ridiculous," I said. "I'm a kami. If Mother and Father said they were going to carry out this switch, they must have changed their minds and not told you."

"The appearance of things is no real proof," Rin said with a shrug. "What the rulers of the kami ask for, the mountain grants, and it has been lending you its energy since you were an infant. You have no more ki of your own than any other human. Even now, a little of Fuji's power lingers in you—and for anything else you feel, I believe you owe thanks to the friend perched in your hair."

Midori. Her wings hummed protectively at Rin's words, but a tendril of her ki wound close to me as she clung on. She gave no inkling of denial. She hadn't been with me when I'd tried to start the fire. And since our flight from the mountain the energy inside me *hadn't* felt the same, had it? My throat closed up.

I shook my head against the sudden doubt. No. It couldn't be true. I belonged with Mother and Father. I belonged to the mountain. I knew that like I knew how to walk, how to breathe.

Rin had turned to Takeo.

"Kasumi and Hotaka have placed a great responsibility on you," she was saying. "But I can see you have learned much of the fighting arts, which are far from my specialty. It is unfortunate that the threat has come upon us so much earlier than we anticipated.

For the true daughter to save the mountain, she must be on the mountain—and she will need training, and the Imperial treasures too. She will have much power even now, but no sense of how to use it. She cannot hope to win back the mountain unless she is properly prepared. You must retrieve her, teach her to use enough of her talents so that she can defend herself out in the world, and then bring her here so I can assist with the rest. I am able to make use of the full extent of my power only here in the valley."

Takeo bowed his head in acknowledgement. Did *he* believe Rin's story?

"Will that be enough?" he asked. "No force has ever overcome Mt. Fuji before, and yet this demon and his ghosts broke its every defense in a matter of minutes."

"It all rests on the girl," Rin said. "And the sacred treasures that will channel her power." She took on the same tone she had when relating the prophecy. "The sword's blade will split open the uneasy dead. The mirror will turn around their attacks. The jewel will amplify all energy used for good. Seek the weapon first, as it may cut the way through to the others."

Takeo still looked uncertain. "So, then, according to your vision, if we bring this girl to the mountain with the treasures, she's sure to win?"

"There are no definites," Rin said in her usual dry voice, her mouth twisting. "A vision is not a guarantee. All that can be said is that if the prophecy is *not* fulfilled, failure is certain."

"Then how can we—" Takeo started, and Rin shook her head.

"Many a thing becomes clear through the doing," she said.

Nothing, she'd said to me. *You have to do nothing at all.*

"Please," Takeo tried again. "Anything else you can tell us—"

Rin's eyes narrowed as she cut him off. "I've said all I can say until I speak with her."

"What about me?" I broke in. "What am I supposed to do during all this, according to you?"

Her gaze barely flickered my way. "That's none of my concern," she said, and then, to Takeo, "This one might be returned to whence she came, to replace what will be lost."

Whence I came. To my supposed human parents? My hands balled.

"All right," Takeo said, the tensing of his jaw telling me he was backing down unwillingly. His fingers found mine beneath the table and squeezed them. "How will I find the girl?"

The gentle touch of his ki reassured me. He believed in me still.

Rin had to be wrong. My parents must have decided not to make the switch. I couldn't accept anything else.

"It should not be very difficult," Rin said. I expected her to offer a tangled series of directions, but instead she stood and walked to the cabinet beside the stairs. She took out a sheet of paper and a small bottle of ink and painted several neat characters.

"She's in Tokyo," she said, handing over the paper. "The more city energy around her, we thought, the easier to hide her ki. Go to this address, and she will be there."

So simple and exact. I stared at her as Takeo considered the paper.

"You're obtuse even in how obtuse you decide to be," I said.

Rin laughed. This time, her gaze lingered on me a little longer. "It's rare that anyone truly appreciates my nature."

"Is there anything more we should know?" Takeo said.

"There is always more to know," Rin said with a huff of breath. "That does not mean you will know it now."

I got up as Takeo did. "We will go, then, at once," he said. "Before the demon takes its plans any further."

The sage inclined her head.

"Yes," she said. "Make as much haste as you can without carelessness. The worst can worsen. As one of the guards of the palace, it was part of your duty to calm the mountain's fire, was it not?"

Takeo nodded. All of the guards took shifts soothing Fuji's volcanic temper.

"Now Mt. Fuji stirs," Rin said. "The ground shakes, the anger builds, unsettled by the binding of the kami and the presence of so many malicious spirits. If the balance remains unrestored, that fire may break its silence for the first time in three hundred years."

The volcano was threatening to erupt. The thought of that fury of ash and lava raining down on all those towns below wiped everything else Rin had told us from my mind. I closed my eyes, unable to shake the images. A flood of molten rock crumbling the walls of the Nagamotos' house. Searing through the park where I'd watched artists painting the spring and autumn colors. Swallowing the cafes once filled with chatter. My stomach knotted.

If the mountain burst, it would not be just the kami under attack, but every living thing in the vast range of the destruction. And once the fire spilled over, nothing any human or kami could do would stop it.

All of Sage Rin's words haunted me as Takeo and I raced toward Tokyo, hoping to reach the city by the end of the day. Even without Mt. Fuji in sight, the heat of its anger seemed to tinge the heavy breeze. And though between Takeo's hand around mine and Midori's tiny feet entwined in my hair, ki thrummed through my body, I couldn't completely ignore the question of how much of it belonged to me. Could I really have been borrowing so much from the mountain all this time, without knowing it?

It serves no purpose wondering that, I told myself. When we saw the girl Rin had sent us to, we would know—that the sage had been mistaken, surely. And then we could move forward from there. Right now, the only important thing was reaching her before the volcano erupted.

As evening fell, I got my first glimpse of Mt. Fuji in the distance to our right, its peak haloed by clouds. We paused for a moment to scan its slopes. The mountain looked no less stable than before. *We're coming,* I thought to it.

Or, at least, Takeo was. The doubts I'd tried to smother crept up again.

I hadn't dared to speak of Rin's claims, and Takeo had respected my silence. Now the question popped out before I could catch the words.

"They never said anything like this to you, did they? My parents? About me being... About any of it? They never gave any sign I wasn't really..."

"No," Takeo said. "I remember the excitement when it was announced that Her Highness was with child, when you were born. Everyone rejoiced. That was part of the reason I decided to dedicate myself to serving the mountain as soon as I was old enough—and I saw the joy they took in you with my own eyes, when I arrived and every day after."

I directed my thoughts up to Midori where she perched on the back of my head. "And you?" I said. "How much power have you been lending me?"

The dragonfly responded with a teasing tickle that amounted to saying if I hadn't insisted on running myself ragged so often, she wouldn't have to assist—although she was quite happy to. Which wasn't really an answer.

"But I don't really *need* you to... to have any power at all, away from the mountain, do I?" I made myself ask.

All she gave me was a mental shrug. I couldn't tell whether she was avoiding answering or whether she honestly didn't know.

"Sora," Takeo said, "do you remember the bear?"

"Of course," I said, the memory rising up. But what did that have to do with this?

"It was such an honor to be chosen as your principal guard," he said haltingly. "I was anxious to prove I was worthy of the honor, to myself as much as anyone, and that distracted me. When you stumbled on that bear and she moved to attack, I was so frightened that she might hurt you that all I could think was to draw her toward me instead. I should have had us both turn ethereal, and she wouldn't even have been able to reach us. Instead I shouted, and she swung toward me, and then *you* threw yourself between us with that blast of ki, as if it were your job to defend me."

"That didn't do us much good either," I said as my cheeks flushed. "It only made her angrier. *I* should have thought to turn ethereal." I hadn't been able to stand the thought of my stalwart playmate being hurt himself, and that had knocked all the sense out of my head.

"You protected us both," I went on. "You did think of it, and you shifted me too, so the bear couldn't touch me. That's what matters."

"And I'll continue protecting you as long as I'm with you," Takeo said. He didn't look at me, but toward the mountain. "That is the duty your parents gave me, and I carry it out gladly. But that story is who you are, Sora. Even as a child, you were brave and strong and willing to give of yourself for others. You've never seemed like anything less than the best of any kami I've known. Until today, no one gave me the slightest reason to think otherwise. And no sage's words could alter my admiration of you."

Until today. In spite of his kindness, the memory of Rin's words pricked at me as if he'd scraped open a cut that had just scabbed over. He wasn't saying it couldn't be true. He was saying that even if it were, it wouldn't matter to him.

I supposed that had to be good enough.

"Whatever happens, I won't let any harm come to you," Takeo added. He turned his head toward me then, his dark eyes so sure that the doubts within me stilled for just a moment.

"I know," I said. "I'm glad you're here." As long as he was, I wasn't completely without my home.

"It is still an honor," he said quietly. Then he glanced ahead of us. "We should keep moving. We have a long way to go."

Who knew how much longer the mountain would hold—or what the ghosts might be doing to my parents and the others even now?

With ki streaming through us, we resumed our dash across the field and on into the forestland on the other side. We'd only been traveling a few minutes more when three figures floated out from between the trees far ahead of us, crossing our path. Two men, one young and one middle-aged, and a young woman. Below their waists, their bodies faded away into nothingness.

Ghosts.

"...all the things I'll do," the young woman was saying.

"I wish Obon were tomorrow, and we could start already!" the young man replied. Then the three of them spotted us and went still.

Takeo tugged at my hand, urging me to run on, but my body had stiffened.

Everything that was happening to me, it was because of them. If not for the ghosts, I would still be on the mountain. I would know my family and friends were safe. I would know who I was.

And we had no idea what they or their demon leader wanted or intended to do next. Maybe I couldn't blame these three for all of my misery, but they had to know at least that much. Surely Takeo and I, with our training and ofuda, could defeat this trio and force the answers from them. Rin had admitted that her vision of victory wasn't guaranteed. We needed every advantage we could get.

As the ghosts stalked toward us, I gripped the charms in my sleeve. "We need this," I whispered to Takeo. "We'll banish two and question the last one. It'll be easier to defeat the rest if we know what they're planning."

"Hmm, look at this," the woman ghost said, coming to a halt several feet away. "Not much of a rescue force, if they're hoping to take back their mountain."

"Check out their get-up," the young man said. "They look like they figure they're royalty. Where are you headed, Miss Fancy?"

Takeo gave me a terse nod. "Stay close," he murmured.

"I don't see that it's any of your business," I said to the ghost, sliding one foot back into a ready stance. My heart started to thump. I'd fought innumerable battles in the palace's training rooms, but never against an enemy who truly wanted to hurt me.

A tingle raced over my scalp where Midori perched. The thick sash and wide sleeves of my robe weighed on my waist and arms. I could have fought the ghosts in their filmy forms while I stayed corporeal, bending my ki and theirs around my solid body, but the fight would be simpler if my clothes weren't holding me back. I shifted, the lightness that came with my ethereal state sweeping through me.

"Could be they're scouts, like us," the woman said. "D'you think we should take them in? You've got the rope, right?"

The older man patted a bag hanging from his shoulder. The ghosts spread out as if to surround us. "Why are you fighting us?" I asked. "Kami have never done anything to you."

"You've never done anything *for* us either," the young man retorted, and sprang.

I stepped to meet him, drawing my short sword to block his knife before it could scrape at my spirit. Ki sparked between the ethereal blades. The young man's knife was smeared with dried blood. On my head, Midori shivered, a wave of revulsion passing from her into me. The blood of a wound, as with any product of sickness or violence, was like poison to kami. As I pressed forward, looking for an opening to use my ofuda, I tried not to notice how little the blood was affecting *me*.

I lashed out with a charm, but my opponent ducked, his shirt collar lifting to reveal the edge of an intricate tattoo at the top of his back. He swung at me and I whirled out of the way. We circled each other. He hissed at me through bared teeth, but for all his ferocity, I could tell he had little formal training. Swordplay was a sort of dance, to a music you had to hear in your head, and there were gaps in the rhythm of his movements. Gaps I could slip through. When he wove to the side and then jabbed his knife toward my neck, I dodged and smacked my ofuda against his face.

The charm hit his nose more than his forehead, but it worked. The lettered strip of bark sank into his ghostly skin, and his form wavered, contracting in on itself. He disappeared with a crackle of ki.

Across from us, the woman grunted in surprise. Takeo wrenched away her striking hand and swiped at her head with one of his own ofuda. She vanished as quickly as her companion had. Beyond her, the third ghost's eyes had widened. He spun around and fled through the trees.

I bolted after him. "Sora!" Takeo called. I couldn't risk slowing. The ghostly man hurtled straight through trunks and branches it was easier for me to dart around, but that meant he moved faster. The distance between us was growing.

Frantic, I threw all the energy in me to my feet and hurled myself at him. I slammed into his filmy body, knocking him to the ground. He scrambled over, shielding his face with a hand that was missing most of its smallest finger, the stubby end mottled with scar tissue. I set the tip of my sword at his neck and drew out another ofuda. My chest was heaving, my limbs trembling with the effort I'd just expended, but I couldn't suppress a small smile of triumph.

"Why are you following this demon?" I demanded. "What do you hope to gain?"

Takeo came up behind me. The man's gaze flitted between us and settled on me. He glared silently. I pressed the sword down with a sharpening of ki. He winced as it pierced his translucent form, but his mouth stayed firmly shut.

I couldn't do any real damage with my blade, only cause his spirit pain—and the thought of attempting to torture him the way his people had the kami made me queasy. My mind skipped back to the conversation we'd interrupted. The younger-looking man had mentioned Obon.

Maybe this one would be less resistant to talking about things he thought I already knew.

"We've heard about your plans for Obon," I said, hoping I sounded convincing. "What makes you think you can hold the mountain that long?"

"Are the two of you going to take it from us?" the ghost sneered. "Omori will crush you in an instant. And when the veil thins, we'll get what we deserve."

He whipped aside his hand and jolted upright. I realized what he intended too late. His head brushed the charm I'd held ready, and he snapped out of our world beneath my hands. I stared at the space where he had been, turning his threat over in my head.

"They're very devoted," Takeo said. "Willing to sacrifice themselves for their cause, whatever it is. That will make them harder to fight."

The lack of blame in his voice dulled the sting of my mistake. "At least we learned something," I said, pushing myself to my feet. "This 'Omori' he mentioned—that must be the demon, don't you think? Now we know its name."

Takeo nodded. "I haven't heard of it, but perhaps Sage Rin will have."

"And he confirmed that they're planning something for Obon. When the barriers between this world and the afterworld are thinnest. The ghosts will have more power then."

"And there may be even more of them," Takeo said. "The dead often return to visit on those three nights." He paused. "These three already had more strength than I would have expected. I thought before that the demon might be lending them power. Now I'm almost certain."

A chill trickled through me. "How much power must the demon have, to be able to share it with so many other spirits?"

"More than any creature I've ever faced," Takeo said grimly.

"Do you think they meant the true Obon or one of the human dates?" I asked. People observed the holiday at different points throughout the summer.

"The dead should know the real time as well as any," Takeo said. "Which leaves us seven days until it begins."

"Seven days to stop Omori, then," I said. "If the mountain can hold that long."

And the weather, and the tides, and all the other cycles the trapped kami should have been tending to. I swallowed thickly.

We knew more than we had just five minutes ago. We knew because of me. Whatever Rin had said, whatever the truth was, I was still strong. But there was also so much more we didn't know. And we had only a week to prepare to challenge a multitude of ghosts, a demon, and who knew what other creatures they had on their side.

FIVE

I WOKE UP to an unfamiliar pain. I lay still on the wooden floor in the small shrine where we'd taken shelter, adjusting to the sensation. A series of sharp pinches ran across my stomach, as if it were being jabbed by little scissors like the ones Ayame used to trim my hair. My thoughts drifted back to my last evening on the mountain, the whirlwind of washing and dressing in my rooms, the smell of the feast drifting through the halls...

My mouth started to water as it had then, and the pain deepened.

Oh. I was hungry. For the first time in my life, I was truly hungry.

I sat up, and my hair slipped unhindered over my shoulders. Sometime during the night, Midori had left—to stretch her wings, to explore the shrine grounds. She had a life beyond me, after all. It shouldn't have mattered to a kami, who could absorb nourishment from the world automatically. But a human—a human who no longer had the energy of the sacred mountain supporting her—

To think that way, even for an instant, felt like giving up. I would not accept that Sage Rin's story was true, not yet. I'd spent the last day and a half in nearly constant motion, fought my first real battle, and held back a multitude of fears. Maybe even a kami would feel hungry after that.

The shrine's guardian, an immense frog kami, was watching me from the top of the cedar altar. I picked up my birthday flute, running my fingers over the lacquered case before slinging it over my shoulder, and got to my feet. "Thank you for the night's lodging," I said, bowing.

The frog blinked and lowered his head in a slight bob. A wisp of friendly ki brushed over me.

As I stepped outside, Midori darted down to take her usual spot on my hair. My hunger pangs ceased at once. I plucked a plum from a tree and walked across the thin grass past a row of lichen-splotched stone lanterns. This small shrine, like so many of the thousands built by humans when they had thought of kami as more than fairy tales, had obviously been forgotten here on its mountainside in the high range that bordered the city. But I was glad it was here at all, with the protections strung and carved around its grounds, keeping out any malicious spirits that wandered this way.

I stopped at the edge of the ridge that overlooked the vast city. It had been past midnight when we'd reached this final slope before Tokyo's sprawling suburbs, and Takeo had suggested we rest and look for the girl by daylight, since she was hardly likely to welcome us if we barged in on her in the middle of the night. Then, the city had looked like a marsh of light, glowing streams winding around stalks of buildings, so bright the stars couldn't compete. Even though it was less striking at dawn, I found it hard to glance away. Energy pulsed off the streets and high rises, so intense that wafts of it drifted over me where I stood. It wasn't the warm caress of ki, but a cool, crackling power. And amidst it lived millions of human beings.

And, possibly, one kami girl all that power had effortlessly hidden.

My fingers squeezed the plum too tightly, and my thumb broke the skin. I forced myself to take a bite, and then another. The flesh was sweet but sticky sliding down my throat. A few drops of juice dripped onto my birthday robe. Since I'd been able to give myself a quick wash at a mountain spring last night, the fabric no longer clung to my skin, but in places it was more brown than blue or golden now. Still, a travel-worn kami robe was a thousand times more regal than any human clothing.

A shudder passed through the ground under my feet. I peered toward Mt. Fuji, though the mountainside hid it from my view. *My* mountain lay miles distant from here, but it was far too easy to imagine the fire bubbling inside it, stirring restlessly. *Wait*, I pleaded silently. *We'll come as soon as we can.*

A sparrow alighted on one of the stone lanterns with a flurry of feathers. It eyed my half-eaten plum. "Are you hungry too?" I asked. I broke off a piece of the yellow flesh and held it out. The sparrow eyed me, then flitted over and snatched the bit from my fingers. It glided back to its perch, gulping the fruit down.

A sparrow had visited me the evening I left Mt. Fuji, I remembered. Could this one know—? Could it have seen—?

But the woods were full of sparrows. It wasn't likely this one had followed us all this way. It didn't know any more about what the demon—Omori—was inflicting on my parents, Ayame, and all those I'd grown up with than I did.

Leaves rustled, and Takeo emerged from the trees beyond the shrine. His hair hung loose and damp, and his face was mottled faintly pink from a recent scrubbing. It made him look less serious, more boyish than usual. When he smiled at me, despite all the reasons I had to despair, my heart lifted.

"Are you ready?" he asked.

I wasn't, but I inclined my head. "Yes."

We made ourselves invisible when we reached the first cluster of houses. The buzz of the city's energy rose around us. It raced over my skin and reverberated into my chest. The ki inside me hummed in response, and a part of me started to believe again. It was a mistake. We would find the girl, and we'd know it really had been me all along.

As we left the suburbs for the city proper, the buildings grew taller and shinier. The sidewalks bustled with people and the roads with cars and bicycles, engines roaring and frames rattling. Takeo's brow furrowed as he examined the paper with Rin's instructions. When he showed them to me, I shook my head. Not knowing the city, the names and numbers in the address meant little to either of us. The sage had managed to be obtuse after all.

"We need a map," I said. "Look for a store with books in the window."

When we found one, I borrowed an atlas of the city while the clerk's back was turned, making it as ethereal as we were with a wisp of ki. I flipped through the pages until I spotted a name I recognized.

"Here," I said, pointing to it. "That's the neighborhood Sage Rin wrote. Once we get there, I think we just follow the numbers."

"Now I'm glad you spent so much time rambling around in town," Takeo said with a squeeze of my shoulder.

We hurried through the streets toward the northwest end of the city, not far from where we'd entered. By the time we identified the location of the address Rin had given us, the sun had already started its descent through the sky. We found ourselves at a large concrete building with three scrawny maple trees out front. The summer heat radiated off the sidewalk and into us, even in our ethereal state. The smell of cooked rice was drifting from somewhere down the street. I ignored the gnawing in my stomach as we read the sign outside the building's doorway.

"A high school?" I said with a noise of anguish. How did Rin expect us to track down one girl inside this place, without even a name? All the sage's talk about urgency, and she insisted on making everything as difficult as possible.

"Let's look inside," Takeo said. We slipped through the door and swept along the empty hallways, stopping to peek through the windows in the classroom doors.

The students sat in neat rows, wearing uniforms of stark white shirts, navy ties, and matching slacks or skirts. Some held themselves straight and attentive; others slouched in their seats, appearing more interested in their neighbors than in the teachers. None of them looked anything other than human.

"She could have given us a classroom number at least," I muttered as we reached the third floor. "There must be a thousand students here. How are we supposed to know which one—"

I glanced through another window and lost my voice.

Ah. *That* was how we were supposed to know.

The girl in the middle of the second row of desks looked unusual even by human standards. Her hair, which was pulled into two wavy ponytails on either side of her head, had been bleached and dyed pale lavender. Her baggy socks bunched around her calves almost to her knees, and her shoes were painted with neon shapes that appeared to be mock lipstick prints.

And she glowed.

The glow seeped from the edges of her body, as if her skin couldn't quite contain all the ki inside her. Around her, her classmates looked dull and faded. Less real.

My throat tightened. Maybe this was why Rin had sent us here, instead of to the girl's house or some less crowded place. Because here, seeing all the human students around her, there was no way we could deny that she was something else. That she was kami.

And there was no reason for any kami to be here, a girl exactly my age, dressing and acting like a human, unless Rin's story was true. Unless my parents had gone through with the switch.

Which meant, beyond a doubt, I *wasn't* kami.

As I groped for words, Takeo touched my elbow. The familiar contact drew me from my daze.

"We can't burst in while the instructor is teaching," he said softly. "When the girl leaves, we'll take her aside. Do you know what time the classes would normally end?"

I grasped onto that concrete question. My eyes found the clock on the classroom wall.

"It might be different at different schools," I said, "but in our town they finished at three thirty. If it's the same here, we'll have to wait a half hour."

"All right," Takeo said. "That's not so long."

I pulled myself away from the door. Away from the view of the girl who glowed. My restless feet carried me farther down the hall. My gaze roamed over the walls without really seeing anything, until it caught on a poster tacked to a bulletin board. I halted.

On the poster was a photograph of the mountain—my mountain—above a spray of cherry blossoms. I stepped closer, reaching out to let my ethereal fingers trail over it. The lettering above the image said, *Visit Mt. Fuji this summer!* One of the clubs organizing some sort of trip, I guessed.

Takeo came up behind me. "I can't imagine how worried you must be for your parents," he said.

"I'm worried about everyone." And I missed them. I missed the familiar halls and the familiar music that so often flowed through them, Ayame's murmuring over my hair, Mother's gentle arms pulling me to her.

The last embrace she'd given me, the way Father had hugged me close, flashed through my mind. I blinked hard. Had they been thinking of me when we were together, or had they been imagining the daughter they'd given up for safe keeping? Their real daughter—the girl in that classroom over there.

"I never knew," I said. "I never even suspected."

No, that wasn't true. I hadn't known my parents were lying to me, but I'd worried there was something wrong. Something different about me, not quite what it should be. But at least before, I'd thought I'd known that they loved me anyway.

I'd wondered why they'd hesitated to let me share in the kami's responsibilities—what better reason could there be than that I'd never really been one of them? Just an inadequate human replacement they passed the time with while they waited for the day their real daughter could return to them.

"They wouldn't have wanted anyone to suspect," Takeo said. "It must have hurt them to lie to you, Sora. They were proud of you—I could see it."

It couldn't have hurt them as much as the truth was hurting me. What had they been proud of me for, anyway—using power that hadn't actually been mine?

"I know they did it for the mountain," I said. "I hope it was enough."

"We will save the mountain," Takeo said. "If the sage says this girl can defeat the demon, it must be possible. And today... you can take the life you were supposed to."

Today? The thought of Takeo leaving me behind hit me with a jolt of panic. "No," I said. "I—I don't want it."

I wanted the bed where I'd slept for the last seventeen years. I wanted the painted silk screens and the scrolls of poetry. I wanted the hum of the mountain's ki close around me.

I wanted, I realized as the ache inside me deepened, to truly make Mother and Father proud. For them to smile at me because of me and not who I stood in place of. Whatever their true feelings were, I'd loved *them*. Even now, it meant far more to me to see them rescued and safe again than to set eyes on the human parents I'd never met.

A sudden hope whispered in the back of my mind. Maybe if I proved myself, they'd take me back. The mountain had lent me power once—it might again. With its help and Midori's, I could protect the palace and help with our duties as I'd always intended to. If they'd have me, it would be far better to live as a fake kami than not a kami at all.

"Sora..." Takeo started.

"I'll stay with you," I said. "Sage Rin said the most important thing is that the girl is properly prepared. We can teach her faster with three of us. And I can still fight—I can help, at least a little, if we run into more ghosts while we're getting the Imperial treasures and when we go to take back the mountain."

Takeo was silent for a minute. My shoulders tensed as I waited for his answer.

"If that's what you feel is best," he said finally, "I'll support you."

"You know you don't have to," I said. "If I'm not really—" It was still hard to say it. "You don't owe *me* anything."

He turned me toward him and brushed a strand of hair back from my cheek. His jaw was set as firmly as I'd ever seen it.

"I swore to serve my rulers' daughter," he said. "But I also swore to serve you, Sora. It would take more than a legion of ghosts to change that."

I stared at him, the tears that had threatened receding. There was a fervor in his eyes I'd never seen before. Could he possibly mean—

A bell pealed overhead. I flinched, and the moment was gone. We hustled to the classroom.

The teacher pushed open the door. Inside, the students had sprung up, grabbing their bags and collecting in groups. The largest group had congregated around the girl with the lavender ponytails. Mostly boys. Her glow might have been invisible to those without kami sight, but clearly they could sense it.

"Hey, Ikeda," one said, "we're going for karaoke tonight. Wanna come?"

"Ikeda, I grabbed you the last of those curry buns you like, if you want a snack," another announced.

"Did you finish the history assignment, Ikeda? I can help you."

"Maybe," the girl said, addressing them in turn as a smile lit up her heart-shaped face. "Thanks! I'm already done."

Then a tall, stern boy with hair cut so short it couldn't help standing up from his head strode into the room, and the girl went from smiling to beaming.

"Haru!" she said, throwing her arms around him. She kissed him quickly, and his serious expression broke with a grin.

"Are these guys bothering you, Chiyo?" he said, and turned to the other boys. "Scram."

The others scowled and grumbled but sidled away. Haru slung a proprietary arm across Chiyo's shoulder. He gazed down at her as they wandered toward us, her bright voice filling the air.

"Mrs. Kaneda forgot to give us our quiz—can you believe it? I'm never going to argue with more time to study. Oh, we should go to the store now! I want to get that phone case for you."

Her voice drifted away as she and her boyfriend headed toward the stairwell. Takeo nudged me forward, and we followed them, my heart thudding in a slow, painful rhythm.

It was time to confront the girl my life really belonged to.

SIX

WE GOT our chance on the second floor, where Haru ducked into a classroom to talk to a teacher. The few other students lingering in the hallway were gathered around another bulletin board, their backs to us, and Chiyo was momentarily alone. Takeo shifted into corporeal form. My body balked, but I curled my fingers into my palms and made myself follow suit.

"Miss Ikeda," I said, and she spun around. Her eyes went wide as she took in my clothing.

"Wow," she said. "Is there a special event going on no one told me about?" Her gaze slid past me to Takeo. "And you're all dressed up too. So cool! Did you bring the costumes from home? I didn't think the drama club had anything that nice."

My mouth opened, but nothing came out. Standing there in front of her, my feet now solid on the floor, the reality of the moment crashed over me along with her effervescent enthusiasm.

The moment we told her who we were, who *she* was, I would truly lose everything.

Thankfully, Takeo's world was not falling apart. "Excuse our intrusion," he said, courteous as always. "I am Takeo and this is Sora, and there's something incredibly important that we need to discuss with you. Is there a place we can talk alone?"

"Okay, now you're weirding me out," Chiyo said, and laughed. "Is he for real?" she asked me.

Haru strode out of the classroom behind her. He stepped to her side with a smooth assurance. "What's going on?" he said, eyeing us.

"I don't know," Chiyo said. "Apparently these two need to talk to me in private about something 'incredibly important.' We should find out what it is. Let's go to the roof."

Takeo frowned. "I don't think your... companion should—"

Haru set a hand on Chiyo's shoulder, and she folded her arms over her chest. "If I'm going somewhere, Haru's coming too."

Takeo looked at me. I shrugged, still too overwhelmed to form speech. What did it matter if one more human heard? One already knew, and no one seemed to mind that.

"All right," Takeo said. "Please lead the way."

We passed several more students on our way up the stairs, all of whom stared at me and Takeo. Chiyo appeared unconcerned. The steps continued on past the third floor landing, ending at a door that opened to a blast of broiling air and sunlight.

As the others tramped out, a squeak below made me turn. I peered down the stairwell. Empty. Just someone passing through, I guessed. I slipped out and shut the roof door behind me.

Chiyo sauntered across the concrete tiles to the wall that bordered the rooftop. She leaned back against the glass and turned the considerable dazzle of her smile on us.

"Hit me," she said. "What's this all about?"

Takeo cleared his throat. "It may be difficult for you to consider," he said. "I know faith in our kind has faded, and for you to accept something so large, so quickly... I'll be happy to answer any questions you have. The truth is, you're more than you think yourself to be. You are a kami."

Haru let out a short laugh. Chiyo just raised her eyebrows.

"Say what?" she said, sounding amused.

"You are a kami," Takeo repeated.

"I heard that," she said. "But you could at least try to make sense if you want to pull my leg. Even if all those myths about spirits in streams and trees were true, I think I'd know if I *was* one of them."

"You were purposefully kept ignorant of your true nature, for your own protection," Takeo said.

"This is pointless," Haru said to Chiyo. "Let's go."

"No, wait," she said in a playful tone. "I'm curious. Let's see where they go with this." She turned to us. "Very fascinating. What else have you got?"

She obviously didn't believe Takeo in the slightest. Of course she couldn't. This news was just as unexpected to her as Rin's proclamation had been to me, wasn't it?

And I hadn't really believed until I'd seen proof my eyes couldn't deny.

"Telling her isn't enough," I said to Takeo. "Show her something you can do." We had only six days left before Obon; we didn't have time for a long debate. And every second this conversation dragged out, the pain inside me prickled deeper.

Takeo nodded. The air shimmered as his ki whirled around him, rippling through his uniform. I thought he might raise himself into the air, or vanish into his ethereal form. But then he gathered the energy between his strong hands, guiding it into a familiar streaming shape. My stomach twisted.

A kite. He was making my kite, *our* kite, for her.

Chiyo gasped as the glinting shape floated up over our heads. Takeo twitched his fingers, and it drifted one way and the other. Then he dropped his hands, and the kite dissipated against the sky.

"How did you do that?" Chiyo said, a little breathless. Haru glanced at her, and I thought I saw a flash of dawning understanding cross his angular face, as if he'd almost known. Then he looked at us and his mouth flattened.

"We're kami too," Takeo said. "I can't say if the tales you've heard are true in their specifics, but we exist all around you, keeping the world in balance with the power I just showed you. And you are one of us."

"I don't know," Chiyo said. "That kite thing could have been a trick. Are you sure this isn't a joke?"

She kept smiling even as she asked. If there was one word for Chiyo, I thought, it would probably be "cheerful."

"Why would we show you tricks?" Takeo said, genuinely bewildered.

"What do you want with Chiyo?" Haru broke in, the uncertainty in his tone offsetting the bluntness of his words. He straightened himself up even taller.

"We've come from Mt. Fuji," I said, "where the most powerful kami live, and many others as well. You know how sacred the mountain is, don't you? We need help. Our home has been attacked."

"Someone attacked Mt. Fuji?" Chiyo said, and turned to Haru. "Have you seen anything on TV about that?"

"It's not something you'd have heard about," Takeo said. "Our attackers would have been all but invisible to humans—an army of ghosts. Only a few of us managed to escape, and the others are in grave danger. The whole world is in danger, if they aren't freed soon so we can return to our duties."

"Kami and ghosts and grave danger," Chiyo said. "This really is quite a story."

"It's not just a story," I snapped before I could catch myself. But Chiyo kept smiling.

"Say it's not," she said. "You didn't answer Haru's question. What are you doing here? Shouldn't you be off fighting those ghosts?"

"How would we know *you're* not ghosts?" Haru put in.

"Because the last thing the ghosts would want is for Chiyo to come home," Takeo said. "And that's why we've come here."

"Home," Chiyo repeated.

"You were born on Mt. Fuji," Takeo said, an edge of frustration creeping into his ever-steady voice. "You're one of us, as I've said. Your kami parents left you in the care of a human family so that our enemies wouldn't be able to harm you before you were old enough to make full use of your power. But we need you now. We need you to fight with us."

"Hold on." Chiyo's tone was still bright, but she sidled closer to Haru. "You're really trying to tell me that I'm some sort of magical being? That somehow I never realized it?"

"You wouldn't have, growing up among humans," Takeo said. "You had no one to teach you how to draw forth your power."

"Okay," Chiyo said, "if this isn't a joke, I'm sorry about your mountain getting attacked. I really am. But I don't think there's anything *I* can do about it. Look, I'm absolutely completely human."

She spread out her arms and swiveled on her feet, and all I could see was her glow. It eclipsed everything around her from Haru to the rooftop wall. She held so much ki she could have lit up the entire school. So much I could believe that this one girl could make the difference against the demon and his army of ghosts.

But she didn't want it. We were offering her everything and she didn't want it.

My jaw clenched. If Mt. Fuji was going to be saved, she *had* to take it.

I raised my hands, giving myself no chance to second-guess. "No, you're not," I said, and hurled a shining ball of ki, which I now knew I had to thank Midori for, directly into her face.

Haru flinched, and Chiyo reacted on instinct, throwing up her arms. Only, because she was kami, she didn't deflect the ball of ki. She caught it. It smacked into her hands and clung there, bound by her own energy.

"Oh," she said, lowering her arms. Glints of light swirled between her palms. Haru was staring at her with open awe now.

"It's me, doing this."

"It's you," I said, like a piece of my soul I was tearing out and handing to her.

She rotated the ball between her short fingers, her grin growing as she watched the light dance. "Then... Then I could..." Turning, she flung it across the roof.

The ball of light whipped through the air toward the stairwell. I had just enough time to notice that the door was now standing ajar before the swirling ki slammed into it. As the door thumped shut, a yelp echoed through it, followed by a mumbled curse.

"Someone was watching!" I said. Takeo was already dashing over, his sword drawn. He yanked the door open.

A teenage boy was crouched behind it, clutching the side of his head.

"What are you doing here?" Takeo demanded.

The boy slowly righted himself, one hand gripping the doorframe. With the other, he grabbed his fallen glasses from the ground and pushed the rectangular frames back over his wide-set eyes. The room at the top of the stairs must have been incredibly stuffy in this heat. The shaggy hair that zigzagged across the boy's forehead looked damp, and the collar of his shirt was loosened, the knot of his tie dangling halfway down his lean chest.

He glanced at the sword pointed at his neck and then up at Takeo, offering a shaky smile.

"Oh, it's just Mitsuoka," Chiyo said with a wave of her hand. "He's the class weirdo, but he's good for a laugh sometimes. Nothing to be worried about anyway." She raised her eyebrows at him. "Don't tell me you've decided to join my league of 'admirers.'"

Haru's expression had tensed. He clearly didn't take that possibility lightly.

"I was just wondering what was up with these two," the boy said, gesturing to me and Takeo. He looked past us to Chiyo and added in the same flippant tone, "You know, you really should be more careful with your magical powers, Ikeda. I thought that—whatever it was—was going to pulverize me."

"The matters we're discussing don't concern you," Takeo said. "It would be best if you left now."

"Don't concern me?" the boy said. "Are you kidding me? You're the one who just said the whole world is in grave danger. Last time I checked, I live here too."

"I guess this story is better than your comic books, huh?" Chiyo said. "But the guy with the big sword said go, so you should probably listen to him." She managed to sound both warning and cheerful at the same time.

The boy tightened the knot of his tie and raised his chin. "No," he said. "Apparently kami are real and Mt. Fuji's been taken over by evil ghosts, and the world might end if we don't stop them. I'm not going to just walk away. Maybe I can help. I might not have some secret magical power, but this is my area of expertise. I've read about ghosts and ogres and just about every supernatural being there is. I might have heard things none of the rest of you have—things you could use."

"You think you know more about kami than kami do?" Haru demanded.

"No," the boy replied. "But give me an hour and I can come up with a list of all the ways demons have ever been recorded being defeated, or what protections work so well against ghosts even regular people can use them, or anything else that'll give you an edge."

Standing there, sweat-damp and defiant, he looked a little ridiculous, especially with Takeo in his formal guard attire towering over him. But the determination on his face and the conviction in his words plucked a chord deep inside me, a sound I hadn't known I was longing to hear. And there probably were human stories about ghosts and demons the kami didn't know that contained some truth.

"Takeo," I said, "he's already heard so much. If he wants to try to help, why *can't* we let him? Don't we need all the help we can get, kami or not?"

Takeo turned to me, and a flicker of confusion passed over his handsome face, as if he hadn't seen me in so long he almost didn't recognize me. But that wasn't it. A prickling ran down through me to my bones. He was finally realizing that I was just as human as the boy in front of him. I made myself smile.

"You're right," Takeo said after a moment of silence. He lowered his sword and sheathed it. "Of course you're right. That is, as long as you—" He glanced at Chiyo.

She shrugged. "The more the merrier, I guess. As long as he doesn't get pushy with me." From my brief observations of her classroom, I suspected that was a problem she encountered a lot.

"He'd better not," Haru said.

The boy swept into a low bow, snatching at his glasses the instant before they slid off his nose. "It is my pleasure simply to be of service," he intoned. But when he straightened up, he was looking at me with open curiosity. I had the conflicting urges to drop my gaze and to stare back at him until he dropped his. His eyes were bright brown, like copper in the sun. They studied me so intently my pulse skipped.

"Keiji Mitsuoka," he said. "You can call me Keiji. Thank you."

"You should thank Chiyo," I said. "It was her decision."

After all, I didn't have any authority now. The real daughter of Mt. Fuji's rulers was standing over there.

Chiyo tossed back her ponytails and pushed off the wall. "Why don't I take you all back to my house and we'll settle this," she said pleasantly. "If what you're saying is true, my parents will know, right?"

Takeo inclined his head. "I hope they can confirm what I've told you. And I can understand your wanting to speak with them before deciding whether to trust us. Given the attention our clothing has drawn, I think it would be best if we accompanied you unseen. It is an honor to have met you, Chiyo."

He dipped into a bow far more graceful than Keiji's had been, forcing me to do the same. As we straightened up, he took my hand, the tingle of transformation already tickling from his skin over mine. Chiyo's mouth dropped open as we shifted into our ethereal forms. We'd turned translucent before her eyes. Haru and Keiji were both scanning the rooftop, looking just as disturbed, but for a different reason. Their human vision wouldn't be able to register our presence at all.

"They've disappeared, just like that," Keiji said. "Now that's amazing."

"Don't be silly," Chiyo said. "They're right..." She trailed off as it must have hit her that she was the only one who could still see us.

"You're kami," I said, and her gaze darted back to me, startled.

From the look on her face, that was the first moment she started to really believe.

On the sidewalk outside the school, Chiyo turned to the right with a discrete motion for us to follow her. Haru strode along beside her. Keiji had stopped to unlock a bicycle and now trailed behind, peering at the air around him as he walked his bike, as if hoping if he looked hard enough he'd be able to make us out. Takeo and I brought up the rear of our strange procession.

Even though I'd slept the previous night and it was still early in the afternoon, I felt worn out. Midori adjusted her grip on my hair, her wings fluttering as she gave me an affectionate nudge. I'd been so lost in my reactions to what was happening to *me*, I hadn't given her much thought.

"Are you all right?" I murmured, directing a thread of concern her way. She answered with a touch of contentment.

"You don't think it's hurting her, do you?" I said to Takeo. "Sharing so much of her energy with me?"

Takeo smiled at the dragonfly. "She's a fine old kami, small as she is. She's got plenty to spare."

I supposed Midori wouldn't have been the one tasked to stay with me whenever I left the mountain otherwise.

The scent of freshly steamed vegetables seeped from the open doorway of a dim restaurant we passed. Next to it, the brightly lit window of a cafe showed off plastic replicas of a vast array of desserts. Chiyo grazed her fingers over them with an avid look, but kept going. A lilting melody whispered through the glass: piano and bass and a woman's high voice. Human music.

I absorbed it as it carried after us down the street. Mr. and Mrs. Nagamoto had often put on instrumental pieces full of strings and woodwinds, not so different from the songs kami played. Their children had usually worn earphones when listening to music at home, but I had vague memories of pounding beats and screeching guitars. This didn't sound quite like any of that.

I'd thought I'd known so much about humans after all the time I'd spent in town, but I didn't really know anything, did I? Nowhere near enough to start living as one myself.

We headed into a quiet residential neighborhood several blocks from the school. Chiyo picked up her pace, and my heart started to beat a little faster. What would they be like—the mother and father who'd raised her in my place? How could I possibly talk to them? Midori send me another wisp of reassurance, but my mouth had gone dry.

Finally, Chiyo stopped outside a beige house surrounded by a low wrought-iron fence. A scuffed red mat lay in front of the door and filmy curtains hid all view of the interior. Chiyo opened the gate. Keiji leaned his bike against the fence.

Takeo glanced around to make sure no one was watching and then nodded to me. We shifted back into corporeal form. Haru flinched, but Keiji just grinned.

“If you can do that, does that mean I can too?” Chiyo asked, cocking her head. “Invisibility would be really useful for dodging questions in class.”

I recognized Takeo biting back a grimace. “It’s how we survive,” he said. “If we couldn’t hide, humans would stumble on us all the time. And we can’t assume all of them would be kind.”

“Is he always so gloomy?” Chiyo asked me. Without waiting for a response, she breezed past us with a swish of her lavender ponytails.

Six days, I thought as we followed her into the house. We had six days to make this girl into a kami focused enough to defeat a demon and an army of the dead.

“Mom!” Chiyo said brightly, kicking off her shoes. “I’ve brought home a couple of kami who want me to save Mt. Fuji.”

A sharp clink sounded from somewhere farther inside, like a dish set down abruptly. A middle-aged woman appeared in the hall. Her searching gaze took in her daughter and the small crowd of us standing behind her. With a twitch of her fingers, she tucked her chin-length hair behind her ears. Hair as thick and straight as mine, by a chin as sharply curved into her slim, pale face. My breath stopped in my throat.

Then I registered her expression. Her eyes and the set of her thin mouth held no surprise or disbelief, only a sort of sad resignation.

I hadn’t given much thought to wondering how aware Chiyo’s adoptive family had been, hadn’t realized I would care, but in that moment the understanding struck me like a blow to the ribs.

This woman had known. She’d known she’d traded one daughter for another. It hadn't been some secret trade in the dark of night, with my human parents remaining none the wiser.

My birth mother had given me up willingly.

"Well," she said, her voice strained. Her hands twisted together in front of her. "Well. Would you come in? I'll make some tea."

SEVEN

CHIYO'S MOTHER—*my* mother, actually, a voice in my head reminded me—insisted that we couldn't talk until Chiyo's father got home. She ushered us into the living room and then hurried to the kitchen. The urgent murmuring of her voice into the phone carried through the wall.

I wanted to protest that we had no time to spare, that the mountain couldn't wait, but the tightness around her mouth as she handed out cups of tea kept those words locked in my throat. Takeo stayed silent as well, though I could see the tension in his sinewy arms as he lifted his cup to his lips.

We couldn't force Chiyo to come with us. She clearly still had her doubts. If we started pushing her or her parents too hard, I could easily imagine her balking completely.

After a stretch of sipped tea and awkward silence, the front door opened. I braced myself as Mr. Ikeda stepped into view, but there was nothing fearsome about the slight, smooth-faced man who nodded to Takeo and me with a stiffness that contradicted his spoken welcome. Plainly our arrival wasn't completely unexpected to him either. Both of my human parents had agreed to send me off to Mt. Fuji, to be parted from me for years.

There wasn't really space for all of us in that small room. Haru, Chiyo, and Mrs. Ikeda were squeezed together on the small couch, and Mr. Ikeda sat in the armchair beside it. I couldn't help noticing the muscles in his long-fingered hands as he clasped them together, wondering if he was the one who played the piano in the corner. Had my love for music come to me through him?

I squashed down that question and the others tugging at my mind. This wasn't about me. It was about saving the mountain. What were Mother and Father going through there as this meeting dragged out?

Keiji had dropped onto the piano bench, and Takeo and I stayed standing. Takeo took one last polite sip of his tea and set the cup on the low table in front of the couch.

"I can see you understand why we're here," he said, briskly but firmly. "It's time for Chiyo to come home. The threat her true parents knew she would eventually face has arrived; she must live out her destiny and save Mt. Fuji. The service you've done for the kami all these years will be rewarded, I'm sure. I'm sorry we couldn't give you more forewarning."

Mrs. Ikeda brought her hands to her face. "I thought—she was supposed to stay with us until she was of age. Twenty years, they said."

"They hoped the threat wouldn't appear until after that time," Takeo said. "Sadly, they were wrong."

"So it's true?" Chiyo broke in. "I'm a... a kami?"

"It's true," Mr. Ikeda said roughly.

Chiyo laughed. "You don't even *believe* in kami. We only go to the shrines for the big festivals, when everyone goes. You never said anything."

"We didn't want to risk you seeing something that would make you realize, or risk some spirit seeing you and recognizing what you were..." He raked his fingers through his thinning hair. "I was so startled when *I* realized that we're not alone in this world, that there truly are beings with powers beyond my imagining—I know it must be such a shock for you, to be told you *are* one. I'm sorry you had to find out this way. Part of the arrangement was that we had to keep it from you."

"Powers," Chiyo murmured. She looked at her palms, and I suspected she was remembering the ball of energy I'd tossed to her an hour ago. Then she shook her head, her smile turning rueful. "It almost makes sense. All my friends would complain about their parents criticizing this and arguing about that, but you let me wear whatever I wanted, go to whatever school I wanted—you didn't even get upset when I dyed my hair! I thought you were just cool. But you were trying to make up for lying, right? Or—was it because I'm not even really your daughter, for you to boss around in the first place?"

"We've tried to be the best parents we could for you," Mrs. Ikeda said. "As far as our feelings go, you *are* a daughter to us. We never wanted to think about you leaving us someday."

My arms tightened where I'd crossed them over my chest. Takeo had suggested I could go back to these people, but they didn't want me. They wanted Chiyo. And why not? She was the daughter they'd watched grow up, that they'd lived nearly half their lives with, not me.

That was fine. I didn't want them either. I wanted my *real* home, safe and filled with love and music again.

"It seems so crazy!" Chiyo said. "I don't feel that different."

"You will," Takeo said, "when we've shown you everything you can do."

"But why?" Keiji said. He leaned forward on the bench, his bright eyes lit up with fascination as he fixed them on the Ikedas. "Why did the kami pick the two of you out of everyone in Tokyo to take Chiyo in? How did it even happen?"

"It was a favor that needed repaying," Mr. Ikeda said. "When I was younger than you, my sister became very sick. She'd been in the hospital for months and she was only getting weaker. I traveled to Mt. Fuji to pray, not really thinking it would make a difference, but desperate to do anything I could. It turned out I should have believed. A woman appeared to me and told me she'd seen that the wish in my heart was pure. She offered me water from a spring to give to my sister, so she'd be well again." The corners of his lips curled into a faint smile. "My sister walked out of the hospital the next day, and she's never had more than a cold since then. So when the same woman came to us and asked for our help—how could we deny her?"

Mrs. Ikeda touched her stomach. "I think they may have repaid us on top of that. We'd only just started trying, but it was right after we agreed that we found out for sure we were having a child of our own." She turned to Takeo. "Where is our other daughter? Is she all right? She wasn't... hurt, by this threat to the mountain?"

The worry etched in her face might have comforted me a little if her words hadn't sent a cold jab of realization through me. Their sacrifice hadn't just been twenty years. She and Mr. Ikeda had given up their daughter knowing they might lose me *forever*. Rin herself had said I'd been set up as Chiyo's stand-in so that if our enemies came for her, they'd find me in her place.

If the attack had happened differently, if I'd been caught up in it instead of able to escape, I might have died. So that Chiyo wouldn't. *That* was what the deal had really meant. My life to save hers.

My stomach knotted. Takeo opened his mouth to answer, and I jumped in. "She's safe," I said. "Chiyo's parents made sure she was out of harm's way."

If they knew it was me, that I was here now, they wouldn't understand why I was going to leave again. Why I wasn't happy to see them. But I could hardly bear being in the same room as them right now. I couldn't handle an argument. It was simpler if they didn't know.

"They did," Takeo agreed, glancing at me. "You needn't be frightened for her. We weren't able to bring her with us, but you can be sure she's looked after, and I'll do everything I can to ensure she returns to you once our mission is finished."

The back of his hand brushed mine, and I passed a ribbon of ki to him, warm with gratitude. Mr. Ikeda considered the two of us, his lips pressed flat. Could he see through my lie? I didn't think the family resemblance I'd noticed was so obvious.

He sighed and looked away. "They said, as soon as they took Chiyo from us, we would have our own—our other—daughter back."

He looked so miserable I felt a twinge of guilt, but I hadn't made that bargain. And where I went should be up to me, shouldn't it? From the moment they'd traded away my life, they'd lost any claim to my loyalty.

"No one's even asked if I'm *going*," Chiyo said, and everyone's attention snapped back to her.

"You have to come," Takeo said. "A sage's vision has shown that you will be the one to defeat those who threaten the mountain. Your true parents—all of the kami—are depending on you."

She spread her hands. "How can they all be depending on me when I've never even *met* any of them?"

"So what if you've never met them?" Keiji said, his voice almost angry. "Your parents did everything they could to protect you, and now you're going to ignore them when they need you?"

I blinked at him, surprised and impressed by his vehemence. If only Chiyo cared that much.

"I don't want you to go," Mrs. Ikeda said to her. "But that's where you belong—where you've always belonged."

"Okay, okay," Chiyo said. "Chill out. It's not like I want people to get hurt. I just don't see how I'm supposed to take on a whole army or whatever, even if I'm a kami." She pointed a finger at Takeo and me. "You're kami, and you couldn't stop them."

"Yes." Haru slipped his hand around Chiyo's, sitting up straighter. "What you're asking Chiyo to do is dangerous, isn't it? Do you know for sure that *she* won't get hurt?"

When he put it that bluntly, it was hard to answer. Rin's words echoed in my head. *A vision is not a guarantee.*

"So she could," Haru pressed. "Who's going to help her fight all those ghosts you talked about—just the two of you?"

"The great sage who foresaw her victory will be helping us," Takeo said. "We'll train Chiyo to use her powers, which are considerable even among the kami, and help her gather the Imperial treasures. With them, she should be able to destroy all who threaten the kami."

"And *you'll* come with us too, won't you?" Chiyo said, squeezing Haru's fingers.

He hesitated, relief, surprise, and uncertainty softening his stern expression in turn. "Of course," he said.

Takeo's composure cracked. "We must begin as soon as possible and move as quickly as possible," he said. "I don't think there is time—"

"Haru and I go together," Chiyo said firmly. "And speaking of time, are you talking about leaving *tonight*? I'll kick some ghost butt if I'm 'destined' to, I guess, but afterward—I can come back here, right? I'm not giving up my whole life."

As if any of us had a choice. My spine stiffened.

"Your true life is as a kami on Mt. Fuji," Takeo said. "But I see no reason why you couldn't visit the city from time to time."

"Visit?" she said. "What about my parents here—what about my friends? I'm going to leave without saying good-bye, and then who knows when I'll see them again? If I'm fated to save Mt. Fuji, it'll happen whether we leave now or tomorrow, won't it?"

"I don't think you understand how grave the situation is," Takeo said. "If the kami aren't released soon, we can't even know all the consequences the world will face."

"Chiyo," Mr. Ikeda started, but she waggled her finger at him.

"I just found out you're not really my dad," she said. "You can't tell me what to do." But despite her teasing, the glow of her ki was contracting, as if she were pulling into herself. Away from us.

"Then by the words of your true mother and father," Takeo said. I held up my arm to stop him, my throat tight.

We needed Chiyo to *want* to learn, to want to use her powers. The more demands we made, the more she would resist. If we couldn't find a point of agreement, then Rin's prophecy would mean nothing at all.

I looked at Chiyo clutching Haru's hand, her shoulder leaning against her mother's. Maybe we'd come at this wrong. The urgency of saving all those kami on the mountain was clear to us, because they were *our* friends and family. We hadn't considered what mattered most to *her*.

"I don't know what might be decided after the mountain is saved—about where you could live or who you see—but I do know that it's not just the kami who need your help," I said, letting a little of my anguish bleed into my voice. "If our enemies aren't stopped soon, every living being will suffer. Every human. The people living close to Mt. Fuji most of all, but the harm will spread everywhere, even here. You'll be saving *everyone*."

Chiyo stared at me, her eyes wide. Her ki shimmered brighter again. I'd gotten through to her, at least a little.

"And we could start the training right here, couldn't we?" I went on, turning to Takeo, before she had to respond. "Sage Rin wanted us to teach her the basics before we brought her to the valley—there is a chance we'll run into more ghosts on the way there, and she'll need to fight. We can start tonight and perhaps be ready to leave tomorrow. As long as we stay in the house it's unlikely Omori's allies will notice us if they're patrolling the cities too. And that will give her more time to get used to all these ideas before she has to leave the home she's used to behind."

"That sounds fair to me," Chiyo said to my relief.

Takeo's gaze swept through the room, and I could tell he was thinking this house was not an ideal setting for training. Nonetheless, he gave a resigned nod. "Now that her powers are awakening, it will be much easier for our enemies to identify her. She should know how to defend herself before we risk traveling."

Chiyo cocked her head. "You know," she said, "if you're worried about people noticing us, those really aren't the best clothes. *Can* you put on other things?"

Takeo eyed his uniform as if it had never occurred to him that there might be a situation it was inappropriate for. "Of course," he said. "We can wear whatever we like."

Even as I fingered the fine embroidery of my robe, I remembered how quickly the ghosts we'd encountered in the forest had identified us as kami—and important ones at that.

"She's right," I said. "We stand out too much like this. We should find other clothes." My outfit wasn't ideal for defensive training either.

"Now that's a problem I'm happy to help with right now," Chiyo said, beaming again as she bounded to her feet. "Dad, can you find something that'll look normal on Takeo here? And Sora, you come with me." She patted Haru's arm. "I know you have that thing with your grandfather tonight, but I want to see you first thing in the morning, you hear?"

He nodded with a small smile, and she bobbed up to kiss him quickly. As he headed for the door, Keiji raised his hand to us. "I'm going to duck out for a bit too. My brother will be checking in on me, and I can grab a bunch of my books for preliminary research on ghosts and demons. I'll be back soon."

Research. My thoughts tripped back to the Nagamotos' house, the computer in the living room where I'd watched Mr. Nagamoto look up potential clients, and his son and daughter run searches for school projects. So much information appearing like magic with a press of a button, about anything they might want to know. Or anyone.

Chiyo was beckoning me. "Do you have a computer?" I asked.

"Sure," she said. "Why?"

"There's something *we* need to research." Our lives might depend on finding out just who this Omori was—if we even could.

EIGHT

THE WALLS of Chiyo's bedroom were painted the same lavender hue as her hair and plastered with posters of young men and women in garish clothing making exaggerated expressions. Chiyo pushed open the door to her closet and contemplated its contents.

"Let's get your fashion situation sorted out first," she said. "You're taller than me, but I think these pants or these shorts should work. You pick." She held up a pair of jean shorts with shredded hems and white calf-length capris.

I pulled my gaze away from the small computer on the desk beside her bed, curling my fingers around my robe's sleeves. I *did* need to change, but her offerings seemed a poor substitute. "I'd like to keep this too," I said.

"Well, yeah," Chiyo said. "I'm not going to steal your clothes! Not really my style anyway."

I studied her as I pointed to the white pants. Her ki was glowing freely again, her eyes sparkling. How could she seem so happy after everything we'd told her?

Then I thought of Ayame, who could find something to fret over even when all was right in the world. Of Mother, whose cool-headedness never faltered. Maybe it was Chiyo's nature to be cheerful and confident no matter how dire life got.

Besides, she was hardly getting the worse end of this deal.

"And this shirt should be good—it's too long on me, really," she said, handing me a loose cotton blouse. "It'll look great with your hair—I wish mine would stay that straight when I grow it long." She fluffed the waves of her ponytails.

The shirt was the same shade of green as the leaves on the cherry trees that bloomed by the entrance to the palace. A rush of homesickness filled my chest. *I'll trade you,* I wanted to say. *My hair for your everything else.*

Instead, I squeezed into the tiny bathroom in the hall, bumping my elbows against the sink and the wall as I untied the robe's sash and squirmed out of the layers of silk. Midori fluttered over me as I folded them quickly and tugged on Chiyo's clothes. The pants had pockets at the hips that I shoved my remaining ofuda into. The fabric hugged my legs, and I could only imagine how tight the pants were on Chiyo's curvier figure. I slung my flute case back over my shoulder and wiggled the narrow sheath of Takeo's short sword through one of the belt loops. The weapon felt unwieldy now that I knew the charms made much more effective weapons, but we might run into creatures other than ghosts—like those ogres in the woods.

Like the demon. Omori.

Changing had rumpled my hair—the smooth, straight hair

Chiyo had admired. I turned away, running my fingers through it and pushing open the door. My parents had called me beautiful on my birthday, but that must have been the glamor of the mountain's ki, the dress, and Ayame's makeup. The girl I'd glimpsed in the mirror now looked completely ordinary.

When Midori and I hurried back into Chiyo's bedroom, I found she'd changed as well, from her school uniform into a yellow tank top and flower-print shorts. She was standing by the window, clutching the cord for the shade.

"Look!" she whispered, waving me over.

My heart started to thud. Had we been found out already? I joined her at the window, but I didn't understand what she'd wanted me to see. The sidewalks and road were still and empty. Then a shiver of movement near the end of the block caught my gaze.

A funnel of wind, slim as a tree trunk and nearly as tall, was whirling beside one of the telephone poles. It veered away, zigzagging across the street, carrying dust and leaves and crumpled wrappers with it. They whipped around and around, so fast they blurred before my eyes.

"I was just going to close the shade, and I saw it," Chiyo said. "Is that... dangerous?" She sounded more curious than scared.

"I don't think so," I said. Nothing about it looked magical, but it wasn't exactly natural either. A chill crept over my skin. The troubles were already beginning. "One of our duties is to oversee the weather," I went on. "A lot of kami were visiting the palace when the demon attacked—and now they're trapped there, unable to fulfill their usual responsibilities. Some of them would have worked with the wind. There aren't enough kami still free to keep control over it."

"So the wind is getting a little wild?" Chiyo said, and I nodded. "I guess it's not so bad."

"It'll get worse, not better, if we don't rescue the mountain," I said.

"Can you stop it?" Chiyo asked, lifting her chin toward the funnel, and I thought I heard a faint pleading note under her good cheer. She believed I was kami too. We hadn't told her otherwise, and Midori's lent ki would be giving me a glow that was more than human. I didn't see any point in complicating matters by revealing I'd lied to the Ikedas.

Maybe, with Midori, I had enough power to calm the whirlwind. I just wasn't sure how to. Because Mother and Father had been waiting for Chiyo to come, so they could teach *her*.

I drew in a breath, groping for an excuse, and outside the window the whirlwind shuddered and scattered. "Wow!" Chiyo said with a laugh. "You didn't even move."

It hadn't been me, just the randomness of the wind. She should have been able to sense that—but at the same time I was desperately glad for that flash of admiration. My stomach knotted.

I scanned the street once more. "Are the ghosts you talked about really looking for us?" Chiyo asked. Her back tensed. "You don't think, if they realized we're here— Would they hurt Mom and Dad?"

"They shouldn't know anything about you," I told her. "As long as we stay where no one can happen to see you, we'll all be fine." We had no reason to believe that Omori had sent his ghosts here—but not knowing what his plans were, we had no reason to assume he hadn't. The others we'd run into had been patrolling far from Mt. Fuji.

"The computer," I said, leaving the window. "Let's see what we can find out."

Chiyo plopped down at her desk. "Okay," she said. "What are we looking for?"

I sat down on the edge of her bed where I could see the screen. "Omori," I said. "We think that's the name of the demon."

"Oooh," Chiyo said in a spooky tone and typed in the name and the characters for "demon." She scrolled through the results, clicking open a few windows. "Hmmm. It looks like there was some warrior guy named Omori got tricked by a lady demon, way back. Do you think that's related?"

"I don't know." It didn't make sense for a man who'd fought demons to now be helping one, but I supposed we couldn't know for sure. "Can you print that information off?"

Chiyo nodded, and the printer beneath the desk hummed. She flipped through several more pages of results and pursed her lips. "It's all just that one story."

"Try looking for just 'Omori'?" I suggested.

Her fingers clattered over the keys, and a new list of results sprang up. "Hmmm," she said, "Omori station, another Omori station, some company named Omori... Hey! Check out this guy named Omori here in Tokyo—he's a businessman, some big exec. And look at this!"

She pushed away from the computer so I had a better view of the window she'd opened. It held a grainy photograph of a slender middle-aged man with short dark hair, shaking hands with an older man in a formal robe. The caption read, *Kenta Omori greets Yamaguchi boss Ryo Shimura.*

"What's Yamaguchi?" I asked.

"Oh, right, I guess you wouldn't know," Chiyo said. "They're yakuza—criminal underworld people? Gangsters. Dragon tattoos and chopped-off fingers. Yamaguchi's one of the top gangs. I wonder if this Omori guy was mixed up with them."

"One of the ghosts we encountered was missing part of his finger," I said, leaning against the bedpost to peer at the screen. I'd seen a tattoo on that other one's back too. "What else can you find about Kenta Omori?"

Chiyo followed a few more links, skimming the articles. "Yikes!" she said. "He was murdered. Shot. Four years ago. If that's how he went, I bet he *was* yakuza. They're not giving many details—the newspapers are really cautious talking about the gangs... Hey, here's a better picture."

The photograph she'd found showed a younger version of the same man. He was just as slender, his hair trimmed as neatly, but his mouth was curved in a broad smile I wouldn't have imagined him making after seeing the first picture. He stood with a relaxed confidence, as if he knew he was going to get things done and no one could change that. It was a few seconds before I could tear my eyes from his face to look at the other people in the picture.

Kenta Omori had one arm around the waist of a woman I assumed was his wife. She looked delicate and graceful in her demure suit, her expression shy but pleased. She cradled an infant in a frilly dress against her chest. Another child, a little boy, grinned where he stood at his father's side.

I stared at them. Could our demon really have once been this man? But if he'd been involved with the gangs Chiyo had talked about, he'd been a criminal too—maybe become one after this picture was taken. The characteristics of the ghosts I'd noticed might be a coincidence, or he might be recruiting his former colleagues from among the dead.

"Chiyo!" Mrs. Ikeda's voice carried from downstairs. "Dinner is ready."

"We can't know for sure who we're dealing with yet," I said quickly. "Let's print off some articles about him too." I could scour them for more clues later, and we could show what we'd found to Sage Rin.

Chiyo tapped a few keys. "I wouldn't have thought kami would know much about computers," she remarked.

"We keep an eye on humans," I said, thinking of Mr. Nagamoto again. Of magma surging down the mountain toward his little house, if we didn't make it back in time.

Paper emerged from the printer, heavy with ink. Chiyo passed the pages to me. Kenta Omori's amused face smiled up at me for an instant before I folded it away and slid it into my pocket.

I might have wanted to skip dinner and rush straight into training if my human body hadn't betrayed me. Even with Midori perched in my hair, when we reached the dining table and the smells of rice and fried pork wafted over me, a stab of hunger cut through my belly. I hadn't eaten since the plum that morning, but obviously now, away from the mountain, my body needed much more sustenance than I was used to. I had to take some of the burden off of Midori. My hands trembled as I waited for the others to assemble so we could start the meal.

I'd eaten feasts at the palace, but no food had ever tasted as rich as that simple dinner. In spite of the screaming of my stomach, I forced myself to chew slowly, to reach my chopsticks toward each new bite gingerly, so as not to give myself away. Still it seemed the pork cutlets, rice, and miso soup disappeared far too fast. To my immense gratitude, Mrs. Ikeda was determined to prove how welcoming she could be. She brought out salad and fish cakes and pickled vegetables. Keiji returned, wearing a blue T-shirt and brown cargo pants in place of his school uniform and carrying a bulging messenger bag, in time to take part in the small dessert of strawberry ice cream. As I swallowed the last spoonful, my hunger finally retreated.

After he'd helped clear the table, Mr. Ikeda turned to Takeo.

"Can you spare us just a few minutes more with Chiyo?" he asked. Takeo nodded briefly, and the older man turned to his adoptive daughter. "Would you play for our guests, just a song or two?" he said. "It'd be nice to hear you one more time before you go."

Chiyo flopped down on the couch. "It's probably my last night here. I'm not going to spend it showing how badly I can mangle the piano keys. That'd be painful for everyone."

His face fell, and an impulse to make it brighten, to do what she wouldn't, lit inside me. A little music would raise our spirits before we began the evening's work. I lifted my flute case.

"I can play something, if you'd like to hear one of the songs from the mountain."

"Yeah, let's hear what kami music sounds like!" Chiyo said. I opened the case, and when I raised my head, the instrument in my hands, everyone had crowded into the living room around Chiyo: the Ikedas, Keiji, Takeo. They were all watching me.

I hesitated. Then Takeo smiled. He looked almost like a stranger in the buttoned shirt and linen slacks Chiyo's father had lent him, but he'd kept his ceremonial belt around his waist and his bow and quiver at his shoulder, and I'd have known that smile anywhere. My fingers found the holes in the polished bamboo as if they belonged there. I brought the flute to my lips.

I meant to play one of the joyful tunes we would have danced to during my birthday celebration. But as I inhaled deep into my lungs, my fingers changed my mind for me. They slipped into the low, gentle melody of the first song I'd learned as a child.

It was the song Mother used to sing to me when I was young and too restless to fall asleep, and it had always soothed me then. Now, the notes floating out into the air sounded only sad. A soft lilting sorrow that swelled inside me and spilled on my breath into the flute. I thought of Mother sitting beside my bed. Of Father, beaming as he handed me this birthday present. And suddenly the sadness was welling up in my eyes, catching in my throat.

I jerked the flute from my mouth, blinking. "I'm sorry," I said, as evenly as I could manage. "I need to go outside for a minute." And then I dashed, half-blind, for the front hall.

Takeo started after me. He reached for me when I stopped to

fumble with the door handle, but I pushed his hand away. "No," I said. "I just need a moment alone. I'll be all right. You—you find the best room for the training."

I ducked outside, hearing him through the door making some excuse to the others. Maybe telling them that I was missing the kami friends and family we'd left behind on Mt. Fuji, that I was afraid of what would become of them if we didn't return soon. But as I brought my hand to my lips just in time to smother a sob, I knew that wasn't the whole truth. That the answer was much more selfish.

As much as I was frightened for them, in that moment I was even more afraid of what would become of me.

NINE

I'D JUST convinced the tears to retreat and the hitch to leave my breath when I heard the doorknob turn behind me. It couldn't be Takeo—he'd never intrude when I'd told him I wanted to be alone. I stepped to the side of the tiny concrete porch, clutching the flute. The evening air shifted around me, thick and tinged with ozone: the smell of a brewing thunderstorm.

Keiji poked his head through the doorway. When he saw me, he seemed to decide it was safe to come out. He closed the door behind him, scooted past me, and hopped up to sit on top of the gate. The heels of his sneakers tapped the metal bars.

"You know, if *I* were the one who just found out I had magical powers, I'd be a lot more grateful to hear it than Chiyo is," he said in his offhand way. "I don't suppose you could tell me I've got some secret ability I never knew about too?"

My fears were still twisted tight inside me, but somehow the arch of his eyebrows and the playfulness of his tone made me smile.

"Sorry," I said. "Not as far as I know."

"Oh well. I guess I've been doing all right as a regular human being so far."

He grinned back at me, in a slow, easy way that lit up his coppery eyes despite the dusk falling around us. As if he really was happy being what—who—he was.

"So what's up with you and what's-his-name?" he said.

"Excuse me?"

"The tall guy with the sword. Are you two a couple or something?"

To my annoyance, I blushed. It didn't seem fair that I could feel scared and amused, irritated and embarrassed, all at once. At least when I'd thought I was kami I'd been able to pretend I had a nature that was somewhat consistent.

"No," I said. "Not that it's any of your business."

"No offense intended," Keiji said. "I just wondered."

Something Chiyo had said came back to me. She'd asked Keiji if he was turning into one of her "admirers." He *had* been paying enough attention to her to notice her talking to us. "Isn't it Chiyo's boyfriend you should be worried about?" I said.

He shrugged, bumping his legs against the gate. "He assumes every guy who hangs around her must be trying to date her. Untrue."

"You had some other reason for watching her?"

"A better one," he said. "I *knew* there was something going on with her. She's cute, I guess, but not so pretty it makes sense that half the boys in school would be chasing after her. And the teachers would never let anyone else get away with hair that wild.

And she never seems fazed by anything, like she just floats above bad grades and arguments and... there had to be more going on with her than met the eye, you know?"

"Yeah," I said quietly. I did.

Keiji fell back into his previous self-mocking tone. "So I was trying to figure it out. I'd already eliminated a whole lot of possibilities—vampire, government cyborg experiment, mystical princess from another dimension. I'll admit, I hadn't thought of kami."

"You seem to be taking it pretty calmly," I remarked.

He paused. "Like I said before, I've done a lot of reading into the supernatural. And if you keep your eyes open, you see things that can't always be explained. It's nice to know I wasn't just imagining all that. And it's pretty hard to argue with the demonstrations you and your sword-wielding friend have given." His grin returned.

My sword-wielding friend might have already started Chiyo's training. I glanced toward the door. "I—"

"So, I guess you lived on Mt. Fuji?" Keiji said before I could excuse myself.

"Yes. All my life."

"That's, what, like a hundred years? Do kami get old?"

"Seventeen," I said. "And they do. Just slowly."

"Seventeen," Keiji repeated. "So if Chiyo's so powerful because she's kami, how did those ghosts manage to defeat all the kami who were already on the mountain?"

I stiffened. "They had a demon leading them," I said. "Takeo thinks it was lending them power. And there were many more of them than there were of us."

The truth was, though, I didn't know exactly how the ghosts had overwhelmed the palace. The mountain had been our safe haven for uncountable centuries. The demon couldn't have more energy than *all* the kami put together. If it had only been a matter of numbers, the kami would have gotten the upper hand as soon as the ghosts exhausted their weaker ki. There had to be something more.

"And Chiyo's the most powerful of any of us," I finished. "And she'll have the sacred treasures."

Keiji leaned forward, and the glow of the lamp over the doorway reflected off his glasses. "So it's really all on her," he said. His smile fell. "Just how messed up is the world going to get if she can't get rid of them?"

"She can," I said, wishing I completely believed it myself. *A vision is not a guarantee.* "But while we're preparing... The rhythms of the natural world have already been disrupted. So many of the kami who helped keep it in order are trapped. It's too much for those who are left. The weather, the tides, the earth, the volcano in Mt. Fuji... but we'll free the mountain before the situation worsens too far." *I hope.*

"Why did this demon and a bunch of ghosts come after the kami anyway?" Keiji said. "I don't remember ever reading about ghosts getting together to fight kami. I'll check my books just in case, but it can't be that common, anyway."

"I don't know," I said. "They never bothered us before." The information Chiyo and I had found about possible Omoris hadn't offered any clue to that either. It still didn't make sense to me.

"None of you had, like, pissed off some ghosts recently or

something? There has to be a reason, right?"

"I don't *know*," I said, my frustration slipping out before I could catch it.

"Sorry," Keiji said, his voice softening. "I'm just trying to understand. From the stories that have been recorded, however much truth is in them, it sounds like ghosts are pretty big on revenge. And demons—take the meanest person you can imagine doing the most horrible selfish things, and that's who'll turn into one. The more you can tell me, the more I might be able to figure out what's going on. How to stop them."

"So... a person can turn into a demon?" I said. I had a vague sense that I *had* heard the idea in a tale somewhere, but we hadn't talked about demons much on the mountain. At least, no one had with me. I'd thought of them as beings like kami or ogres, who simply came into existence as they were from the start.

"I don't know how common *that* is," Keiji admitted. "And maybe those myths aren't true at all. But there's more than one story where something happens around a person's death that makes them so incredibly angry or vengeful they become consumed by the emotion and it transforms them. Did it seem like this demon was created that way?"

"Maybe," I said. *Kenta Omori.* "We don't know a lot about it."

"Well, I can try to find out more about different types of demons too. I think I'd better leave the physical combat to your friend with the sword. I'm surprised he left the mountain—he seems like the type who'd want to stay and fight."

"He did want to," I said. "So did I. But someone had to come for Chiyo."

Keiji cocked his head, and a moment of silence stretched between us. I should be going back in to help with Chiyo's training right now, but the intentness of his gaze behind the shine of his glasses held me in place. My fingers tensed around the flute.

"Both of you had to come?" he said casually.

"It'd be risky to send only one," I said. "What if something happened on the way here?"

"I guess that makes sense," he said. "Or... maybe you came because you're the girl they switched Chiyo for."

My throat closed up. In that first second, all I managed to do was stand there, lips parted and soundless, like a fool.

Keiji dipped his head. "I thought so. Don't worry, I don't think anyone else has a clue. But I saw how you looked when Chiyo's mom asked about her real daughter—and Chiyo just turned seventeen—and the way you ran out here—"

"I'm worried about my family," I said roughly, scrambling to recover.

"Except they're not your actual family."

"You have no idea—"

"No," he agreed, and stood up with a thump. "I know that. I just have more of an idea than everyone in there. I won't say anything, of course."

He touched my arm, just for a second, his palm warm against my skin. A gesture of reassurance. My heart stuttered despite myself.

"There's nothing to say," I insisted, jerking back.

A tremor rippled through the ground beneath us. *The mountain is so unhappy*, I thought.

And inside the house, Chiyo screamed.

As her shriek pierced the air, light blazed from the house, so bright it seemed to sear straight through the walls. It burned into my eyes. I groped for the door handle and dashed inside.

"What the—" Keiji said behind me. Chiyo was lying on the living room floor, her knees curled to her chest. The light was coming from her, flaring from her body in quavering streams, hundreds of times more intense than the usual glimmer of ki that seeped out of her. I dropped my flute and shielded my eyes as I dropped down beside her. Takeo was already there, Mr. and Mrs. Ikeda hovering behind him.

Chiyo let out another cry. "It hurts," she whimpered. "It hurts, it hurts, it hurts..." The last word trailed off in a hiss. I touched her shoulder gingerly, and her skin singed my fingers. I flinched. The light emanating off her grew even brighter.

"What's happening?" I said to Takeo.

"I don't know," he said. "A moment ago she was fine, and then... this. I've never seen anything like it before. It's almost as if her ki is on fire."

"Can you stop it?" Mr. Ikeda demanded. "Whatever it is, it's hurting her!"

He'd hardly finished speaking when Chiyo shrieked even louder. Heat was wafting off her now, prickling against my face.

Takeo lay his hands on Chiyo's abdomen and closed his eyes. A cool wash of ki slid off him into her. The air chilled, the burning light dimmed slightly, and Chiyo's eyelids fluttered open. I reached for her arm. She was still feverish but no longer flaming.

Midori tugged at my hair, sending an urgent wave of energy

through me. I directed it into my hands with thoughts of ice and snow. The ki raced through Chiyo's flesh and smashed against a white-hot wall inside her.

It wasn't enough. This had to be some sort of magic, and it was too powerful for Takeo, Midori, and me to subdue, even together.

My gut twisted. I could think of one being who'd shown seemingly immeasurable powers. But how could the demon have known to target Chiyo? How could he have found her from so far away?

"We can ease the pain," Takeo said to the Ikedas, "but we can't stop it. If she had full control of her powers, she could shield herself from within, but..."

Chiyo squirmed, gasping. Eventually the three of us would be too drained to continue offering what little help we could now. What if Omori had something even worse up his sleeve? We'd have nothing to protect her with.

Nothing here.

"A shrine's protections keep out ill-meaning spirits," I said quickly. "Would they destroy dark magic too?"

"They very well might," Takeo said. "Good thinking." He turned to the Ikedas, keeping one soothing hand on Chiyo's side. "Leaving may be the only way we can help her. We'll return if we can, but if our enemies have found us somehow, it won't be safe for us here until we've defeated them."

Mrs. Ikeda nodded. "We understand," she said shakily. "Just look after her, please."

She bent to brush her fingertips over Chiyo's hair, and Mr. Ikeda did the same, in a silent goodbye. Then they stepped back, tears shining in their eyes.

"Chiyo," I said, leaning close, "we're going to help you get up. We have to go, but we're going somewhere that should stop the pain, okay?"

All she managed in response was a grimace. As Takeo and I lifted her to her feet, she sucked in a sharp breath. I set her arm over my shoulder and slid mine around her back, and Takeo did the same. Ki hummed between us.

"Where's the nearest shrine?" I asked Keiji, who'd stopped gaping long enough to sling his messenger bag over his back.

"There's one a few blocks from the school," he said, coming with us to the door. "It's really small."

Chiyo's blazing glow flooded the street as we darted outside to a crackle of thunder. "Over here," Keiji said, pointing to the left. We'd just stepped onto the sidewalk when two dim, legless figures drifted into view farther down the road.

Before I could speak a warning, one of them turned our way and let out a shout.

"Ghosts!" I said, and abruptly I understood. This *had* to be Omori's doing—and it wasn't just to hurt Chiyo, but to track her down as well. When she'd first flared up, the light must have been visible from miles around. It was a signal fire to the demon's ghostly allies.

"Sora," Takeo said as the ghosts raced toward us, "you go ahead, feel for the most powerful shrine close by, and find a clear path to it. Keiji, take Chiyo's other arm. Hurry!"

I lifted Chiyo's arm from my shoulder to set it on Keiji's and bolted away from the ghosts to the opposite corner, pulling an ofuda from my pocket as I ran. "This way is open!" I called. Takeo sprinted after me, his ki speeding along both his and Keiji's feet.

We tore down the street toward a faint sense of stillness I sensed amid the city's buzzing energy, which I guessed—and Midori agreed with a tickle of affirmation—was a shrine. In that moment I was glad that humans had build so many everywhere they went, even if their belief had faded. But we'd only made it a few blocks when a trio of ghosts charged out in front of us. I spun around. Two more had joined the couple lagging behind us. Ethereal knives flashed in their hands.

We might have been able to fight them all, but not while dampening the fire in Chiyo. If she flared up again, who knew how many others would find us?

I rushed to a side street. We might be outnumbered, but any kami could outrun a ghost.

"Here!" I said. "Faster!"

I led the others through a maze of alleys at a frantic pace. After several breathless minutes, we darted out across a wider street and nearly barreled into a group of half a dozen ghosts. "Hey!" one hollered, and they lunged at us in a mass of filmy bodies. I managed to whirl around them. A translucent blade nicked my elbow, the pain stinging through my ki. Takeo drew his sword with his free hand just as another ghost heaved a net at him. He managed to wrench it to the side with a grunt, but his protection over Chiyo faltered. Her body flamed brighter, and Keiji yelped as if he'd been burned.

We dashed on across the sidewalk, my heart thudding as quickly as my feet. My lungs were starting to ache. A rasp had crept into Takeo's breath. He managed to dampen the fire in Chiyo's spirit again, the light within her shuddering dimmer, but she whimpered.

More legless figures slipped through the gates and walls, converging around us. How much of Omori's force had he sent to Tokyo? If we stopped moving for a second, they'd overwhelm us.

"The city's full of them," I said to Takeo as we whipped around a corner. "We can't stay here. There's no way we can get enough distance to escape them completely. Even if we make it to a shrine, they'll know exactly where we are. Do you think we can reach the mountains? We'll have a better chance if we can get a long head start on them and then lose them in the forest." And there were shrines there too, like the one we'd slept in last night.

"I think that's our best chance," Takeo agreed. "Join your ki with mine—if we can keep her dimmed enough, it'll be harder for them to continue tracking us once we pull farther ahead."

I ducked close to Keiji, who threw his other arm around me. "I'm sticking with you," he declared, even as his voice shook. I reached behind his back toward Chiyo and found Takeo's hand. Midori's wings trembled against my hair. Ki surged through me and back to Takeo. The light inside Chiyo contracted. I sent every particle I could spare into my legs and *ran*.

We fled through a parking garage and under a bridge. When we seemed to have lost the ghosts momentarily, we veered toward a train track where we could speed unimpeded beside its snaking path through the suburbs. The wind buffeted us, yanking at my hair. My chest ached and my legs throbbed, but I pushed myself forward. All that mattered was reaching the vast stretch of trees I could now see beyond the urban sprawl.

We raced on for several minutes, bracing ourselves when a train roared past, but as the dark line of the forested slope grew, we had to slow down. Our energy was fading. Midori's fatigue echoed through me, and I sent her a wisp of apology.

Then a cluster of ghosts drifted through the track-side fence ahead of us.

"There!" one of them said. "I told you I saw something."

I knew without a word spoken between us that neither Takeo nor I had the strength to outrun them, not anymore. We had to face them, exhausted as we were.

In a swift movement, Takeo shrugged off Chiyo's arm and laid her on the ground beside the tracks. Keiji crouched next to her, panting. I dug out the rest of my ofuda, and Takeo drew his from his belt.

The ghosts charged at us. My body repositioned itself automatically with the moves I knew by heart. I struck one figure across the belly, sending ki to my hand so my corporeal body would connect with her ethereal form, and shoved her into the path of one of her companions. Both fell. I slapped ofuda against their foreheads as they tried to scramble around, and a third ghost hurled himself at me with a swipe of a switchblade. I ducked, heaving him across my back. The charm I struck out with missed by an instant. He spun around and raked at me with his knife. The tip caught my wrist. I grabbed his forearm, fast enough this time, and yanked him into my waiting charm. His body dissolved, but my wrist still panged. I didn't have enough energy left to heal.

A *bang* thundered through the air. Takeo flinched as he struggled with a burly ghost carrying an axe, a circle of blood blooming on his shoulder.

"That one's got a gun!" Keiji yelled, waving his arm.

A ghost at the fringes of the fight had used his ki to turn corporeal so he could make full use of his weapon. With newly formed feet planted solid against the ground, he was sighting along the pistol as he waited to get another clear shot.

One of his ethereal companions leapt at me, wrenching my hair dangerously close to where Midori perched. I swung around, slamming my fist into the ghost's ribs with a jagged edge of ki. He staggered backward, and I darted around him.

The gunman saw me at the last moment and jerked around, but I slammed into him, ofuda in hand. He disappeared beneath me.

The wild lash of the ghost's ki had licked over my body as I'd felled him. So strong, even while he should have been using most of his energy to stay solid. It must be all that power the demon was lending his ghostly followers.

Maybe I could gain a little power for myself here. Confirm who the demon was, at least.

The ghost who'd grabbed my hair was charging at me again. He'd unfolded a net like the one the earlier ghost had been carrying. A strange, rotten smell hit my nose as he hurled it at me.

"Kenta Omori will never succeed!" I shouted as I dodged to the side.

"He's better than any of you," my opponent snapped.

That was all I'd wanted—I didn't have the time or energy to press for more. But even that small delay cost me. As I threw out my hand with its clutched ofuda, the ghost managed to whip his net at me again. Just before my charm hit his forehead, the interlocked ropes swept over me, brushing Midori's thin body. At the contact, she flinched, and the last flicker of her ki connecting to me went out like a snuffed candle flame as the ghost vanished.

"Whoa!" Keiji said. "Not one more step. Back off. I mean it!"

I swayed around, every muscle in my body quivering, my limbs feeling abruptly heavy. Midori adjusted her grip on my hair, but she must have been too drained of ki to share any more. Takeo had just banished the man with the axe, but two more ghosts were springing at him from opposite sides. Three had ignored us and were flying straight for the spot where Chiyo lay crumpled, writhing in agony.

Keiji's human eyes couldn't have made out more than three faintly glowing streaks of ghostlight, but he must have recognized what they meant. He'd braced himself in front of Chiyo as if he'd be able to hold them off on his own, his jaw tight and his hands balled into fists. I felt a twinge of admiration, seeing him display such nerve, but they'd be able to sweep right through him.

Still not the slightest ribbon of energy traveled from Midori into me. My vision of the ghosts was fading. My skin turned cold. I was losing my grasp on the spirit realm.

But I couldn't stop now.

I reached down inside of me and clamped onto a shiver of energy that came with a touch of Mt. Fuji's warmth. The last shred of the ki the mountain had lent me. Without that, I was nothing. But we were nothing without Chiyo anyway.

I pushed that ki into my legs and hurtled my body forward, thrusting out with a charm in each hand. I knocked into two of the ghosts, and they snapped out of this world with a shimmer. The final ghost swerved past me, her knife aimed at Chiyo's chest. I kicked out and knocked her to the ground. Rolling over, I wrenched out one more ofuda. It caught the back of her head. Her body disappeared into the air.

I slumped, aching and empty. Takeo halted a few steps from me, his arms sagging to his sides, his hair come loose from its knot and drifting to his shoulders. I forced myself to look around.

We were alone on the train tracks. We'd defeated all of them. A rush of unsteady laughter tickled up my throat.

Chiyo's breath was ragged with pain, and there was no shrine in sight, but we'd protected her. I'd held my own. Takeo would tell Mother and Father. Chiyo would tell them. Then my kami parents would have to say that I could stay, that I'd earned at least that one reward.

If we rescued them. If we saved Mt. Fuji. As I hauled myself to my feet with no power but my own human muscles, I felt just how far away that goal still was.

TEN

I WOKE UP the next morning with a sense of peacefulness that seemed strange, considering that every part of my body was aching. A bird was twittering outside. Leaves rustled in a soft breeze. I arched my back, stretching out my arms, and reached instinctively for my flute case. My hand found only bare floor. Because I'd left it in Chiyo's living room last night. The memory of our flight from the city rushed back to me, and I sat up abruptly.

We were safe now. I had only blurry impressions of our last exhausted dash through the night, but here I was in the inner room of the shrine where we'd taken shelter, on a mountainside just beyond the edge of the suburbs, though it didn't appear to be the same one Takeo and I had stopped in before.

The summer heat was already rising through the dark wooden walls. I pressed my hands against the cooler floorboards and willed myself fully awake. A wisp of ki tingled through me. I swallowed hard, remembering how drained I'd been after our final battle. Midori wasn't here right now, but she would have recovered some of her energy as she rested. She must have passed a portion on to me before she'd gone out. Yet it didn't quite reach all the way down to the deepest ache inside of me—the hollow spot where I'd been holding the last of Mt. Fuji's gift without realizing it.

The room around me held a small altar ringed with faded paper charms and coated with dust, a row of built-in cupboards along the back wall, and Keiji, lying at their foot. Takeo and Chiyo must already be up. How would Chiyo be feeling now? The one thing I remembered clearly was the firelight washing out of her body the second we'd stepped onto the shrine grounds.

Keiji was still dozing, his bag tucked under his head like a pillow. His glasses had fallen off during the night. I reached over and righted them so the lenses wouldn't get scratched. He shifted with a murmur, the wiry muscles in his arms flexing.

Asleep, his face looked much softer than it had last night when he was grinning and offering to keep my secret. Or when he'd grimly faced the ghosts he could barely see. Chiyo and Haru shouldn't have been so dismissive of him. I suspected most humans would have run screaming at the sight of all those ghost-lights. Keiji had been terrified, clearly, but he'd stayed with us. He'd been willing to fight for us even if he didn't know how.

Unbidden, my mind conjured up the image of his copper-bright eyes opening, his lips curling into that slow, knowing grin. An unexpected warmth washed over me. Shaking myself, I stood up.

I walked to the open door and stepped onto the narrow platform outside. My breath caught at the view. I hadn't realized Mt. Fuji would be visible from here. Pine trees towered over the shrine grounds on three sides, but to the south the land sloped away, and the familiar craggy peak rose between the two nearer mountains.

A mournful shudder seemed to pass through the air, from it to me. *I'm coming back,* I promised, my fingers curling into my palms. *Just hold on.*

Chiyo's voice carried across the wide yard in front of the building. "Yes, I get it; I know the whole plan." I turned to see her and Takeo standing by the torii, a plain structure of unstained cypress wood. The tall pillars of the gate and curved lintel fixed over them were designed to soothe the spirit of anyone walking through, but it didn't appear to have had an effect on Chiyo. Her hair had frizzed overnight, her bangs puffing from her forehead in a lavender cloud. She was twisting the rest back into her usual ponytail. An energetic flush colored her cheeks.

"I *know* I can't hang out in the city anymore," she continued. "Last night was awful. Believe me, I'm looking forward to taking down a whole world of ghosts now. We just need to go back quickly and get Haru, and then we can start."

Takeo shook his head. "I understand that he's very important to you," he said. "But it's too dangerous for any of us to go back to Tokyo so soon, even briefly. Our enemies know we were there—they'll be combing the streets for us."

"But we agreed that Haru would come with me, remember?" Chiyo said. "I don't want him to think I've run off on him. And he'll be a lot of help. He's the top competitor in our school's kendo club, and he practices with real swords too—he could teach those spooks a lesson." She sliced the air with her arm.

"The one destined to save the mountain is you, not him," Takeo said. He was speaking calmly, but I could hear his voice becoming ever so slightly strained. "We can't risk losing you for the little assistance he may give us."

"You're just not going to listen, are you?" Chiyo let out a huff of breath and gave Takeo a fiercely cheerful smile. "I'm going to go see if those kami ladies who're looking after the shrine have any way for me to call him and my parents, but this conversation is *not* over."

She marched off around the side of the building. As I watched her go, a thread of uneasiness wound around my stomach.

The city had already been swarming with ghosts last night. The ones we'd encountered must have been in Tokyo when the spell had started—otherwise, even with Omori's demonic powers strengthening them, they couldn't have followed the light to Chiyo's neighborhood that fast. Had they somehow known the girl they wanted was in Tokyo? Or did Omori have so many ghosts at his command that he could send thousands of them all across the country while holding Fuji's palace?

How had he known to target her at all?

Takeo sighed. I walked down the wooden steps to join him, noticing the rot creeping through the cracks on the railing. Grit and pine needles scattered the granite tiles between the four stone lanterns in the courtyard. This was another shrine humans no longer cared much for.

"Chiyo looks as if she's recovered from last night's attack," I said, but Takeo's grave expression didn't budge.

"She is well," he agreed. "I just don't see—" He grimaced, raking his fingers through his unbound hair. "Why can't she understand how urgent this situation is?"

Only five days left until Obon. His frustration echoed through me. But that was the problem: Chiyo didn't feel it. "We grew up knowing the responsibilities of being kami," I said. "We grew up knowing kami were *real*. She didn't. But I think she's starting to see."

"She is," he said. "And we have put a lot on her. Of course it's difficult for her. But I don't see why she has to seem so... *happy* all the time."

I looked up at his solemn face and had to clamp my lips together to stop an unexpected smile. Apparently the greatest challenge to Takeo's steadfastness was one cheerful girl.

Well, I could be the strong one when he needed that, couldn't I?

"We need to get her to Sage Rin," Takeo went on. "Perhaps she can get through to Chiyo. But I worry the demon's magic will reach us again."

"Do you have any idea how Omori knew about her—or what sort of spell could have affected her like that?" I asked.

"I've been thinking on it," he said. "The best answer I can come up with is... There's a sort of magic that allows a connection between two things. One might build a figure with a specific person in mind, using a part of them in its construction: a hair or a fingernail, or an item they had a strong emotional connection to. Blood sings to blood, heart to heart, spirit to spirit. If done correctly, the sorcerer could act on the figure and have the effects travel to their victim."

"But Omori shouldn't have had anything like that of Chiyo's," I said. "He shouldn't even have known she *exists*."

"No," Takeo agreed. His jaw worked. "And if it were as small a connection as that magic allows, Chiyo's instinctive defenses should have been enough to block it. So I suspect the demon drew on deeper ties of blood, heart, and spirit."

His tone turned my skin cold. "What do you mean?"

"Any kami in the palace could reveal that the daughter of their leaders must have escaped—the demon would only have to break one. Even without knowing of the prophecy, this Omori would suspect that girl would try to fight back. He must hope to disable her before she has the chance. He meant to get at *you*. But to do so, in a way to create such an immense effect, I think he must have acted on one of your—her—parents. He... must have set one of them on fire and cast that fire into their daughter's body. So it hit Chiyo."

My throat closed up with a sudden swell of nausea. If he'd put Mother or Father through such torment— If he was *still* doing it, trying to strike out at Chiyo again— How long could they survive, even as strong as they were?

I drew in a breath, trying to bury that horror under my determination. If we were going to get to them in time, there was still so much we had to do.

"Then we need to start training Chiyo right away," I said, managing to keep my voice from quavering. "We wanted to teach her the basics before we started traveling anyway. We'll begin right away and go to Sage Rin when she can defend herself."

"That requires we get Chiyo to agree to the training at all without her young man here," Takeo said.

I reached for his hand. "She'll come around," I said. "It's been less than a day."

His fingers tightened around mine. Ki hummed between us, warm with gratitude. And I felt what he was too loyal to my parents to say out loud.

He wished their true daughter, the girl of the prophecy, was me.

The shrine platform creaked behind us. I started, dropping Takeo's hand.

Keiji was watching us from the doorway, his shaggy hair sticking up in tufts across his head. He gave me a crooked grin.

"I don't suppose there's anything like breakfast here?" he said.

Takeo paused. "I apologize," he said. "I hadn't thought of that. We kami don't need to eat as you do. I'll see if the shrine guardians can help."

"Don't worry about it then—I packed supplies just in case," Keiji said. He bobbed his head and ambled off. "Good morning, Ikeda!" he called as he disappeared behind the building, and a moment later Chiyo strode into view. The shrine's kami trailed behind her: two willowy figures with waterfalls of pale hair.

"So," Chiyo said brightly, halting in front of Takeo. "About Haru. There's no way for me to even talk to him from here."

I didn't want her to get any more caught up in that argument. "Chiyo," I said, stepping forward, "even if we did go back for him, you'd need to be able to fight off our enemies first—you know that too. Why don't you let us begin the essential parts of your training, and after that's finished, we can decide what our best next step is?"

Chiyo considered me. Then she clapped her hands together. "All right," she said. "Fine. Teach me about this 'ki' and how to use it to stop demons from messing with me, and then I'll take down anyone who gets in my way."

We arranged ourselves in the middle of the courtyard. Takeo let me take the lead. I supposed my mastery of ki work meant something, even if the energy I'd moved through myself had come from the mountain. Now, Midori settled close on my head with a tickle of curiosity. I wondered if she even remembered the long ago time when she hadn't been fully competent in her powers.

I thought back to my earliest lessons with Father, his rumbling voice filling the training room as he guided me. Then a different image wavered into my mind: the ghosts stabbing him with their knives the way they had the palace guards. I swallowed thickly. It was by training Chiyo that we would save him and everyone else.

As much as I wanted to hurry, I knew if I tried to rush Chiyo and she tensed up, her progress would take longer. I reached inside me for the calm, reassuring tone my teachers had taken with me. "The most important step is being able to feel your ki," I told her. "Once you have a sense of it inside you, all you have to do is learn to control it."

"What does it feel like?" Chiyo asked, peering down at herself.

"Like a sort of energy, rippling through you... It's almost like standing under the sun with its beams raining down on you, warm and bright, except the glow is inside you. Close your eyes while you're looking for it," I suggested. "That makes it easier to focus."

Chiyo lowered her head. After a few seconds, the faint shimmer that never quite left her body quivered and intensified, and then contracted into her skin. "I think I've got it!" she said. "Wow. That's—that's so cool. So weird I never noticed it before." She opened her eyes. "You know, I never really got cold in the winter, even when I'd forget my hat or gloves. I bet this is why."

She had so much ki radiating through her, of course she'd find it quickly. "Good," I said. "Now let's try one of the basic practice exercises."

"What about going invisible? You've got to teach me that."

"Shifting out of our corporeal state takes a lot of concentration until you get used to it," Takeo said. "It's better if you learn how to manipulate your energy in simpler ways first."

"Fine, fine," Chiyo said. "Lead on!"

"Let's try exchanging ki with direct contact," I said, taking her hand. "Pick a feeling or an image you want to share with me. Picture it flowing with your ki from your mind through your body to my hand. It might take a while, so don't—"

A jolt of pain shot up my arm and blasted into my chest so violently it rocked me on my feet. My fingers slipped from Chiyo's. I gasped, clutching my shoulder. The burning aftershock seared through me and slowly died away.

"I'm sorry, I'm so sorry, I didn't mean to do that," Chiyo was saying. "I was getting ready to send this gorgeous flower I saw by the fountain, but all of a sudden I remembered last night, and everything got mixed up."

The pain had left a tingling in my palm. I drew in a breath, gathering myself.

She had so much power. I'd never felt anyone's ki that intensely before.

Well, she was going to need that power to be able to crush a demon and an entire army of ghosts.

"It's okay," I said. "That's the control part you need to work on. Want to try again?"

"If you want me to—" Takeo began, and I shook my head quickly. Was he already doubting me?

Had he seen how completely I'd drained myself last night?

"I'm fine," I said. "It just startled me."

I expected control to take a lot of trial and error, and braced myself as Chiyo and I linked hands again. But her mistake seemed to have made her determined to avoid any others. She sent me a shaky image of her gorgeous flower. Then she shared the taste of her favorite ice cream, the jangling harmonies and sweep of lights at a stadium concert, the rush she got on the school track just before she crossed the finish line. With each attempt, the impressions became clearer, until I was almost there with her in her memory.

"You're a runner?" I asked, letting the last sensation linger. The exhilaration of it felt almost like dancing.

"Sprinter for the track team since my first year of junior high," Chiyo said, giving me a thumbs up. "So the next time we've got a pack of ghosts chasing us, as long as I don't have some crazy magic burning me up, you can be sure they won't catch me."

"You may have inherited that talent from your mother," Takeo remarked. "Her affinities to air and water make her the swiftest of any on her feet."

"So you two know my... my kami parents?" Chiyo said. She looked down at her hands, clenching and relaxing her fingers. "I guess everyone does, if they're the leaders of all the kami. Is everyone going to be okay about me just showing up out of nowhere?"

"You'll have saved them," I said. "And they would welcome you anyway, once they hear the story."

"What else do they do?" Chiyo asked, raising her head, her expression avid now. "My parents. Other than whatever rulership things, I mean. Do they—"

My chest tightened so sharply for a second I couldn't breathe. "We can talk about that later," I said, cutting her off. "Right now we have to focus on the training—to make sure they're still alive for you to save."

The glint in Chiyo's eyes wavered. "Oh," she said. "Yes, of course." She set her hands on her hips. "What's next?"

I paused, willing my scattered emotions aside. "Why don't we try sending without touching?" I said. With a thread of thanks to Midori, I held out my hand and let a thin, silvery ribbon rise from it into the air. It swayed gently to a melody I felt more than heard.

"You send your energy out, just like you sent it to me," I said. "But because there isn't a place right there for it to go, you have to concentrate on shaping it and holding it in that shape. If you stop paying attention..." I let my mind go blank, and the ribbon disintegrated.

Chiyo stared down at her hands, her brow knitting. Then she laughed. A tiny, swirling ball of ki danced in her grasp. She drew her palms apart, stretching the ball larger, and tossed it up in the air. "This isn't so hard. It feels like—like I could have done it all along, but I forgot I knew how. Hey, I bet you I could—"

The edges of her body glimmered. "Chiyo!" I said, but my alarm was unnecessary. Her body faded into a gleaming after-image of itself. She blinked, and then grinned at me, even more luminescent than usual in her ethereal state.

My mouth had dropped open. It had taken me *hours* to learn how to do that, with Mother and Father explaining and demonstrating patiently, after I'd spent months mastering other more basic skills. And they'd told me I'd picked it up faster than most did. Chiyo had managed it in a matter of minutes.

"Most of the ghosts were like this when they attacked us, weren't they?" Chiyo said. "How do you fight people you can't really touch? Can *they* hurt *you*?" She waved her ethereal arm through a stone lantern.

"Ki can touch ki, just as matter can touch matter," Takeo said. "Whether you keep your physical body or shift to fight with energy only, you can direct your ki to affect them, and they can twist yours with theirs. You have to concentrate more, and it feels a little different, but many of the techniques are the same. The ghosts prefer to stay in their natural state because it requires a great deal of energy for them to form physical bodies. But their ki is more limited than ours, so even if we're fighting them on their own plane, we usually have the advantage."

"That makes sense," Chiyo said. She jabbed at the air with a crackle of ki. "Can we try that now?"

"Why don't you take over for a bit?" I said to Takeo. "Combat is more your area than mine."

He was a good teacher—I'd learned most of what I knew of martial arts from him. And if Chiyo touched me again, our energy mingling, I wasn't sure I'd be able to keep her from seeing the mess of emotions now churning inside me.

She was born for this, I reminded myself as I climbed onto

the shrine building's platform. She had nearly two decades of suppressed ki clamoring to be put to use. We'd have no chance at all of saving Mt. Fuji if she couldn't handle it so well. And no matter how strong she was, I could still help, as long as I had Midori with me.

I knew all of that, but my stubborn human feelings wouldn't settle. They whipped around inside me like branches in a storm. I leaned against the worn wooden railing, wrestling with myself as I watched Takeo teach Chiyo how to fight.

She was picking that up quickly too, maybe because she was already an athlete. She moved easily and precisely, and when Takeo demonstrated how to angle her hand or position her stance, she always did it just as he'd shown her from then on. She was still grinning, but there was an intensity in her expression that made her beautiful.

They looked right together, I realized as Takeo cupped her elbow and explained how to use ki to more effectively escape an attacker's grasp. The smile he flashed at her when she successfully broke from his hold, as warm as those I'd seen so often directed at me, made my gut clench.

He wasn't frustrated with her now. He was impressed. Wouldn't that make the perfect story: the palace guard falling in love with the girl he'd been tasked to bring home?

Footsteps tapped across the platform toward me. Keiji threw his arms over the railing and looked into the courtyard. After a minute, he rolled his gaze toward me.

"Are you just lost in thought, or is something actually happening down there?"

"They're sparring," I said. How strange it must be to see only the empty yard. As I would have, if not for Midori.

"Do you want to watch?" I asked, offering my hand. Keiji glanced at it, at me, and then took it.

His skin was smooth and dry against mine. I sent him a wisp of ki so light I doubted he'd even feel it, but enough to give him a hint of kami sight. My own vision shivered, and the forms in the courtyard dimmed slightly, but I resisted the urge to draw more energy from my dragonfly friend. She was giving me so much of herself already.

Keiji's grip tightened. "Hey!" he said. "That's amazing. They really are there."

Like all living things, he had his own ki. It whispered against my palm. He didn't have enough to use it for anything more than staying alive, unless he trained like the human warriors and monks Ayame had told me stories of. But it was there, as my own must have been even when Midori left me.

I caught the quiver of his awe, a mix of pride and fear at finding himself here, and underneath the rest, a pang of sadness. A sort of sadness I recognized too well: loss, and desperately missing what was gone. It made me want to curl my fingers between his, as if I could somehow ease the pain. I looked over at him, wondering where *his* sadness came from.

"How can you do this?" he said, turning to me in the same moment. "If you're not even—"

His gaze shifted to the back of my head.

"Ah ha! The dragonfly's a kami, isn't it? It's helping you."

I had the urge to rip back every shred of ki I'd shared with him.

The closest I could manage was to pull away my hand.

"I told you before, I don't know what you're talking about," I said.

His smile went crooked. "Ack, sorry. I wasn't trying to upset you."

When I didn't answer, he dropped to his knees, as easily as if it were something he did every day. "Please forgive me," he said, holding out his hand beseechingly. "I meant no offense."

"Does that usually work?" I asked, keeping my eyes fixed on the courtyard. From the corner of my vision, I saw Keiji shrug.

"I haven't tried it enough to draw a clear conclusion. Should I kowtow to the floor? Would that help?"

He started to without waiting for a response, and I found myself grabbing his shoulder before his forehead touched the ground. "Stop it," I hissed. "You look ridiculous. Chiyo can still see *you*, you know."

He glanced up at me, his expression fraught but a mischievous gleam in his eyes. "I'll stop if you smile."

My lips twitched of their own accord. "Okay, that'll do," he said. He pulled himself to his feet and leaned back against the railing.

"Anyway," he said, "I already told you I'm not after Chiyo. So I can make a fool of myself for you if I want."

My pulse skipped in an oddly giddy way. "Well, *I* don't want you to," I said, ignoring it. "We're trying to save the world's most sacred mountain from an invasion of demons and yakuza ghosts and who knows what else—I don't think foolishness is going to do us any good."

Keiji's head jerked around. "Yakuza ghosts?" he said. "What does that mean?"

"It seems the demon who's leading the ghosts, he used to be a man, a man who was murdered." *Kenta Omori.* "And he was a criminal when he was alive. Chiyo and I did some research on the computer—she called him *yakuza*. From what she said, some of the other ghosts might be too." I paused. Curiosity itched at me despite myself. "If you don't care about impressing her, then why was it so important to you to come with us?"

"I don't want to see the world taken over by some demon any more than you do," he said, and hesitated, tweaking his glasses. Suddenly he looked almost as vulnerable as when he'd been sleeping on the shrine floor. "And I was kind of hoping, if I do help... Do you think maybe afterward the kami would do something for *me*?"

"I—I don't know," I said. I'd been thinking the exact same thing for the last day, but hearing the idea come out of his mouth caught me off guard.

"It's not even for me," Keiji said hastily. "I mean—it's my brother— A couple years ago he had this, ah, accident, and now he can't do most of the things he used to. He always looked out for me, you know? But now it's so much harder for us to even hang out, and he'd just like things to go back to more like they were before. And I would too. If they could."

The loss I'd felt in him. He lowered his eyes, as if embarrassed to have said so much, but his wish was so much less selfish than mine.

"I'd imagine Chiyo's parents would do what they could," I said. "They did heal Mr. Ikeda's sister. And of course they'd want to repay you for helping Chiyo."

"You really think so?" he said.

"I'm sure of it."

He gave me that slow grin that made my heart thump, as if we were conspirators together, and held out his hand on the railing.

"Let me see again?" he asked, tilting his head toward the courtyard.

I'd almost forgotten about Chiyo's training. My emotions seemed to have scrambled into a completely different but no less tangled jumble. Maybe it wasn't fair to blame Keiji for that, though. I laid my fingers over his. He kept watching me for a moment longer before turning to the yard. It hurt a little, for no reason I could explain, to lose his gaze.

Takeo and Chiyo were standing side by side near the edge of the courtyard, using one of the stone lanterns as a target. At first it looked as though they were simply staring at it. Then the lantern rocked and tumbled over, and Chiyo raised her hands with a cheer.

He was teaching her how to send out ki without moving. Shifting your energy was ten times harder when you didn't use your limbs to direct it. And she had just toppled a stone figure that had to weigh more than she did.

Maybe we could leave for Sage Rin's valley as early as this afternoon. That was something to be glad for.

"I'm starting to think it's the ghosts who should be scared, not me," Keiji said with a laugh, but a tremor of anxiety echoed through his palm into mine. "When we go to get the Imperial treasures—is it going to be like last night? That was pretty freaky."

"There'd be no reason for the demon to send ghosts to protect the treasures unless he knows about the prophecy," I said, "and I can't see how he could. My— Chiyo's parents would never give that information up, and none of the other kami know."

"Good to hear," he said. "Oh!" He dug into his pocket with his free hand. "I had some convenience store sweet breads in my bag. Figured you might be hungry too. You want one?"

At the sight of the doughy circle in its plastic wrapper, my stomach growled. My hand twitched, and I caught myself just before I reached out.

He was offering because he assumed that, like him, I needed food. Because of his guess that I was human, not kami. If I took it, I'd be proving him right.

Suddenly the thought of keeping up the charade any longer exhausted me. What did it matter? He'd figured out the truth; he didn't believe my evasions. He didn't seem to have any intention of giving away my secret to Chiyo. And I *was* hungry.

"Thank you," I said.

Even though he couldn't see anything there while my hands were otherwise occupied, Keiji surveyed the courtyard as I unwrapped and wolfed down the sugary bun. When I'd finished eating, my mouth sticky but my stomach satisfied, he turned back to me.

"Did they tell you?" he said. "When you were growing up on the mountain—did you know you'd been switched?"

There was a relief in being able to admit it. "No," I said. "I found out three days ago."

He winced. "That's got to suck. You think you're the star of the show, and it turns out you're only the understudy."

"Understudy?" I said.

"Like in theater." When my confusion didn't fade, he went on. "I was in drama club one year. When you put on a play, you have all the actors, and then you have understudies for the biggest roles. People who learn all the lines and cues just in case the real actor gets sick or something. But they don't usually end up doing anything more than prompting lines from the side of the stage. I had to do that a few times."

The awful sorrow that had overwhelmed me when I'd played my flute yesterday welled up again. "It's not so bad," I said, to myself as well as to him. "They needed me. They still do."

As my words drifted out into the air, Chiyo flashed back into her corporeal state with a shudder. "Hey," she said, frowning at Takeo even as her voice stayed bright. "You broke my concentration. No fair."

Takeo returned to the physical plane as well, his dark eyes troubled. "Omori isn't going to care about fairness," he said. "If we're to leave here safely, you'll need to be able to hold that shield up much longer. Let's begin again—we have a lot more work to do."

ELEVEN

OVER THE next hour, Takeo pierced Chiyo's inner shield five more times. Each time it took him a little longer, but fifteen minutes was still far from enough for us to safely make the journey to Rin.

After a while, my worries made me so restless I couldn't stand to watch anymore. It seemed we'd found weakness in Chiyo after all: for all her power, she lacked endurance. And she was going to need an awful lot to survive a full onslaught.

I collected more bark and burned more wood for charcoal, and sat inside the shrine building inscribing a stack of ofuda. When there was enough that each of us could carry a large sheaf of the charms, I distracted myself tending to the shrine. With each minute I spent there, its neglect pained me more. Taking on the jobs human priests were meant to do, I washed the dust from the red altar cloth, swept the floors, and rubbed clean the walls and railings. The shrine kami drifted around me, puzzled but murmuring their gratitude.

During my work the ground trembled twice with Fuji's anxious stirrings. By mid-afternoon, the sun had burned all the clouds from the sky and the breeze had died, leaving a sharp heat that crackled against my skin. Summer was always hot, but not like this. In the absence of so many kami, the weather was starting to echo the fire churning inside the mountain.

Another yelp carried from the courtyard as Takeo knocked down Chiyo's protections yet again. My fingers tensed around the cloth I was holding.

"Do you know anything about a demon named Kenta Omori?" I asked the shrine kami. The two women shook their heads. I dug out the article Chiyo had printed off for me and read it over twice, but nothing in the folded pages gave me a better sense of the man who'd become our demon.

Keiji had been sitting in the shade of the trees behind the building, but he must have gotten uncomfortable after the breeze had disappeared. When I came back inside, I found him bent over a book he'd propped up on his bag, three more scuffed but sturdy volumes stacked beside him. There was something arresting in the earnest dedication with which he studied the page that made me stop and watch a moment before I forced myself to interrupt.

"Have you found out anything more about demons and ghosts?" I asked.

His head snapped up; he clearly hadn't heard me come in. Then his face relaxed with his usual crooked grin. "I've read all these before," he said. "Just refreshing my memory and seeing if I can make any new connections. It's definitely unusual for a demon and ghosts to be working together like this."

I sat down on the floor across from him. "What about just the demon?" I said. "He's the source of most of the ghosts' power anyway. It'd be easier to fight him if we understood why this Omori attacked Mt. Fuji at all."

"Well, if he started as a guy who was murdered, there's always the revenge thing I mentioned before. You see a lot of that in the folktales."

"But why would a criminal businessman from Tokyo want revenge on the kami? None of us would have hurt him."

"Yeah." Keiji rubbed his chin, considering his books. "Well, if demons are filled with negative emotion, I'd guess that's got to cloud out logic. He might not be thinking straight. Or... kami have a lot of power, right? Maybe it isn't really about Mt. Fuji—he just wants to use the power there for something else. Like revenge on the people who *did* hurt him."

"I don't think there's any way he could take that power," I said. "And he's already got lots of his own." A chill trickled through me. "What if he's so angry and spiteful that he *wants* to see the whole world fall into chaos?" His plan could be nothing more than to watch from the palace as all the kami's work fell to ruin.

"That's possible," Keiji said.

All we had were possibilities, nothing definite. I made a noise of frustration and got up. "I'm going to see if Takeo can use any help." I paused. "Thank you for looking for answers."

"It's my pleasure," Keiji said, nudging his glasses up. For once he sounded serious, not teasing. "I hope I can find something more useful."

The sun had long set when Takeo finally called an end to

Chiyo's training, with a tentative note of victory. Even with both of us working on her, she'd managed to hold her ethereal shield steady for a full two hours, without so much as wavering even at the end. Now she sprawled on the steps of the shrine building near Keiji, who was licking the last bits of juice off his fingers from his dinner of fried lotus root, bamboo shoots, and wild mushrooms. My stomach pinched. He'd told the shrine kami that he was particularly hungry to ensure they brought enough for us to share the meal, but I hadn't gotten the chance to sneak away from Chiyo's curious eyes yet.

"So, are we leaving to see this sage person now?" Chiyo asked.

Takeo glanced at the sky. The near-full moon and the brilliant stars cast a faint light over us, but within the trees all was dark. "As much as I hate to delay, I don't think we should risk traveling now. You're worn out, and if Omori penetrates your shield at night it'll be much easier for his ghosts to find us. We'll rest and leave at dawn."

"I thought you wanted to go back for Haru," Keiji remarked.

Chiyo shook her head. "I didn't really know... I've learned a *lot* today," she said with a wry smile. "I'm sure he'll understand. He doesn't have any way of making shields of ki or whatever. I don't want to bring him into the middle of this fight until I'm sure I can protect myself *and* him."

Takeo's gaze settled on me. Thinking of how I needed extra protection too? "We'll be coming back to Tokyo within a few days anyway," I said quickly. "The jewel is kept in the Imperial Palace's shrine."

"Right," Chiyo said. "I'm supposed to get the sacred treasures before we go take back the mountain." For just an instant, her easy confidence seemed to falter. Then she clapped her hands together with a fierce grin. "No problem."

"We'll save the jewel for last," Takeo said, "since it only amplifies the others' powers. And if the ghosts in Tokyo spot us and realize what we're doing before we have the sword and the mirror, they'll get in our way."

"So the treasures really are super-magical?" Chiyo said. "I thought that was just a myth... but I guess a lot of things I thought were myths aren't."

"They were all the possessions of one of the first great kami," I said, my mind slipping back to long-ago evenings perched on Ayame's lap. "Amaterasu, who guided the sun. The mirror was clear enough to reflect her full beauty, and the jewel captivating enough to draw her out of hiding when her brother offended her."

"He's the one who found the sacred sword, before he gave it to her," Keiji added when I paused. "If the stories I've read are true, anyway. It was in one of the eight tails of this huge dragon he killed—so strong the blade chipped the sword he already had and so sharp it could slice through grass like the wind."

Takeo inclined his head in acknowledgement. "And all three were given by Amaterasu to the first emperor, to show her support of his rule. They've been in the care of humans ever since."

"So how far do we have to go to get the sword and the mirror?" Chiyo asked.

"They're kept in shrines dedicated to Amaterasu," I said. "The sword in the city of Nagoya, and the mirror at the large Ise shrine."

"How long exactly do we have?" Keiji said. "People observe

Obon at different times in different places."

"Humans pick the dates that are convenient to their interests," Takeo said. "The symbols are what matters the most to them. But the true Obon, when the barrier between the worlds thins, changes every summer, depending on the moon. Tomorrow we have four days left."

Hearing him say it out loud made me shiver. Four days seemed like hardly any time at all.

A similar uneasiness crossed Keiji's face, and he looked as if he was going to say more. He was interrupted by a staticy melody that started to play from somewhere near where he sat. He leapt to his feet.

"My phone," he explained, and headed down the steps as he dug it out of his pocket.

Chiyo's eyebrows rose. "You get reception up here? What company are you with?"

Keiji didn't answer, already opening the phone to his ear. His shoes rattled over the pebbles as he disappeared around the side of the building. "Hi. Yeah, of course it's me. Hold on."

"I wish I had *my* cell," Chiyo said. She tipped her head back against the platform. "I feel like I could fall asleep right here."

I slipped past her before she could decide to head into the shrine building for the night. As promised, Keiji had left part of his dinner on a plate in one of the cupboards. A package of corn puffs that must have come from his personal stash of snacks lay beside it.

I grabbed a handful of the vegetables, so hungry I hardly missed having chopsticks to eat properly, and popped them into my mouth. As I gulped them down, and then more, the grumbling in my stomach subsided. I willed the flow of ki I was drawing from Midori to shrink.

"If you want to leave for a little while, you can," I told her. She replied with a flicker of contentment.

A ruffling of feathers by the side door caught my eye. Palming the last of the meal and tucking the corn puffs under my arm, I stepped outside.

A familiar sparrow was perched on the corner of the shrine's roof. *You again*, I thought, studying it. Maybe it was only a coincidence, but I was starting to feel sure it was the same bird. I sent a thread of ki toward it, wondering if I'd managed not to notice it was kami, but my silent greeting provoked no response. Maybe it had been helped by a kami once, and now it took comfort in our presence. Even a regular sparrow might have been frightened witnessing the ghosts swarming Mt. Fuji. And Takeo and I would have been the only ones it'd seen escape.

"Hoping for food again?" I asked, holding out a mushroom. The sparrow tilted its head. When I set the mushroom on the platform's railing, it swooped down to peck at it.

As I wandered off the platform and along the edge of the forest, a voice reached my ears: Keiji's, raised.

"If you won't even tell me— Okay, okay, I'll try. I know. I'm sorry. Right. Okay. I'll see you."

Footsteps crunched through the fallen pine needles, and his form emerged from the darkness amid the trees. His expression was grim as he snapped his phone shut. When he saw me, he came to a halt.

"Sorry," I said. "I wasn't trying to listen—and I didn't hear much. I was only walking by."

"That's okay," Keiji said.

"Are you all right?" I asked. "You sounded... upset."

His shoulders hunched. "I'm not really. I just— That was my brother. Who was being a typical older brother, thinking he knows everything, not really listening. But he does know a lot more than I do, so maybe he's right and *I* should listen more."

"Is *he* upset?" I asked, suddenly curious. "That you're out here, I mean? Do your parents know where you are?"

"My parents are dead," Keiji said matter-of-factly. "Since I was two. And my aunt and uncle are probably glad to have one less 'problem' on their hands for the moment. At least my brother cares. I shouldn't get on his case—if he hadn't been trying so hard to make things better for me, maybe he'd still be fine."

"I'm sorry," I said. Here I'd been wishing I didn't have two sets of parents, when he had none.

"Hey, don't be," he said, a trace of his usual smile returning. "It's because of you I'm going to get my chance to fix things for him. May I escort you back to the shrine? I promise to stay off my knees."

"I should hope so," I said, falling into step beside him as we ambled toward the shrine building.

"You know, it's really not so bad kowtowing, if you've got the right girl in front of you."

"What's *that* supposed to mean?"

"I'm not sure," he said easily. "I just thought it sounded good. Did you like it? If not, I'll keep trying."

"No!" I said before he could make good on that offer. "I mean, no, don't keep trying. It was wonderful."

He laughed, and as I watched the light coming back into his face, I wondered what else he would have said, if I'd told him to keep going.

***

The sun was blazing overhead late the next morning when the five of us reached the valley of the doves. The forest around us felt like an oven, baking us as we climbed to the final ridge. The dry soil crumbled at the lightest touch of my feet, and the leaves on the bushes and saplings were starting to yellow.

I counted back through the days and realized I couldn't remember the last rainfall. Certainly it hadn't rained since Omori had taken Mt. Fuji. Even the thunderstorm I'd smelled brewing two nights ago had dissipated without a drop.

Between the dryness and the unusual heat, the crops must be starting to die, the streams shrinking. Was the absence of so many kami only affecting us here, near the mountain, or was it already echoing throughout the world?

Maybe Rin would know. I wanted to leap straight into the valley, but we were already racing along as fast as our legs and ki could carry us. Ahead of me, Chiyo gripped Keiji's wrist, lending him energy so he wouldn't slow us down. She'd suggested leaving him behind as we'd been getting ready to set off, and I'd blurted out that we could hardly abandon him miles from any means of getting home. Takeo, managing to stay loyal to both of us at once, had pointed out that this way would give her extra practice controlling and maintaining her energy. But we'd both been watching her closely in unspoken agreement, checking for any sign that Omori might have resumed his magical attack. It seemed too much to hope that he would have given up on that strategy after just one failure.

At the top of the ridge, Takeo stopped. His hand dropped to his sword. The rest of us slowed behind him.

"Something's come through here," he said. "I sense ki I don't like the feel of."

I sidled around Chiyo. As I reached Takeo, I caught a discomforting quaver in the energy around us.

We separated, scanning the brush. After a few steps, a tug of uneasiness drew my eyes to a footprint in the cracked earth. Midori's wings buzzed unhappily.

"Takeo," I said.

The print looked almost human, but it was too wide across the ball of the foot and too narrow at the heel, and the toes ended in jagged points. I held my hand to it. A stronger waft of ki lingered in the dirt. My nose wrinkled as if I'd tasted something bitter.

"Whatever made this, I don't think we want to meet it," I said.

Takeo leaned toward the footprint. "Ogres, maybe," he said.

I remembered the monstrous figures I'd seen from a distance, tramping toward Mt. Fuji, and shuddered.

"Ogres?" Chiyo said. "Right, if kami and ghosts and demons are real, of course ogres are too."

"The world's full of all sorts of beings," Takeo said. "Not all of them are friendly to kami. I don't know why Sage Rin would allow ogres into her valley."

"Maybe she couldn't stop them," I said. To have lived as long as she had, Rin must have great power, but no kami was invincible. "How many do you think there were?"

Takeo eased forward, closing his eyes as he absorbed the energy. "More than one. They were heading toward the bottom of the valley. I'll go on ahead and make sure it's safe."

He strode forward, drawing his sword. The trees rustled as he rushed down the slope with ki-sped steps. Chiyo tsked her tongue, letting go of Keiji. "Wait for me!" she called. "I'm ready to take on a few ogres."

She dashed after Takeo so swiftly the ground sparked beneath her feet. I grabbed Keiji's hand and we hurried after them, Midori clutching my hair. The two of us supported by one already-tired kami were hardly a match for Takeo's energy, let alone Chiyo's. In a few seconds, I'd lost sight of both of them in the denser vegetation of the forest below. I pushed myself faster, threading more ki down to my feet and through my hand to Keiji. Midori's small body tensed with a glimmer of strain. I hesitated.

"Let's just walk," Keiji said. "They'll come back for us when they've made sure the coast is clear, right?"

"I don't like being left behind," I snapped, and clamped my mouth shut. I'd been thinking as much, but I hadn't meant to say it.

"Do not fear," Keiji said with a squeeze of my hand. "I will never leave you."

I looked at him, and his crooked smile and the teasing glint in his eyes stopped any retort I might have made. The truth was, I would much rather have him here with me than be straggling behind alone. And if we were attacked by ogres, we'd be better off if Midori wasn't completely exhausted.

I released the flow of energy I'd been drawing. The dragonfly's gratitude wisped over me like a gust of cool air, and guilt curdled in my gut. I'd been so worried about my own capabilities that I hadn't been paying enough attention to hers. A real kami would never make another living thing suffer for her benefit. That was an unpleasant human trait I was going to have to break myself of.

My hand felt abruptly empty. Keiji had let go to tramp through the trees to a small outcropping. He gazed down toward where I knew the waterfall and its trio of pools lay. "Wow," he said, his voice awed. I folded my fingers into my palm and picked my way down the path past him.

"So what other supernatural creatures do we have to watch out for?" Keiji asked as he caught up with me. "Shape-shifting foxes? Slimy kappa? Two-tailed giant cats?"

"Probably all of them." The thought made my skin crawl. But Keiji glanced around eagerly as if he hoped to spot one. "You didn't know those things really existed until two days ago," I said. "Why did you bother learning so much about them?"

"I might not have known, but I believed it was possible," he said. The path narrowed as it cut through the forest along a particularly steep section of slope. The ground below us fell away amid the knobby roots of the trees and stalks of bamboo. "And also, ah, it totally annoyed my aunt and uncle—they didn't think I should be reading anything except my school books until I was getting top marks. When I was little, there was a while when I'd decided *they* had to be evil spirits and if I just found a way to prove it, my brother and I would get to go live someplace else. Ha. After that it just sort of stuck. It's kind of reassuring to imagine there's more to life than grades and getting some upscale office job and working until you die, you know. Ogres or not, I'd rather be out here than back there."

He swung his arm toward the vista beyond the trees.

"This sage we're looking for," Keiji added, "she's the one who had the vision? What exactly did she see?"

"She didn't tell us a lot," I admitted. "There was something about darkness coming over the mountain, and then Chiyo takes up the three treasures and drives it away."

"So she saw a vision of a girl with purple ponytails and puffy socks? I guess that helped narrow it down."

The corner of my mouth twitched up. "I don't think so," I said. "It was more... metaphorical, but we know it's Chiyo because—"

A black shape shot out of the underbrush near Keiji's feet. He flinched away with a yelp and tripped over a root. I caught his wrist as his arms flailed, but he was falling so fast he pulled me off balance too. We toppled over the edge of the path together.

TWELVE

WE SLID several feet down the slope, Keiji on his back and me on my side, before my hand caught a bamboo stalk. My elbow twinged as we jerked to a halt. Midori, who had leapt from my hair as we fell, hovered above us.

A large black rabbit hopped across the trail of broken ground left in our wake and darted off through the bushes. Keiji watched it go and started to laugh.

"I thought—" he said. "I thought—" He was gasping too hard to finish the sentence. I looked down at the two of us, dirt-smeared and breathless for fear of a rabbit, and all the tension I'd been holding in broke with a giggle.

Keiji shook his head, moving as if to squirm upright, and his shoulder bumped mine. He froze. I turned to find his face only inches away, his bright eyes fixed on mine. The air he exhaled grazed my cheek.

It was the perfect time for him to make one of his jokes. I braced myself for it. But he just looked at me as if I were as magical as the creatures he'd spent his whole life wishing to meet.

My heart started to pound. Gazing back at him, I could almost believe it myself. I wanted to fall into that look in his eyes.

Before I quite knew what I intended to do, my head dipped. I caught myself. And in that moment's hesitation, Keiji seemed to wake up beside me. He shifted the short distance upward and brushed his mouth against mine.

My lips parted in surprise, the gentle contact sending a ripple of warmth through me. I'd never kissed anyone before. Not like this.

Before my uncertainty could take over, Keiji slipped his hand around the back of my neck, tilting his head to bring our mouths closer together. His fingers were gritty with earth and the edge of his glasses bumped my face, but I found I didn't mind at all. His lips were warm and a little rough, and as I kissed him back my head spun in a way that seemed totally out of proportion to what was happening, but *oh*—the shivery slide of his thumb tracing the line of my jaw, the fresh peach he'd eaten at breakfast on his breath, the softness of his skin as my palm found his cheek—my pulse was singing, my blood dancing—

And then *I* woke up. I was lying there kissing a boy I'd met two days ago, when the one I'd loved for years might come dashing back at any moment.

I jerked away. My lips tingled as if all the energy in my body had pooled there. Heat flooded my face, and I stared up at the path we'd fallen from, willing the sensation to pass.

Keiji's hand had dropped to his side, but otherwise he didn't move. I could feel him watching me, hear the soft rasp of his breath. The silence stretched on. My heart stuttered.

"We should keep going," I said, hauling myself to my feet. "We—we don't have much time."

Keiji swallowed. He shoved himself into a sitting position. I refused to look at him, but all I could see was him crouched there at the edge of my vision.

"Time," he said. "Right." He took off his glasses, wiped the smudges off them with one of the few clean parts of his T-shirt, and set them back on his nose. Then he reached for his messenger bag, which had tumbled off his shoulder. Grabbing another bamboo stalk, he managed to stand. I scrambled up to the path ahead of him. Midori fluttered down and landed over my ear. I didn't dare reach out to discover what she thought of my unexpected diversion.

"Sora?" Takeo's voice called. He emerged from the trees farther down the path. Panic washed over his face when he saw me. "Are you all right?" he said, rushing over. His eyes scanned the forest and came back to rest on me.

"I'm fine," I said around the lump in my throat, though I wasn't really. Someone had rearranged all my vital organs. Nothing felt like it should. I wanted to close my eyes and lean into him until everything settled back into its proper place.

"Oh, wow," Chiyo said, coming up behind him. "What have you two been up to?"

"We fell," I said quickly, and motioned to Keiji, who had just staggered onto the path. "A rabbit startled us. It was stupid. Did you find Sage Rin? Is *she* all right?"

Takeo still looked worried, but my questions seemed to deflect his concern. I became suddenly aware of a prickling that might have been a dusty handprint on the side of my neck.

"I'm not sure," he said as I wiped it away. "There were a few more footprints and traces of ki along the way to her house, but no other sign of the creatures it came from."

"Good," I said.

"So c'mon," Chiyo said, snatching Keiji's wrist. "You've slowed us down enough already, dirt boy."

They breezed past us with a gust of ki. Takeo offered me his hand. As I curled my fingers into his familiar, steady grasp, my mind flashed back to the taste of peach and the gentle pressure of someone else's lips. That unwelcome heat tickled through me.

Was this just one more horrible human thing: the inability to remember who you'd dedicated your heart to?

I tightened my grip on Takeo's hand. "Let's go."

We'd nearly reached the stream at the base of the valley when Chiyo winced, her steps faltering. I tensed. "Are you all right?" I said.

She nodded, smiling tightly as she tapped her chest. "I think our friend Omori just took another stab at me. But I felt it coming. He's not getting in here, not today."

That meant Omori was hurting Mother or Father again. Blood singing to blood, heart to heart, spirit to spirit, in a tortured harmony. My throat tightened.

I thought Chiyo proceeded across the stream a little more

slowly than usual, but by the time we reached the tree that held Rin's home, I couldn't tell if she was still warding herself or if Omori had let up his attack already. Her eyes glittered with anticipation as she took in the immense cypress.

Takeo knocked on the bark. We waited outside for a minute, but the sage didn't appear. Takeo touched the trunk again and shimmered into his ethereal state to slip inside. Keiji's eyes widened.

"I've got you," Chiyo said, and tugged him through the outer wall with her. I looked around once more, tasting the same bitterness in the air that I'd sensed from the footprints. Then Midori and I glided in after the others.

I stopped with a jerk on the other side of the wall. Torn papers and broken porcelain scattered Rin's once-tidy room. The bench in the corner lay on its side. Blotches of soil had been tracked across the polished floorboards.

"Honored One?" Takeo was calling as he hurried up the stairs. The rest of us followed, over shards of pottery and trampled herbs. The table where Rin had taken tea with us was smashed in half; the cupboard doors dangled askew from wrenched hinges.

"There was a fight," Takeo said.

"And if Sage Rin won," I filled in unwillingly, "she'd still be here. They've taken her." My gut twisted.

"Do you figure Omori is behind this too?" Chiyo asked.

"We did see ogres before who looked as if they were heading to Mt. Fuji," I said, glancing at Takeo. "What if Omori sent them here?"

"That could be," Takeo said.

Rin had hardly been kind to me when I'd met her, but I would never have wished harm on her. And we'd needed her to share her wisdom and experience with Chiyo, to expand Chiyo's understanding of her powers beyond Takeo's and my capabilities. What were we supposed to do without the sage?

"Is there some reason that the demon would attack this sage?" Keiji said slowly. "I mean, I thought the prophecy was a secret? Or is the sage an obvious target?"

"He knew to come after me," Chiyo said, with a flex of her jaw that made me suddenly sure she was fending off his magic even now.

"Yes," Takeo said, his brow knitting, "but we believed he was targeting you only because he'd found out an important kami had escaped the mountain. No one but your parents knew about the prophecy and Sage Rin's connection to it. I can't imagine any circumstances under which they would have given up that information, no matter what he did to them."

"They'd have died before they risked the lives of everyone on the mountain," I agreed, hugging myself. "But there *isn't* any other reason for him to have attacked Sage Rin that I can think of."

Chiyo paled. "Okay," she said to Keiji, holding out her hand. "I need your phone, now."

His shoulders stiffened. "What?"

"Your phone! I have to call my other parents. *They* knew about the prophecy too."

"Oh. Oh!" He handed over the phone, and Chiyo flipped it open.

"The ghosts could have figured out which house was hers," I

said to Takeo. "At least a few of them saw what street she lived on. We did talk about how a sage had prophesized Chiyo's victory—did we mention that we would be going back to her?"

"I can't remember," he said grimly. "But the rest might have been enough."

"No signal," Chiyo said, her voice squeaking. She snapped the phone shut. "Maybe the top of the ridge would be better."

"Wait," Takeo said. "You shouldn't go alone. If you two keep guard while Sora and I check the rest of the house—quickly—then we can all leave together."

Chiyo frowned. "If those ghosts have hurt Mom and Dad..." she said. The glow of her ki flared to the surface of her skin. I wondered if Omori could sense her distress. An image of the smoothly confident man from the photo chuckling over the destruction he'd wrought flashed through my mind, and I shivered.

Takeo strode to the staircase. I hurried up after him, through a room as ransacked as the ones below, and up another flight, and another. I hesitated on the fifth floor, nudging the heap of robes strewn across the boards with my toe. The ogres had left nothing useful behind.

"Takeo," I said, "I don't think we're going to find—"

"I know." He rested his hand against the wall and grimaced at the floor. Then he raised his head. "I wanted to talk to you alone for a moment. I think you should go, Sora."

"Go?" I repeated.

"Back to the city. To your real parents, if the ghosts haven't found them. To wherever else you can take shelter if they have."

"But... why?" I protested. "The Ikedas don't want me. I don't want them. Takeo, you said you'd support whatever decision I made. I want to be here." Without Rin, Chiyo was going to need my help more than ever.

"I did say that," Takeo acknowledged. "And I wish I could keep my word. But I promised I would keep you safe too, and that's far more important. I don't think I can do both. If it was just a matter of strolling into the shrines... but it's not. You see, don't you? If Omori knows about Sage Rin, he may very well know everything. An army may be waiting for us when we arrive to look for the treasures. If you let Midori go, and you stay far away from us, no one will know you had anything to do with Mt. Fuji. You've helped us so much already."

Not nearly enough. But Takeo was right. If Omori knew about the prophecy, he'd also know how Chiyo was to defeat him. He'd tell his thousands of allies to do whatever they could to stop her.

How could she fight his whole army before she had even one of the treasures?

"It's too dangerous," Takeo went on. "We can't know what we'll face at Amateresu's shrine in Nagoya."

I blinked, my eyes going hot. "And you don't think I'll be able to manage. Because I'm human."

"Sora." He made a strangled sound and turned toward me. Suddenly his arms were around me, solid and secure as always, his face bent close to mine.

"That doesn't matter to me," he said. "My decision has nothing to do with that. I don't know if any of us will come out of this alive, even Chiyo. Sage Rin said nothing is certain. And now, with her gone... I can't let you come when I don't know what'll happen to you, when our enemies are too powerful for even a sage to defeat. If you were hurt because I failed you... If I *lost* you..."

I'd never heard him sound so anguished before. My hands found their way around his back. My world had tipped over. The only clear things were the strength of his embrace, the tremor in his voice, and his words. He cared about me so much. More than I'd let myself hope. But I couldn't—

Of course I could. In the midst of all the fear and uncertainty, I calmed as I clung to that one definite thought. I could erase in one moment all memory of the kiss that never should have happened and replace it with something right. Something I could hold on to, no matter what else the demon threw at us.

I eased back, my nose brushing Takeo's jaw, and looked up at him.

"I'm sorry," he said. "I'm overstepping. I have no place—"

"Takeo," I said, and when he stopped talking to hear what I would say, I rose on my toes and kissed him.

Takeo responded at once, his arms tightening around me. His lips were smoother, firmer, than Keiji's, and as they parted against mine I prepared for that spinning, singing feeling to race through my body.

Except the music didn't come.

I felt sheltered in Takeo's embrace. Like waking up from a nightmare with Mother's lips against my forehead. It was warm and comforting and not at all the uncontainable rush I wanted it to be. I leaned closer, trying to pull everything I could out of the kiss, but my heart kept beating in the same steady rhythm.

What was wrong with me? I wanted Takeo. My mind knew

that. So why didn't the rest of me?

It seemed like a betrayal to be kissing him and not feeling all the things I'd felt with someone who wasn't him. *That* was wrong. I braced myself to pull back, to apologize, to I-don't-know-what.

Then a cry echoed up the stairs.

I flinched away from Takeo with far less grace than I'd intended, but it didn't matter. We were both running for the stairs before I had time to think about it.

"Get out of here!" Chiyo shouted, and something clanged, and Keiji said in a tone so grave and terrified it made my chest ache, "I really think you should listen to her."

A pungent, oily smell filled my nose as we dashed past the third floor. I skidded down the next flight and caught myself just before I hit the bottom step.

Two tall, gangling creatures, one with a shock of white hair and the other bald and lumpy-headed, were circling Chiyo and Keiji, who were trapped in the middle of the room. Another, with curved horns that jutted along its shoulders, stood at the top of the stairs that led to the first floor. It glanced at me, and I saw it had no nose, only yellow reptilian eyes and a grin full of jagged teeth.

Ogres.

Chiyo stood in a defensive stance, her hands raised, ki glowing between them. Our enemies weren't attacking yet—she shouldn't have been wasting her energy. But she hadn't had time to learn that, had she? Beside her, Keiji brandished a bamboo walking stick that must have been the only weapon he could find. It quivered in his grip.

Takeo had slid his bow from his shoulder. He nocked an arrow and drew back the string in one fluid movement: a perfect line from him to the nearest ogre's head.

The ogre by the lower staircase leapt at us, faster than I'd have thought a creature that large could move. Its knobby fingers wrenched at my side as I dodged it. I shifted into the ethereal state instinctively, but the thick ki that oozed off the ogre's body dragged on me as if I were still perfectly solid. I stumbled across the floor, pulling the short sword Takeo had lent me from its sheath.

With a thud and a *crack*, Takeo's arrow twanged into the wall over my head. I whirled around. The ogre had pinned him down, and Takeo was struggling to draw his own sword while keeping the thing's hands off his neck. His bow hung in two limp pieces over the stairs.

"I think we should bring these ones back," his attacker said in a rough warbling voice like water over gravel. It slammed both of Takeo's arms against the stairs and turned its head to its companions. "The kami, at least. They match what our new friends said to look for, don't you think?"

"Ogres running errands for ghosts?" Keiji said, his voice shaking. "Well, now I've got no respect for you at all."

"The human dead are claiming the spirit world," said the creature closest to him. "Only the stupid don't join the winning side." It swiped at Keiji's stick. Keiji winced and dodged backward, jabbing the bamboo staff toward its abdomen. The ogre snapped off the top third, sending the piece clattering to the floor.

"Stop!" A blast of energy rippled from Chiyo's hands and hit the ogre in the chest, so hard it staggered backward. As she struck out with another surge of ki, I raised my sword and lunged at the ogre that held Takeo.

It hadn't expected me. One of its arms thrashed out as I grabbed its legs and plunged the sword into its calf. I clung on, holding my breath against the stench of its skin, and heaved back. At the same moment, Takeo kicked its belly. The creature gave an *oof* and we both toppled over.

My tailbone jarred against the floor, my ankle twisting. I bit back a gasp of pain. Midori's wings hummed by my ear, anger winding through her distress. The ogre whipped around, and I threw a ball of ki into its eyes. It reared back, sputtering, right into the swing of Takeo's sword.

The kami blade sliced straight through its neck. The ogre's body slumped over me, its head rolling across the floor to smack into Rin's broken table.

"Mitsuoka!" Chiyo shouted, and reached out to Keiji. He tossed the walking stick to her and ducked. Ki flared along the length of the bamboo staff. As the second ogre charged at them, she rammed the end of the stick into its face. The wood sizzled through the mottled flesh of its forehead. The creature spasmed and crumpled to the floor. Chiyo stared at its shuddering body.

That had to be the first time she'd killed anything. And in her distraction, the last of the ogres hissed and stabbed out at her with its knife-like claws.

I squirmed out from under the headless body, reaching for the sword still imbedded in its leg. Takeo jumped down the stairs. The ogre must have heard the whistle of his blade. It spun suddenly and flung itself under his strike and toward me, just as I dashed forward.

I tried to stop, but my feet slipped on the polished floor. As I threw myself backward, the ogre caught the flying strands of my hair. Midori's ki pulled away from me like roots ripped from the earth. The ogre's fist closed around her with a sickening crunch.

"No!" I choked out. I slammed at the creature's leg with my heel, but it was already wrenching me around as it dodged Takeo.

"Let go of her," Chiyo yelled as I raised my sword to hack at the fingers that held me. A blinding glow seared through the room. The ogre gurgled and grabbed at the only solid thing within its reach: me.

With its last gasp of life, it dug its claw under my chin and slashed straight through my throat.

I fell. The ogre did too, fouling the air with the stench of its burning flesh. My mouth opened, but no sound came out. My throat was full of pain and a hot, wet rush. My head hit the ground, my cheekbone cracking.

My lungs seized. I stared across the floor toward Midori's mangled body. Her wings had been crumpled like tissue paper, her exoskeleton smashed. The facets of her round eyes gazed dully at nothing. My own eyes filled with tears.

If you hurt them badly enough, if they're already weakened, kami can die. Midori had given me so much of her ki for so long, she hadn't had enough left to heal from an injury that serious.

And I wasn't any kind of kami.

I watched the scarlet puddle spreading out from under me.

That's my life, I thought. My life spilling out and slipping away, just like that.

Icy, spidery fingers wound through my spirit and gripped on. They tugged at me, down, down toward the gaping darkness of the afterworld. It was so big, so big and so dark and so *empty...*

Panic jittered through my mind. *No.* I tried to reach, as if I could hold myself in the world of the living if I found something to grab on to, but my arms wouldn't move. I couldn't feel my feet. A chill crept through my chest.

I was sinking, sinking far too fast to catch.

THIRTEEN

As MY VISION hazed, figures scrambled around me in a blur of motion. Shouts echoed past my failing ears. The room grayed.

A shaky touch brushed my temple. A voice babbled frantically. The light contracted, swallowed up by the cold, empty dark—

A brilliant glow burst in my head, sending a blast of energy rippling through me. It faded, and then sparked again. My muscles jolted. The taste of rot flooded my mouth. I gurgled, shuddered, and wretched. The brightness flared once more, and my lungs heaved. Air rasped into them down my newly sealed throat.

I coughed, the effort rattling my body. My stomach turned over. As I gagged, my lips brushed a pool of something viscous soaking the floor beneath me. The hands that had touched me flitted away from my face.

"Sora?" Takeo said. "Sora!"

I turned my gaze slowly. My vision doubled the figures around me and then blended them back into one. Takeo was crouched at my side, his jaw tight. Chiyo knelt by my head, smiling even as her shoulders trembled. And Keiji stood by my feet, his hands fisted, his mouth set in a firm, pale line as if he were trying not to vomit.

Which maybe he was. That stuff on the floor—that was blood. My blood. He'd just watched me all but die.

The only reason I *hadn't* died was that Chiyo's ki had saved me.

The memory of that yawning blackness rose up, blotting out every other thought, and I started to shiver. Once I started, I couldn't stop. My body quaked as I drew my knees to my chest. My arm was wet, my cheek sticky. More blood. Strands of hair streaked crimson across my shirt. I shivered harder, squeezing my legs and pressing my face against them.

I was supposed to have centuries before I faced that place. Millennia. So many years I got weary counting them. Not seventeen. Seventeen was nothing.

But I was human, and this was how humans died. In an instant, a claw ripped across a throat.

My neck still ached. When I swallowed, my throat stung. My eyes burned, but crying seemed somehow pointless. Crying didn't even begin to express the terror knifing through me.

Terror, and a swell of shame.

I hadn't died, but Midori's body was still lying crushed and strewn on the floor, too far gone for even Chiyo's power. Midori, who had stayed with me, played with me, and guided me on my adventures for as long as I could remember. Who had let me keep up this charade of being kami at the expense of her life. How many years had *she* had?

I closed my eyes. A fresh bout of tremors swept through me. Next time Chiyo might not be here. Next time the darkness might take me too, and I would never come back.

"Is she all right now?" Chiyo asked.

"Physically, she's weak, but she'll recover," Takeo said, his voice strained. "But she's never... When you're a kami, it's so hard to be killed, you never really think about death. You never worry— The shock—"

There was a pause. Then Chiyo said, faintly, "So she isn't a kami then, right? Or she'd have been able to heal herself. You were helping her seem kami with some trick that stopped working. But why would you bring a human girl—?" She paused. "She's the one, isn't she? The one they switched me for. That's how she knew how to act like a kami. Why didn't she say something? My parents—her parents—she's supposed to be with them!"

"She wanted to help you," Takeo said. "And she did. But I've already talked with her. She's going back to Tokyo. This is my fault. I should have made her stay behind before."

"Isn't that up to Sora?" Keiji broke in. "You can't just decide something like that for her. If she wants to—"

To fight more ogres? To face more ghosts with their blades and guns while only the thinnest dribble of ki moved through me? To risk tumbling down into that void, where my spirit would gradually disintegrate into the vast pool of energy that fueled the world. Until I was gone completely.

The thought made my eyes well up and my fingers curl, clutching at the air. I wasn't ready for that.

"No," I said. My knees muffled the word. I turned my head. It felt like a great weight on my neck without Midori's buoyant presence.

"No," I repeated. "I'll go back."

We couldn't go anywhere right away. My limbs were so weak I could barely sit up, and the presence of spilled blood was upsetting Takeo's and Chiyo's ki. In just a short time, their skin had turned sallow and their movements gone shaky. I suspected they felt almost as sick as I did.

Chiyo tried to follow Takeo and Keiji as they went to get water from the valley's stream, and collapsed to her knees by the stairs. "I'll be fine, I'll be fine," she said, but the battle and the energy she'd expended healing me had obviously taken their toll. Takeo brought her to the first floor and left her there to gather herself as he and Keiji continued their errand.

With the bowls they brought, I washed my clothes and hair. Then they rinsed Rin's floor until the water ran clear. Despite their efforts, dark stains marred the smooth boards. I wondered if this house would ever be clean enough for Rin to return and live here comfortably.

If she still lived at all.

My mind darted back to the rising cold and the blackness, and I bit my lip.

As we left the old cypress, Takeo carrying me on his back as if I were seven years old again, Chiyo gasped and stumbled against a tree. "Omori," she gritted out. Takeo clasped her shoulder, and the distress in her expression softened as he must have helped her reconstruct her inner shield.

"We'll find a shrine," he said. "You both need to rest, somewhere we don't have to worry about his magic intruding."

We came across a tiny shrine on the other side of the valley, with a wooden structure more for presentation than to provide any real shelter. But the protections did their work. Chiyo lay down at its base and immediately fell into a deep slumber, her body and ki finally relaxing. I set myself down on a mossy patch of rock by the stone trough of the shrine's small purifying fountain. Human visitors were supposed to rinse their hands and mouths with its water to cleanse themselves inside and out, but I couldn't believe that would purify my spirit, not right now. When I blinked, I still saw the broken pieces of Midori's body.

I should have released her from her service. I should have accepted what I was, stayed where I belonged.

"I'll search the forest for any kami who might know what's become of Sage Rin," Takeo said, and vanished amid the trees.

Keiji paced by the edge of the narrow grounds. He approached me once, right after Takeo left. "Is there anything I can do?" he asked. "Cup of water? Sweet bread? Magic tricks?"

He wanted me to smile, but his grin was so hesitant, his posture so awkward—so different from his usual easy composure—that I had to look away. That was also my fault, wasn't it? I'd acted as if I wanted him, wanted something more than our tentative friendship, and then I'd shoved him away. In my thoughtlessness, I'd broken him too.

"I don't need anything," I said shortly. "Thank you."

After that, he left me alone.

Every few minutes, I tested my strength. Without Midori's ki, the ground beneath me was muted, as blank of feeling as the breeze that grazed my face. At the same time, my awareness of the world *inside* my skin had sharpened. Delicate bones, so easily cracked. Trembling strings of muscle on the verge of tearing. My human body was a fragile husk that one harsh breath might split in two.

It took two hours before my legs would hold my weight. Another before I could take more than a few steps. I hobbled to the shrine building. A stubby pencil and a few sheets of rice paper lay on a shelf in its shed-like interior. I tore the papers into strips and poured all my focus into printing the characters Takeo had taught me. Every ofuda was a death possibly averted.

I didn't notice Chiyo had woken until she leaned over my shoulder. "Got another pencil?" she asked.

"I'm almost done," I said. "How do you feel?"

"Ready to blast a whole lot of ghostly butt," she said, her eyes sparkling. I wondered what her ki would have looked like if I could see it. "Where'd Takeo get to?"

I told her and added, "I'm sure he won't be gone much longer."

She picked up a stick to poke at the earth beneath us. "So you didn't just know my kami parents," she said after a long moment. "They looked after you."

"Yes," I said, my fingers tensing around the pencil. I hardly had the energy to sustain that old rush of jealousy, but ever fiber of my being resisted this conversation.

"What are they like, as parents?"

"They're wonderful," I said truthfully. "Patient and kind and caring. You'll be happy with them."

"I wish—" Chiyo started, but I didn't have to find out what she wished about the parents I would probably never see again, because Takeo emerged from the forest just then. A small group of kami followed him: a marten, a pheasant, and a finch with bright yellow spots on its wings, a doe that regarded us with a slow blink of its dark eyes, a boar snuffling its long snout over the ground beside it, a monkey that chittered what sounded like a remark of excitement, and two humanoid figures who must have pulled themselves from trees or flowers.

"You brought company!" Chiyo said.

"No one is certain what happened to the sage," Takeo said, "other than there was a great commotion here this morning. But they've offered to come with us to Nagoya and help us retrieve the sword in any way they can."

My spirits lifted a little. It wasn't an army, but it was much more support than we'd had before. I pushed myself to my feet, stiffening my legs to keep myself from wobbling. "So you'll go straight for the sword now?"

"I think we should at least discover what waits for us there. We've already lost most of a day. If Sage Rin is... unable to join us, then we must push forward as well as we can. When we're able to."

His gaze settled on me. He had to see the effort it was taking me to hold myself upright. I hoped he'd believe it was only grief and worry affecting me now. The thought of the ghosts and ogres roaming beyond the shrine's boundaries sent a stab of fear through me, but I held my tongue. Chiyo was obviously recovered. They couldn't delay any longer on my account.

"I'm well enough to leave," I said.

Takeo hesitated. "Are you sure?"

"Definitely."

⁂

Takeo held my hand during the run toward Nagoya, steadying my body if not my mind. As night fell, every shifting shadow made my heart thump out of rhythm. It was fully dark when we reached the edge of the city that held the sun kami's shrine and the sacred sword within it.

Chiyo immediately demanded Keiji's cell phone, which had refused to locate a signal in the mountains, and gave a little cheer when she checked the display. She dialed, bobbing on her feet as we hurried toward the train station.

"Mom? Are you okay?" She gave us a thumbs up, beaming, and scooted a little ahead as she lowered her voice. "You wouldn't *believe* what we've been doing."

The sight of her joy broke me from my daze. I wasn't worried that she'd tell them about me—I'd asked her to let me be the one to explain, and she'd immediately agreed. But her reaction had a bigger implication. "The ghosts didn't hurt the Ikedas," I said. "Then how...?"

"They might have simply spied on Chiyo's parents and overhead them discussing the situation," Takeo said. "Which means they may not know everything." He exhaled with what sounded like relief.

Maybe they could retrieve the sword safely. A pang echoed through my chest. After I left, I wouldn't know. I'd have no idea what was happening.

I touched the raw skin along my throat, and those worries quieted under an icy flash of panic.

To anyone walking by as we approached Nagoya Station, it would have looked as if we were a group of four. The kami Takeo had gathered had made themselves ethereal as soon as we'd entered human habitation. We did have one fully visible companion, though. I caught sight of a sparrow darting between two telephone poles and wondered if it understood what we were doing here.

Two towers rose over the roof of the boxy station building, looking like massive tree trunks that had been cut just below their branches. I released Takeo's hand and headed to the nearest doors, but stopped just outside them. People were scattered throughout the wide, bright hall on the other side, streaming this way and that. I had to walk in there as if I were one of them. I didn't even know *how* to take a train. Wouldn't we need money to buy a ticket?

Chiyo tugged open the door next to me and ambled inside. I pressed my palms to the glass, watching her go, so confident and at ease. As the last strands of Takeo's energy slipped away from me, my awareness of the surface beneath my fingers numbed, as if a layer of cotton separated my skin from the door. The spot on my head where Midori used to perch felt horribly light. I blinked back the tears that sprang into my eyes.

I could still feel the high rises with their glowing advertisements all around me. We were in the midst of a human forest made of neon, metal, and concrete, its energy so blatant I wouldn't have needed eyes to sense it. But I didn't feel a part of it at all.

Chiyo returned a minute later, bounding past the doors. "The last train for Tokyo already left," she said. "But there'll be another at six in the morning."

"All right," I said. So what was I going to do for the rest of the night?

Takeo paced to the edge of the sidewalk, where a line of taxis stood waiting, and back toward the station. His jaw tensed when he looked at me.

"I should have taken you straight to Tokyo myself before we came here," he said. "It was my mistake. I'll take you now."

"And waste another day?" I protested. "No. You can't."

I wanted to be away from here, I wanted to be somewhere that felt secure, but Mt. Fuji *needed* him. Chiyo needed him. And not even Tokyo was safe until the mountain was recovered.

"What's so awful about her waiting until morning?" Chiyo said. "She can hang out here, we'll drop by the shrine and get the sword, everyone's happy."

Takeo shook his head. "I have a duty," he said. "I have to— I can't just—"

My heart wrenched. He did have a duty: to *her*, to everyone on the mountain, to all who were already being harmed by Omori's scheme. Any loyalty he felt to me should have been a distant fourth. But it wasn't. It was nearly overwhelming him.

That was my fault too.

"Takeo," I said, the words like stones in my mouth, "we should talk. Alone."

Without waiting to see if he'd follow—of course he would, it was in his nature to do as I asked—I walked away from the others, past the corner of the station building. Lights shone from several of the high windows overlooking the street. I stared up at them, focusing on them instead of the darkness. Those were what humans used for stars.

I turned when Takeo's footsteps halted behind me. He set his hand on my shoulder. Beyond him, Chiyo was brandishing a stick she'd picked up in the forest—a sturdier version of Rin's bamboo staff—in mock-battle with one of the kami I couldn't see. Keiji just stood there, watching Takeo and me, his arms folded tightly over his chest. *He'd* insisted he was staying, I assumed still hoping for that reward to help his brother. But then, his efforts on the kami's behalf hadn't gotten anyone killed.

I made myself look up at Takeo's face. At the dark eyes that had always reassured me. And said what I'd known since the moment before the ogres had attacked.

"What happened in Sage Rin's house," I said, "I shouldn't have done that. I thought—I thought that was how I wanted things to be with you."

His hand dropped to his side. That was the only sign I'd hurt him. "But it isn't?" he said.

"I love you," I said softly. "I've loved you since my first memory of you. But... I don't think I do quite like that. I love Mother and Father and Ayame too. I just assumed..." I'd assumed, because he was young and handsome and *there,* that he was exactly what I wanted. Maybe he had been, before all this. But I couldn't ignore what I'd felt and what I hadn't when we'd kissed. I couldn't let him take more risks for me when my heart wouldn't sing for him. "I'm sorry."

"Don't be," he said. "*I'm* sorry. I shouldn't have presumed. You're having to deal with so much."

"And I'm dealing with it," I said. "What you need to deal with is rescuing everyone else we love. We're running out of time. If Omori doesn't already know our plans, he may figure them out soon. Go with Chiyo to get the sword. I'll..." I considered staying behind here, alone, while the others vanished into the night, and my gut clenched. "I'll stay out of the way, somewhere near the shrine. And first thing in the morning, I'll go to Tokyo."

Takeo lowered his head. "I feel as if I'm failing in both of my duties as a guard of the palace."

"*No,*" I said firmly, and managed to smile. "Of course not. I'm alive. You have Chiyo. Tonight you can see her one step closer to saving the mountain. So let's get started. I'd like to know she has one of the treasures in her hands before I go."

* * *

Amaterasu's shrine lay in almost a direct line along the train tracks, so we followed them rather than the streets where we'd have to dodge the traffic and pedestrians. With Takeo's hand around mine and Chiyo's clamped on Keiji's wrist, we slipped through the fences. Thanks to Takeo's ki, the world beyond the boundaries of my body snapped back into focus. A peaceful murmur emanated through the city's frenetic energy.

"Come on!" Chiyo said.

We dashed past the massive office buildings and department stores that filled the city's core. They gave way to smaller apartment complexes mingled with individual houses and shops, dark and still beneath the clouds that streaked the sky. We had just come into sight of another long train station when the shrine's murmur swelled, beckoning us.

On the other side of the station, streetlamps washed the road with a yellow light. Across the street from us, trees rustled overtop a short stone wall. Other than the occasional passing car, the area appeared deserted. But it was impossible to make out much in the shadows beyond the wall.

"We'd be able to see more from higher up," I said, motioning toward a concrete walkway that was angled over the road like a bridge. Takeo nodded and we walked over. My body had continued recovering during our travels from Rin's valley, and I found I could climb the steps almost as steadily as I normally might have.

The shrine grounds encompassed what amounted to a small forest within the city. Even from above, the sweeping branches of the trees blocked any glimpse of the buildings. Only a narrow asphalt drive was visible, penetrating the trees as it veered through a gap in the shrine's wall.

As I peered through the dim light, the shadows on the drive shifted and swirled. A cold sweat broke over my skin.

They weren't shadows at all. They were ghosts. A swarm of translucent, legless figures was drifting across the inner road, in and out of the forest.

"Oh, wow," Chiyo said. She raised her stick defensively. "I thought ghosts couldn't go into shrines—isn't that what all the protections are for?"

"They *can't* go in," I said as the realization hit me. "Not really. They're sticking to the edges of the grounds. They mustn't be able to pass the line of torii—that's as far as they can manage. You'd just have to get past the gates, and then they wouldn't be able to reach you."

But in that gap of fifteen or so feet between the wall and the first of the gates, hundreds of ghosts were gathered. I swallowed thickly. Omori must have known exactly what we were planning. Were just as many waiting near the sun kami's shrines in Ise and Tokyo while thousands still held Mt. Fuji captive? Or had he correctly determined that we'd want the sword first, and this was the largest portion of his army?

How much else had that demonic businessman with his assured smile determined about us, while we still knew so little about him?

"Should we wait until morning?" Chiyo asked. "Do ghosts have anything against sunlight?"

"Not from what I've read," Keiji said, his face drawn.

"I'm not aware of a weakness like that," Takeo agreed. "And I'm sure their orders are to stand guard indefinitely. More may join them if we give them time."

So many unsettled spirits—where had they all come from?

"Then we should go in tonight," Chiyo said. She paused, studying the flow of ghostly bodies. "There are a lot of them, but I bet I can blast through. I feel totally strong again. And we've got help." She turned to her small troop of kami. "Are we ready to fight?"

The kami raised their voices in a cheer. The two human figures waved the ofuda we'd shared with them.

"Oh," Keiji said, and dug into his messenger bag. "We also have..." He thrust a half-full bag of salt toward the woman-shaped kami with petal-like hair named Sumire, who I'd gathered was the spirit of a violet. "I, ah, borrowed it from my aunt and uncle. Salt is purifying, so it should repel malicious spirits. I'd have brought other stuff too, but I didn't have a chance to go shopping."

Takeo still looked uncertain. "If we had more time..." he said. "But we don't. I suppose ghosts require little subtlety. It *would* be a matter of simply 'blasting' through." He eyed Chiyo and rested his hand on his sword's grip. "Don't try to engage them—any time you slow down, you give them a chance to get the upper hand. Use your energy to repel those that come near you, and don't stop until you reach the gates. The rest of us will protect your sides and back." He glanced toward the drive. "I don't think they've noticed our arrival yet, so we'll have an element of surprise. That may carry us through."

Chiyo waved her stick in the air, her face set with determination. "Let's go smash those ghosts back to where they belong!"

"Good luck," I said, squeezing Takeo's hand. He held on for a second longer before letting go.

Chiyo darted down the walkway, ki glittering under her feet. The other kami followed her charge. Without Takeo enhancing my sight, they faded away before my human eyes. The figures on the drive blurred into a shimmer of ghostlights: glowing spheres that bobbed through the motions of their patrol, most so faint I could only make them out if I squinted. I stepped to the railing, my fingers closing around the cool metal.

When Chiyo's force reached the sidewalk, the kami shifted into corporeal form. Without hesitation, they raced up the drive.

I flinched as ghostlights flared along the edge of the shrine forest. They swirled around the drive so densely that in a moment I could no longer see Chiyo or Takeo except for blazes of ki and glints of sword. Here and there a light blinked out as an ofuda must have found its mark, but in less than a second, another glow replaced it. I leaned forward, the railing digging into my palms, trying to follow Chiyo's progress.

Keiji was still standing on the other side of the walkway. "You could have gone with them," he said. "It doesn't matter whether you're a kami or not. I've seen you—you can fight. You didn't have to listen to him."

"I'm not staying back because of Takeo," I said, more sharply than I meant to. I dragged in a breath, fear prickling down my throat and into my lungs. "If the others had to look out for me, it'd be so much harder for them to fight. And what can I really do by myself? Without a kami helping me, the ghosts can hurt me without me even being able to touch them."

They could *kill* me. I could imagine too clearly how their weightless hands would reach into my chest, grab, and twist... I closed my eyes, suppressing a shudder.

"What about you?" I said.

"I don't know anything about fighting," Keiji said. "After this morning, I'm glad just to have all my limbs still attached."

When I looked again, the ghostlights were circling like a whirlwind around a ki-bright center where Chiyo and the others must have been struggling on. They were maybe halfway to the gates now. Had the ghosts managed to stop them completely?

"Hey!" Keiji said. At the same moment, my gaze snagged on a figure running up the drive from the street—a tall, lanky figure carrying a basket over his arm. He burst into the front ranks of the shimmering army of ghosts, reaching into the basket and throwing something that made the lights around him wince away. Then he turned to throw another handful, and the ghostly glow lit his stern face with its topping of spiky-short hair.

"It's Haru," I said, staring. "How did he—? We mentioned going to get the treasures. He must have come here to wait for Chiyo." And decided to join in the fight when he'd seen her.

Keiji bent over the railing. "What's he doing?"

Haru tossed another handful at the ghosts, the soft objects glimmering pink. "He's got flowers," I said.

"Lotuses! Nice. He must have looked that up—the ghosts will be afraid of them because they're sacred. At least, it looks like it. I wasn't sure if that one would work."

"It does seem to," I said with a flicker of surprise. But that was Keiji's area, knowing these things. That was how he was going to help. Me...

A couple of forms solidified around Haru. Knives flashed in their hands, and my shoulders stiffened. The sacred flowers might repel the ghosts' energy, but they wouldn't block a physical weapon.

Haru brandished the flowers at them, but as he turned one

way and then the other, the ghosts followed. Another solidified, and another. Any second he'd make a wrong step and give one of them an opening. And no one was coming to help him. Chiyo was pressing on so intently that she and the other kami probably hadn't even noticed him.

"They're going to kill him," Keiji said faintly.

They were. Because he'd dared to attack them, dared to stand by Chiyo, despite his human frailty. My fingers clutched the railing.

He was so brave, and he was going to die for it.

FOURTEEN

ALL AT once, I felt sick. I was the one who'd been raised to face battles like this, who'd trained for it. And now I was cringing up here while Haru put his life on the line—for Chiyo, for the mountain, for *my* home.

What was I so scared of? The memory of that cold gaping darkness still made my chest clench up. But so did the thought of living just a few more days only to watch Fuji's fire spill down, knowing thousands of humans and kami were dead and I hadn't even tried to stop it. I didn't like being this weak, cringing thing.

Maybe I wasn't kami, maybe I wasn't so strong after all, but I wasn't completely helpless. I could do what was right.

I forced my legs to move, propelling myself toward the far end of the walkway. My muscles felt heavy. Perspiration beaded on my forehead. I kept walking, faster, almost jogging now. My heart was beating at the back of my mouth, my stomach churning, but the idea of seeing Haru fall was so much worse.

Keiji hurried after me. He caught up by the top of the stairs.

"You don't have to come," I said as I started down.

He kept pace, offering me a shaky smile. "If you're going, I'm going."

We sprinted downward. My palm was slick against the railing, and the impact of each step rattled through my feet. Keiji skidded and stumbled as we hit the sidewalk. He caught himself against the stone wall.

"I'm fine, let's go," he said.

We ran.

Around the curve of the drive, we came up on the mass of ghostlights. Keiji hesitated, but I hurled myself straight into their midst. I heard the scuffing of his shoes as he followed. The dim orbs whirled around me in a clotted fog, their chilly edges brushing my skin like dusty cobwebs. Bile rose up in my throat.

Then I spotted Haru to my left—Haru, and a solid ghost-woman slashing at his rectangular jaw with a knife. I had no time to think. My well-honed instincts kicked in, and I lunged forward.

Without the boost of ki, my limbs responded more slowly, as if moving through water rather than air. But I was fast enough. My elbow rammed into the woman's side, and she teetered back with a grunt.

"The ofuda!" Keiji shouted behind me.

My hand was already darting to my pocket. I grabbed the last few I'd kept, wishing I hadn't given most of them away. As the ghost-woman turned toward me, I smacked one against her head. She wisped away, but more of the ghosts-turned-corporeal were closing in around us. My teeth gritted, my pulse thundering in my ears. I was afraid to know what sound might slip out if I opened my mouth.

I was here. That was what mattered, however terrified I was.

"Mitsuoka!" Haru said, startled. "Sora!" It wasn't the time for greetings or explanations. We edged away from the approaching ghosts, back to back in a cluster of three. Keiji's shoulder pressed firmly against mine, but his breath was ragged. Haru dug into his pocket and pushed a small silk bag into my free hand.

"Put it on," he said, passing another to Keiji. "It's an amulet against evil spirits—I bought them at the shrine this morning." A similar bag dangled against his broad chest. I yanked the ribbon over my head.

A man with a gun sprang at us, pointing the muzzle at my face. My legs locked, but my arms remembered what to do. I snapped his wrist aside an instant before his finger could pull the trigger. The gun clattered onto the pavement. Haru tossed a lotus flower at him, and the ghost staggered backward, fading into his ethereal form.

To my right, another ghost leapt at Keiji with a switchblade. Keiji dodged, waving an ofuda, but there wasn't much room for him to maneuver. The blade sliced across the skin above his elbow. He yelped. But as the man drew back his knife to strike again, Keiji hurtled forward and whipped the charm at the ghost's forehead. The strip of paper smacked the bridge of the man's nose, and he vanished.

A four-legged form lurched through the ghostlights beyond our attackers. The deer kami. She reared and twisted as the ghosts around her battered her from all sides. My heart sank.

We'd brought the other kami into this, but none of *them* would have been trained to fight. Most of them weren't even built for it. What was happening to the rest of our "army"?

"Run!" I shouted to her. "Get out of here while you can!" I grabbed a flower from Haru's basket and pitched it toward her. The ghostlights momentarily broke away, and the deer dashed for the street.

Haru lashed out at the ghosts around us with a fistful of petals. They edged back, but didn't leave. They were simply being more cautious now that they knew we could banish them. As we glared at them, several more lights shimmered into solid bodies. I licked my dry lips. I only had four ofuda left. I wasn't sure how many Keiji was carrying.

"I'm out of flowers," Haru said quietly. "Do you think Chiyo has made it through?"

From where we stood, I could no longer see the space where she'd been fighting. Maybe she had made it to the gates, and we could flee now. Or maybe she still needed whatever small distraction we were providing.

"I don't know," I said. "Do you think you can keep going a little longer?"

He reached behind him and pulled a surprisingly authentic-looking katana from a sheath slung across his back. Keiji let out a wobbly laugh.

Kendo club—that was what Chiyo had said, wasn't it?

"It's only a practice sword," Haru said, his face sallow but his expression resolute. "It's not very sharp, but it'll hurt if I hit them hard enough. I'll keep fighting until she's safe, or die trying."

"Same here," Keiji declared. He feinted at the ghosts around us with a handful of ofuda. A few beads of blood dripped off the tip of his elbow onto the pavement.

Then a cry split the air, so high and victorious it rang in my ears like music.

"I got it! Watch out, you ghouls—I've got a magic sword now."

Chiyo. Relief washed over me. The lights around us shivered, and the corporeal ghosts glanced from us to the inner shrine grounds, apparently not sure where they were needed most. As they faltered, I took a gulp of warm night air and stepped out, slamming a charm against one man's forehead, kicking the feet out from under the woman next to him, and throwing another ofuda down on her. Both blinked out of the world of the living.

When I looked up, Chiyo was plowing through the sea of ghosts. The straight sword in her hands glowed as she swung it in a wide arc. Every ghostlight the blade touched didn't vanish, but shattered into sprays of glinting mist. Grinning, Chiyo spun around. Dozens of ghosts scattered in her wake. Our attackers abandoned us to charge at her, only to be disintegrated by another swing of the sacred sword.

A tingle of ki I recognized as Takeo's rippled over me. He touched my back.

"Come this way," he said, his tone betraying no hint of emotion at finding me there. His hand clasped mine. A few of the other kami gathered around us with a rush of ki. We dashed onto the street, Chiyo circling us with the sword held high, and then on toward the train tracks, faster than any ghost could follow.

When we finally came to a halt at a shrine far beyond the fringes of the city, the rest of the kami shifted back into corporeal form. That was when I realized not all those who'd come to Nagoya with us had made it this far. There was no sign of the pheasant or the marten. The doe immediately sank to the ground and lowered her graceful head to her haunches, and the monkey limped past her, examining a cut on its chest that hadn't quite healed. One of the human-like kami was hugging the other, who was shivering.

My skin prickled uncomfortably. We might have gotten what we wanted, but the assault had left us far from unscathed.

The shrine's guardian, a sturdy, dour-faced tree kami who lived in the equally sturdy oak at the back of the grounds, cringed over the blood on Keiji's arm. He healed the cut with a brush of ki and led him to the purifying fountain to wash it. The other kami settled on the smooth stone platform that surrounded the shrine building. And Chiyo stopped admiring her new sword long enough to notice Haru standing in our midst.

She froze, her eyes going wide. Haru stiffened. He smiled with an awkwardness at odds with his usual physical ease, as if he wasn't sure how he'd be received. Then Chiyo's startled expression broke with a grin so huge it nearly split her face. She dropped the sword and flung her arms around him.

"I tried to tell them we had to go back to Tokyo to get you," she said. She pulled back to look at him, bobbed up to kiss him so soundly my cheeks warmed as I watched, and then squeezed him in another embrace. "But you came and found me!"

Haru laughed, hugging her back. "I knew you were going for the treasures, so I figured I'd stake out one and wait. And I guessed you'd go for the sword before the others."

"Ha!" Chiyo said. "Who says you're not a smart one?"

As she started asking him about her friends, Takeo walked past us, deep in conversation with the oak kami. He shot me a reassuring glance before they disappeared behind the shrine building, and understanding struck me. He was explaining the need to get me home.

My gut knotted. I imagined sitting in the Ikedas' cramped living room with the narrow couch and the piano, my "real" parents hovering over me, while kami who'd never before encountered a blade or a fist fought on. I'd face no ghosts, no ogres, no demons. It would be so easy. Easy, and cowardly.

My heart thumped louder even as I thought those words, but I hurried after Takeo.

I reached him near the oak tree just as its kami disappeared back into it. Takeo turned to me. He'd pulled his hair back into its formal knot, and even though his human clothes were dust-smudged and his expression weary, he looked as gallant as always.

"I'm staying," I said before he could speak. "With you and Chiyo and the others. I'm going to keep fighting."

His lips parted soundlessly. But he couldn't have been completely surprised after he'd seen me in the midst of the battle.

"You promised you'd go home," he said after a moment.

"I didn't *promise*," I said. The anguished look he gave me made my throat tighten. I folded my arms over my chest. "I only said I would. I changed my mind."

"Sora—"

"Do you think I'd want to live knowing I was letting you and

Chiyo and everyone else fight my battles—*die* in my battles—for me?" I interrupted. "We did something good, Haru and Keiji and me, didn't we? There will be fewer ghosts next time because we banished some. Maybe even one or two kami survived who wouldn't have without us drawing some of their attackers away. I know not all of them made it back."

He lowered his gaze. "Some of those who joined us... I should have realized they would not have the capability to withstand the ghosts in that number."

"But I can, for at least a little while." I dropped my voice. "You keep calling Tokyo my 'home.' It isn't. Mt. Fuji is. Even if I never set foot on the mountain again, it's the only true home I have. And if we don't save it, any other home I could make will be ruined too. We lost Sage Rin. The only other kami we can find have no practice fighting. Chiyo's going to need every bit of help she can get if she's going to make the prophecy come true. I only agreed to give up because I was scared, and I'm still scared, but I'm a lot more scared of what will happen if I let that stop me from doing everything I can."

A quiver had crept into my voice. I paused, fingering the silky amulet that hung from my neck. A sweet floral scent wafted from it. "I have this now," I said. "Haru gave me and Keiji two of the extras he bought. I think they repelled the ghosts enough that they couldn't attack us with ki. We won't be defenseless."

"You could still be hurt again," Takeo said.

"Even if I am, even if I... die, it'd still be better than standing by and letting Omori win."

"I don't like it."

"I know," I said. "But can you accept it?"

The moment stretched on. Then he sighed. "I'll have to, won't I? It's not my place to order you around. I know we need any help that's offered. But I—I hope you'll be careful, Sora."

"I will be," I said.

"I only wish..." He trailed off, but I thought I knew how he'd have finished that sentence. If only I weren't human. If only we didn't have to worry that one bullet, one swipe of a blade could kill me.

"Only two more treasures," I said. "Two more, and this will be over."

Takeo nodded. "I need to teach Chiyo how to handle that sword most effectively. It is incredibly powerful, but... the ghosts know how to weaken us. The weapons they came at us with were stained with blood from elsewhere. If even one got too close to her..."

I'd noticed that about the weapons they'd carried before. "Omori must have learned how much spilled blood weakens kami."

"He knows far more than I like," Takeo said. "I'm thinking perhaps we should risk going back to Tokyo for the jewel next."

I frowned. "But Ise is so much closer, and the mirror will do more to protect Chiyo."

"Exactly," Takeo said with a grim smile as we started to stroll back around the building. "It makes more sense. It's what we already planned. So it's possible the demon will send the bulk of his force there next, leaving the Imperial Palace less defended. I think the chance is worth the lost time. All the same, we should leave right away. The journey will take at least half a day."

Keiji walked out of the forest at the edge of the shrine grounds ahead of us. He was either too distracted to notice us, or we were too hard to see in the deeper darkness cast by the roof's curved awning. He stared down at a silvery object clenched in his hand—his phone, I recognized after a second. Then he looked back toward the woods, his arm rising as if he meant to throw it away. His jaw twitched. He shook his head and shoved the phone back into his pocket before stalking off to rejoin the group out front. Another argument with his brother, I guessed.

We followed him into the front courtyard a minute later. The kami, sprawled across the platform and the grass at its foot, looked as defeated as before. Chiyo was smiling, but she was leaning into Haru's arms, as if too tired to stand on her own.

Takeo stepped onto the platform. "I know we've been through a lot tonight," he said. "But we must press on to Tokyo as soon as possible. We can't afford to wait until morning."

Wait until morning. The phrase sparked a memory of our conversation outside the train station. "Wait," I said. "We don't have to travel to Tokyo by our own power. There's a train that goes straight there from Nagoya—faster than any of us can run. We could rest now and catch the first one in the morning, and get there at least as early, without expending anywhere near as much energy."

Takeo blinked as if he couldn't quite make sense of my words. It probably would never have occurred to him that kami might travel using human machines. Until tonight, it might not have occurred to me. But why shouldn't we? If the kami stayed ethereal and shifted Keiji and me too, we didn't even need to worry about tickets. No one would see us there.

"Yes," Takeo said slowly. "Yes, that would be possible. Good thinking, Sora. Then for now we will rest."

"That's it?" Chiyo said. She raised the sacred sword in the air. "We took on all those ghosts and won—I think we deserve a little victory party. How do kami celebrate?"

Part of me balked, but I noticed the other kami raising their heads at her suggestion. Maybe a celebration was just what we needed, to lift our spirits before the next challenge that awaited us.

"We dance," I said.

* * *

We lit a campfire amid the white pebbles of the yard's central path. The oak kami arrived with a basket of wineberries, which he passed around the circle. I palmed a few gratefully. The tart juice burst in my mouth, easing the hunger pangs I'd managed to drown out until now.

Across the fire from me, Keiji gestured to Haru's katana and pulled an exaggerated face of shock and awe. Haru chuckled in his reticent way, and Keiji laughed too. He leaned back on his hands, tipping his face toward the indigo sky. Whatever had upset him earlier, he appeared to have put it behind him.

Takeo turned to me. "To dance we need music. Do you have your flute?"

"I had to leave it in Tokyo," I said, and he nodded as if it didn't matter.

The petite kami with petal-like curls of hair stepped onto the platform. The bush warbler and the finch fluttered onto her shoulders. She opened her mouth, and a high, shimmering voice pealed out in a wordless song. The birds joined in with a lilting harmony. And the rest of the kami in the courtyard, in all their forms, started to dance.

Chiyo swayed this way and that, her arms around Haru, then dragging Takeo over. The doe and the boar and the others pranced in a circle around the wavering fire. The even tapping of their steps formed a solid rhythm under the melody.

Even without words, I understood the song. *Darkness was upon us,* it said, *but we fought, and we survived, and we will be victorious again.* The feeling of it tingled through me, drawing me to my feet. Then I halted.

My muscles throbbed from the fight and lack of sleep, which my body needed far more than those fueled by the earth's ki. Part of me longed to leap into the midst of the dance, but my legs had locked, refusing to move. The kami danced on, not one of them noticing me standing there—not even Takeo.

Why should they? Even if I'd held on to my flute, even if I matched their steps, I'd never belong with them again.

My stomach twisted. I turned and slipped away through the shadows.

In the small clearing behind the shrine building, the mingling of moon and starlight glinted on the grass. I could still hear the music faintly. Here, there were no watching eyes to wonder why a human danced the kami way or to notice if I faltered. I held up my hands to the sky and let the melody sweep through me.

My bare feet pattered over the grass. The breeze became my fickle partner, whispering around me and then flitting away. The smell of cedar and summer flowers filled my lungs. I closed my eyes.

I'm back in the palace's great hall, I told myself. *It's still my birthday. Everything since then was only a dream. It's time to dance, to celebrate another year, to honor the time I've been on this Earth.* I could picture the lanterns gleaming on the walls, Mother and Father whirling around each other with eyes for no one else. All the other kami in their colorful robes or shining pelts, spinning like autumn leaves on a stream.

The soreness of my body retreated into the distance. The music would flow on without end, one song blurring into the next, and I needed nothing to sustain me but the soaring of my heart and the rhythm rippling through my bones...

A shoe scraped over stone, and my eyelids popped open, the illusion falling away. My hands dropped to my sides.

Keiji was sitting down on the edge of the platform. I could hardly see his face from where I stood, only a sliver of moonlight reflecting off his glasses.

"Sorry," he said. "I was trying my best not to distract you. You don't have to stop."

"It's all right," I said. Now that I was aware again of my limbs, my breath, an even deeper exhaustion was settling over me. I stepped toward him.

"It's gotten a little crazy over there, hasn't it?" he said with a half smile, gesturing toward the front courtyard.

"It's not crazy," I said. "I just don't fit in there anymore."

"You fit in a lot better than I do," Keiji said. "I bet half the time they forget whether you're kami or not."

I looked at the ground. "I don't."

"Is it really that bad being human? I kind of like it. I guess being able to instantly heal and, okay, turn invisible and all that is pretty neat, but—"

"It's not about that," I broke in. "You couldn't understand—you have no idea what it's like, to know who you are and what you can do and then none of it is true, none if it's really *yours*, it's just..." I didn't know how to finish.

In the silence that followed, I heard Keiji swallow. "I'm sorry," he said. "I didn't want to make you upset."

It was strange the way he could be irreverent one moment and serious the next. Because I was used to talking with kami, whose natures were clear and unwavering. Because he was human, and that was what being human meant, wasn't it? Changing, all the time.

Like me, right now, wanting to run from his words and to hear more of them, both at the same time.

He moved to get up, and I grasped his wrist. His pulse drummed against my fingers. He met my eyes with a question in his.

"Don't go," I said. "I—I'm not angry."

He sat back down, watching as I released his arm.

"You're right," he said. "I don't really understand how it's been for you. But I do know a little about what it's like to feel you don't fit in. My brother and I, we weren't what my aunt and uncle wanted at all. Our marks were never high enough, our chores never done fast enough. But he— He managed to figure out what he wanted to do, who he wanted to be, at least. I'm still working on that. I'm not one of the athletic guys, or the charmers, or the geniuses. I know I can't pull off any of those. So I make people laugh. I collect a lot of facts about a lot of weird things. And I can pretend pretty well not to care about anything else. That's what I've got so far."

"You care," I protested. "You—" The memories welled up too fast for me to put them into words: the whisper of loss I'd felt through his palm, his joy when exploring Rin's valley, his determination as he'd followed me into battle last night. The awe on his face just before he'd kissed me.

He glanced up at me then, with a full smile this time. "I don't seem to be so good at pretending with you. I think I'm okay with that."

The hurt he'd tried to keep out of his voice when he'd talked about his family lingered in his eyes. Was it worse to feel you had a place and then to lose it, or to never have felt you belonged? Maybe I was lucky I'd had what I was missing as long as I had.

"I shouldn't have snapped at you," I said. "It's just—it's taking a while to get used to the idea that I'm so much less than I grew up thinking I was."

Keiji shook his head with a short laugh. He slid off his glasses, rubbed the lenses with the hem of his shirt, considered them, and set them on the platform beside him. Without them, his face looked even more open.

"Just because you aren't kami doesn't mean you're less than

them," he said. "You're definitely the most amazing girl I've ever met, Chiyo included. And, okay, I haven't met *that* many girls, but I can judge at least a little."

He raised his head, and the look he gave me knocked the breath out of me.

"But—" I couldn't help saying. "Chiyo, she *glows*."

He arched his eyebrows. "What are you talking about? You do too."

"What? Can you even see without those on?" I motioned vaguely at his glasses.

"If I'm close enough, sure." He shifted off the platform onto his feet, so we stood just a few inches apart. "Anyway, I'm pretty sure there's more than one way to glow."

I held perfectly still, my heart pounding, unable to tear my eyes from his. Keiji's gaze dipped down to my mouth and up again, but he didn't move. "If I—" he said. "Could I—"

I reached for his arm, my fingertips skittering up to the soft skin above his elbow. My touch seemed to give him the answer he'd been seeking. He leaned across those last few inches and kissed me.

His lips brushed mine cautiously, but his other arm slid around me, steady against my back. For an instant, my mind leapt to Takeo—what he would think if he saw this? But why had I told him no if I wasn't going to take the feeling I wanted when I had it? I shoved all thought of him away and kissed Keiji back.

With a rough sound in his throat, he pulled me closer. My arms slipped behind his neck of their own accord. The wineberries had left his mouth sweet, and his skin smelled like smoke from the fire. The warmth of him radiated through me. Every nerve in my body started to hum, and I could have believed right then that I really was glowing. I kissed him again, more deeply, wanting to lose myself in this one thing that I had chosen.

Then the ground shuddered beneath us, tipping my feet and bringing me back to Earth.

We broke apart, Keiji stumbling backward. I caught my balance against the platform. The ground heaved and trembled for a few seconds longer before it quieted. I stared down at it, struggling for breath.

None of the earlier quakes had lasted that long. The mountain's fury was growing.

A wave of nausea swept through me. While I was letting myself get carried away by my careless human emotions, the fire inside Mt. Fuji was swelling, ready to rain down on the Nagamotos, their friends and neighbors, and thousands more. For a few minutes, I'd actually forgotten that. Forgotten even my kami friends, the ones I'd considered family, who were still being tormented and maybe even dying at Omori's hands.

Good or bad, none of my feelings mattered right now. If I was really going to help and not become a burden, I had to put them aside until this war was over. Shut off every part of me—the fears, the delight—except those that supported our efforts. Strength. Focus. I had to be as kami as a human could be.

"I should make some more ofuda before I sleep," I said. "There's not much time left before we'll be leaving."

Keiji paused and offered me a shy grin.

"Need a hand?" he asked.

"Thank you," I said, but I couldn't quite return the smile. There'd been a moment in the midst of the music when I'd felt so sure we'd come out of this horror safely. But the truth was, even Rin hadn't been certain what the future would hold. I'd never forgive myself if one of those kami in the courtyard, or Haru, or Keiji, died because I'd gotten distracted from doing all I could to make ready for the battle ahead.

FIFTEEN

WE REACHED Tokyo in the middle of the morning. Keiji stashed his books in a train station locker, and we detoured to a grocery store where we bought up all their bags of salt with his and Haru's pocket money. The rest of us with arms purchased cheap satchels to carry our defensive materials.

Everywhere we went, I heard murmurs about the weather, the tremors; saw worried glances at the ground and sky. Browning grass mottled the park we gathered in to portion out our supplies. Scattered on it were dead crickets and beetles for whom the heat and lack of water had been too much. The sight of their fragile carcasses brought a lump to my throat. They reminded me far too sharply of Midori.

If we didn't succeed in retrieving Amaterasu's sacred jewel from the Imperial Palace's shrine today, the crisis would only get worse.

I'm not sure any of us felt completely ready as we headed across the palace's parking lot. Of the kami we'd met around Nagoya, only Sumire the violet, the oak, the monkey, and the boar had followed us here. The others Takeo had felt were more likely to be hurt or killed than able to help. He held my hand, Chiyo Haru's, and Sumire Keiji's, using their ki to make us invisible as we approached the two broad gates leading into the palace grounds. My pulse started skittering. We skirted the visitors dawdling on the paved bridge that crossed the still, murky water of the moat. A guard stood by the high stone wall, oblivious to our presence.

Chiyo clenched the sacred sword at her side. I sucked in a breath as we stepped past the old wooden doors onto the grounds.

No ghosts rushed to meet us. Nothing met us at all but the heat rising off the baked asphalt. A squat, modern building stood ahead of us by a branch in the road, near a lawn spotted with trees and rounded bushes. Tourists strolled by as the breeze stirred the leaves.

"Maybe the ghosts are waiting for us farther in?" I said. Surely Omori hadn't completely failed to defend this treasure?

Takeo inclined his head. "The grounds cover acres, and only the small area around the shrine is fully protected. We can't know where our enemies will make their stand."

"So we're going to just wander around until we stumble onto them?" Keiji said, his mouth slanting nervously.

I didn't like that idea either. "Maybe there's a kami on the grounds who can tell us what they've seen," I said.

"Just got to find them," Chiyo said. "Too bad kami don't use cell phones!"

A small streak of cloud streaming across the sky caught my eye. There were other ways of sending a message across a distance.

"Use a kite," I said to Takeo. "You can make it with a message on it."

"Perfect!" Chiyo said. "Like people used to do way back during wars and stuff. I guess this *is* a war, isn't it? Here, I can do it."

Before she'd even finished speaking, she was stretching a cylinder of ki between her hands. Rough characters sparkled across its side: *Imperial Palace kami, we need your help*. She tossed the ki-drawn kite up over her head. It caught as if on a gust of wind, swaying higher and higher. Chiyo's eyes narrowed, watching it.

"Don't drain yourself," Takeo warned. She nodded and then let the kite dissipate.

We continued down the road tentatively, taking the wider branch. We'd just reached the building when a brief burst of ki sparked in the sky.

Here.

"It worked!" Chiyo said.

"Definitely kami," Takeo said as he absorbed the sense of the ki. We hurried forward in the direction the message had indicated. The road led us around an inner wall of mossy stone and through another gate. We passed wide hedges and old-style wooden guardhouses with gently curved tiled roofs. If it hadn't been for the boxy shapes of high rises hovering in the distance over the treetops, I could have believed we'd slipped back into an earlier time.

Not a whisper of a ghost rose to challenge us. My fingers curled into the palm of my free hand. Even if the dead were keeping themselves dim and hidden, kami eyes would spot them. So where were they?

The road curved through a grove of cherry trees. There, a tall kami with bristling hair and arms roped with muscle stepped out to greet us. A pine, I thought, or maybe a fir. He looked young, even younger than Takeo, and his eyes widened as he took in our group.

"I am glad to help you," he said haltingly, and paused as if struggling with his words. He must not have been around humans or speaking kami often enough to have fully picked up the language. "There is... You look for the jewel?"

"We do," Chiyo said. "Do you know where it is?"

He bobbed his head in a jerky motion and gestured for us to follow. "It is not far. It is... moved, for safety."

"Away from the ghosts?" I said, and he nodded.

Chiyo bounded forward to walk beside our guide. The kami walked on without hesitation, but there was something out of rhythm about his gait. Uneasiness crept over my skin. I scanned the gardens, dragged air into my lungs, and strained my ears. None of my senses caught anything worrisome, even with Takeo's ki enhancing them. He looked perfectly confident as he strode along beside me. All the other kami appeared alert but untroubled.

It was just the overactive emotions that had come with this human body, then—my fears trying to make me jump at shadows. I squared my shoulders.

The young kami turned off the main road onto a narrow path. The flowering shrubs that lined it gave off a delicate perfume. The path wound toward a three-story keep on the edge of an inner moat. The roof bowed over the keep's white-washed walls. Solid panels sealed off most of the windows.

"The jewel," the kami said, and cleared his throat. "Inside." I supposed the palace shrine kami must have secreted it here when they'd seen the ghosts converging on them.

The keep's door opened at Chiyo's nudge. As we eased inside, the oak kami sent up a ball of energy to cast a dim glow over our surroundings. We'd come into a long, high-ceilinged hallway that led to what looked like a stairwell at the other end of the building. Several inner doors broke the blank white stretch of the walls. The floors were clean, but the place felt abandoned. An ideal hiding spot.

Now that we were away from other eyes, Takeo released my hand to set his fingers on the grip of his sword. He and the other kami turned corporeal. My body settled back into the physical world with a wash of heat and the smell of dust.

Our kami guide stopped before the third inner door and bowed. His eyes stayed fixed on Chiyo.

"Here," he said. "This is where."

As Chiyo reached for the doorknob, a cry leapt into my mouth. *No!* I gritted my teeth and scanned the hall again. An army of ghosts couldn't conceal themselves in this darkness. And if there *was* something wrong, Chiyo was hardly defenseless. I had to get over my nerves. It was my decision to be here in the midst of the danger.

Then Chiyo turned the knob, Takeo at the ready beside her, and I happened to glance at the young kami. My body went rigid.

The way he was watching her, as if he were afraid to look away. The strain in his jaw. I recognized the feeling in that expression, because I'd felt it more than once in the last few days.

It was desperation.

"Chiyo!" I said, but she'd already pushed open the door. Her nose wrinkled.

"What—" she started.

She never had the chance to finish her question.

In a blaze of light so intense I thought the ceiling had caught fire and fallen on our heads, hundreds of ghostlights rained down on us. The thickest whirl of them smacked straight into Chiyo and Takeo, slamming them through the doorway and yanking the door shut. One solidified, jamming a key into the lock. The swarm of ghostlights blurred around me. Waiting for Chiyo and Takeo to burst back out, I fumbled with my sheaf of ofuda. A solid door couldn't stop kami, locked or not.

But they didn't emerge.

All around me, ki glinted where the other kami must have been striking out at the ghosts. I thrust out my trembling hand, smacking charms against the spirits closest to me. A liquid sound came from behind me, something sloshing on the floor, but I didn't have time to look. Haru was leaping forward, snatching at the door Chiyo had vanished behind, and a ring of ghosts solidified around him.

A sound of protest escaped my lips. I threw myself toward him, but my legs couldn't move fast enough. He banished three of his attackers with quick snaps of ofuda, reaching to his satchel for his salt. Before he could pull it out, his fourth charm missed. The woman he'd aimed it at ducked beneath his arm and plunged the thick blade of her knife into his side.

His amulet gave him no protection against steel. He sagged against the wall as if deflating. Gasping, I slapped an ofuda against the side of the woman's head before she could turn around and spun as another ghost turned corporeal behind me.

A wire flew over my head and jerked against my neck. Against the spot where the ogre's claw had cut. A cold surge of panic flooded my mind. As the figure that held the wire pulled it tight, I flailed back wildly. The wire dug into my flesh, cutting off my air. A third ghost stepped toward me and bashed something hard against my forehead.

My legs buckled. A hazy shape with Keiji's voice flung itself into view, shouting, "Stop! Stop!" And then the world went black.

* * *

I came to on the floor of a small room. Sunlight too thin to give me a sense of the time seeped through a narrow window high on the wall behind a stack of cardboard boxes. My mouth tasted like ash. I turned my head, and a jagged line of pain sliced across my neck where the wire had nearly strangled me.

Somehow, I was still alive.

I tried to move my arms, and my wrists strained against thick strands of rope. My ankles were bound too. My forehead ached. Ignoring my various pains, I wiggled my limbs, testing the knots. They didn't budge. Something rough and powdery flaked off the rope against my skin.

As I squirmed, my gaze caught the other body lying by the wall. It was sprawled there limply with its back to me, but in the dim light I made out Haru's short, spiky hair and the collared shirt he'd been wearing. The image of the knife stabbing into his side flashed through my mind. I stared at his chest, willing it to rise.

"Haru?" I said. The name came out in a croak.

He offered no response.

Dizziness swept over me. I let my head tip onto the floor.

How had we ended up like this? The ghosts must have dragged us here after the fight. After they'd tricked us. That *kami* had tricked us. Why had he helped them? They'd been waiting for us on the floor above the entire time, until he'd gotten us exactly where they wanted.

Even that didn't make sense. Chiyo and Takeo should have been able to use their ki to slip through the walls of the room the ghosts had shut them in. But if they'd managed to escape, Haru and I wouldn't be lying in this room.

And Keiji... A sudden chill filled my chest. If he wasn't here with us... How badly had the ghosts hurt *him*?

I bit my lip. I couldn't assume the worst. Right now I had to just think about getting out of this. We needed Chiyo. If she faced the ghosts with the sacred sword, the balance could tip in our favor. I had to find her and Takeo.

And to do that, I had to find a way out of these ropes.

The pain in my head had dulled to a mild throbbing. I inched my feet forward until I could see my legs. A heavy cord circled my ankles in several tight loops. It was an odd color, dark and mottled. No, that was something smeared *on* the rope—it had smudged my skin where the rope touched me. I bent at the waist, peering at it, and my stomach turned.

The dark substance looked like blood. As if the rope had been soaked in it and left to dry.

A putrid metallic smell reached my nose. I closed my eyes and took a few breaths through my mouth. The rough powdery stuff against my wrists—that was dried blood too, no doubt. Revulsion welled up inside me, but I found I wasn't surprised. The ghosts had used the stuff on their weapons to make them more effective against kami, so why wouldn't they treat their bindings the same way?

Blood from the wound of something living was bad enough. Blood from a creature who'd died unwillingly, which I could only guess was how Omori had obtained so much—nothing was more toxic to kami. A rope or a net drenched in that blood would have burned the flesh of any it touched, rotted their ki, and left them sapped and helpless. This must be how the ghosts had overcome the kami on Mt. Fuji, and perhaps the kami who'd fought with us here in the keep too.

Because I was human, it didn't affect me the same way, but nausea turned my stomach all the same. How many innocent creatures had Omori already ordered killed just to coat his army's weapons and traps? So much destruction wrought by that slight man with his brilliant smile.

I groped along the rope at my wrists, cringing at the feel of the dried gore crumbling beneath my fingers. I couldn't reach the knot.

By jerking and shoving myself against the boxes, I managed to work myself into a sitting position. Maybe one of the boxes held something sharp enough to cut rope. If I could manage to open them.

With another bout of squirming, I hauled myself onto my

knees. My arms were no help behind me, so I nuzzled at the flaps of one of the lower boxes with my chin. A whiff of dust made me cough. I worked open the flaps, but inside there was only a heap of fabric that looked like some sort of costume.

As I turned to the next box, a movement by the window caught my eye. I froze, peering toward it as surreptitiously as I could.

A small brown shape swooped from the window ledge down to the floor beside me. A sparrow. I sank back against the boxes.

"You," I said. "I'm not sure you should have joined me in here."

The sparrow cocked its head at me as if it understood. I paused. I'd assumed because I could tell the bird wasn't kami that it was just a bird. But I knew by now there were many other forces in the world, and I wouldn't necessarily have recognized all of them. No ordinary bird would have followed us this long, this far.

"What are you?" I asked, leaning closer. "You're more than a sparrow, aren't you?"

The air around the sparrow sparked. I flinched backward as a shimmering figure formed in the air over the feathered body.

It was a middle-aged woman, her hair pulled back into a braid that looped at the back of her head, what had once been smile lines around her mouth now tight with worry. She wore a rose-pink dress that ended just below her hips... where all of her ended.

My sparrow friend had been home to a ghost.

The edges of the woman's body wavered. She must have had just enough energy to make herself visible to me, but not enough to become completely corporeal. She dipped down until her moist eyes were level with mine.

I stared back at her. I'd seen her face before—I was sure of it.

Had she been one of the Nagamotos' friends, or another woman I'd observed in town? Maybe a traveler who'd visited Mt. Fuji? Whoever she was, some kami had guided her spirit into the sparrow when she'd died, through the same process I'd wanted to use with Mr. Nagamoto.

"How do I know you?" I said. The woman motioned with her graceful hands, but I couldn't follow what she was trying to convey.

If she was a ghost, then she could have been acting as a spy for the others all along. She could be the one who'd told them about Chiyo, about Rin, about the prophecy.

But then, if she was loyal to them, why was she here now, revealing herself to me?

"The ghosts," I said. "The ones who attacked the mountain. Are you—"

She seemed to realize what I meant before I finished the question. Distress flickered across her face, and she shook her head so vehemently I believed her. Her hands fluttered again, sketching in the air.

"I don't understand," I said. "Can you speak?"

She opened her mouth. A little cry jolted out of me.

There was nothing left of her tongue but a ragged stump.

"I'm so sorry," I said. "I didn't know."

Strangely, the woman smiled, a little wistfully. She held out her arms as if to say, *Does it matter now?* Then she brushed the top of the sparrow's head with her fingers. The outline of her body faded until it was nothing more than a ghostlight, which glided down into the bird. It stirred and glanced up at me. Leaping onto the edge of the nearest box, it let out a burst of song.

"That's why the kami gave you a bird," I said. "So you could sing again."

Maybe that was why she'd sided with us: gratitude. A kami had been kind to her, and now she was repaying us. How much had she observed of our enemies?

"Have you seen Omori?" I asked. "Do you know what he's planning?"

The sparrow let out a distressed-sounding squawk and ruffled its feathers. I guessed that was the best answer I was going to get. But my friend might be able to help me in other ways.

"I need to find something to get me out of these ropes," I said.

As I leaned over another box, the sparrow alighted on one higher up. It levered the flaps open with its body and dove inside, fabric rustling as it poked around. The one I pushed open held only a stack of file folders. I craned my neck, checking for writing on any of the boxes that might identify their contents, and noticed a metallic glint on the other side of the stack.

"Over there," I said to the sparrow with a jerk of my head. "Can you bring that thing on the floor to me?"

The sparrow fluttered down. It leapt up a moment later and dropped the object on the floor beside me: a small box cutter someone had left behind. Rust spotted the blade, but I wasn't about to be picky.

"Thank you," I said. The sparrow darted back to its window ledge perch with a chirp.

I managed to maneuver the box cutter between my hands

until I could extend the blade. Then I twisted my fingers to rest it against the ropes. I sawed at them tentatively, and then pressed harder when the blade held. Relief bloomed inside me at the feel of the first strands parting.

My forehead was damp when I finally broke through the first layer of rope. I wriggled my arms until the cord began to unwind, and pulled my hands free. Then I sawed through the cord around my ankles and kicked that away too.

I hurried to Haru, kneeling by him to touch his arm. His skin felt warm, but the air around us was warm too. Blood stained the front of his shirt and was pooled on the floor beneath him. His eyes stayed closed. Only the threadiest of pulses, if it was a pulse, pattered through his wrist against my probing fingers.

I hated to step away from him, but without the ki to heal him, I'd do us both more good out there than in here.

The door opened when I tried it. The hallway beyond was lit with only a faint haze that emanated from behind a door standing slightly ajar near the opposite end. Given the height of the window in the room I'd just left, I guessed I was in a basement. If the ghosts hadn't moved us from the keep, then Chiyo and Takeo might still be trapped right upstairs.

I crept toward the light, squinting at the shadowy walls, goose bumps crawling over my skin. Could the ghosts make themselves so dim that human eyes couldn't catch even a hint of their glow? I checked my pockets, but they held only the folded printout of the Kenta Omori article I'd stuffed deep inside. Someone had taken my ofuda, my protective amulet, and the satchel with my bag of salt. Takeo's short sword was gone too.

If there *were* ghosts in the hall, they made no move to stop me. A dull clanging sound rang out as I neared the ajar door, like metal striking wood. I could see now that the stairwell lay just past it. As I hurried toward that, voices slipped from the lit room, one of which I recognized.

"Would you stop that?"

Keiji. I halted, my heart thudding.

The clanging stilled, and then started again in slower, more even strokes. "It's not a bad sword," a deeper voice said casually. "Not bad at all. Interesting friends you've made. You didn't tell me about this one earlier."

"I don't know if Haru Esumi would call me his 'friend,' exactly," Keiji replied. "Anyway, it didn't seem important."

He sounded tired and tense, though not as scared as I'd have expected while he was being interrogated by a ghost. I peeked through the gap between the door and its frame.

A fixture on the ceiling flooded the room with artificial light. In the sliver of space I could see, an arm was swinging Haru's katana against the side of a wooden table. The blade left a nick with each impact. On the table itself lay a single key on a ring. Keiji was out of my view.

The key—was that the one they'd used to lock up Chiyo?

As I eyed it, the figure with the sword shifted in front of the gap. I stiffened.

The skinny young man in his sharp gray suit, collar flipped high under an equally sharp grin, was holding himself completely corporeal. But I knew he was a ghost, because I'd seen that sharp grin and that crimson-streaked hair before. I'd seen him in Mother and Father's chambers, legless and translucent, directing the charge against the guard who'd fallen while Takeo and I had escaped the palace.

He glanced toward the other end of the room. "It's my job to decide what's important, little brother."

SIXTEEN

I CLAMPED MY teeth together to trap my expression of shock. I must have heard wrong. Or the red-haired ghost was only calling Keiji "little brother" to tease him. It wasn't as if Keiji could have failed to notice his brother was dead.

"Fine," Keiji said. "But I think we've gone over everything now. You could have been clearer about what you were planning before."

"It still worked out well for us," the ghost said. "Omori has been impressed by all my inside info—that's what got me made captain—and what we've done here is going to blow him away. I had to keep it under wraps in case things fell through, but a couple of my guys are heading to the mountain to tell him about it now. I just want to make sure I have all the loose ends tied up when we get his instructions for next steps." He cocked his head, and his smile turned even sharper. "What's the glum look for, Kei? Haven't I thanked you enough?"

"I just wish you'd told me what was really going on from the beginning," Keiji said quietly.

I choked on my breath. I hadn't misheard. This *was* Keiji's brother. The brother he looked up to so much, the only person he'd bothered to contact since he'd left home. The one he wanted more than anything to help...

Fragments of our past conversations surfaced in my memory. *A couple years ago he had this, ah, accident. It's because of you I'm going to get my chance to fix things for him.* And what the ghost had said, just now: *All my inside info. Haven't I thanked you enough?*

I leaned my shoulder against the wall, my legs suddenly weak. We'd assumed a kami trapped on Mt. Fuji had given away the fact that I'd escaped, that the ghosts had learned about Sage Rin and the prophecy from spying on Chiyo's parents. But the Ikedas hadn't known we'd be coming to the Imperial Palace instead of Ise. No one had known that except for the handful of kami with us, me, Haru... and Keiji.

The way he'd insisted on joining our group. All those prying questions he'd asked. It seemed so obvious now. He'd been trying to help his brother, yes—help his brother defeat us.

And I'd fallen for his act. I'd let him win me over with his grins, his flattering words. How much had he learned from *me*?

Even as I wondered, my thoughts tripped back to last night at the shrine near Nagoya, to the look on his face when he'd told me I was the most amazing girl he'd ever met, and my heart skipped despite my queasiness. My stupid, fickle human heart.

The voices warbling on in the room before me brought me back to the present. I couldn't do anything about my past mistakes. All that mattered was how I reacted now. I made myself edge closer to the door.

"There's nothing special about this Haru?" Keiji's brother said. "He's just a regular human kid?"

"As far as I know," Keiji replied.

My gaze dropped to a pale lump on the floor behind the table. My breath caught. My satchel—and Haru's too, alongside Takeo's short sword. Someone had tossed them in a corner. Had the ghosts dared to open the satchels with all that salt inside? I'd stashed extra ofuda in mine. The charms might still be there.

All I needed was one. One, and I could banish Keiji's brother back to the afterworld while there were no other ghosts around to interfere. Then I could make Keiji tell me where Chiyo and Takeo were. I'd have the key. I could free them.

My mind was still whirling. I pressed my hand to my jaw. If I was going to get across the room in time, I had to think like a kami, act like a kami. Not let my human nature get in the way.

But a kami would have had the power to blast right through, to fend off the ghost while she grabbed the satchel. I wasn't sure I could even reach the table before Keiji's brother was on me, and I wouldn't be able to accomplish much then. I didn't even know if there *were* ofuda still in my satchel. Doubt melded my feet to the floor.

"And they haven't said anything else about the powers in this jewel?" Keiji's brother was saying now.

"No," Keiji said. "What does it matter?"

"Well, it would have been nice to know sooner about the magic sword—we didn't expect to be losing people, not for good."

Losing people for good—what did he mean by that? They'd

lost plenty to our ofuda too.

"Still, you've done well, Kei," the young man went on. "Don't doubt that."

Keiji's voice was so low I couldn't decipher his tone. "Thank you, brother."

"Why are we back to formalities?" the ghost said. "You know you can call me by my name, conventions be damned. We're equals."

"Sorry, Tomoya."

"Do you remember the first time Uncle heard you calling me 'Tomo'? That was some epic rage. The man has no sense of priorities. But we never let him stop us."

He set down the katana on the table. Beside the key. My hands clenched. One way or another, I *had* to get it, to make this right—to make up for believing in Keiji, for losing Chiyo this morning, for all my weaknesses.

I couldn't get to the key without the ghost interfering. So I needed to get rid of the ghost. So I needed an ofuda.

I could make a new one. Back in the room where I'd woken up—I could tear a few strips off the cardboard boxes. There might be a pen or a pencil lying around, or... or if there wasn't, I'd prick my finger with the box cutter and write the characters with my own blood.

Before I could move, the ghost spoke again. "I think I'd better see what I can get out of our captives. They might know more they didn't tell you."

Chiyo and Takeo—so they *were* still here? I hesitated.

"I'm sure they didn't know anything I don't," Keiji said. "We talked about everything."

"You shouldn't assume that," his brother said. "We can't trust anyone outside the two of us, Kei. Remember that."

"But—"

"Come on. It shouldn't be too difficult to 'convince' our human prisoners to talk now."

My pulse stuttered. *Human* prisoners meant Haru and me. They'd see I'd escaped. Steps were approaching the door in a smooth steady rhythm: the ghost's feet, still corporeal against the floor.

I didn't have time to run down the hall. The stairwell was closer—but that would only serve me until they reached the room and saw the scraps of rope I'd left behind.

If I didn't want them to catch me, I had to use my only advantage: surprise.

I braced myself, my gaze fixed on that satchel beyond the table. I didn't know if I could do this, but I had to try. As the ghost's footsteps sounded just behind the door, I threw all my weight against it.

The door slammed into his corporeal form. As he grunted in shock, I was already bolting across the room.

I was less than a stride from the table when a swift kick knocked my legs out from under me.

My elbows jarred against the tabletop as I caught my balance. That minor pain was nothing compared to the sense of failure that pierced through me. But the katana was right there. I wasn't going down without a fight.

I snatched up the sword and spun around. Keiji's brother leapt back, just out of reach. Then he pulled a sleek black pistol out of his jacket pocket and aimed it at my face.

I hesitated, my palm sweating against the sword's grip. He stood between me and the door. There was still the entire table separating me from my satchel. I suspected he could pull the trigger faster than I could lunge—and even if I lunged *at* him, Haru's katana couldn't truly hurt someone who was already dead.

Keiji's shoes scraped the floor somewhere to my left, but I didn't dare take my eyes off his brother. "Tomo," he said, his voice strained. Ignoring him, the ghost dipped his head to me in a mockery of a bow.

"Tomoya Mitsuoka at your service," he said. "So I finally get to meet Miss Sora in the flesh. I've heard a lot about you."

From Keiji. My jaw tightened. Up close, the family resemblance was noticeable. They had the same wide-set eyes and rounded chin. But Tomoya's face was narrower, his cheekbones more prominent, giving him a slightly malnourished look. A thin scar sliced across the bridge of his nose just below the jagged sweep of his red-streaked hair.

When I didn't answer, he made a tiny gesture with the gun. "You'll probably feel more comfortable if I stop pointing this at you. And I'll stop pointing it at you if you put down the sword."

"How about you go first?" I suggested. Tomoya's smile returned.

"Sora," Keiji tried, closer now. I could almost see him from the corner of my eye. My hand tensed around the sword grip.

"Back off," I said. "I can use this on a human even more easily than a ghost."

"You should be nicer to him," Tomoya said. "If it weren't for Keiji, you'd be dead, you know."

The muscles in my hand were aching from the effort to hold the sword steady. "I should appreciate being tricked into walking into a trap, tied up, and thrown in a storage room while my friends are dead or dying?" I said.

"Well, if you don't want to be here, we could arrange something else." His eyes skimmed my body. "Omori would definitely approve of you as a specimen."

Specimen? "For what?" I asked.

"Oh, you'll find out. It's just a few more days until Obon."

He was smirking at me now, as if there were something funny about the rain ceasing to fall, Mt. Fuji threatening to erupt. I still didn't understand. He didn't have to fight us any more than the woman in the sparrow had needed to help me.

"Why are you doing this?" I said. "Why are you helping him? Why hurt the kami at all?"

"Why not?" he said. "What have the kami done for any of us? All those souls they've left to the darkness of the afterworld—we've got no reason for loyalty. Omori's already saved more of us than they ever did."

"Saved you how?"

"I'm here, aren't I?"

I didn't understand, but he didn't seem interested in explaining. "What about everyone else who's going to be hurt?" I asked. "You have family, friends, people who are still living. Doesn't it matter to you what happens to them?"

"That's exactly why I'm doing this," Tomoya said, his cocky

expression darkening. "For my family."

"Tomo—" Keiji started again, but I wasn't interested in what he had to say.

"Doing *what*?" I interrupted. "What's going to happen during Obon?"

Tomoya shook his head. "You'll just have to wait and see."

"And you trust a demon to keep his word?"

"A demon?" he repeated. His eyebrows rose. "Is that what you're calling Omori? He's as human as the rest of us."

In his amusement, his gun hand dipped, just an inch. A slim chance, but better than none at all.

I ducked and thrust out with the katana. The tip of the blade missed Tomoya's chest as he jerked back. In desperation, I wrenched it to the side with all the strength I had. The back of the blade slammed into his wrist. His hand twitched, and the pistol fell.

As I lashed out with my foot to shove it away, Tomoya came at me, sliding a knife from a sheath hidden in his sleeve. I dodged and kicked at his knee. He followed me, his blade whipping back and forth, his heel ramming into my ankle. Losing my balance, I smacked against the edge of the table. I needed to be around it. I had to get enough of an opening to go for the satchel.

But unlike the ghosts I'd fought before, Tomoya obviously had both training and practice. I barely flinched out of the way of his descending knife. When I struck out with the sword, he deflected the blow with a chuckle. He started backing me away from the table, into the opposite corner. Farther from my goal.

"If I really wanted to hurt you," he said. "I could wisp away like the ghost I am, where you can't touch me. But this is more fun."

I made to dash around him, back toward the table, but he was too fast. He snatched at my forearm and yanked me backward with a *crack*. Pain exploded in my wrist and spiraled up my arm. A voice shouted something, but my heart was pounding too hard for me to process the words. I swung around, tears blurring my vision. My blade clattered against Tomoya's knife.

I jabbed out with the katana again, and he caught it. His fingers glowing with ki, he clutched the blade and heaved it out of my hand. As I groped after it, he smashed his elbow into the back of my ribs, forcing a gasp from my lungs and knocking me to the floor.

"All right," he said, lowering his knife to my neck. "That's enough playing. Now *you* need to answer some questions."

He'd only just finished speaking when a figure crashed into him, throwing him to the side. I scrambled away, disoriented. A yelp rang out behind me, and a hand grabbed my bad arm with a tug that sent another jolt of pain searing up it. As I swiveled around, Tomoya twisted my broken wrist. A whimper broke from my throat.

But he couldn't do anything more to me. In a glance, I made out Keiji crouched on the floor beside his brother, his fingers clamped around Tomoya's knife hand. Blood was seeping down his chin from a nick at the corner of his jaw.

The edges of Tomoya's body shimmered. He jerked his arm free and shoved Keiji into my way. And I saw the one thing that could save me.

Keiji still had his ofuda. The end of one was poking from his pants pocket. He might not be willing to use it on his brother, but I had no qualms at all.

As Keiji stumbled toward me, I braced myself against the pain in my arm, dodged around him, and snatched the slip of paper. A flash of recognition passed through Tomoya's fading eyes a moment before I slapped the ofuda against his nearly translucent forehead. He opened his mouth as if to protest, and then his ghostly body vanished. Keiji gave a startled cry.

I bent over, holding the side of the table as the effort of my final offensive caught up with me. My left arm hung limp by my side, my wrist twinging just from the pressure of brushing against my hip. I hadn't registered the place where Tomoya had hit my ribs before, but now a stinging pain radiated through my abdomen with every breath. The longing rose up inside me to curl up into a ball and rock until my body felt right again.

But I couldn't.

Keiji had dropped back onto the floor. He reached out, staring at the spot where his brother had been, as if he might feel Tomoya there. "He's gone," he started, his voice raw. "You..." Then he glanced at me, and his face went even grayer.

"Sora." He pulled himself to his feet. His gaze darted to his brother's last location once more, and then he shook himself. "I... You're obviously not okay. What can I do?"

I turned away from him to the table, the anger I'd squashed down while I fought flaring up in a white-hot flame. There was the key I'd done all this for. I stuffed it into my pocket. Then I knelt to pick up Takeo's short sword and pushed it through the belt loop by my hip. The motion was less agonizing than the idea of looking at Keiji. My satchel felt far too light as I lifted it. Empty after all. I spotted Haru's katana where it had fallen and collected that too, my fingers curling around the leather bindings on its grip. At least Tomoya hadn't wrecked my stronger arm. I should count my blessings.

"Stay here," I said to Keiji. It wasn't worth the time trying to restrain him somehow. I doubted he could stop me even with my injuries.

I headed for the doorway, testing my legs, and found that other than a pang in my right ankle, they were functioning pretty much normally. Another blessing.

Keiji trailed after me into the hall, dabbing at the dribble of blood along his jaw with the collar of his shirt.

"I'm sorry," he said as I reached the door to the stairwell. "I didn't know. I didn't mean to— Tomoya said he needed me to tell him what we were doing so he could try to help us. I had no idea he was already working for Omori. He's been into some messed up things, but he never— I never thought he would—"

So much fury blazed through me that suddenly I wasn't afraid of looking at him anymore. Let him see what I felt.

"You *knew*," I bit out. "Even if it's true that you didn't know he was with Omori from the start, he said things that upset you, didn't he? You knew he was asking about our plans, and as soon as you told him, our enemies knew them too. Maybe you didn't want to think it, but you *had* to put that together. And you kept telling him everything anyway. You kept—"

You kept pretending you cared about me.

Keiji's expression was as wretched as if he'd swallowed a

mouthful of pine needles and they were stabbing their way into his gut, but he didn't look away from my glare. And I still, I *still* wanted to touch his cheek, to make that awful expression leave his beautiful coppery eyes. To believe he hadn't ruined everything on purpose.

I clamped down on the feeling, burying it under my anger.

"I'm sorry," he said again. "I did wonder for a second, when we found Rin's house, and after... But he's my brother. You can understand, can't you, why I didn't want to believe it could be him? There was always some other explanation. If I'd realized... I'm *so* sorry."

"I don't care," I said. I pushed open the door and headed into the darkness cloaking the stairs.

On the first floor landing, I placed my back against the wall and edged to the door to peer through its wire-laced window into the hallway.

A dim glow streaked the darkness there—the light of a hundred ghosts or more, drifting around each other in a steady stream. The katana wobbled in my hand.

"Are we still in the keep where they attacked us?" I asked as Keiji crept up alongside me. "Are Chiyo and Takeo here?"

"Yes," he said. "They're still shut in that room, as far as I know. This woman ghost, Tomoya called her his lieutenant, he told her to keep the other ghosts guarding the hall."

"What happened to the kami who were in here with us?"

"I couldn't see a lot of the fighting," he said. "And I was... I was trying to keep the ghosts off of you. Some of them were carrying these buckets—they splashed stuff on the floor and the walls, and it seemed like the fighting stopped after that." He swallowed audibly. "I think they were using blood."

I grimaced. Like the ropes, like their weapons. They must have splattered the hall with gore so the kami would either sicken or flee.

Blood couldn't stop me, but a hundred ghosts could. A human girl with a fractured wrist and no protective amulet—even with Keiji's ofuda, I couldn't fight them all. Charging out there would be suicide.

So if I was going to save Chiyo and Takeo, I had to make the ghosts leave. I had a feeling asking nicely wasn't going to work.

At least, not for me.

I glanced back at Keiji where I could sense him in the darkness. "That 'lieutenant,' she knows you're Tomoya's brother?"

"Tomoya made a pretty big deal about it," he said, "to make sure they left me alone."

His voice was still rough, an echo of his repeated apology running through it. Why shouldn't I use his guilty conscience? However little I trusted him now, he obviously didn't want to be responsible for my death. He'd fought his brother to keep me alive. I was pretty sure he wouldn't turn back on that decision and offer me up to the figures out there.

And I didn't exactly have a multitude of options.

"All right," I said. "Then I need you to go get rid of them."

"What?"

"Go find the lieutenant," I said. "Give her a story—that Tomoya had to run off without consulting with her first, that he asked you to tell all the ghosts here to follow him. Say there was a surprise counterattack on the ghosts at Mt. Fuji. Or that Omori called some urgent meeting. Just convince them to leave."

There was a rustle of fabric as Keiji shifted his weight. "They're not going to believe it," he said. "Tomoya going off and leaving *me* in charge? They'll never listen to me."

The composure I'd been holding on to so desperately started to crack.

"Maybe not," I said, "but if you're really so sorry, why don't you at least *try* to fix this mess you got us into?"

There was silence beside me, and then an exhaled breath. "Okay," Keiji said. "Okay."

I flattened myself against the wall as he stepped past me into the hallway. The ghostlights clustered around him as he walked through them, giving his skin and clothes an eerie sheen. He stopped several paces into their midst.

After a moment, one of the ghosts solidified in front of him. Her sleek, shoulder-length bob obscured her face from where I stood.

Keiji launched into his story with a flurry of impatient gestures and worried expressions. The woman tapped her pointed shoe on the floor. I could only tell when she spoke because those were the few moments Keiji stilled.

All at once, she spun around and marched toward the stairwell. I flinched away from the door and sucked in a hiss of pain as my broken wrist bumped the wall. Ducking low, I darted through the darkness, up the stairs toward the second floor. The door sighed open below just as I scooted out of sight around the bend.

The woman ghost strode into the stairwell. "I *told* him he

should talk to you himself," Keiji was saying, hurrying after her. "But he wanted to make sure he got to Omori as soon as possible."

The woman made a dismissive sound. Her faint light faded away as she tapped down the steps. I held myself perfectly still. The ofuda left no sign of the ghost it had banished. There was no way she could know what had happened.

Unless she decided to check the room where I was supposed to be and discovered one of the "human prisoners" was missing.

Finally, the door swung open again. The hard soles of the woman's shoes clattered back up the stairs. She pushed into the hall. I waited five seconds, ten, and when she didn't return, crept back down and peered through the window.

The ghostlights had stopped meandering about and were flowing toward the opposite end of the hall. They looked like a cloud of hazy fireflies gusting away in a sudden breeze. As they vanished through the front entrance, I tipped my forehead against the wall and sighed.

Hinges squeaked below me. Tentative footsteps padded up.

"It worked," I said. "They're gone."

"Really? She didn't seem very impressed." Keiji came up beside me, close enough that I could feel the warmth of his presence even though we weren't touching. My skin prickled.

I edged to the side and peered through the window. My hand tightened around the katana.

"Mostly gone," I amended.

Five ghostlights still floated around a spot I judged to be more than halfway down the hall. By the room where they were holding Chiyo and Takeo, no doubt. Tomoya's lieutenant had believed

Keiji enough to take the majority of her force with her, but not to leave their valuable captives unguarded.

I weighed the sword in my hand. It wasn't going to do me any good, not against a bunch of ethereal ghosts. I set it on the floor.

"How many ofuda do you have?" I asked.

Paper crinkled as Keiji dug them out of his pockets. "I'm not sure. Twenty-ish?"

"Give me half."

He held them out, the edges of the scraps of paper tickling my arm. I shoved a few into my own pocket and palmed the rest.

Compared to what I'd already faced in the last few days, five ghosts was hardly anything. But my mouth had gone dry.

"What now?" Keiji said.

I studied the hall. "Go out ahead of me," I said, "and see if you can get them to turn corporeal to talk to you. It'll be easier if I can see them properly."

Without any argument this time, he nudged open the door and headed down the hall alone. The darkness was even thicker now that the main hoard of ghosts had left. After just a few seconds, I couldn't make out more than the edges of Keiji's body.

As he approached the ghostly guards, two of them flickered, taking on solid forms. Two was as much as I could hope for. I slipped into the hall.

I meant to approach the ghosts quietly to give them as little warning as possible. But after a couple of steps, my heel hit a thick, tacky patch on the floor. It made a little sucking sound when I raised my foot.

The blood the ghosts had splashed here. I'd been breathing

through my parted lips, but even so, a rancid metallic smell started to fill my nose. Fighting the urge to gag, I hurried on. If I didn't have the element of surprise, I'd have to rely on speed.

"Who's that?" one of the corporeal ghosts said to Keiji, and Keiji shrugged and said, "Oh, just a friend." Before any of them had time to wonder where his "friend" had come from, I was smacking ofuda into their midst.

Two of the ghostlights blinked out in an instant. Keiji whipped out his own charms, banishing the last ethereal ghost and slapping the closest solid ghost's face while her attention was on me. I was raising another ofuda when the final ghost grabbed my elbow. His other hand wavered translucent and dipped into my chest.

My lungs seized as he caught the thin thread of ki inside me. He squeezed, and my fingers spasmed, the ofuda slipping from my grasp. The rest of the ghost's body started to fade. He grinned at me, twisting the core of my spirit so my pulse wobbled and my legs sagged. An icy haze washed over me. I shook my head against it. If I let fear overwhelm me this time, I really would die.

As I wrenched against his grasp, the ghost's head snapped forward. He winked out of the world of the living, revealing Keiji behind him lowering the hand he'd thrust an ofuda with before the hall went fully dark.

I stumbled against the wall. In an instant, Keiji was at my side. "Sora?"

"I'm all right," I rasped. Or at least I hoped I would be soon. Pain was searing through me as if my internal organs had been scraped raw. I fumbled for the key. "Let's get them out. Is there a light around here somewhere? I can't see a thing now."

Sticky footsteps pattered down the hall. I traced the wall to the edge of the doorframe, a handle, a narrow hole beneath it. Keiji made a triumphant sound, and electric lights hummed on overhead. I pushed the key into the lock. For a second it jarred, and my heart stuttered. Then the deadbolt slid over. I shoved the door open.

The smell hit me first: a rotting stench that made my stomach lurch. Chiyo and Takeo were huddled together a few feet from the door, surrounded by a cracked red paste that coated every inch of the walls, floor, and ceiling: layers of blood and gristle and I didn't want to know what else. Chiyo was shivering, Takeo wheezing, their faces wan and shining with sweat.

Dropping the key, I held my breath and rushed inside. As I took Chiyo's arm to help her to her feet, Keiji burst in. He jerked to a halt and stumbled out again. Through the doorway, I heard him heave and a splatter of vomit hitting the floor.

"Sora," Chiyo murmured. She clung to my shoulder, swaying as she stood. She was still clutching the sacred sword in her other hand, as if she didn't dare let go of it. "Where's—where's Haru?"

"Downstairs," I said, trying not to remember how he'd looked when I left him. "Don't worry about him yet. You have to—"

A tremor passed through her as I helped her to a patch of untainted floor in the hallway. "I'm fine," she said, her voice faint but brighter. "He needs me."

She nudged past me and started to shuffle down the hall. I glanced between her and the door, judged that it would be a while before she made it there, and ducked back into their prison room to assist Takeo.

He was even weaker than Chiyo had been. My knees jarred when I tried to support the weight of his much taller and bulkier body. Keiji slunk back in, his face pinched, and leapt to help. Together, we hauled Takeo out of the room and set him on the same clear patch I'd brought Chiyo to. He coughed, slouching over.

Chiyo had made it partway down the hall, quivering as she darted around the splashes of gore. What was she going to do when she saw Haru? She wasn't in any condition to heal him.

"Walk Takeo outside," I said to Keiji, and he nodded.

"Chiyo!" I called, running after her. I caught up with her just as she reached the stairwell. She paused, wiping her damp bangs from her forehead. Her eyes were slightly glazed, but no less determined.

"He's down here?" she said.

"You have to rest before you can do anything for him," I said.

"I can handle this," she insisted. She shoved aside the door and trudged across the landing. The walls and floor were unbloodied there. As she headed down the stairs, her posture drew straighter, but she still had to push three times to open the door to the basement.

While the bloody prison had sapped her ki, I was battered and aching from head to toe. I was afraid if I tried to hold her back, she'd use up even more of her energy fighting me, and then still keep going. So I just followed.

I didn't need to tell her which door Haru was behind. She hustled down the hall on teetering legs as if he were a beacon only she could see. When we reached the room I'd escaped from, she charged right in. Then she dropped down beside his slumped body with a cry.

“No,” she said, finally releasing the sword. She pressed her hands to his face and shook her head. “No no no no. You’re not going anywhere. You’re staying here with me.”

“Chiyo,” I said around a catch in my throat, “I don’t know if he’s even—”

“He’s alive,” she said. “I can feel it. Right...” Her fingers skittered down to his chest. “But it’s slipping away. I have to catch it.”

She inhaled with a gasp, and the room exploded with light. Haru’s body twitched. A breath rattled over his lips. He groaned and rolled over, and Chiyo collapsed beside him.

SEVENTEEN

I CROUCHED at Chiyo's side for several long minutes, feeling her back tremble under my anxious hand and wondering how long it would take for Tomoya's lieutenant to discover our lie and come charging back here with the rest of Omori's ghostly army. Rescuing Haru from the brink of death had left Chiyo completely drained, and Haru, though alive, was so weak he crumpled over the first two times he tried to sit up. There was no way I could carry both of them, and no way Chiyo would allow me to separate them. Finally, Keiji came for us with the oak kami.

Takeo met us outside in the early afternoon heat, his tan skin still off-color. "We should leave here immediately," he said. His gaze fell to the wrist I was holding limply by my side. Before he could remark on it, a gangly figure appeared on the path behind him: the pine kami who'd tricked us into entering the keep.

Chiyo managed to spring onto her wobbly feet, raising her sword, and my hand dropped to the hilt of mine. The young kami bowed as low as his waist allowed, stretching his arms toward us.

Cupped in his hands was a necklace composed of sparkling curls of green jadeite.

"The Imperial jewel," I murmured.

"I most greatly, greatly am sorry," the kami stuttered. "They—my tree—they started to cut, to chop—they said if I did not say what they asked—"

"If you'd told us that," Takeo said, "we would have stopped them."

Chiyo wavered forward, and Takeo accepted the necklace to fasten it around her neck. "Thank you for bringing this to us," she said to the pine kami in a reedy voice. "I'm not angry. I know you must have been very scared."

She beamed at him despite her weariness, and he bowed his head again, blushing. Then she turned her grin on Takeo.

"A little more trouble than we were hoping, but we got what we came for in the end."

"Let's make sure we don't lose it," he replied. "Omori's forces could return at any moment."

He and the few other kami who'd come with us to the palace gathered around Chiyo and the three of us humans. As their ki swept through me, my thoughts started to fragment. I hadn't realized how weary *I* was, but between my injuries and the fight and so many nights of sleep cut short, it suddenly took all my energy just to stay upright.

We whisked through the city streets to a wide forested park surrounding one of the largest shrines I'd ever seen. In the separate sanctuary building off limits to the average visitor, Takeo bent over me and slid his fingers across my broken wrist. That was the last thing I remembered before sleep dragged me under.

When I woke up, my head felt clearer. Sunlight was filtering through the paper panels of the door near my feet. The sounds of a ringing bell and clapping hands carried with it. That would be the human visitors at the worship hall nearby. We hadn't taken shelter at an active shrine before. Takeo must have arranged with the resident kami some way of preventing the priests from noticing our presence.

Beside me lay my satchel and a bundle of clean clothes: a green tunic of a similar shade to the now-filthy shirt I'd borrowed from Chiyo and a pair of pale jeans. Brought by one of the kami as well? Had I only slept a few hours, or had we lost another day?

I dressed quickly and slid open the door. Before I could step out, a tremor rippled through the floor. The door rattled in its frame. I waited, gripping the wall and counting off the seconds. I reached ten before the ground stilled.

Oh, Fuji, I thought. *What are they doing to you?* I pictured the walls of the palace I'd grown up in splattered with gore, and shuddered.

I hurried to an entranceway that led to a grassy yard behind the building. From the angle of the sun, it was late afternoon—the same day, then, not the next morning. Still three days left until the first night of Obon.

Haru was sitting on the steps leading down to the yard, watching Chiyo and Takeo, who were standing by a small pond. They both looked well enough. The pond's water was low, the soil dry and cracked along its edge. Keiji squatted on the bank, tossing bits of bread to the koi.

I stiffened when my eyes fell on him. I hadn't told the others yet. They didn't know the part he'd played in leading us into that trap.

Keiji had to realize I would tell them, but he was still here. I didn't know what that meant.

"It was too great a risk," Takeo was saying. "However important he is to you."

"It wasn't a risk at all," Chiyo replied, smiling. "I knew I could do it. We still have time, and there's only the mirror we still have to get, right?"

"Your ki was already exhausted and you pushed yourself even further," Takeo said. "Omori will be sending every ally he can spare to Ise to stop us from reaching the mirror. You'll never be able to fight through an army if you have nothing left."

Chiyo rolled her eyes. "I haven't *lost* it. Look." She raised her hands, and a ball of glinting energy formed between them. But after a few seconds, its surface quivered. Chiyo's fingers tensed as the ball fizzled away into the air.

As I pushed myself on toward them, Chiyo frowned at her hands and then shrugged. "I just need a little more rest, and I'll be good as new."

"We have little enough time as it is," Takeo said. "We can't be sure the mountain will even hold until Obon."

Chiyo turned at the sound of my steps. "Sora!" she said. "I never really thanked you before. So thank you, thank you, thank you." She threw her arms around me. "When you got us out of that horrible room, the only thing I could think of was saving Haru."

"I know," I said, awkward in her embrace until she stepped

back. "How are we going to tackle Ise?"

"We were about to discuss that," Takeo said, his voice softening. "But first, how are you?"

With his familiar gaze on me, my scrapes and bruises prickled. I could have asked him to heal all of them as he had my wrist, to make every ache and pang disappear—at least, the physical ones. But then I'd be suggesting I couldn't carry on without help. I needed to get used to the limitations of my human body.

"I'm all right," I said. "And you?"

He grimaced. "Recovering. I should have realized the ghosts might resort to trickery."

My hands balled. *I* should have realized. I'd known something was wrong.

Except I hadn't known, not really. I'd only had a feeling that something was off. I'd had lots of other feelings in the recent past: the fear that froze up my mind, the... whatever it was that had blinded me to Keiji's lies. Even if some of my instincts were right, how was I supposed to tell which inclinations to listen to and which to ignore?

"How did you manage to get rid of all those ghosts anyway?" Chiyo asked. "Can we do the same thing at Ise?"

My eyes darted to Keiji, who had gotten up to join us. He met my gaze uncertainly.

"It wasn't really me," I said. "Keiji convinced most of them to go. I only had to fight a few. But I don't think that trick will work a second time."

Chiyo's eyebrows leapt up. "'Convinced' them to go? Have you got some super power of persuasion you forgot to mention to me, Mitsuoka?"

A flush crept up Keiji's neck. He lowered his head, his hair falling over the top of his glasses. For a second, I thought he was going to make me say the rest. Then he forced himself to look up again.

"They listened to me because the ghost who planned the surprise attack was my brother," he said, his voice strained but steady. "It's my fault. That they—that they knew where we'd be and when, the whole time. That they knew about Chiyo and the treasures." His mouth twisted. "I didn't mean for anyone to get hurt, I promise you. He'd never said anything about Mt. Fuji or Omori—it never occurred to me, at the beginning, that he could be involved in that. I was only telling him things and answering his questions in case he knew things about ghosts that I could use to help, and I was hoping if I helped enough, then afterward maybe the kami could help him somehow. He wanted his life back. That's all *I* wanted."

Takeo's hand had leapt to his sword. "Omori knows everything because of you? This morning... Nagoya... Sora almost *died*. Any of us could have died. Fuji could be lost completely now because of you!"

Keiji cringed. "I know. I should have figured it out sooner. I just didn't want to think he could be part of something that awful."

"Wait," Chiyo said, sounding amused even as she crossed her arms over her chest. "Your brother's a ghost? You figured *that* out right away, didn't you?"

"Of course I knew he was a ghost," Keiji said. "He... died two years ago. He'd gotten in with a bunch of guys running a lending company, and he was going to make enough money so he could get his own place. A place for him and me, to get away from our aunt and uncle. But—I don't know exactly what happened—the group he was with was connected to one of the syndicates, and someone there must have pissed off someone in a different syndicate. There was a big fight and..."

He made a jerking motion with his hand, as if it were a figure toppling over. Dead.

"A little while after that, he appeared in my room—he told me he'd wanted to keep an eye on me still, and he thought since I already believed in spirits and all that, maybe I could handle talking to him. I freaked out a bit, but, well, it was so good to have him back."

"The syndicates," Haru said in his abrupt way. I hadn't heard him walking over. "You mean yakuza."

Keiji nodded. "When you mentioned some of the ghosts were yakuza, that was the first clue I had," he said to me, a plea in his eyes. "I know I should have said something, even if I wasn't sure. I wish I had."

But he hadn't. Those regrets didn't mean much when the damage was already done.

"Wow," Chiyo said. "It sounds like Omori's set himself up as the big boss, then, recruiting all the dead yakuza members he can find."

Recruiting. The word brought back Tomoya's odd comments. "We already know he's helping them by lending them his power," I said to Keiji, "but how is he finding so many of them at all? Your brother talked about Omori *saving* them. What does that mean?"

"Yes," Takeo said, still gripping his sword. "We need to hear everything he told you about Omori's intentions."

"Tomoya didn't tell me much this morning," Keiji said. "He said he'd explain more later, when everything was in place. I just know he's proved himself to Omori and been put in charge of a bunch of the other ghosts..." He paused. "He did mention something before all this started, though. Months ago. He said he'd made friends, and that one of them was so powerful he could guide spirits right out of the afterworld. Maybe he was talking about Omori."

My mouth fell open. "Then Omori isn't turning just to spirits who've lingered here—he's dragging back those who passed away properly but haven't been dead long enough to fade away. No wonder he was able to raise such a large army."

No wonder that army felt so indebted to him. He *had* saved them, if only temporarily, from the cold, dark emptiness I'd glimpsed as my life drained away.

Keiji nodded. "You're right. It must be. But Tomoya didn't give me any details back then either. I just know he was trying to find a way to come back for real. He was always talking about how there might be forces in the world that could make that happen."

"Hmmm," Chiyo said. "So where is your brother now?"

"I banished him," I said before Keiji had to answer. Maybe it was more weakness, but I didn't want to see the expression he'd make saying it. "But... if Omori knows how to bring spirits over from the afterworld..."

"He could come back," Keiji filled in, his eyes widening. Then his jaw set. "If he does, no matter what he says, I swear I'm not going to tell him another thing. I never would have in the first place if I'd known the whole story. I'm on your side. I want to keep helping, better this time... if you'll let me. I'll do whatever I can."

He was watching me as he said those last words. I looked away. Being near him was making my chest increasingly tight. But maybe his brother had let something slip that we didn't realize was useful yet. That was more important than my wounded heart.

We stood there in silence for a moment, Takeo looking as if he were still considering driving Keiji out of the shrine at sword point.

"How were you even telling your brother things?" Chiyo said abruptly. "Secret meetings in the woods?"

"My phone," Keiji said. "He did something to it, with ki I guess, so it always works for him no matter where I am."

"All right." Chiyo held out her hand. "Give it here." As Keiji passed over his phone without argument, she added, "I don't think we should be talking secret plans with you around until we're sure you're really sticking with us. So…"

She made a dismissive gesture. Keiji blinked and then ducked his head as he ambled toward the shrine building.

"Do we want to head for Ise right away?" Chiyo said to Takeo and me.

"I don't want you that close to Omori's army until you've recovered more of your power," Takeo said. "As much as I hate to delay, I think we should hold off on our travels. I suppose... if we leave first thing tomorrow morning, that should be sufficient time." He didn't sound entirely sure.

"We can do everything possible to prepare in the meantime,"

I said. "Make more ofuda, collect salt and lotus flowers and whatever else can repel the ghosts..."

Takeo rubbed his chin. "I could speak with whatever kami live here in the city. Perhaps there are a few powerful enough to be of service in a fight, and willing."

Would that be enough? Tomorrow, with just two days left, we'd have only one real chance at retrieving the mirror and making it to Mt. Fuji before Obon. And it wasn't just the huge force that would be waiting for us at Ise that we needed to worry about. We'd assumed before that Omori and his ghosts would be predictable in their attacks, that they'd try to overwhelm us with brute force alone, but they'd surprised us today. Out-thought us.

He's as human as the rest of us, Tomoya had said about Omori. In the moment, I'd dismissed that remark as delusion, but there was some truth to it. The demon and his ghosts, none of them were straightforward—they were all at least partly human too. I should know better than anyone else here how annoyingly complex a human mind could be.

And we still didn't know what Omori was truly after.

"Maybe," I said tentatively, "we should also try to learn more about Omori as he was before he died. At Chiyo's house we didn't have time to do very much searching, and we weren't even sure yet we had the right man."

Chiyo's eyes lit up. "Yeah! We could go back home. I could—"

"No," Takeo said firmly. "Omori will definitely have ghosts watching that place, especially now that they know we're back in Tokyo."

Chiyo opened her mouth, and then stopped and looked at her

hands—the hands that had failed to hold a simple ball of ki for more than the length of a breath.

"Right," she said. "And if they caught me with my parents, they might attack Mom and Dad too. So we could find an internet cafe instead. There are tons of those around the city. We won't have to go far."

"And if we see any ghosts, we can run straight back to the protections of the shrine," I said. I would have offered to go alone, but I'd never used a computer before. I didn't even know what an internet cafe looked like. And from Takeo's frown, I doubted he'd have liked the idea of me wandering the city alone either. "We have to find out more about Omori," I went on. "Either the information will help us understand what he wants and what tactics he might use next, or... or maybe it'll lead us to someone who knew him, who could tell us those things. Keiji's brother came to him—Omori might have visited *his* family since his death, told them what he was doing. We'll be so much better prepared if we can predict his next move."

Takeo sighed, and I knew I'd pushed the right button. "We would," he agreed. "All right. But please, be careful."

"Of course," Chiyo said, linking her arm around mine with a renewed smile. Haru stepped forward, but before he even spoke, she reached up to give his shoulder a playful push. "You go rest some more. You need it even more than I do. I've already had to save you once."

"Sorry," he said, wincing.

"There's nothing to apologize for. Those ghosts got me too, didn't they?" She let go of me long enough to give him a quick kiss.

"Okay," I said when she rejoined me. "Let's see if we can turn the tables on this Kenta Omori."

⁂

The shrine's forest had blocked out all sight and sound of the city around it. I'd almost forgotten we were still in the middle of Tokyo until we stepped past the gate onto the bustling sidewalk. People were peering through store windows, ambling in and out of restaurants, and crowding the intersections. The trill of bicycle bells and the rumble of engines filled the air. Traffic lights glared and advertisement screens flashed. With the sun beating down on my head, a wave of dizziness washed over me.

Chiyo sauntered forward, apparently undisturbed by the hustle and the noise, but after several steps her legs wobbled, and she caught herself against a signpost.

"Chiyo!" I said, but she waved my concern away.

"I just have to stretch these muscles a bit," she said with her usual cheer. My stomach remained knotted as we continued down the street at a slower pace.

Chiyo stopped once to paw through a rack of dresses by a shop door, and again to ogle a display of silver jewelry. I suppressed my impatience, suspecting that she was pausing not so much out of idleness as to rest her feet. My gaze slid over the display and caught on a charm shaped like a streaming kite. Glinting in the sunlight, it looked almost like the one I'd made from ki for Takeo in our last little game. Or the one he'd made for Chiyo, or the one *she'd* made this morning. That shape wasn't mine anymore.

"You want to get something?" Chiyo asked. "I picked up a ton of cash from the shrine—they had a huge box for offerings in front of the altar. We can use it for train tickets and amulets and all that, but we should be able to have a bit of fun too." She pushed a wad of bills into my hand.

"But... it's shrine money," I said, my fingers curling around the textured paper. Offerings to the kami didn't include me.

"It was," Chiyo said. "And then it was mine, and now it's yours. Even if you don't buy anything now, we should all have some on us for emergencies, right?"

That made sense. I shoved the money into my satchel.

On the next block, Chiyo nudged me and pointed upward. A sign protruding from the second floor of a building up ahead read, *High speed internet.*

We squeezed up a narrow flight of stairs beside the first floor shoe store. An erratic beat filtered down to us, threaded with a winding, dipping melody. As we emerged into the cool artificial-smelling blast of air conditioning at the top of the stairs, my body swayed with the music, drawing resolve from the rhythm.

Bright orange paint covered the room's walls, broken by posters of cartoon figures, hulking beasts, and soaring spacecraft. Several customers, most of them our age or a little younger, clustered around a few of the flat-screen monitors on the tables that lined both sides of the room.

As we approached the front counter, the floor jumped and rattled beneath us. I grabbed Chiyo's arm, keeping us both balanced until the tiny quake faded.

"Another one," the thinly bearded man behind the counter

said, eyeing the ground uneasily. "All these tremors and a rainy season with no rain—I don't care what they say on the news, it's kind of freaking me out. And now there's that gigantic typhoon that looks to be brewing near Okinawa. Crazy summer, isn't it?"

Okinawa—the Nagamotos had talked about their son heading there on vacation. But of course, Omori didn't care any more about that than he did about the forests and farms dying or the fire growing in Mt. Fuji. My hands clenched.

"It has been," Chiyo said. "Can we get on one computer?"

"Sure. 300 yen for fifteen minutes, 500 for half an hour." The guy tapped the glass-doored fridge behind him with his heel. "There's water, tea, and soft drinks if you want."

"Thanks." Chiyo handed over a few bills from her wad of cash. She tugged me to a computer in the far corner, away from the window overlooking the street. "Don't want any spooks spotting us while we're busy," she said in a conspiratorial whisper. "Okay, let's do some digging. Who do you think Omori would be talking to?"

"If anyone, his family?" I suggested. "Or maybe—he seems to still have ties to the yakuza, so someone who was part of his gang?"

"I'll start with the wife," Chiyo said, typing into the search box.

"I might have her name in that article we printed," I said. By the time I'd pulled it out of my pocket, Chiyo already had a page of results in front of her. She clicked on one of the links.

"Hey, this is kind of sweet," she said. "He organized and paid for a bunch of workers to bring supplies to Sendai after the big earthquake, and he dedicated the emergency aid effort to his wife. Emiko. Maybe we can find out where she's living now."

Why would someone who'd once tried to save people from natural disasters now be causing them without a care? Maybe he'd never cared, only put on a show to cover up his criminal activities?

I glanced at the print-out I'd unfolded in my lap, and all those thoughts fled my mind.

The papers were smudged from my first charcoal-drawn ofuda, and somewhere along the line they'd gotten a little damp, so the edges of the image had run. But Omori still grinned at me with that warm blast of a smile, and beside him his wife...

...looked shockingly familiar.

"I don't think Emiko Omori is living anywhere right now," I said, setting the pages on the table between us. "She's dead."

EIGHTEEN

"WHAT?" CHIYO said, peering at the printed photo. "How do you know?"

Those soft eyes, that gentle mouth—I couldn't have forgotten them if I'd wanted to. "When we were trapped in the keep..." I said. "There's this sparrow that's been following Takeo and me since we left Mt. Fuji. It has a spirit in it. She appeared to me for a moment. It was Mrs. Omori—she looked a little older than here, but I'm sure it was her."

Chiyo's eyebrows leapt up. "The ghost of Omori's wife has been following you? That doesn't sound good."

"I don't think she's on his side," I said. "If it wasn't for her help, I wouldn't have been able to escape. And..." The horrified expression she'd made when I'd suggested she was working with the other ghosts. "Maybe she doesn't agree with what he's doing. Maybe she's scared of him. He wasn't a demon when she married him." Seeing us escaping Mt. Fuji, she must have assumed Takeo and I were her best chance to see him overthrown. "She couldn't exactly explain. Someone had cut out her tongue."

"Yikes," Chiyo said, wincing. "That sounds like a yakuza move. They can be really vicious." Her fingers flitted over the keyboard again. "Emiko Omori, death... Oh."

Prominent Tokyo businessman and family slain in daytime attack.

"This is from an independent paper," Chiyo said. "They're less scared of talking about yakuza stuff."

My stomach twisted as we read through the article Chiyo had found.

"It sounds like Omori was in with the yakuza big time," Chiyo said after a moment, her tone more subdued than usual. "Probably just below the big boss of his syndicate."

"But why would someone have killed his wife and children too?" I said. I swallowed thickly, still feeling sick, though few details of the deaths had been given. It was the housekeeper who'd called the police after finding the bodies. The attackers had left no one in the house alive. "It says none of the yakuza groups would take responsibility for his death."

"Look." Chiyo pointed to a paragraph farther down. "The writer thinks that because Omori's syndicate didn't step up and take anyone down afterward, they might have killed him themselves. Maybe he did something that made the head boss angry. But wow, being murdered by your own colleagues—I bet his plans now have something to do with that. I've heard that ghosts can get stuck on whatever they were feeling right before they died. Like, this girl who drowned herself because her boyfriend cheated on her, her ghost could only think about how betrayed she was, nothing else. If that's true for demons too, Omori could be stuck on that betrayal. Maybe he's bringing back ghosts from all the other syndicates to get back at his own."

"Keiji said something about that," I said, ignoring the twinge that came with the memory. "That a person could become a demon if they were so angry when they died that it consumed them."

"There!" Chiyo said. "That's got to be it."

"But how does Mt. Fuji fit in?" I said. "Why wait until Obon when he already has so many spirits with him? He doesn't need kami to get revenge on the people who killed him and his family—he could murder any of them *himself* if that was all he wanted."

We scrolled through several more pages of search results, but none told us any more details about the circumstances around Omori's death. Chiyo sat back in her chair and sighed. "Well, we can't ask his wife what he's thinking, but maybe he *has* been in touch with someone he worked with—someone still alive."

"But the articles don't give the names of any of his yakuza coworkers," I said. "And even if we found some out, we don't know who might have been involved in *murdering* him. What are they going to do to us if we start asking questions?"

"I can take on any yakuza jerk," Chiyo declared, but I remembered how she'd faltered on the way here. She wasn't even strong enough to walk at full power yet.

If only we had something to direct us... Or someone. My gazed darted to the window, seeking a small, feathered form. I didn't see the sparrow, but she'd stuck close to us every step of the way before now. She had to be nearby.

"Omori's wife might not be able to tell us anything, but maybe she could point us in the right direction," I said, standing up.

We hurried down the stairs and back along the street the way we'd come. "Emiko!" Chiyo called out, drawing a few stares. "Emiko, we need to talk to you!"

We'd just come into sight of the shrine gates when a brown shape fluttered over them. "There she is," I said, my heart leaping. The sparrow landed on a window frame beside us and bobbed its head.

For a second, I had trouble finding words. "You're Omori's wife," I said. It gazed back at me, its black eyes glinting. "You helped me before," I went on. "Now... we want to understand everything we can about what Omori wants with Mt. Fuji, what's driving him... If there's anything you can show us that might give us some answers, we'd be incredibly grateful."

The sparrow bobbed its head. Then it chirped and glided across the street to a telephone pole on the opposite corner.

"Do you think she understood?" Chiyo asked.

"We'd better go with her and find out," I said.

I was worried Chiyo wouldn't be able to handle an extended walk, but we'd only gone a couple of blocks before the sparrow veered into a small train station building. It tapped a spot on a route map by the ticket vending machines, and Chiyo bought our tickets.

The train rumbled south for twenty minutes before we got off. The sparrow rejoined us and led us down a series of broad streets between towering apartment buildings in shades of ivory and peach. "Pretty posh neighborhood," Chiyo said.

She'd paused for a moment to catch her breath when the sound of piano notes drifted from a second floor balcony door. The player stumbled, and the music cut off with a mumbled curse. Chiyo gazed up toward the apartment, her fingers moving against her hip. Her face had taken on an oddly melancholy cast.

I thought of the piano in the Ikedas' living room. The one she might never play again.

"I'm sorry we couldn't go see your parents," I offered. "It must be hard."

She pulled her eyes away. "Takeo was right. And I can call them again tonight. They know I'm okay, and I know they're okay. That's what really matters."

But then, as we followed the sparrow around a bend, she wiped the sweat from her forehead and said, "This probably sounds silly, but... my other parents, the ones on Mt. Fuji—I keep trying to picture them, but I don't know anything about them really. Not even what they look like."

Because I'd tried so hard to avoid talking about them with her. An ache swelled in my chest as I finally let the jumble of memories rise up.

"Your mother is tall and thin and graceful, and very beautiful," I said slowly. "She's kind and calm. And very smart. Whenever there's a disagreement among the kami, she sees the best way to solve it so everyone's satisfied. And she has the most lovely voice when she sings." A voice that still echoed in my head. "Your father is large in presence and in body, tall but broad, like Fuji itself. He has this way of making everyone who talks to him feel as though they're the most important person in the world, and he can't stand to see a single kami mistreated. When he laughs, you can hear him right across the palace. Everyone looks up to both of them—that's why they were chosen to lead." I hesitated. "I'm sure they can't wait to meet you."

Chiyo lowered her gaze. "You didn't have any idea either, did you? That they weren't *your* real parents."

The ache rose up. It took me a moment to answer. "No."

"Well," Chiyo said, "you should know that your actual parents are great people too. They did everything right for me—always looking out for me, but never too bossy or strict. I think you'll be really happy with them after all this is finished."

She beamed at me, but I'd heard the hint of a quaver in her voice. An uncomfortable sort of acceptance opened inside me as I looked back at her.

She might have taken my life, but I had also taken hers. And even if her cheerful nature was too ingrained for her to acknowledge it, I wasn't the only one missing the home I'd thought was mine.

The sparrow swooped right past my face, jerking me from my thoughts. It alighted over the front door of a pale yellow apartment building. When Chiyo and I pushed into the entryway, it fluttered in after us and pecked one of the entries on the list of apartment numbers. Kobayashi.

"That name came up in one of the articles," I said to Chiyo. "Omori's housekeeper, I think. It's a common name, but why else would his wife have brought us here?"

"Not quite as exciting as a gangster," Chiyo said.

She pushed the button beside the name. After a moment, a slightly hollow voice came through the speaker. "Yes?"

"We're here to see Mrs. Kobayashi," Chiyo said.

"Who is this?"

"It'll be easier to explain in person," Chiyo replied.

Her upbeat tone must have eased the woman's concerns, because the inner door buzzed. The sparrow didn't follow as we headed across the gleaming floor of the lobby to the elevator.

When we emerged into a hallway, I could see the door of one apartment standing ajar. A wiry middle-aged woman with brown-tinted hair peered around it.

"Are you the ones who buzzed?" she said.

"Yes, ma'am," Chiyo said with that brilliant smile of hers. "We need your help."

"My help?"

Chiyo nodded. "We'd really like to speak with you."

The hallway was empty, but there was no telling who was home behind the other doors. "The subject is a little private," I said. "Could we talk inside?"

Mrs. Kobayashi looked from one of us to the other and seemed to evaluate us as nonthreatening enough. "Well, I won't make you stand out here," she said. "Come in."

Though the building's lobby and halls had been elegantly decorated, the living room Mrs. Kobayashi led us into was plain, furnished with only a tan rug, a cushioned bench, and two wooden chairs. Chiyo and I sat down on the bench. "So," the woman said as she sank onto one of the chairs, "what is this about?"

"We need to know about Kenta Omori," Chiyo said. "You were his housekeeper, right?"

The woman's hands twisted together in her lap. "Kenta

Omori?" she said. "I don't believe I know that name."

"I'm pretty sure you do," Chiyo said. "It would be hard to explain how we ended up here, but you don't need to worry—we aren't yakuza or anything. We just want to know a little more about him."

She was smiling away, as if we weren't asking about a criminal's murder. "Chiyo," I said, and she blinked at me, oblivious.

Mrs. Kobayashi was getting up, her lips pressed flat. In a second, she'd tell us to leave. Maybe she thought we were thrill-seekers or gossipmongers, or worse, that we really were associated with Omori's former gang. She had no reason to trust Chiyo, especially when Chiyo was treating the whole situation so casually. Why couldn't Chiyo see that?

Because she was kami. She didn't know any approach other than her constant cheerful confidence. Eager as *I* was to find out what this woman could tell us, I was human enough to be able to hide it.

"Now, I think you should—" Mrs. Kobayashi started.

I stood up quickly, pulling Chiyo with me. "Excuse my friend," I said, bowing. "I didn't explain to her just how serious this matter is. She means no disrespect."

"Of course I don't want to be disrespectful," Chiyo said. "I was only—"

I caught her gaze. "I think it'd be better if just one of us talked. Could you wait for me in the lobby?"

She hesitated, her brow knitting, but her good-naturedness overrode her confusion. "Well, this *was* your idea. Don't take too long!"

When the door had closed behind her, I turned back to Mrs. Kobayashi. She was braced in front of her chair, her expression uncertain.

"I'm sorry," I said. "I know this must be difficult to talk about. We didn't mean to scare you. She... she doesn't think sometimes."

Well, she did. She just thought like a kami.

"I don't believe I can help you," Mrs. Kobayashi said stiffly, but she didn't move.

If it were me, asked by a stranger to bring up horrible memories, what would convince me to agree? Unbidden, my mind slipped back to the slash of the ogre's claw across my throat. A shiver ran through me. But despite that fear, I was still fighting. Because I'd known I could make a difference between so many other people living or dying.

"Mrs. Kobayashi," I said, "I am very, very sorry to ask you to remember what must have been a deeply disturbing time. But it's important for me to know everything I can about Kenta Omori and his death. His spirit... It hasn't settled. He's already hurt people I care about. You've felt the tremors, noticed the heat, the lack of rain? It's all because of him and what he's been doing. I need your help to make sure he doesn't cause an even worse disaster."

I kept my eyes fixed on hers, hoping she would accept my explanation. Praying she had enough belief in the spirit world to think it was possible.

"Causing a disaster?" she said, her forehead furrowing. "That doesn't sound like Mr. Omori."

"I came here with the guidance of other spirits who want to stop him," I said. What else could I use to convince her? I paused.

She'd been the one to find the bodies. We both knew things that hadn't been reported in the newspapers. "It was Mrs. Omori's spirit, actually, who brought me. I've seen her. I know what they did to her tongue."

Mrs. Kobayashi flinched. She stared at me, speechless.

"Please," I said. "Anything you can tell me."

She drew in a breath and exhaled in a rush. "All right," she said. She lowered herself into her chair. Her hair shadowed her face. "I worked for the Omoris for seven years. There are many things I could say that I can't imagine would be relevant. What do you want to know exactly?"

"What was important to him?" I said. "What did he want to accomplish? What did he care about the most?"

"Well, that... I assume from your friend's comments that you know the sort of connections he had?"

"Yakuza," I murmured.

"Yes," she said. "But he kept that part of his life out of the house, never spoke of it in front of me. He did talk about the legitimate side of his business, developing real estate properties. He took a lot of pride in his ability to land any deal he was pursuing with favorable terms. When he wanted a building or a piece of land and the current owners were resisting, he was always able to determine one key person he had to sway and direct all his attention there. By focusing so effectively, he liked to say, he got results much faster than those who tried to cater to everyone."

So business success had motivated Omori. How far had he gone to achieve it? "Did he hurt people to encourage the sales?" I said.

Her lips pursed. "I'm sure as much as possible he persuaded them simply using words—he knew how to talk to people so well. And he wasn't a cruel person. He liked to talk about fairness and justice, and it wasn't just talk. There was a time when my husband lost his job because the manager wanted to promote a nephew, and when Mr. Omori heard about it, he didn't just demand they take my husband back, he arranged that they had to change the wording of their corporate directive so that no one would think of doing that again. I don't know how he managed it—I didn't want to know—but he did it even though it didn't benefit him at all."

I hesitated. This man was now a demon holding all of Mt. Fuji's kami hostage while risking the lives of people across the world. What sort of justice did he see in that?

"And his family, of course, was very important to him," Mrs. Kobayashi went on at my silence. "Mrs. Omori liked to tell the story of how he courted her. He was sure he wanted to marry her after they'd dated each other for six months, but she wasn't ready to settle down. She even broke up with him for being too serious! So he waited. He told her he couldn't imagine being as sure about any other woman, so he would give her whatever time she needed to be ready. He didn't go out with anyone else. They would see each other socially every few months, and he would be kind and courteous but not pushy. And after a couple of years, she realized she was ready for that sort of commitment, and that she had always liked everything about him except for that. Even ten years after they married, the way they looked at each other..." She laughed faintly. "I'll admit sometimes I was a little envious."

And yet now his wife seemed afraid of him. My stomach had

knotted. "What about right before he was murdered?" I said. "Had he changed at all? Started to act differently than usual?"

Mrs. Kobayashi frowned. "I wouldn't say so. In the last month before it happened, I heard him arguing on the phone more than once—with a colleague, I think, because he was talking about a decision they'd made about his current building project. Something he felt was to save money at the expense of people's safety. He kept saying it wasn't right and he would find a better way. The project was the biggest one he'd ever worked on. I... I think maybe the trouble he was stirring up over it might have been why they came for him. It sounded as if he'd taken matters into his own hands, made arrangements he knew his superiors hadn't approved of."

"It was his own gang that killed them?" I said, remembering what the article had suggested.

"He knew the men who came," she said. "He sounded so horrified..." Her voice trembled.

My heart stuttered. "You were there," I said. "We thought you only found them, after."

She lowered her head. "I was in the kitchen preparing the children's lunch boxes for school," she said, "and the family was having breakfast together. They always did, you know, no matter how busy he was. And then I heard a crash. The men broke the door down—as if they had no fear of being seen! I didn't know what to do, I was so frightened, so I squeezed into the closet and hid there."

She stopped, her hands clenching. I hated to ask her to go any farther, but Omori's last moments might hold the answer we needed. "And then...?" I said softly.

"I could hear everything," she whispered. "Mr. Omori telling them to be reasonable, saying his boss couldn't really want this. The men saying he'd stepped too far out of line. And then they shot him. Not to kill him, only to hurt him and make it impossible for him to fight back. He yelled until his voice got hoarse as they did all those unspeakable things to Mrs. Omori and the children, but they wouldn't stop..."

She paused again, blinking hard. My own eyes had gone hot. How awful for Mrs. Kobayashi to have witnessed that scene. And how awful for Omori, no matter what he'd become, to lie there helpless, watching his family tortured. To know it was happening because of him.

"I suppose his superiors wanted to punish him in every way they could," Mrs. Kobayashi murmured after a moment. "It was a mercy when the men finally shot Mrs. Omori and the children. Then they must have turned the gun on Mr. Omori again. But even then, he didn't sound frightened, only angry, and so *sure*... I can still hear the way he said his last words. As if they were a threat. As if he'd have the chance to follow through."

I straightened up. "What did he say?"

She wiped her eyes and looked up at me. "*I will never be this powerless again.*"

The words rang through me in a cold peal. So that was what Omori had been thinking about as he died: power. Was that what he got out of controlling Mt. Fuji—knowing he held so many lives in the palm of his hand?

But maybe there was a way we could use what Mrs. Kobayashi

had told us to our advantage, even if he was so far gone from the man she claimed he'd once been. I just wasn't sure I knew enough yet.

"Thank you for sharing that with me," I said. "I hope it will help us. I don't suppose you have anything of Mr. Omori's from back then? Letters, business documents... anything, really." Anything that might show the connections he'd been making just before his death.

"I have a few things." A faint flush colored the woman's cheeks. "I don't know if they'll be of any use. Just a moment."

She disappeared into one of the other rooms and returned with a small leather box that she handed to me. I opened it to find a simple gold ring set with a modest but brilliant emerald, a bulky pen with gold detailing, and a sheet of lined paper that appeared to be a shopping list: *screws, sandpaper, wood stain*.

"I was supposed to pick up some items so Mr. Omori could fix the leg of one of the side tables," Mrs. Kobayashi jumped in to explain. "He liked to take care of those sorts of concerns himself. But I didn't know if it might turn out to be meaningful to the investigation somehow... The pen was his favorite, given to him by a professor in university, and he used it to sign all his business documents. I thought he would hate the idea of his enemies having it. And the ring was Mrs. Omori's. The first birthday present he ever gave her. It'd been at the cleaners—I had the receipt to pick it up. To be honest, I had been thinking of selling it, but then I found out Mr. Omori had been very generous to me in his will." She rubbed the knee of her linen pants, and suddenly I understood the fancy building and the apartment's understated interior. She didn't feel entirely comfortable with that generosity.

I didn't see how any of these could offer us much, but the more I learned about Omori, the more obvious it became that he was too complicated to assume anything for sure.

"Could I borrow these?" I asked tentatively. "I would bring them back, once his spirit is settled again. We're willing to try anything to accomplish that."

"I— All right," Mrs. Kobayashi said. "I suppose they aren't truly mine as it is. And if it might help Mr. Omori, I'd be glad of it. He's a better man than you think, I promise you."

I reported to Chiyo everything Mrs. Kobayashi had said as we rode back to the shrine on the train. "Wow," she said when I was done. "What a story. What do you think it means as far as fighting him?"

I'd been mulling that over since I'd left the apartment. "There might be some way we can exploit his obsession with power. And... the thing she said about him picking a key person to target when he wanted a deal done—he has been focused on capturing *you* from the beginning. I'm sure even more so once he found out about the prophecy. You're the one person who can stop him, after all. His ghosts didn't even try to restrain the other kami after you were captured with Takeo in the keep, just let them escape."

Chiyo hummed to herself. "It did seem like, when we were going for the sacred sword, most of the ghosts only bothered with the others when they were in the way of getting at me. But it was hard to tell when we were all so packed together. And then there were the jerks who decided to go after Haru." She bared her teeth.

"So it won't be a perfect strategy," I said, considering. "But... maybe if we could somehow trick him into *thinking* you were captured when you really weren't, he'd let down his guard?"

"Oooh, that sounds like fun," Chiyo said. "How would we do that?"

"I don't know," I admitted. I was hoping inspiration would hit me before we left for Ise tomorrow morning—or maybe Takeo would have an idea.

Evening was falling when we walked back through the shrine gate. Chiyo seemed to have continued to recover during our foray into the city—she bounded toward the sanctuary building on steady legs. I ducked around it into the back yard and found Haru waiting for me with a yellow amulet in hand. An identical silk pouch hung from a cord around his neck.

"Mitsuoka and I picked up new ones for the three of us," he said. "And some backups. They came in handy before."

I couldn't stop my gaze from seeking out Keiji. He was meandering along the pond in the glow of the sanctuary's lanterns, his own pouch bright against his blue T-shirt.

"Thank you," I said, dragging my eyes back to Haru and accepting the amulet. "We're going to need them."

"You think it's going to be brutal at Ise," Haru said, his flat inflection making the words a statement rather than a question.

"I don't see how it couldn't be," I said. Even if we came up with a strategy that exploited Omori's weaknesses, we had an entire army of ghosts to contend with, almost certainly more than we'd ever faced before.

I had to remember what I'd learned at the Imperial Palace—to pay attention to my human instincts, not just blunder along thinking of being strong. Maybe if I could figure out a way to judge which instincts were right, I'd be able to do more than banish a few ghosts, even if I'd never be half as capable as the kami warriors.

I ran my thumb over the soft fabric of the pouch, the one thing that would stand between my life and a ghostly death grip. Haru was wearing a new collared shirt, a pale gray one someone had brought him, but I could still picture the dark splotch of blood that had stretched across his abdomen this morning.

"Does it bother you?" I found myself asking. "That, I mean, Chiyo can take down ten ghosts with one swing of that sword and heal her own wounds, but all it takes is one knife and you—or me—we're done?"

His mouth curled into a wry smile. "All we can do is our best. It's not our fault her best is a thousand times better."

He'd put it even more baldly than I'd dared to. "You almost died," I pointed out.

"True." He sat down on the edge of the platform, stretching his lanky legs over the lawn. His head turned toward the forest. Chiyo was standing at its edge with Takeo, probably telling him what we'd found out. Haru ran his hand over his hair, making it stand up even straighter than usual.

"I'm not going to say the idea of taking another knife in the gut doesn't scare me," he said in a low voice. "I do wish she didn't have to worry about me. But at the same time, this feels... *right*. When I met her, I could tell she was a girl worth fighting for. My friends, my sisters, they've hassled me about being too hung up on her, and I'd ask myself if they had a point, but I'm okay with it now. The folk tales are full of guys who devoted their lives to protecting amazing women. Nobody makes fun of them. I'm glad to fill that role. As long as she wants me here..."

I laughed. "I think you can be pretty sure of that."

His smile turned sheepish. "I was nervous when I got to Nagoya that she'd be upset I'd thrown myself in there, tell me she had no use for me anymore. But she didn't. And now I can really fight for her. So I know this is where I have to be."

Yes. The sentiment washed over me with a certainty that reverberated through my bones.

"We're never going to be kami," he added. "But that doesn't mean we're nothing."

"Of course," I said. I'd done my part. If not for me, after all, Takeo and Chiyo might still be locked in the keep.

"Haru!" Chiyo called, and he waved to her. We were just getting up when a slender figure solidified at the edge of the yard and stumbled toward us.

"Sora!" she cried, holding out her spindly arms. "Sora!"

"Ayame!" I leapt forward to meet her. Her hair was tangled, and the indigo robe she'd been wearing when she applied my birthday make-up was torn and stained. But her embrace was firm as she caught me up.

"You got away from the ghosts," I said, hugging her back tightly. The words couldn't tumble out fast enough. "How did you know where we were? Are Mother, Father, everyone—"

"Still trapped," she gasped against my shoulder. "I almost didn't— I haven't stopped running since— If they caught me—" Her thin voice cut off with a shudder. "I wish I could have freed them all, Sora, but I knew it would be hard enough escaping on my own, and the most important thing was finding you."

She pulled back and held up her hand. A thick black hair circled her index finger. As she touched my cheek with it, it dissolved against my skin. "From your brush," she said. "I had it with me when they attacked. Your hair led me to you."

Takeo's remark about magic came back to me: *Blood sings to blood, heart to heart, spirit to spirit.* Every part of me was singing just seeing my honorary auntie safe.

The others had gathered around us. Ayame glanced away from me, and her gaze veered straight to Chiyo. Her tiny frame stiffened as she stared. Then she reached out to touch one of Chiyo's wavy lavender ponytails. I half expected her to criticize Chiyo's choice of hair color. Instead, her eyes teared up.

"It's true," she murmured. "I heard the ghosts say there was another girl, that Their Highnesses had exchanged their daughter for a human to protect her, but I could hardly believe—"

Her eyes darted back to me. I could feel the lack of ki in my body as if I were a hollowed-out tree. Dread dampened my joy. "It's true," she said again. "Sora, you're—"

"I know," I said, more sharply than I meant to. Ayame didn't seem to notice. She'd already returned her attention to Chiyo, bowing low.

"It's an honor to meet you," she said.

"Who *are* you?" Chiyo asked, her eyebrows arched in amusement.

"She is one of the mountain's kami," Takeo said. "One of your parents' most devoted subjects."

"Ayame," Ayame said with another bow.

"Well, I'm Ik—" Chiyo caught herself as if realizing for the first time that her last name no longer applied. "I'm Chiyo. Pleased to meet you too."

"What's happening on the mountain right now?" I said, cutting in. "What is the demon doing? How did you get away, Ayame?"

She hesitated. I didn't understand why until Chiyo nodded and said, "Yes, tell us everything," and Ayame drew in a breath. To tell *her*.

Because I didn't count anymore.

I hadn't thought my heart could break any more than it already had. Apparently I was wrong. It felt as though it had just cracked down the middle. But even if it was only Chiyo's opinion Ayame cared about now, I needed to hear this.

"It's awful," Ayame said. "Bad enough, being so close to so many of the dead, but then the ghosts brought their bloody nets and ropes and smeared the walls of our beautiful palace with more of that dreadful stuff, until we could all barely breathe. Most of us couldn't move after a few hours. I only got away because I was lucky. The demon sent some of the ghosts to look for kami who would do as they asked. I said I would, just to see what would happen, and they let a few of us start to recover in a room they'd left clean. They didn't think much of me, a little woman with combs and pins, until I stabbed them with my hair sticks and ran. I don't know how I made it. Fuji must have lent me strength."

"We're glad you reached us safely," Takeo said gravely.

"Pretty stupid of Omori," Chiyo said. "Why would any kami want to help *him* after everything he's done?"

Ayame's face pinched. "It's not so much wanting as... Your mother and father. The demon has ordered that they be tortured. He's weakening them until he can kill them. And we can hear them, their cries... There are those among us who won't be able to stop themselves. We've held out so long, but the worse it gets, the harder it is for them to resist. They would sooner accept the demon's demands than let one of our rulers die."

Understanding struck me like a kick to the gut. That possibility hadn't occurred to me, but if it meant saving Mother or Father, even Takeo would agree to anything. His sense of loyalty would overcome all logic. Omori was using the kami's natures against them.

Mrs. Kobayashi had said he was good at "persuading" people to do what he wanted, hadn't she? I suppressed a cringe. So he was torturing Mother and Father, over and over... Closing my eyes couldn't shut out the images Ayame's story had conjured in my head.

"What does he want the kami to do anyway?" Chiyo asked.

"That's the worst part of it," Ayame said. "When they first came, the demon demanded that we bring them all back to life, him and his ghosts. Your mother tried to explain that we don't have that sort of power—all we could do for a spirit that seemed worthy was let it share the life of another being for a time. And then the demon asked about sharing life with another human."

Takeo startled. "That can't be done. It isn't done."

"It isn't done," Ayame agreed. "And she told him that. But he insisted we try. He thinks, during the days of the dead when their power is strongest, it will work."

My skin had gone cold. When a spirit was given to an animal, like Mrs. Omori's sparrow, the bird's life remained, but the human spirit could see and feel all it did and direct it when it wished. That was how Mrs. Omori had followed us. If a human spirit were put into another, living human—what would happen to the spirit already there?

"He's readying us for his first attempt right now," Ayame said. "That's why he was letting some of us regain our ki. And if he's happy with the outcome, he says he wants living bodies for every one of the ghosts with him come Obon."

NINETEEN

I WAS IN the middle of a dream full of ghosts and blood and tortured screams when someone shook me awake. I flinched, my hand darting to Takeo's short sword. Then I made out Ayame's worried face in the faint pre-dawn light.

"What's wrong?" I said, sitting up. It was too early for us to be leaving to catch the train to Ise. When I'd gone to sleep, I'd chosen one of the sanctuary's smaller rooms so I could be alone. Now I wished I could see Takeo and Chiyo to know they were all right.

Ayame was wringing her hands. "I was so relieved to find you that I completely forgot until now. I woke up and remembered that I hadn't told you."

"Told me *what*?" I said.

"To prepare for his test of transferring spirits, the demon sent some of his ghosts to collect people they found apart from the tourist crowds on the mountain," she said. "They were keeping those captives in the room next to the one where they were letting the few of us kami recover. There was one middle-aged couple I heard them dragging in—the wife was saying they only wanted their daughter, that she'd been living in the palace with the kami."

Her frantic eyes met mine directly for the first time since she'd realized what I was—and what I wasn't—last night. My mouth went dry.

The Ikedas. My birth parents. When we'd spoken with them, we'd left out the details of the threat the mountain faced, let them believe their daughter was still there. At the time it had seemed simpler that way.

But they hadn't wanted to wait any longer, and they'd gone looking for me.

They must have realized there would be some danger involved, but they'd been willing to risk it. To get me back. I brought my hands to my face. Now they were trapped along with the kami, waiting to be used as—what was the word Tomoya had used?—*specimens* in Omori's horrible experiment.

"Have you mentioned it to anyone else?" I asked. As soon as Chiyo knew, it'd be like yesterday at the keep. She loved her human parents as much as she loved Haru. She'd drop everything to try to rescue them.

Maybe that wouldn't be so awful. If Omori was focusing all his energies on the most crucial obstacle to his plans, he'd have sent almost all of his force to Ise, so there might not be many ghosts patrolling in the palace itself. From Ayame's earlier description, the kami were so subdued no guards were really needed now. If we skipped Ise and charged straight to the mountain—

No. My stomach lurched. Then we'd be going in without the sacred mirror. According to Rin's vision, Chiyo needed it with her to save the mountain. *If the prophecy is* not *fulfilled, failure is certain.*

If she faced the demon now, he might hurt her so badly she'd never recover in time for Obon. He might even kill her. Too many other lives depended on her.

On *her*.

Ayame was shaking her head. "I thought you were the one who should know. They were looking for you. But that's true—Chiyo, they raised her. Of course."

"Don't tell her," I said quickly.

"But..." Ayame started.

"Don't tell anyone," I repeated more firmly. I grasped Ayame's wrist. "Chiyo has a duty to carry out. We can't distract her from that. If she rushes over there unprepared, there's no way she can defeat the demon. Do you see?"

After a long moment, Ayame nodded. "You're right," she said. "It wouldn't do to worry her."

"Thank you," I said, and paused. "The room you were in, where was it in the palace?"

"At the front," Ayame said, looking puzzled. "About halfway between the main entrance and the hallway leading to your chambers."

I nodded, and she took the gesture as a dismissal. As she slipped out, I stared past her toward the faint glow behind the paper panels.

If I'd told the Ikedas who I really was when we were at their house, they would never have gone to the mountain. I'd been thinking only of myself, of my pain, not even considering their feelings. They'd wanted to see me so badly, and now they could lose their lives to Omori's ghosts before the day was out.

Chiyo couldn't take the risk of rescuing them, but *I* had no part in the prophecy. I didn't really matter in the grand plan to save Mt. Fuji. My human parents needed me. Maybe it was time I found something useful I could do on my own instead of tagging after the kami with my meager contributions. Chiyo and Takeo could go for the mirror as they'd intended, and I could go to the mountain and try to extricate the Ikedas from the fate I'd accidentally led them into.

The ghosts would pay no mind to a human girl. From what Ayame had said about the rooms, I should be able to reach them quickly after I entered the palace. Maybe I could even learn more about Omori while I was there. And if I failed, Chiyo and the others would fight on without me.

At least I'd have tried to set things right.

I stood gingerly to prevent the boards from creaking under my weight. If I left now while the others were sleeping, I could avoid the explanations and arguments and all that lost time.

I pulled out one of my ofuda and scrawled a quick message on the back. *I've found another way to help. I'll meet you in Ise.* Leaving it on the floor where I'd been sleeping, I scooped up my satchel and slipped into the hall. I darted around the corner and sprinted the last short distance to the front entrance—

—and nearly tripped over Keiji.

He was sitting on the front steps, his chin propped on his hands. When I caught myself, he glanced up, and we both froze. Cautiously, he eased onto his feet.

"Where are you going?" he said.

"A walk," I said, throwing out the first lie that came to me. "I couldn't sleep any more."

He studied me through the panes of his glasses. "No," he said. "You're leaving."

His careful scrutiny made my heart thump. "It's none of your business what I'm doing," I said, keeping my voice low.

He hesitated. Then he said, "Takeo might think it's his."

"Well, it isn't."

But if Keiji went to him, there was no way I could outrun a kami.

"If you tell me where you're really going," Keiji said, "I won't tell him. I won't tell anyone."

I couldn't sense whether he meant it, but I had to leave before this conversation caught someone else's notice.

"I'm going to Mt. Fuji," I said. "Ayame saw the Ikedas there. They went looking for me, and the ghosts caught them. I'm going to get them back."

I braced for a debate, but Keiji just looked at me a few seconds longer, his expression strained. Then he lowered his head.

"Good luck," he said.

As I left him behind and raced across the shrine grounds, a strange little ache formed behind my ribs, as if part of me wished he'd said more.

Beyond the walls, cars were roaring down the street. Even this early, the city kept moving. I halted by the gate, abruptly uncertain. It would take days to reach Mt. Fuji with no ki to hasten my feet.

A city bus rattled by, and I could have laughed at myself if I hadn't been so worried. Of course. I could get to the mountain the same way any other human would—I just had to find the right station.

⁂

A couple of hours later, I was sitting on a tour bus roaring up toward the drop-off spot partway up the mountain. The vehicle was less crowded than I'd expected. I knew from watching tourists arrive in past summers that the buses were usually packed during the peak season, but only half the seats around me were taken. I had a pretty good idea why. The woman in front of me had turned to her husband not long after we'd left the station, her brow knit, and said with a Hakata accent, "The hotel clerk said they've felt several tremors recently. You don't think there'll be another earthquake, do you?"

"I'm sure if there were any serious danger, they wouldn't be running the tour routes," he'd replied, sliding his arm around her shoulder. "There's always a little risk."

I guessed a lot of the other tourists had decided the risk wasn't worth it.

I couldn't make out any ghostlights between the trees beside the road, but I was sure at least a few of Omori's followers were there, keeping watch. I'd tucked my amulet under my shirt and the sheath of the short sword inside my pants, tugging the bottom of the blouse low to hide it.

During the journey, I'd worked out the details of my plan as much as I could. I'd make my way to the hidden opening in the mountain as if I were just another tourist wandering off the paths. Then I would sneak in and find the room where the human prisoners were being kept. I'd free the prisoners and hurry them back out. Once we were outside again, any ghosts who happened across us might not even realize we were escapees. As long as I didn't run into more ghosts than I could banish with my ofuda, it could work.

But only if I took Omori's strategy of narrowing my focus. I hated the thought of all the kami suffering in the palace, but I'd seen how weak Chiyo and Takeo had become after just a few hours surrounded by gore. I couldn't possibly carry even one kami out without being noticed. A lump had formed at the base of my throat when I'd considered that, one I couldn't swallow down.

Chiyo would come for them tomorrow, I told myself, with everything she needed to fulfill the prophecy and reclaim the mountain. I was making sure of that by doing this in her place.

When the bus jerked to a halt in the parking lot, I hopped out with the other passengers. They all headed into the courtyard with its snack booths and shops. Tour guides barked instructions to their groups and engines growled as more cars and buses pulled in. Fewer people might be traveling to Mt. Fuji this week, but its main stop was still busy.

My pulse thudded as I slipped away to the edge of the parking lot. I stopped where the concrete gave way to earth, and for one instant, my apprehension vanished. The wind rustled along the branches of the pines and birches I'd played amongst as a child and whipped through my hair, welcoming me home with the smells of dirt and stone and everything that lived upon it. The sensation was so achingly familiar that tears sprang to my eyes.

I blinked them away. I had no time to revel in this homecoming. Omori might start his "test" at any moment.

I strode across the stretch of grass by the side of the road and ducked into the forest. Twigs crackled under my heavy human feet. Other than the noise I was making and the whisper of the wind, the mountain seemed strangely quiet. No birds called overhead; no insects buzzed through the air. Had they all fled when Omori's army had come?

As I picked my way down the slope into the thicker forest, I glimpsed a few glints of light hovering amid the trees. There were the ghosts. I didn't think there were anywhere near so many here as when they'd first attacked the mountain, but there could be dozens my human eyes were missing. The sweat dampening my skin turned cold in spite of the intense summer heat.

I walked on, schooling my gaze to skim over any ghostlights I noticed. As long as they didn't know I'd seen them, they wouldn't realize there was anything odd about me.

When the gurgling of water reached my ears, I paused and wiped my forehead. Was that the palace spring?

A ghostlight drifted close to me, barely visible amid the sunbeams. If I hadn't been watching for them, I wouldn't have realized it was anything supernatural. I walked onward as if I hadn't seen it, resisting the urge to cringe as the edge of it brushed my shoulder. My hand dropped to rest over the ofuda in my pocket. The ghost must have decided I seemed harmless, though, because after a few more seconds it glided away.

As I hurried on, my eyes caught on more glints of ghostlight than before. Omori certainly hadn't left the mountain unguarded.

I scanned the landscape, ignoring the invisible soldiers. A few steps later, my shoes squished into damp soil spotted with mossy rocks. I'd almost stepped in the stream without noticing it. It was shallower than I was used to, but a steady trickle ran over the pebbles.

I'd come too far down—the entrance I was aiming for lay a short climb above me. Kneeling, I splashed water on my face and cupped it in my hands to drink. The coolness filled me, clearing my head.

Pure running water was as much a bane to evil spirits as blood was to kami. As long as I stayed close to the stream, the ghosts should avoid me.

I ambled on up, passing the main entrance without a glance. From the corner of my eye, I could see the cave was clotted with ghostlights. Even if I could have gone through that way now, I'd have been caught before I reached it.

But there was another way I didn't think the ghosts would have discovered.

I had to veer away from the stream as I left the cave behind, retracing the route Mother had led me along when I was younger so I would know the way if I needed it. I spotted the old cedar tree first, its swooping branches leaning into the cliffside, and then the jagged boulders like a line of teeth beneath it. I pushed past the thicket around the stones until I was hidden from the rest of the forest. No ghostlights lingered here. Relieved, I squeezed behind the trunk of the tree. My fingers caught on the edge of the crevice hidden there—the emergency passage for kami who'd been too badly injured to enter the palace through ki.

I slipped into the tight space. In the darkness, the passage appeared to end just a few feet from where I stood. Only if you walked right up to that wall could you make out the sharp turn that led farther into the mountain. If things had been as they should be, a kami would have been guarding this spot to ensure no human or malicious spirit accidentally found its way in.

I trod across the rough stone. The passage twisted and widened, ending at a sliding door. The light of the palace glowed through the panel. I eased close to the wooden frame and listened.

The hall on the other side would once have been echoing with footsteps and friendly voices. Now there was only dull silence—broken, abruptly, by a hoarse cry. It echoed through the wall and then sputtered out almost as quickly as it had risen. My back went rigid.

That had sounded like Father's voice.

Ayame had said they were torturing him and Mother to the brink of death. If only I could save at least them… I ached at my helplessness.

Tomorrow. Tomorrow, Chiyo would free everyone.

If she was able to get the mirror today. If, even with the sacred treasures, she was able to make Rin's vision real.

I shook those anxious thoughts away. Maybe what I observed here would help her accomplish that.

I nudged the door open and peered through the gap. Normally too, the palace would have been humming with the mountain's soothing ki, but my human senses had no awareness of it. I doubted it would have felt soothing right now, but the absence made the hall seem doubly empty.

If Ayame had described her room's location accurately, the one the human prisoners were in should be just a few down to my right. I crept down the hall. The rancid smell of long-dried blood seeped through the closed doors. Here and there, the gore had been spattered so thickly it showed through the painted screens like shadows marring the delicate images. Dark smears colored the floorboards. I caught a low moan and a pained murmur, and had to force myself to keep moving. Ayame's room had been clean. When I found that one, I'd know the human prisoners were beside it.

A flutter of movement overhead made me press against the wall. I had the instinct to sink right inside it—but of course I couldn't do that as a human. My gaze found a small brown body perching on a wooden beam. Mrs. Omori's sparrow. I hadn't expected her to follow me back here.

Just then, a swarm of ghostlights emerged from a room up ahead. I froze. There were more than a dozen of them, all swirling around a cluster of solid human forms. At least a few of the figures had their wrists bound behind them with rope, while others were shoving them on down the hall, away from me. Guns or knives hung from those figures' belts. Corporeal ghosts directing their human prisoners, I guessed.

My pulse skittered. I was minutes too late. And if even one of the ghosts glanced my way, I'd be caught. There was no way I could banish so many of them on my own before one of them used a weapon on me.

Maybe they were only moving the prisoners to a different room, and I'd get my chance later. I held my breath until the ghostly caravan had turned a corner leading deeper into the hall, and then I slunk after them. I'd just come up on the corner myself when a voice carried from behind me.

"Hey, you lost one!"

I whirled around to see a corporeal ghost striding toward me. My hand leapt to my pocket again, but I already heard the thud of footsteps behind me. My fingers clenched. I could try to fight my way out of this, and undoubtedly die. Or I could play along with the mistake he'd made. Play just one more harmless human until I had a better chance.

I let my arms go slack. "Why are you doing this to us?" I protested as the first ghost grabbed my wrist. My voice quavered of its own accord. "Let me go! I want to go home."

One of the ghosts who'd come up behind me frowned. "This one wasn't in the room when we got the others," she said.

"Well, she must have managed to wander off before you showed up," the first ghost said. "Good thing I noticed before Mr. Omori did."

"What's going on?" I said with a panic I didn't really need to fake.

"Come along," the woman said brusquely. She gripped my shoulder and propelled me around the corner. The cluster of ghostlights there parted, and the groping fingers of the other corporeal ghosts dragged me into their midst. I bit back the protest that rose in the back of my mouth.

I ended up inside the ring of ghosts next to the four figures with bound wrists: a young woman whose bleeding forehead showed she'd put up a fight, a stout older man who was trembling uncontrollably, and the thin, smooth-faced man and short, bob-haired woman who'd been introduced to me as Chiyo's parents. The Ikedas stared. Catching their eyes, I pressed my lips flat together, pleading wordlessly for their silence.

They both lowered their heads. As the ghosts hustled us down the hall, I kept my own head low and flicked my gaze from side to side, my heart thudding. I counted ten corporeal ghosts around us, some already with blades in their hands. At least as many ghostlights floated around them. And the deeper we went into the palace, the longer we'd have to run to reach our escape route. At least the ghosts hadn't bothered to tie my wrists—a small mercy. I brushed the grip of Takeo's sword through the fabric of my shirt, trying to hold on to hope.

After a minute, I realized we were heading to Mother and Father's suite of rooms. The ghosts ushered us through their outer chambers, leaving my exit point farther and farther behind. As we approached their audience room, a rich, measured voice rang out through the open doorway. Even though I'd never heard it before, its expansive timbre immediately brought to my mind the smiling figure from the photograph in my pocket.

"I've given you time to recover your strength. You've had many demonstrations of what will happen if you refuse. But if those demonstrations haven't been enough to convince you, I can arrange another. It's entirely in your hands."

Omori. It had to be. I'd wanted to learn what I could about the man, but suddenly I felt completely unready to meet him. My skin tightened as we stepped over the threshold.

After the emptiness of the palace's halls, the audience room felt suffocatingly crowded. Corporeal ghosts stood in a semi-circle turned toward the platform where Mother and Father would have sat. Ghostlights glowed amongst them. A kami crouched by the platform's edge, flanked by three other ghosts. One was training a gun on him, another a knife. A third was poised with a thick net caked with dried blood.

The kami wore the same guard uniform Takeo had for my birthday celebration. Omori had known the right kami to target, as precisely as he'd conducted his business ventures, I thought with a chill. Who would be more loyal, more unwilling to let their rulers suffer, than the ones who served as their protectors?

Only one figure stood on the platform itself. Omori's head was cocked, his arms crossed loosely over his chest as he studied the guard. He looked even more slight in person than he had in the photographs: his shoulders were narrow within his charcoal suit, his nose and mouth almost dainty. But the sight of him made my heartbeat shiver. Thin as he was, an aura of power flowed around him like a dark flame, so fierce even my human eyes could see its course. The hairs on my arms rose at the hum of ruthless energy rolling off of him. I could believe he was lending strength to thousands of ghosts just from the sense I got standing across the room from him.

His gaze slid over us, and I shifted behind the Ikedas. He wouldn't identify me as a threat, but the kami guard would recognize me.

"Thank you," Omori said to the ghosts who'd brought us in. "Now we can begin."

He turned back to the guard. The ghost with the knife dug the tip of her blade into the kami's shoulder. His face tensed with the effort to suppress a wince.

"Enough, Inoue," Omori said with an eerie calm. "We aren't here to hurt this gentleman. He simply needs to make his choice. Your lord continues to suffer the more you delay," he added, directly to the guard. "Why do you hurt him?"

"I've told you, what you ask for can't work," the kami said.

"You've told me you've never tried it," Omori said. "That's all we're going to do today. Try."

At that moment, the feathered shape of the sparrow flew across the room toward him, looking as if it intended to land on his shoulder. My breath caught. Would he see his wife? Would that—?

She dipped toward him, and he brushed the tiny bird aside with a wave of his hand and a ripple of his awful energy. It propelled the sparrow off toward the wall. He didn't even glance at the bird, his gaze fixed on the kami guard as if nothing had happened.

"You must release us," the kami was saying. "To imprison the mountain and its guardians like this—we can't tend to the wind and the rain, we can't soothe Fuji's temper. Everyone in the world is suffering because of your actions."

Omori shook his head. "We could be gone by the end of Obon, if you do as we require quickly enough. We only took the mountain at all because it was clear you wouldn't help us without an incentive. If you had been willing to reason, this could all have been avoided. What are a few thousand lives—lives we are owed—in comparison to the whole world?"

"The people you want to take over deserve their lives too."

"Well, whichever spirit is stronger will win, I suppose," Omori said. "It will be a fair struggle. Is that not the way of nature—to struggle to survive? If they want that life more, they will keep it. I'll ask one more time. Will you do as I've requested, or do you require further convincing?"

The kami didn't speak. The hum of Omori's energy heightened, reverberating through to my bones. He made a gesture so quick I barely saw it. One of the ghostlights disappeared into the wall. A second later, a hiss of pain filtered in from the neighboring room, followed by a strangled groan.

Father. He was so close. I balled my hands as a broken cry split the air. He sounded nearly dead already.

The kami guard looked toward the wall. With each noise, he quivered. There was a crack that sounded like bone breaking, and then a gasp and a muffled whimper, so hopeless and unlike my image of Father that I had to grit my teeth to hold in a cry of my own.

"All right." The kami extended his arm to Omori. "All right, I'll try, just stop!"

"Good," Omori said. With another gesture, the sounds on the other side of the wall ceased. He stepped off the platform and strolled toward our group. A fresh sweat broke over my skin.

The ghosts around us parted so Omori could look each of us over. His attention seemed to settle at once on Mrs. Ikeda. He rubbed his chin, an unearthly glint in his eyes.

No. My mind raced, thinking back through everything Mrs. Kobayashi had told me. She'd mentioned repeatedly how much he'd cared for his family. Had any fragment of that emotion lingered? He'd watched his children dying at his wife's side...

His lips had just parted as if he were about to speak when I blurted out, "Would you steal someone's mother from them?"

His gaze snapped to me as the energy around him flared. "What do you know about loss?" he demanded, fury crackling through his voice. My muscles had tensed, and it was all I could do not to cringe backward. But as I ducked my head, the waves of power settled against his body again. I saw his thumb curl across his palm to rub the thick gold wedding band on his finger.

"Let's start with her," he said.

Panic jolted through me in the instant before one of the ghosts cut the rope on the arms of the young woman with the bleeding forehead. He'd pointed at her. I swallowed thickly as Omori strode back to the platform, the ghost shoving the young woman after him. She stumbled, her head bowed. No fight was left in her slumped shoulders. I hadn't meant to turn his eyes on her. But how could I save all of us?

As the woman stopped in front of Omori, the other ghosts edged forward, eager to watch. After a few seconds, only one stood directly between me and the doorway. And everyone's attention was on the spectacle in front of them, not the remaining human prisoners.

This might be the only chance I'd get.

I displaced my shirt and carefully pulled the short sword out of its sheath, hiding the blade against my forearm. "Who gets the honor of being first, Mr. Omori?" a ghost who looked no older than fifteen called from the crowd. "Who gets to have her?"

Omori chuckled, but as his gaze roved over his assembled followers, an odd expression passed over his face. He looked almost lost. The flow of energy around him ebbed just slightly.

His thumb rose to rub his ring finger again.

"Something is missing," he murmured.

Then he drew himself up straighter, and all hint of confusion vanished. I kept watching him, tensed, searching for another clue to what I'd just seen. What had happened? Something had affected his power.

"Inoue," he said. "You've served well. Would you like her?"

The young woman flinched as the ghost walked up to her, knife still in hand. Inoue grinned, showing a row of uneven teeth, then turned to Omori and bowed.

"More thanks than I can give, Mr. Omori," she said.

Lowering my eyes, I set the sword against the thin rope that bound Mr. Ikeda's wrists. I didn't have time to observe further. This father, my human father, I might be able to save.

His arms twitched, then stilled as he realized it was me. The rope frayed quickly under the pressure of the blade.

The other two ghosts who'd been minding the kami guard propelled him forward. He considered the young woman, and she stared back, her eyes blank, like a rabbit gone numb with fear.

"I'm sorry," he said.

The coil around Mr. Ikeda's wrist split. He caught the rope so it didn't patter on the floor. I eased half a step to my right so I could reach Mrs. Ikeda's arms.

The kami guard raised his hands, shimmering with ki. He slid them into Inoue's chest. My eyes widened. I'd never seen the spirit transfer done, only heard about it.

Inoue whispered a prayer under her breath. Her body started to fade. Within it, the kami's fingers clasped around the spot where her heart would have been. A light sparked between them. As he drew it out, the ghost's form contracted around it until it was gone. He turned toward the human woman, placed his palms over her chest, and pushed.

The young woman gasped. Her body spasmed. My sword broke through the last strands of the rope at Mrs. Ikeda's wrists. I glanced toward the man standing beside us. He was a stranger to me, but he didn't deserve to be here any more than the Ikedas did. I set my sword against his bonds as well.

The young woman's legs buckled. She fell to her hands and knees. Coughing and gagging, she dribbled spit on the floor. The kami knelt beside her, smoothing his fingers over her brow, and her sputtering subsided.

The old man shuddered with the breaking of the rope. As I jammed my sword back into its sheath and palmed several ofuda from my pocket, the woman by the platform swayed to her feet. She looked down at her hands, flipping them over before touching her cheeks, her collarbone, her belly. An awed light filled her face.

"Thank you so much, great one," she said, bowing to Omori. Her voice had a distant quality, as if it came from another room.

My gut twisted. The transfer had worked. The ghost, Inoue, had wrenched the young woman's body away from its proper spirit.

And any moment now, the others were going to stop staring at her and start deciding which human they'd take next.

TWENTY

"RUN!" I murmured with a brief jerk of the Ikedas' hands toward the door. Then *I* was running—smacking an ofuda against the cheek of the ghostly man blocking our way, spinning to banish a second who turned at the sound of my feet. My pulse thumped in my ears. My parents rushed past me, the older man stumbling after them.

"Straight through the chambers and then down the hall to the right," I called to them. A third ghost leapt at me, and I caught him with another ofuda.

Before any of the other spirits reached me, I bolted through the doorway. The others had already made it to the end of the next chamber. Our feet pounded across the woven tatami floors. I was suddenly glad the ghosts hadn't bothered with the politeness of closing the sliding doors after they came into a room. We had a clear path all the way to the hall.

A blur of ghostlight flickered around me, and cold fingers penetrated my skin. A faint warmth flowed from the amulet at my chest, deflecting them. The chill receded, but a ghost solidified beside me, her finger on the trigger of her gun. I tossed an ofuda into her face. Three more ghosts shifted into corporeal form between me and the other escapees, charging after them. I pushed my legs faster and threw myself at the ghosts with charms fanned in my hands. As their forms blinked away, I rolled across the floor and back onto my feet with an ease that surprised me.

This body might be slower and heavier without the aid of ki, but now that I was adjusting to that, I knew the dance of combat as well as I ever had.

Still, it was also a body that tired quickly. My muscles burned as we burst into the hall. I glanced behind us. A stream of ghostlights was pouring out of the audience room in pursuit.

"Keep going!" I shouted to the others. My parents were hustling onward, but the older man's strength appeared to be flagging. I caught up with him as I dashed to the corner that led to the palace's long main hall. His breath was coming in wheezes.

"Just a little farther," I said to him.

A figure whipped around us with a blast of ki so strong it tingled to my core. The kami guard who'd transferred Inoue's spirit held out his hand to me. I guessed he'd slipped his minders in the confusion.

"Thank you," I gasped, shoving a bundle of ofuda to him. He whirled around me again, banishing a cluster of ghostlights right behind me.

We raced down the hall. Up ahead, Mrs. Ikeda stumbled, and Mr. Ikeda slowed to steady her.

"Hurry!" I said. "We're almost there." The door was just beyond them, the painted crane with its wings spread beckoning us from the paper panel. I leapt to make sure they didn't run past it.

A fresh wave of ghostlights surged around us. As they started to solidify, I dug into my satchel and tossed salt in a circle around us. The dim shapes cringed back with a hiss, but a group of them had fallen on the older man behind me. He collapsed to the floor as they swarmed over him.

"No!" I cried, reaching for another handful of salt. Before I could close my fingers around it, the air reverberated with a gunshot.

Mr. Ikeda lurched against the wall. Blood welled through his shirt where he clutched his side. My stomach flipped over.

With a silent, pained apology to the man we were abandoning, I sprinted the last few feet and hauled open the door. "We can make it," I said, wrapping my arm around Mr. Ikeda's shoulders to urge him through the doorway. Another shot rang out as we squeezed inside. I didn't dare look behind me. If we could just get to the tourist stop with its shops and buses, we'd find help there.

Mr. Ikeda's breath had gone ragged, but he hurried on, Mrs. Ikeda close behind him. I jerked the door shut before running after them, sprinkling more salt on the floor as I went. That should at least stop the ghosts from following us directly.

We hurried through the cave and staggered from the narrow crevice into the forest. "This way," I said, clambering along the slope. It wouldn't be long before the ghosts warned the sentries outside.

One materialized in front of me and vanished just as swiftly with my thrust of an ofuda. Others turned corporeal above us, their shoes crunching over the pine needles. I urged the Ikedas in front of me along a winding path through the trees, hoping the trunks would shield us from bullets. Mr. Ikeda was still holding his side, his face streaked with sweat. Mrs. Ikeda gripped his arm. She cringed as a gunshot crackled behind us and pulled him along faster.

A ghost charged up behind me, and I whipped around just long enough to banish him. Another shot rang out. Bark burst on the pine I'd just passed. I ran on, my thoughts rattling through my head. Were we leading a pack of murderers straight into a crowd of innocent tourists? Should we head for the road instead—surely someone there would stop and help us? The ghosts couldn't outrun a car.

"Sora," Mrs. Ikeda whispered, looking up. I followed her gaze and blinked, not quite believing my eyes.

A scarlet kite was soaring above the treetops. Dark green paint streaked across the fabric. The wind shifted, and I saw the name written on it.

Sora.

Someone had come for us. For me.

Whoever it was had to be at the tourist stop—that was the only place nearby there'd be room to send up a real kite. With renewed vigor, I scrambled onward. Mr. Ikeda teetered. I lunged between two ghosts who appeared by his side and banished them. I only had four ofuda left, clutched in my right hand. My left closed around my last fistful of salt. But with a few more steps, I made out the shining colors of the cars in the parking lot through the tree trunks.

The sharp snap of a gunshot split the air behind us, and my shoulder jerked forward with a lance of pain. My fingers twitched, dropping the salt. I cried out and pushed myself faster.

We burst onto the thick grass between the forest and the parking lot. Amid the buses and cars, the kite's string sliced down from the sky into the hands of a shaggy-haired boy in a rumpled blue T-shirt.

My heart stuttered. "Keiji!" I yelled.

He turned as we reached the pavement. "Keep after them!" a voice shouted behind us. Keiji must have seen the panic flash across my face. The kite string slipped from his fingers, and he dashed to a car parked a few feet away. Mrs. Ikeda and I helped Mr. Ikeda over the low fence surrounding the lot, ignoring the stares of the tourists.

A slate-gray sedan jolted to a halt in front of us. Keiji waved us in from the driver's seat. I yanked open the back door and pulled Mr. Ikeda inside, Mrs. Ikeda clambering in after us.

"Go!" I said as she slammed the door. The car lurched forward and roared toward the road.

"I can't drive too fast," Keiji said. "If I'm speeding... Technically the fact that I'm driving at all is illegal."

"I think this is fast enough," I said, glancing through the back window. If the ghosts were still following us, they were staying hidden amid the trees.

Mr. Ikeda groaned, slumping in the middle seat. Blood was seeping over his fingers. I pulled out my short sword and cut a strip off the bottom of my tunic. Then I leaned over and wrapped the fabric around his middle as tightly as I could.

"We'll get you to a hospital," I said. And then, to Keiji, "There's one in the first town this road passes through. We'll have to turn at the first major road and watch for the signs."

He nodded, his knuckles pale where he was gripping the steering wheel. They whitened further as the car bumped over an uneven patch in the asphalt. I hesitated, watching the profile of his face.

He'd come. Not Takeo or Chiyo or any of the kami, who might have had half a chance of taking on an army of ghosts alone, but him.

Of course, they would never have thought to bring a car. Which was exactly what we'd needed.

My own wound throbbed. I examined my shoulder. The bullet appeared to have only grazed me, but the short sleeve of my shirt was damp with blood. I cut another strip off the bottom and wound it around the side of my shoulder until the ends were short enough to tie. It still hurt, but at least that should contain the bleeding.

My mind tripped back to our dash through the palace's hall, to the older man who'd fallen. What had the ghosts done to him? What *were* they doing to him right now? If only I'd...

But I couldn't think of any way I could have gotten all of us out alive. It seemed like a miracle any of us had escaped.

Mrs. Ikeda rubbed her husband's back. He sighed. I glanced over at them and found them both watching me.

"Thank you," Mr. Ikeda said. He laid the fingers of his unbloodied hand over mine. "Daughter?"

My arms stiffened. They were looking at me so earnestly.

Hopeful, even after everything we'd just been through. This was what they'd come to the mountain for, after all. To find their real daughter.

"Yes," I said. My throat was so tight the word came out in a whisper.

Mrs. Ikeda—my mother—leaned forward. "I am so sorry," she said. "I should have known, *we* should have known, the moment we saw you. To not even recognize our own child... I can't blame you for keeping your distance."

I opened my mouth, but no sound came out. Compassion told me to reach out to her, to reassure her that everything between us was fine now. Except it wasn't. They were my birth parents. I hadn't wanted them to die. But they were still the people who'd given me up, who'd traded my life for Chiyo's.

"It'll take time," my father murmured. His head drooped against the back of the seat, but his gaze was steady as he held mine. "You don't know us. And we don't really know you yet."

"But we want to," my mother broke in. "We want to very, very much. Every night, we looked toward Mt. Fuji and prayed that you were safe and well. We talked about what you might be doing, how you'd be growing up... I kept an album for you, with photographs and notes. To help you get back what you missed, when you returned to us."

The tangle inside me loosened just a little.

"The kami were good to me," I said. "I was happy on Mt. Fuji. I have to keep trying to help them. But I do want to know you too. When this war is over..."

She nodded. "You must come by. We'll look at the album

together, and we'll talk, and it'll get easier. I'm sure it will. There is a space in our home waiting for you, whenever you're ready to take it."

"I'll come," I said. It seemed better not to make any promise more specific than that.

The slope of the road flattened as we left the mountain behind. Keiji drove through the thinning forest and into town. A few minutes after he turned off the highway, passing within a few streets of the Nagamotos' house, we spotted the hospital's sign.

My mother and I helped my father out of the car and into the Emergency waiting area. As a nurse hustled over to help, I squeezed his hand and slipped back outside. I watched my birth parents be ushered down the hallway by a doctor. Then I opened the front passenger door of the car and sat down beside Keiji.

"Okay," I said.

He didn't ask what I meant. He just hit the gas and swung the car toward the highway.

"Are *you* okay?" he asked after a minute.

"Yes. Getting there." But I might not have been if he hadn't shown up. I groped for the right words, but nothing seemed adequate. "Thank you," I said.

He shrugged, his gaze darting to me and then back to the road. "I figured I owed you. Got you into trouble before, maybe this time I could get you out of it."

His light-hearted tone sounded forced. The memory of the "trouble before" hung between us. I ran my fingers along the edge of the leather seat. "Where did you get the car?"

Keiji hesitated. "It's—it was—my brother's. He started taking me out where there weren't many people around and teaching me how to drive when I was, like, twelve. Even kept up the lessons now and then after... you know."

Tension strained the corners of his eyes and mouth, as if he didn't know whether to be sad or angry. The feeling echoed inside me. I thought of my human parents and of Mother and Father, decisions made and lies told, and how far I'd fought for them all the same. Betrayal didn't stop you from caring about someone.

"He mattered a lot to you," I said.

"He wasn't a bad guy," Keiji said in a rush. "Obviously he's got his priorities all out of whack now, but he was always there for me, even when I was being a dumb little brother. I don't know if I'd have made it as long as I have without him."

Looking at him, my pulse skipped in a now-familiar way. It wasn't so hard to believe that he could have been misled by his brother without actually meaning to hurt us, was it? That he could have managed to ignore his suspicions about Tomoya's true intentions? I'd missed the hints that Keiji was hiding something from me because I'd been so wrapped up in the idea of how he felt about me, and I'd known him less than a week. He'd depended on Tomoya all his life.

But that hadn't stopped him from rising to my defense when his brother had attacked me. From staying by my side after I'd banished Tomoya. Even now, he'd known he could be arrested for driving, he could have been swarmed by hostile ghosts, but he'd come anyway, for me.

Something opened up in my chest, as if a shell protecting my heart had cracked open and fallen away. Keiji had picked me. And it wasn't out of some inherent need to be loyal, like Takeo, but because he'd decided to.

At the thought of Takeo, my muscles tensed. Despite the note I'd written, he wouldn't have been happy about my disappearance. "What did you tell the others when you left?" I asked.

"I kept my promise," Keiji said. "I didn't say anything about you. Actually, I didn't tell them anything at all. You left, and I was sitting there, and I thought of the car and how in dangerous operations people always need a getaway vehicle, and... I didn't want something to happen to you because I couldn't get my act together in time. So I just went. They probably figure I ran off to find my brother."

"Well, when we catch up with them, they'll see that wasn't true. We should go back to Tokyo and check whether they've left a message for us, and then follow them to Ise." If the fight went long or Takeo felt Chiyo needed more recovery time before rushing in, we might even be able to help there.

"I don't really care what they think," Keiji said. "As long as..." He nudged his glasses up on his nose. "I know I was stupid, and I screwed things up. I lied about what was happening with Tomoya. But I want you to know, everything else, all the other things I said to you—I really meant them."

My lungs felt suddenly empty. I grasped for something to say, but all that came out was, "Okay."

He swallowed. "I know everything with us is probably too messed up now, and I'm not as strong or as brave or as whatever as Takeo is, but—"

"Of course you are," I interrupted, the words startled back into me. "You're just as brave as him."

"Right," Keiji said with a disbelieving laugh.

"I mean it," I said. "Takeo just is the way he is, the way kami are. His nature tells him how to react. When the people he's loyal to are threatened, he defends them. It's not really about bravery." I remembered with a pang how I'd wished to be Sora the strong, charging into every situation without worries or fear. "Being human, the answers aren't obvious. You have to choose whether you do the difficult thing or the easy thing. It takes a lot more courage to do the difficult thing you don't have to do, that scares you, than to just... follow what you automatically know to do. So you're *more* brave than he is, or Chiyo, really."

I stopped. Maybe I could have said the same thing about myself.

Keiji's lips curled slightly upward. "So... you don't hate me then?"

"Hate you?" The way I'd spoken to him in the keep, the way I'd avoided him afterward. Yes, it could have looked that way. "No," I said. I'd felt anger, confusion, and hurt, certainly, but not hate. But saying that didn't seem like enough. "I'm glad you came. It would have been really hard getting out of there without you."

He was definitely smiling now. I hadn't seen his usual grin since we'd arrived in Tokyo, and I'd missed it.

Then a shadow crossed his expression. "What your kami friend who escaped said about Omori's plans... Did you see— Are they really—"

The memory of the young woman's body shuddering leapt into my mind, and bile rose to the back of my mouth. "They're doing it," I said quietly. "I saw— Omori forced one of the kami to put a ghost into a woman they'd kidnapped. It looked like, afterward, the woman's spirit was just gone." Smothered by the invader.

"I don't understand how Tomoya can think it's right to take someone else's life," Keiji said. "I guess Omori has them all convinced... Maybe he'll think twice now that he's seen how humans can fight back."

"I don't think he'd be that easily swayed," I said. What *had* Omori made of our escape? I'd been too busy fending off ghosts to notice his reaction.

Maybe he'd already put it out of his mind, focusing on the next steps of his plan. If the dead could become so wrapped up in their last thoughts they hardly noticed anything else, and Omori had already been inclined toward intense concentration, his mindset might be even narrower.

But it had appeared as if there were still something more in him. I'd seen that moment of confusion. If any part of the man he'd been remained, if what Mrs. Kobayashi had said about him were even partly true, I couldn't imagine he'd have felt at ease with his current methods. Was there some way we could reach that part of him, that was barely more than a glimmer?

I rubbed my face. It wasn't likely Omori would give us a chance.

Keiji pulled a CD out of a thin binder attached to the flap over his head and inserted it into a slot in the dashboard. "You're into music, right?" he said. "This band is one of my favorites."

A rumble of drums rolled from the speakers in a slow but powerful rhythm. One guitar and then another sprinkled the beat with a twisting line of notes. The soft keen of a violin lifted to meet them. Finally, a voice at turns smooth and ragged wound out between the instruments, singing his love for the town he called home. I let my head sink back, breathing in the song.

"I like this," I said, and Keiji's smile returned.

"Ah," he said a few minutes later as the road curved past the first block of glinting high rises. "Back in the big city."

I peered out the window. Shops and office buildings whipped by. And then, in the window of a travel agency, a poster featuring a vibrant photo of Mt. Fuji.

The sight broke me out of the music's reverie. All those tour buses, the tourists wandering the parking lot and the courtyard, climbing to the peak. The tremors hadn't put that much of a dent in the crowds.

Tomorrow night, the veil between the afterworld and the world of the living would dim, and Omori's army would have a hoard of unsuspecting bodies right there for the taking.

Keiji had to park the car on a street a few blocks from the shrine. We hurried the rest of the way back, impatient to be continuing to Ise. Despite the torn hem of my shirt fluttering around my waist, the sword slung at my hip, and the dappling of blood surrounding the makeshift bandage on my shoulder, I received only a few brief stares from passers-by. For a couple of minutes, being lost in the city crowd was almost relaxing. No ghosts, no guns, no demons or ogres. The urban bustle wasn't so bad.

Then we slipped down the shrine's walkways and darted

around the back of the sanctuary building, where we found Ayame pacing by the pond.

"Sora!" she said when she saw me. "You're all right! Takeo will be so relieved. The poor boy. When he saw the two of you were missing, he was ready to rip the city apart."

"What?" I said, my heart sinking. "But they went to Ise, didn't they?"

"My dear, he and Chiyo and that human boy of hers have been searching for you all morning," Ayame said. "I don't think they meant to go anywhere until they found you. Chiyo said she thought you had to be all right, because you always looked after yourself just fine, but Takeo wouldn't hear of leaving."

Oh no. "*You* must have realized where I was," I said.

She lowered her eyes, her dainty fingers fidgeting with the sleeve of her robe. "You said I shouldn't tell Chiyo what I'd told you. If I'd said you'd gone to the mountain, they'd have gone too, wouldn't they? Without all they need to defeat the demon? I couldn't be responsible for that."

She was right—the outcome probably would have been worse if she'd spoken up. But what was Takeo thinking? I'd left that note so he'd know I'd gone of my own accord. Even if he'd worried about my vague explanation, how could he have put finding me ahead of saving Mt. Fuji?

A weight settled in my gut. I'd just said it to Keiji, hadn't I? Takeo didn't decide, he just followed his nature. He still felt loyal to me, even if he shouldn't. Maybe even more loyal than he felt to the mountain itself, since he'd been specifically assigned to watch over me. I'd thought he would put Chiyo, as the real daughter of his rulers, first; I'd thought, when I'd told him we wouldn't be more than friends, he'd let go.

I should have realized it would take more than that. I knew how unshakable kami nature was. Maybe some part of me had liked feeling he was looking out for me still. Liked knowing I hadn't lost that one last piece of my old life.

I had to fix this. I wasn't the one who needed him, not anymore.

"Do you have any idea where they are now?" I asked. "Or any way to find them? We can't miss the last train to Ise."

Ayame started to shake her head, and then paused. "I brushed Chiyo's hair last night before she went to sleep. I think..." She dashed into the building and returned a moment later with a lavender strand of hair pinched between thumb and forefinger. "This will lead me to her as yours led me to you. And Takeo said he'd stay with her."

"Go," I said. "Quickly. Mt. Fuji depends on it."

Her delicate face hardened with resolve. She darted away, fading into her ethereal state as she murmured to the strand of hair.

Trying not to stew over how long it would take Ayame to reach Chiyo, I went to the pond to wash the blood from my shoulder. When only a dull stain remained, I squeezed my shirt sleeve dry and sat down on the platform to prepare ofuda to replace those I'd used on the mountain. I couldn't stop my feet from tapping restlessly.

"Do you need more salt too?" Keiji asked, bringing out a new bag. A hint of uncertainty had crept into his expression, as if he were afraid the peace we'd made in the car might not extend here.

"Yes, please," I said, and made myself smile. "Do you want to help with the charms?"

"Whatever I can do," he said as he sat down beside me. The way he smiled back sent a warm tingle through me, and for that moment my own smile didn't feel so forced.

Close to an hour had passed when voices reached us from around the side of the building. I leapt to my feet and ran to meet them.

"You see," Ayame said when I came around the corner. "She's here, perfectly safe."

"I told you," Chiyo said to Takeo. She slung her arm around Haru's waist and raised her hand to me with her fingers spread in a victory sign.

As Takeo's dark eyes found mine, they held nothing but relief. But before I could say anything, his gaze slid to something behind me, and he stormed forward, drawing his sword.

"Takeo—" I started.

"You!" he said, pointing the sword at Keiji, who'd come around to join us. "What did you do to her? Where did you take her?"

The color drained from Keiji's face. He took a halting step backward, holding up his hands.

"I was *helping* her," he said.

Takeo made a derisive noise. My chest clenched up. I hadn't considered how it might look, with both of us gone. Of course Takeo would assume we'd gone together. He must have thought Keiji had forced me to write that note.

"Stop it," I said, stepping between them. Takeo flinched as the tip of his sword brushed my shirt, and he jerked it back. "Keiji's telling the truth—he was helping me. And we're both fine."

"You're hurt," he said.

"I went to the mountain," I said, as calmly as I could. "Ayame told me that my parents—my human parents—went there looking for me, and the ghosts took them for Omori to use. So I got them out. They're okay," I added, glancing at Chiyo.

"The ghosts grabbed Mom and Dad?" she said. "Why didn't you tell me? I'd have sliced and diced the whole bunch of them."

"I knew I could get in there without being noticed," I said. "And you're not meant to face Omori until you have all three of the sacred treasures. You were supposed to go to Ise this morning."

Takeo frowned. "We couldn't leave Tokyo when you—"

"You *could* have," I said. "You're kami; you serve Mt. Fuji. I'm human—I have nothing to do with that anymore, not really. You should have been doing what was best for the mountain and all the kami there."

"Sora," he protested, and my throat closed up. I could barely remember a time before Takeo had been my best friend, my playmate, and my protector. He would have died for me. I couldn't even tell him how thankful I was to have had him in my life. But that bond had to be broken now.

I held his gaze, tensing my arms at my sides. "There is nothing more between us," I said firmly. "Any ties you feel to me, sever them. I am not family, I am not a friend, I'm only a fellow traveler. Until Mt. Fuji is reclaimed, that's the only way you'll think of me. Have I said enough?"

For a moment, there was only silence and the pressure of five pairs of eyes, staring at me. I looked only at Takeo. His jaw had tightened and his face darkened, but then he inclined his head. Accepting.

And so the last bit of loyalty he gave to me was to take that loyalty away.

My own eyes felt abruptly hot. I turned. "Now let's catch the next train to Ise. We can't risk losing a minute more."

TWENTY-ONE

THE SUN blazed over us as we approached the courtyard that led to Ise's massive shrine. Even though it was late in the day, heat rose in thick waves off the streets. Hundreds of people brushed past us and the tourist shops done up with old-fashioned roofs and dark wooden frames, wandered across the courtyard, and ambled along the wooden bridge that arced over a shallow river to the shrine grounds.

"I've heard this is one of the most popular shrines in the country," Keiji said. "Looks like that's still true."

"Popular not just with the living, today," Chiyo said. "There are so many ghosts out there. And people are walking right through them! It's pretty creepy. Can't you see them at all?"

I squinted, but I could only make out the faintest glimmers amid the crowd. Anyone not looking for them would have assumed it was only the sun catching on buttons, zippers, purse clasps. The daylight hid the ghosts nearly completely.

"They appear to be using the same strategy as in Nagoya,"

Takeo said. "Surrounding the borders of the shrine in large numbers. Larger numbers than before."

"We just have to reach the bridge, right?" I said. A huge torii shaded this end of the crossway. Once we passed under the gate's protection, the ghosts shouldn't be able to follow.

Takeo nodded, but he looked solemn. In Tokyo, he'd found a few other kami who were capable and willing to join us, even obtained swords for those with hands and taught them a few basic moves, but we were still vastly outnumbered. We didn't even have Ayame's support, as she'd been so exhausted after her escape yesterday and tracking down Chiyo today that she'd stayed behind.

"It's a good thing this place will be closing soon," Chiyo remarked. "I wouldn't like to try to fight all those ghosts with so many people in the way."

The ghosts weren't bothering anyone now, only waiting for Chiyo to appear. The possibilities that had been stirred up by my conversation with Mrs. Kobayashi itched at me.

"The ghosts could have more planned that we can't see," I said. "I want to take a look around. I don't think they'll worry about one more human."

Takeo bowed his head. "Retreat immediately if they show any hostility."

"Do you want—" Keiji started.

I quickly shook my head. "I'll be less likely to catch their attention alone."

I skirted the edges of the courtyard, my stomach knotting as I realized just how many of those glints I was catching from the corners of my eyes. In the packed parking lot, they danced amid the reflections on the car windows. But none stopped me as I trod past the stretch of trees along the river bank and stepped beneath the torii.

The moment I crossed under the gate, my heart leapt. I peered along the bridge's pale length toward the forested grounds on the opposite bank. Maybe I could just stroll on over there myself...

Something moved within the thick vegetation along the river. A body too tall and hunched to be a person. I caught only a glimpse, but it was enough to chill me.

It wasn't only the ghosts we had to worry about today. The shrine's protections mustn't have been enough to keep out ogres… and whatever other creatures Omori might have summoned to his cause as word of his invasion of Mt. Fuji spread. Even if I could have convinced the shrine kami to give me the mirror if I headed in there alone, I doubted I'd make it to their sanctuary alive.

The crush of tourists on the bridge was already thinning, all of them heading back to the courtyard as closing time approached. I walked a little farther and peered down the river. On our side, glints of ghostlight showed all along the tree-lined bank. They didn't want to give us the chance to take an alternate route. Not far down from the bridge, a strip of wide, flat stones made nearly as easy a path across the river.

I considered that for a moment, and then I made my way back to my companions.

"If there are other creatures lurking in the shrine, we'll deal with them there," Takeo said after I'd shared my observations. "Our first concern is getting past the ghosts."

"Sora had a cool idea yesterday," Chiyo said, nudging me. "It's me Omori really wants to stop. So if the ghosts think I'm already captured, they won't stick around."

"They're not going to believe us just telling them that," Haru said.

"I'm sure they've been warned not to listen to me again," Keiji said. His forehead furrowed. "Could a kami pretend to be a ghost, and tell them?"

"We couldn't make our legs disappear completely to imitate their appearance," Takeo said, but Keiji's suggestion had sparked an inspiration of my own.

"But a kami could pretend to be another kami," I said. "Maybe we can't convince them that Chiyo is already captured, but what if we convinced them she's somewhere she's not? All they'll be looking for is a young woman kami holding a sword. Pushing all your ki to the surface of your skin and into the sword, any of you could give the impression of being that powerful. If they think Chiyo is trying to cross the river at a different spot, they may leave the bridge... not unguarded, but less so."

Takeo glanced to the side, where our ethereal kami companions must be standing. "Sumire says she will help in any way she can," he said.

I hesitated as an uneasy realization struck me. We were going to send a substitute into harm's way in Chiyo's place—again. "She could be hurt," I said. "Badly. If she and most of the other kami make a run for that path of stones as if they're trying to sneak across there, the ghosts will attack her with all the strength they have."

Takeo tipped his head, listening to the violet kami. "Sumire says it will be worth that sacrifice to see Chiyo reach the mirror and recover Mt. Fuji." He turned to the rest of us. "We'll need to send most of the kami with her for the deception to be convincing. If the ghosts don't fall for the ploy, we'll be at an even greater disadvantage. You are the only one who has been in Omori's presence, Sora. How sure are you that this will work?"

I thought of the slight yet immensely powerful man I'd spoken to in the palace audience room. The precision with which he'd targeted the kami guard. His total dismissal of his wife's spirit.

"He'll have told the ghosts that only Chiyo matters," I said. "To ignore every other kami unless they're in the way of getting to her. To stop at nothing to capture her again. I'm sure of it. And the last thing they'll want to risk is disappointing him."

"All right," Chiyo said with a pump of her fist. "Let's do this."

Keiji raised an eyebrow. "Just a thought—maybe we should cover your hair. Someone might notice *that*."

Chiyo rolled her eyes at him, but she found a stretchy cloth hat in one of the shops and managed to stuff her ponytails into it. Her jeweled necklace was already hidden under her blouse, and her sword in a cloth carry bag Haru had helped her pick out earlier. There was nothing to indicate she was anything but another kami follower.

With evening creeping in, the cars and tourist buses were leaving, and the shops starting to carry in their displays. The glimmers of ghostlight were easier to see now that the sunlight was dimming and there were few people in the courtyard for them to hide among. They were bunched so close together that they formed an eerie glow in the open space. The remaining tourists gave the area confused glances before hurrying off.

"All except the monkey and the oak have gone with Sumire," Takeo reported to the rest of us. "When we decide to move forward, we should form a ring around Chiyo to help hide her from view. Chiyo, keep your sword concealed and attack only with ofuda, unless you have no other choice."

We all watched the courtyard as the last human visitors slipped away. The ghostly glow churned and rippled. What if I'd misjudged?

Then all at once the ghostlights surged to the north, where Sumire had headed. Takeo smiled grimly. "They're calling for help, saying they've spotted her."

As the lights streamed out of the courtyard, more streamed in from farther south. We waited, braced to run. The glowing haze in the courtyard dimmed before my eyes. Chiyo winced as if she'd heard a painful sound my ears couldn't make out.

"They'll discover the deception soon," Takeo said. "We've got some advantage—we must use it now."

We hurried forward, our feet thudding far too loudly over the stone tiles. I gripped several ofuda in one hand and Takeo's short sword in the other.

Several of the ghostlights converged around us, whipping away again as they brushed against our amulets. My spirits lifted. We didn't matter at all to them, not when they thought they had Chiyo within their grasp elsewhere.

We were ten feet from the bridge when Takeo flinched. "They know!" he whispered, and sprang forward. Even as the rest of us raced after him, a wave of ghostlights crashed into the courtyard.

Chiyo let out a battle cry and drew her sword. Her hat fell off, her lavender hair spilling loose.

The greatest mass of ghosts rushed into the narrowing space between us and the bridge. As Chiyo slashed through them, I kept close to her side, whipping out charms as quickly as I could. Several ghosts turned corporeal around us, weapons ready. I knocked the knife from one's hand with my sword, caught it, and threw it into the wrist of another corporeal ghost just before he could shoot his gun. The blaze of ghostlights all around us began to blur my vision. Heart pounding, I grabbed another handful of ofuda from my satchel, just in time to banish a ghost who'd lunged at Keiji while he was fending off another. Other than him at my right and Takeo at my left, I didn't have time to look around to check on the others.

Chiyo grunted, and a rancid droplet struck my cheek. One of the ghosts had tossed a bloody rope into our midst, catching Chiyo's arm. Before her sword could falter, I chopped through the rope with mine. Chiyo flung it away, her hand wavering and then steadying again. She swept through the last line of ghosts, scattering them into glinting dust, and staggered beneath the gate onto the bridge.

I had no chance to rejoice. The whirlwind of ghosts contracted even tighter around the rest of us without Chiyo's sword slicing them away. I tossed ofuda into their midst and grabbed Keiji's wrist, hauling him toward the bridge. Takeo was just stepping onto it when a row of ghosts turned corporeal around us humans. One jabbed at Haru's amulet, severing the cord. Three more struck out at Keiji at once. Two charged at me. I stumbled to the side. Haru's legs wobbled as a ghost reached into his body. Even as he managed to hit her with an ofuda, two more barreled in to take her place. A blade raked across my ribs and my lungs clenched. There were too many of them. We weren't going to make it.

Then a voice shouted, "Off with you!" and a small, shining figure whirled around us, parting the crowd of ghosts. We dashed under the gate. Takeo and Chiyo caught us and dragged us up the bridge. Keiji was panting, and Haru grimaced as he leaned back against the railing, his cheek red where a ghost had rammed him with a knife hilt. The glowing figure somersaulted after us, landing on the boards with a patter of leather sandals. Rin gave us a satisfied smirk.

"It appears I arrived at a most beneficial time," the sage said in her dry voice.

Before I could ask how she'd gotten here or where she'd been, Keiji made a startled noise. I followed his gaze back toward the courtyard.

The ghostlights had settled, several corporeal figures standing in their midst, all of them watching us. One near the back of the crowd was walking toward the bridge. He strode right to the edge of the gate, the red streaks in his hair clearly visible even in the fading daylight.

Tomoya.

So it was true. Omori had taught the ghosts how to come back.

"A nice trick," he said. "I applaud your ingenuity. I don't think the allies you set us on are enjoying themselves quite so much."

"Tomo," Keiji said, his voice a rasp. He swallowed audibly. "You have to stop this!"

"You don't understand yet, little brother," Tomoya said. "You will. Once we've taken care of these insurgents." His gaze rested on Chiyo. He smiled his sharp little smile as if he weren't worried at all, and a fresh chill washed over me.

"*If* you make it through the shrine, we'll be waiting for you," he said. "You won't trick us a second time."

He drew back into the crowd, his physical form fading. "Tomoya!" Keiji called, but his brother had already vanished. To our sight, at least.

"He has even more of the demon's power in him than the others," Takeo said. "I think he is acting like a river, carrying the main flow of energy across the distance before it streams from him to his associates."

That sounded like Omori's sort of efficiency. Maybe carrying all that energy had corrupted Tomoya's mind even faster.

"We should go for the mirror as quickly as possible," I said. "Before they come up with a plan for our return."

"Hold on a second," Chiyo said, peering down at Rin. "Who are *you*, anyway?"

"This is the sage Rin," Takeo said hurriedly. "The one who foresaw you saving Mt. Fuji."

"Oh!" Chiyo said, her eyes widening. "We thought the ogres got you," she told Rin. "They made a real mess of your house in the tree."

"Hmmm," Rin said. "What is merely broken can be fixed. The ogres could hold me but not destroy. They all moved here on the demon's orders, and within the shrine, I had the strength to avoid further holding." She gave Chiyo a measured look. "You have learned some, but not all I would have liked. But the days for training are past."

"I can handle this, no problem," Chiyo said, hefting her sword. "We've taken down ogres before."

"Our enemies multiply," Rin muttered in her obscure way, but I could guess what she meant. My skin crawled as we marched over the bridge to the shrine grounds.

A second after our feet crunched onto the gravel path, I got my confirmation: a hulking figure with a mane of maroon hair and horns jutting from its cheeks burst from between the trees beside us. Chiyo leapt forward, her sword blazing as it plunged into the ogre's chest. Three black dog-like creatures sprang over the hedge on the other side of the path, their eyes shining red and their fangs gleaming. They were followed by an immense cat with two snaking tails. A shriek split the air above us, and a pack of body-less heads, streaming dark hair and gnashing their teeth, descended on us.

"Nukekubi," Keiji muttered, edging closer to me. Now that he was actually faced with the monsters from his books, he looked as though he'd preferred keeping them in his imagination. I swiveled on my feet, trying to track all of our enemies at once.

The oak and monkey kami sprang to our defense. They caught one of the demon dogs between them, the oak man stabbing it awkwardly. Takeo leapt to meet the monstrous cat. I held out my blade and shoved Keiji behind me as the second dog snapped at my arm. Its breath smelled like burnt meat. As I thrust the beast away, Keiji slapped an ofuda against the nose of one of the nukekubi that had dived at us. The wan face cringed and circled away, but it didn't disappear.

"Damn," Keiji said, his voice shaking. "I figured it was worth a try. The salt might repel them."

"Even if it doesn't, throw it in their eyes," I suggested. I stuffed my remaining ofuda into my satchel and palmed a handful of my salt.

Chiyo sliced her sword through the air, cutting two of the flying heads in half. The pieces fell to the ground with a sickening patter. Takeo shoved aside the dead body of the two-tailed cat.

"Push on," he said.

We ran down the path, Rin taking the lead with a speed I wouldn't have expected from her aged body. She might not have trained in the martial arts as intensely as Takeo, but she still had skill. When another ogre lurched out in front of us, she dashed up its gangly body in a blur of motion, kicked out at its collarbone, and twisted its neck at the same time. It collapsed, its spine cracking.

The sage stumbled as she hit the ground. She pressed her palm to the path before pushing herself upright, and I remembered her comment about her power being connected to her valley. And who knew what the ogres had done to her to keep her imprisoned until now? How much longer could she keep fighting?

Two demon dogs charged at Chiyo with a snarl. She spun around, ki arching from her sword and shattering through their bodies. But even as they crumpled, four more ogres stormed out of the forest on either side of us.

"Don't let them halt us," Rin said. "Clear the way and make for the shrine!"

Easier said than done. Takeo and Chiyo slammed through the two ogres in front of us with their blades, but the ones behind us charged at us three humans. Haru whacked one in the face with his sword. The oak kami managed to ram that ogre in the chest before the second tackled him to the ground. He groaned as he waved at us to leave him behind. My gut twisted, but I spun around and gestured to the others to race after Chiyo.

We burst into a yard ringed with shrine buildings that were shuttered for the night. More screeching heads dove at us. Keiji and I threw salt at the ones near us, and their features contorted. They dipped, sputtering and blinking furiously, low enough that Haru and I could stab them with our swords. Chiyo chopped through another one as the last sank its teeth into her hair. She yelped, and Takeo slammed it to the side, his fist lit with ki. The horrific face sizzled and plummeted to the ground.

More monsters were flooding onto the path both behind and ahead of us. There was nothing to do but run on. Sweat streaked down my back and into my eyes. My shoulder throbbed where the bullet had caught it this morning. I gritted my teeth against the pain.

The gravel skittered under my feet as I smacked away a demon dog with the flat of my blade. Keiji whipped another handful of salt into a swarm of nukekubi and nearly tripped. I caught him by his elbow, tugging him onward.

The monsters had gathered for a final stand on a series of wide stone steps at a bend in the path. At least half a dozen ogres waited for us, demon dogs and two-tailed cats stalking between them, a cluster of nukekubi circling against the darkening sky. At the top of the steps loomed a wooden gate and a roof marked with two boards forming an X at its peak.

"The sanctuary!" I said.

Chiyo darted up the steps, smashing through four ogres without a pause for breath. Before the other monsters could try to stop her, the rest of us hurtled in to cover her. The sanctuary gate's hinges creaked as Chiyo pushed into the compound.

Two flying heads screamed down at me, and I flung salt at them as I held up my sword to block them. They hissed and veered away. Rin leapt into the air and mashed their skulls together. One demon dog clamped its jaws around Takeo's sword arm, but he flung his blade to his other hand and plunged the weapon into the creature's side.

A tall, spindly ogre with claws as long as its fingers threw itself up the stairs after me. I scrambled higher. My sword clinked against the ogre's claws, which sounded hard as metal. I ducked and jabbed at its belly, and felt one of those claws graze the top of my head.

I jerked back, swallowing a cry, just as Keiji slammed into the ogre's side. They both toppled. The ogre slashed out at Keiji the second before they hit the ground. I chopped at its arm, an instant too late. Keiji rolled away, gasping and clutching his stomach.

My heart stopped. Another demon dog chomped at Keiji's leg, and I kicked it in the muzzle as I grabbed his shoulders. "Come on!" I said. He stumbled with me over the last few steps and through the gate Chiyo had left hanging open. The sanctuary compound's additional protections appeared to be too strong for any of the monsters to follow us inside.

"Chiyo!" I yelled, but she didn't answer. Within the high fence, there was not just one sanctuary building but a row of them, spread out across a yard of white stones. Any one of those buildings could have held the mirror. She might be searching too far away to hear me.

Keiji was straightening up. "Lie down!" I said, gripping his arm. I knelt beside him. His shirt was mottled with dirt and blood, but I couldn't tell how much of the latter was fresh or even his. Bracing myself, I tugged up the hem.

His pale skin was smudged scarlet. The blood had seeped from a thin line that curved across his abdomen just above his belly button. The cut was so shallow the bleeding had already slowed. My shoulders sagged in relief. Not fatal. Not even all that concerning.

"Should I start coming up with my brilliant last words?" Keiji asked, staring up at the sky.

"It's just a scratch," I said. "I think you'll live."

"Oh," he said, and sat up despite my wordless protest. "It didn't feel *that* bad, but then you hauled me in here, so I figured the pain just hadn't sunk in yet."

I flushed, remembering my panic. I hadn't even stopped to see what was happening to anyone else. They were still fighting. I should get back to the battle.

"It was very valorous of me, though, wasn't it—leaping in like that?" Keiji went on. "I'm practicing the bravery thing."

"I already told you," I said. "You're brave enough."

"But that was bonus points level brave," he said as I shifted my weight to stand. "Can I at least get a kiss of gratitude out of it?"

He said it in that joking way of his, but his eyes were serious. They flickered nervously when I met them. Something twinged in my chest, and all at once I felt like crying. So much time I'd spent being angry and uncertain when my heart had never wavered in what it wanted.

"You idiot," I said, "you don't have to try to get yourself killed for that."

His face tilted up to catch my lips as I quickly dipped my head. His fingers slipped into my hair, and a happy shiver ran down my spine. I kissed him hard, reveling in just how warm and there and real he was for that brief moment before I had to pull away.

I didn't want to. Right now, for this one moment, we were safe—who knew what might happen after? But the others needed me too.

"Sora," Keiji said, "I'm sor—"

"Don't," I said before he could finish the apology. I pushed myself to my feet and offered my hand to help him up. "You don't have to say it again. It's not as if I haven't made mistakes too. Now let's make those monsters see what a mistake it was to challenge us."

A grin flashed across his face. He sprang up. We were just turning to the gate when a low, wrenching cry carried through it.

We hurried forward. "Haru!" Chiyo yelled, charging across the yard behind us. She held an eight-sided mirror of brilliant silver under one arm. Together, we burst through the gate onto the top of the stairs.

There, we all jerked to a halt, staring at the scene before us. Takeo and Rin had been forced to the sides of the stairs, Takeo eyeing the two ogres who loomed over him. A monstrous cat and a demon dog circled Rin on the ground, a nukekubi above. And at the base of the stairs, the largest ogre I'd ever seen had its sinewy arm squeezed tight across Haru's chest and one of its claws pressed against his throat, deep enough that blood was already dribbling onto his shirt collar.

The ogre's gaze fixed on Chiyo. It bared jagged teeth. "Our red-haired friend requested I take this human if you escaped us," it said in its rough voice. "I bring him back to the ghosts now. Tomoya says if you want to fight for his life, you will leave your special toys behind before you reach the bridge. Otherwise, he dies."

It turned and loped away, Haru still clutched in its grasp.

"No!" Chiyo cried. She raced down the steps, blasting through the creatures that sprang at her. As she passed the katana Haru had dropped, she snatched it up. "I'll kick you all into the afterworld, just you wait!"

"Chiyo!" I called after her, my heart in my throat. We couldn't let her go alone.

But as I moved to the steps, even more monsters swarmed from the woods. Our stand here had given those spread across the shrine grounds time to reach us. I swung my sword so swiftly I barely saw where it struck, trusting my body to follow the rhythm of the fight, tossing salt in every direction. Around me, grunts and thumps told me the others fought on just as hard.

It wasn't enough. With every moment, Chiyo was farther away.

Then, with a gruff mutter, ki blazed across the steps. The light was so harsh it blinded me. I stumbled, gasping.

When my vision cleared, the smoking bodies of our enemies

littered the stone stairs, filling the air with a caustic oily stench. Amid them, Rin slumped on her side. Her breath rattled over her lips, and her skin was gray.

"Go!" she rasped. "Stop her before all is lost!"

Takeo dashed down the path on ki-sped feet. I ran after him as quickly as I could, hearing Keiji's erratic breath behind me. We passed the limping monkey and the oak-man, sprawled and weak but alive, not stopping until we reached the bridge. I pounded across the boards. Takeo had already halted beneath the first torii at the edge of safety.

Ghostlights clogged the courtyard. They surged toward the bridge, and I could imagine all those hostile eyes studying us, anticipating our next move. But I couldn't spot a single solid body among them—not the ogre, not Haru, not Tomoya. Not Chiyo.

She was gone.

TWENTY-TWO

"WHERE'S YOUR leader?" Takeo demanded of the ghostlights. "The one with the red in his hair."

At an answer I couldn't hear, his jaw set. "Enough. I can bring the sacred sword to deal with you if that's all you're willing to offer."

Whatever the ghosts said next, it wasn't good news. Takeo's broad shoulders sagged so slightly no one but me might have noticed. "Is there—" he started, and then leapt back as a figure turned corporeal in front of us.

The burly man who'd shifted his state grinned and waggled a net matted with crimson stains. "Next time we'll get *you*," he said. The rest of the ghostlights surged even closer behind him.

All three of us withdrew farther up the bridge. "What did they say?" I asked.

Takeo was frowning. "After some mockery, they seemed happy to inform me that we have no hope of finding Tomoya. He told none of them where he intended to take Chiyo, so that there would be no one we could force to help us. And he specifically told them to tell us that."

He lowered his head, rubbing the side of his face. I'd never seen him look so wretched.

"Tomoya can't have killed her," I said, the most reassurance I could offer. "Not so quickly. She's too strong for that." So he'd have brought her to a place where he could... take his time. Another room smeared with gore? A continuous string of torture, the way Omori had been whittling down Mother and Father's lives? Nausea trickled through me.

Dragging steps rasped over the wooden boards with the tap of a stick-turned-cane as Rin limped toward us.

"Chiyo took Haru's sword," Keiji said. "Even without the other one, couldn't she still manage to defeat a bunch of ghosts? Maybe they just took the fight farther off."

"The spirits fear the sacred sword far more than the girl," Rin said, reaching us. "It can do what charms cannot."

"What do you mean?" I said.

"Charms banish. The spirit remains, elsewhere. The sacred blade is like running water. It purifies. The ki returns to its source."

I remembered Tomoya in the keep, complaining that the sword had taken too many of the ghosts "for good."

"So when she cuts them with the sword, they're completely destroyed?" I said. "Their ki is absorbed back into the world—they can't return?"

Rin inclined her head.

If the sacred sword didn't just send the ghosts back to the afterworld but dissipated their ki in a way more final than death itself, it was no wonder Tomoya had wanted Chiyo to leave it behind. Haru's katana wouldn't even banish the spirits.

"Perhaps she just needs more time," Takeo said, but even he didn't sound as if he believed that. I swallowed thickly. Obon began tomorrow night.

I turned back toward the courtyard. "We have to go after her," I said, but the sea of ghostlights before us made my gut knot. *Next time we'll get you*, the ghost had said. They had no intention of letting us pass easily. And without Chiyo or the sacred sword—

"Where *is* the sword?" I said as the thought stuck me. "And the other treasures? If she left them behind as Tomoya asked..."

"That with the power of water was returned to water," Rin murmured in what I'd come to recognize as her prophesying voice. I glared at her, wishing she could find it in herself to speak plainly, and then realized I knew exactly what she meant.

I hurried back across the bridge and up the gravel path to the huge stone basin of the purifying fountain. Blurred shapes glinted beneath the flowing water. I leaned over, my hands braced on the slick rock.

The sacred sword lay at the bottom of the fountain, the necklace and the mirror beside it.

Chiyo might have been desperate to save Haru, but she'd still known we couldn't afford to lose the treasures. She'd left them behind in the purest place she could think of, where no malicious thing could touch them.

As the others came up beside me, my hands clenched. We couldn't afford to lose *her* either. How could she have taken such a risk—

But even before I'd finished that thought, I knew. I remembered all too clearly how the idea of Keiji being hurt had burned every other thought from my mind. Beneath her cheer and confidence, Chiyo must have felt even worse seeing that claw digging into Haru's throat.

I drew myself up as straight as I could, ignoring the protests of my beaten body. "All right. We have the treasures. We'll get through those ghosts out there... somehow, and then we'll track Chiyo down. We could ask the kami in the lands around Ise. Maybe one of them saw something."

I'd just finished speaking when the ground lurched. I tripped, and would have fallen if Keiji hadn't grabbed my arm. Rin turned toward Mt. Fuji, invisible in the distance. How badly had the ground shaken there if we could feel it even here, hundreds of miles away?

"The mountain's fire is close to bursting," Rin said. "When time is of the essence, it cannot be wasted on maybes."

I stared at her. "Well, do you *know* where Chiyo is?"

"I cannot always see what I wish to," she said, her dry voice still thready from the ki she'd expended earlier.

"It sounds like you're saying that we shouldn't look for her at all," Keiji said.

Rin gave him a crooked smile.

"What?" I said. "Of course we've got to find her! We should already be searching, not standing around talking in riddles."

"There is no 'got to,'" Rin replied calmly. "We have the treasures we sought. We make do with what we have."

"You're not making any sense," I said. "You told us before

that if the conditions of your vision aren't met, we'll fail to save the mountain. What does it matter that we have the three sacred treasures if we have no one to carry them?"

Rin inspected me from head to feet as if I were a painting she was considering where to hang. Then she met my eyes, a little light dancing in hers. "Are you sure?" she said. "I believe we do."

For an instant, I couldn't breathe.

"You can't mean—"

"I also told you before that a prophecy is far from fact. The specificities are often blurred. I saw a young woman with power, carrying the treasures. We have a young woman. We have the treasures. We have kami who would go beside you to lend you ki. And there is strength in you. I can see it. You have only to accept the role."

"But—you saw a girl 'born of all the elements,'" I said. "That has to be Chiyo."

Rin shrugged. "Truth be told, the image I saw could have signified one *raised by* Kasumi and Hotaka as well as *born of*. It was a vision, not a treatise. We must take the best chance we have."

I looked to Takeo, who had been standing there silently. "You can't think she's right. You know we need Chiyo."

"There is reason in Sage Rin's words, Sora," Takeo said slowly. "You have the training—far more than we were able to provide Chiyo with in our limited time. You love the mountain. If we go now, we can attack Omori when he least expects it, defeat him and his ghosts before the first night of Obon falls. The longer we wait, the stronger they become, and the weaker the mountain. We can seek out Chiyo after. She... should be able to withstand their torment that long."

The strain in his voice told me he wasn't sure of that, though. And what if we couldn't make it up the mountain without Chiyo's power on our side? It would be difficult enough *with* her now that Rin was exhausted and Takeo weary. If the vision had meant only her, and the demon slaughtered us, what would become of the world then?

"But—" I started, and Rin plucked the sword out of the fountain. She spun it in her deft hand with an arc of droplets and held it out to me, hilt first.

Instinctively, I reached to take it. The water-cooled grip immediately warmed against my palm. My fingers curled around it, my heart racing.

"Accept that which you have so wanted," Rin said, almost kindly.

I *had* wanted this. Oh, how I'd wanted it. For Rin to be wrong, for me to be the kami I'd always believed I was. To feel ki moving through me the way it used to, as easily as it had come to Chiyo. I imagined myself soaring up the mountain, power humming through me, slicing through every ghost that had caused my loved ones harm. Watching them fall back before me in awe.

I hefted the sword, testing its weight. It moved like a beam of sunlight. Mt. Fuji's weapons were fine, but I'd never trained with a blade like this. Whichever kami had forged it had been not just a great craftsman and artist, but a genius as well.

And yet, it didn't look quite right. In Chiyo's hands, the sword had gleamed like fire. Blazed with ki. But not the faintest tingle passed through my palm. It lay dormant, waiting.

For her. Because the fire had been hers.

My fingers tightened, but all I felt was that hard surface against my skin. To push energy through the blade, I'd need to take ki from our allies. Leach off their lives the way I had with Midori. How would that be so different from what the ghosts intended to do to their human captives?

A certainty settled over me with that thought, easing the tension in my chest. Even if I charged up Mt. Fuji with the aid of a thousand kami, I would never be the slightest bit kami myself. This wasn't my sword. It wasn't my role. The mountain needed the *right* girl to save it, and that girl was Chiyo.

As I lowered the sword, I realized I could accept *that*. As Haru had said, there was nothing wrong with being someone who supported the true hero. Chiyo was counting on me, on all of us, to back her up.

I handed the sword to Rin. "No," I said. "We have to find Chiyo. The mountain needs *her*."

"And they call me obtuse," Rin muttered.

"We must begin the search at once," Takeo said, a little of his usual vigor returning at the prospect of taking action.

Of course, we still had a more immediate problem. "How are we going to get past all those ghosts?" I said. "We barely made it through them when we had Chiyo's help and a distraction."

After a moment of silence, Keiji dipped his hand into the fountain. "If the sword is like running water," he said slowly, "then water destroys the ghosts too? Do you think there are any boats around here? We could take the river and sail past them."

Takeo's face brightened. "An excellent suggestion," he said. "I don't believe we'll need to search for a boat."

He led us along the path to where it veered down to the edge of the shrunken river. There, Takeo knelt and reached toward the water. The ghostlights on the opposite bank bobbed and drifted in the darkness. I could feel them watching us even if I couldn't see their eyes.

I paced the cracked earth as we waited. Once we got away from the shrine, we couldn't just wander aimlessly if we were going to find Chiyo in time. Tomoya would have a plan. He always did. He'd tried and failed and kept trying, changing his strategy as he learned more about us. Because he was as human as I was, and he didn't have to act in just one way.

As blood sings to blood, I should be able to understand him and his strategies. How had he beaten us? He'd observed Chiyo's confidence, recognized her devotion to Haru, and turned those things into a weakness. But he could be over-confident too, couldn't he? There were people he was devoted to. When I'd accused him of not caring about anyone other than himself, he'd said, *That's exactly why I'm doing this. For my family.*

For the little brother he'd expected to join him; the one he thought would eventually come around.

I glanced at Keiji. "You know Tomoya. Where would he hide, if he didn't want to get caught?"

"He's mentioned places he used to work sometimes," Keiji said, looking startled. "But he wouldn't go somewhere he'd told me about, would he?"

"I don't think he sees you as a threat," I said. "He thinks he's going to win you over to his side in the end, that you're still loyal to him underneath. He might even *want* to be somewhere you could find him."

Keiji nodded. "I could see that. And ghosts *are* supposed to be most comfortable in places they knew when they were alive. There were a couple districts south of Tokyo where he did a lot of business. I don't know the exact spots, but that would give us a direction, right?"

"It's a starting point," Takeo said. "And once we're close enough to her, I may be able to sense her ki."

Of course, then we'd have another ghostly army to face. Tomoya wouldn't have spirited Chiyo and Haru away on his own. And he'd have his followers ready with nets and blood to weaken Takeo and Rin and any kami allies we gathered.

I turned toward the main path, where the forms of the monsters we'd slain earlier were sprawled. Even those felled with swords had started to melt into stinking, oily masses. The smell prickled in my nose.

Maybe we could learn something else from the demon and his ghosts. Omori had been open to using *every* creature willing to join his cause so that he could attack us where his main army could not. Tomoya hadn't orchestrated his kidnapping alone.

"We haven't been able to find many kami able to fight," I said, "and those who are, the ghosts can use their old tricks on. But if they can ask ogres and demon dogs and nukekubi to help them, why can't we ask for help outside the kami? There are other friendly creatures who'd join us if we asked, aren't there?"

"I suppose there are some who might be willing to take up our fight," Takeo said. "But kami don't make a habit of asking for favors outside our kind."

"I think it's time they did," I said.

He hesitated, and then bowed his head. "We should not turn away any help we can gain."

A gleaming body broke the surface of the night-darkened water in front of him. Takeo leaned over to speak with the fish—a kami who'd responded to his summons, I assumed. After a moment, it swished away. In a matter of seconds, it had gathered a mass of neighbors. Tight rows of finned bodies lined up in the water before us, forming a makeshift raft.

Rin hopped on without hesitation. I followed cautiously. The scaly bodies formed a ridged but firm surface under my feet. I sat down on them as gently as I could. Keiji clambered on beside me, the oak-man and the monkey kami scrambling after him. I wasn't sure what had become of Sumire and the others who'd gone with her, but I hoped they were only wounded and recovering.

Takeo stepped on last, moving to the center of the raft with the sacred sword ready in his hands. The water rippled as the fish began to swim. They carried us to the middle of the river and then swiftly down it. A breeze ruffled my hair. As the trees on the bank flew by, the ghostlights shivered through them, chasing after us.

"They don't look happy," Takeo said.

A gunshot rang out, but Takeo deflected the bullet with a burst of ki. One of the nearby figures solidified—a scowling young man running along the bank. Just as we reached a bend in the river, he sprang at us, knife raised. Takeo shifted into a fighting stance, but the ghost had underestimated the distance. He plummeted downward a foot from the edge of the fishy raft.

The second he hit the water, his body shattered into a sparkling mist. It faded into the breeze, and then he was gone, his ki returning to the world from which it had come.

"Wow," Keiji said, peering into the water as if the man might have reformed there.

We swept under another bridge and out into the midst of Ise city. The scenery on the banks changed from forest to grassy soil to concrete and back again. Soon we'd left the ghosts and the shrine grounds far behind us.

Takeo must have sent a request to the fish, because they drew up to the bank. "Thank you," he said when we'd hopped off, and I gave a quick bow beside him. Then he turned to Keiji. "You said south of Tokyo? We should see if any kami northeast of the shrine saw your brother leaving in that direction."

The oak-man and the monkey spread out to search. Keiji and I stayed with Takeo, as did Rin, who hadn't loosened her grip on her stick-cane. We rambled across the countryside, stopping when the two of them sensed a fellow kami was near. None reported having seen anything that sounded related to Tomoya.

Finally, the monkey came scampering back to us. Takeo bent to confer with it. When he straightened up, a glint of hope shone in his eyes.

"A swallow saw a transport truck drive away from Ise City around the right time," he said. "The driver looked like a normal human being, but he had short hair with red streaks."

There weren't many people with Tomoya's sense of style. "The other ghosts with him must have been hiding in the truck," I said. "He knew we'd be looking for them."

"We'll just have to hope other kami took note," Takeo said.

We rushed onward, but after another hour, we hadn't found any more witnesses. We stopped near a train track that cut through the fields around us. A train whipped by, rattling the metal slats.

"Tomoya might be nearly to Tokyo by now," I said. "We'll have more time to search that area if we take a train before they stop running for the night." And more energy. Takeo and Rin were already looking even more weary than before. At least riding the train would allow them to recover some of their spent ki.

"If we go to Tokyo, I could get Tomoya's car," Keiji said, apparently thinking along the same lines. "That'll drive faster than you can run, right? Then we can cover more ground. Assuming he did go to one of the same districts as before."

Takeo stared along the line of the tracks. "We must take the best chance we have," he said. "If the kami can't tell us where the ghosts have gone, we'll rely on your knowledge."

We found a station a short dash along the tracks. As we waited for the next train, Takeo disappeared briefly with the other kami to recruit whatever creatures they could find nearby. When the train finally arrived, I sank into my seat. I was exhausted now, but my pulse was still thrumming with urgency.

"You will need your strength for the times ahead," Rin said with a surprising gentleness, and touched both me and Keiji on the forehead. A moment later, I was asleep.

I woke up just as the lights of the great city began to streak through the train windows. Keiji was still sleeping, his head resting against mine. When I eased away to look around, his cheek dropped to my shoulder. His glasses dangled by the tip of his nose. I pushed them up and he shifted closer, a faint smile curving his mouth. A strange ache filled me, fierce and tender and breathtaking all at once, as if, while I was looking at him, nothing in the world could be wrong.

Then the earth shook beneath the tracks, the train stopped abruptly, and all the things that were wrong came rushing back to me. The faces of the other passengers tensed, their hands gripping their seat arms. A little boy started to cry, so frantically no word from his mother calmed him. *It'll be over soon,* I wanted to tell him, but I couldn't actually promise that.

When we reached the station and disembarked, the kami sped us along to the spot where Keiji had parked his car. He drove us through the city, nervously checking the traffic around us, until we passed the southwestern suburbs of Tokyo. Then he turned us down the winding back roads that scattered the peninsula where he thought Tomoya had conducted most of his business while alive.

Takeo sat in the front seat, staring through the windshield. We passed farmland and fringes of towns and rolling forested hills. Whenever he or Rin felt the presence of a shrine of any size or another kami habitation, we stopped so they could consult them. No one reported on Tomoya's passing with any certainty—many trucks followed these roads, some said. But several of them agreed to help us with our search, heading out in the directions we hadn't yet tried.

As dawn colored the sky, Mt. Fuji came into view through my side window, then slowly slipped away behind us. In the thin light, I could see stalks bowing and leaves withering in the fields.

Heat was already rising from the earth, strangely distant with the car's air conditioning system sending its steady stream of cool air over us.

"I can't sense her at all," Takeo said, his brow furrowed. "I'm extending my senses as far as I can."

"We haven't covered the whole area yet, not even close," Keiji said, but his arms quivered as he adjusted his grip on the steering wheel. None of us had gotten more than an hour's sleep on that train ride.

"We'll find her," I said. "We have to."

The words had barely left my mouth when the ground bucked beneath us. The car lurched. My shoulder smacked the door hard enough to send a lancing pain down my arm. Keiji jammed on the brake.

The tires screeched, but we stopped—in the middle of the road, with the engine rattling in time with the shaking of the earth. Beside me, Rin turned to peer back the way we'd come. "The fury arrives," she said.

I craned my neck to follow her gaze and choked up. Mt. Fuji loomed over the trees beyond the rear window. Smoke was billowing above its upper reaches, rolling out across the sky around it.

"It's erupting?" I managed to force out. "Now?"

"Very soon," Rin said.

I spun on her. "*How* soon?"

She looked at me as the ground finally stilled, with a flat expression that suggested I should know better than to ask. "As soon as the fire climbs from the depths to the peak. As soon as the last strands of control break. *Soon*."

I wondered if she wanted me to say I'd changed my mind. That I'd take up the sacred treasures after all, race to the mountainside right now. But even faced with that horrible image through the window, the idea felt utterly wrong. I'd let myself second-guess my feelings too many times in the last week. Almost all of my mistakes had come down to that. I had to believe I could see what was right—and what wasn't.

"Then we'll have to move faster," I said. And if we didn't find Chiyo in the hours we had left... I wasn't going to let myself think that.

TWENTY-THREE

"SO WE keep going?" Keiji asked from the front of the car. Takeo stayed silent.

I was about to tell him to drive on when a furry red body amid the trees by the road caught my eye. A fox. It was staring toward the mountain, as if it understood what the scene before us meant as well as we did.

"Wait," I said, and leaned toward Takeo. "There are foxes here. They like to involve themselves with human lives, don't they? And they're clever. If any creature would have noticed odd activity in the region, it's them."

"Can we trust them?" Keiji asked. "If they're like the stories say, aren't they always playing tricks?"

"They do often enjoy misleading more than guiding," Takeo said. "I've preferred to avoid their kind."

It was true that most of the tales I'd heard of foxes involved them leading humans astray. But from what I remembered that had usually been out of mischief rather than true malice. And why should we assume that was all there was to them? Even Omori held more concerns and cares than I'd first assumed.

"I think we should give them a chance," I said. "They live on this land too—they could lose their homes. Do you really believe they'd prefer to play tricks on us now if they could help us?"

Takeo grimaced. I grasped the door handle. "*I'll* go ask them."

I hopped out of the car. As we'd talked, the fox I'd seen had vanished into the forest. I marched the way I hoped it had gone. "Foxes!" I called, as loud as I could. "If any of you can hear me, I beg you to come. I wish to speak to you on behalf of the kami of Mt. Fuji."

After a few moments, I strode deeper into the woodland. Takeo's steady footsteps crackled over the dry leaves that scattered the ground behind me. I shouted out my summons again as he drew up beside me. My back tensed.

"You are right," he said quietly. "I should not let old prejudices prevent me from seeing solutions to our problems."

But the minutes stretched, and no answer came to my call. My heart sank. I was just turning back toward the car when a sleek, red-furred body rustled out of the underbrush. The fox halted in front of us and straightened up into the form of a lovely woman in a red kimono.

"Kami," she said with a bob of her head to Takeo, and then to me, "and you who speak for them. What is it you seek from us?"

When Takeo didn't immediately respond, I pushed onward, hoping I was choosing my words carefully enough to avoid mischief. "You can see Mt. Fuji is threatening to erupt. You may have heard that a demon has taken control of the mountain. We are searching for the one kami who can stop him and prevent the disaster. We believe those who took her, a group of ghosts led by a young man with red-streaked hair, have brought her somewhere in this area to imprison her. They would have arrived in a truck. They would have picked a location away from living humans. They would likely be using blood, lots of it, to help weaken her. The effects of the demon's rule are hurting everyone, including you. We hope that the foxes will consider lending their efforts to our cause. Any clue you or your kind can find that might lead us to the one we seek, we would be immensely grateful for."

The woman's nose twitched. She offered a sly smile. "Blood we could scent out. I have not seen those you speak of, but there are many I can ask. Kami, do you extend this request too?"

Her bright eyes settled on Takeo. He bowed lower than she had to him. "I do," he said, with only the slightest hint of an edge in his tone. "Indeed, if you are able to help us, I believe I can speak for my rulers when I say that they would welcome you to the palace to thank you personally."

I blinked at him, startled that he would speak that boldly on behalf of Mother and Father, though I had no doubt he was correct. The fox-woman appeared equally affected. "Well," she said, with a brush of her slender fingers over her flowing hair, "I will do as I can. We will find you in your smoke-creating vehicle if we have news."

"Please hurry!" I added, but she'd already dropped into her fox shape to dart off through the trees.

We hurried back to the car and continued our own desperate search. Every time I glanced back, more smoke-tinged clouds clotted the sky and shadowed the mountain. The sour taste of fear filled my mouth. *Hold on,* I thought at the mountain. *Please, just a little longer, hold on.*

Had Omori even noticed how close his invasion had pushed Mt. Fuji to eruption? Even if he couldn't bring himself to care about the people who'd be hurt, didn't he at least realize there'd be no tourists to use in his plan now that the volcano's fire was so obviously building? Or was he so caught up in the thought of regaining the power of life that he'd lost all sense?

We passed another town, Takeo shaking his head. "Nowhere near here," he said.

"Can't you 'see' anything?" I demanded of Rin.

She turned her sunken gaze toward the road ahead of us. "This far from my valley, my vision is dim. I see... Water may put out a fire. That is all."

As I bit down on a noise of frustration, the earth trembled again. Keiji slowed the car. The ground had just settled when a fox sprang through the tall grass ahead of us onto the road. It transformed into a woman, a little older than the one we'd spoken to before but just as elegant. As Keiji stopped the car completely, she sauntered over to us. Takeo fumbled unsuccessfully with the window controls and then simply opened the door.

"My cousins told me of your search," the woman said, halting. Her black eyes and pale teeth gleamed in the rising sun. "There is an abandoned factory near Mishima that smells of blood where none was before. The chill of the dead is upon it too. I can show you."

Without waiting for our response, she slipped back into her

fox form and loped ahead. My heart thumped as Keiji drove on.

The fox trotted down roads that grew narrower and more pot-holed, and finally onto a gravel track that angled through a vast field of scrub. In the distance, a cluster of broad dun buildings stood around a concrete yard.

Takeo jerked forward.

"She's there," he said, and his mouth twisted. "They're hurting her."

As we crept down the road toward the factory compound, a scattering of the kami Takeo had talked to earlier caught up with us, along with a few beings I wasn't as familiar with: wolves that moved across the terrain like gauzy phantoms, the child-sized tree fairies with their slingshots and tiny crossbows, and a strange creature with a bear's furry body, an elephant's trunk, and the striped legs of a tiger. When it crossed the road in front of us, Keiji gaped for a moment before murmuring, "Dreameater."

At least we weren't going into this completely alone.

About a half a mile from the factory, Takeo motioned for Keiji to pull the car into the field. We stepped out onto dry soil and yellowed grass. The twenty-some allies who'd joined us trailed behind as we circled around the back of the compound. I eyed the buildings, watching for glints of ghostlight or shivers of movement in the dark, dusty windows.

"She's in that one," Takeo said, motioning to the most easterly building. We crept closer, my hand tight around my ofuda. After a minute we stumbled onto a streambed, little more than pocked, muddy earth. A trickle of water little wider than my hand ran down its center. We hopped over and hurried onward.

We were some fifteen paces from the building when several dozen ghostlights streamed out of its walls and those of the neighboring structures. They charged straight at us, so swiftly I didn't have time to suck in a breath before I had to throw out my hands, trying to banish every one that raced near me. A few turned corporeal and tossed one of their gore-stained nets over the kami beside me, but one of the spirit wolves smacked it aside with its massive paws. The ghosts shuddered and turned ethereal again as the tree fairies pelted them with needles and stones imbued with their own sort of magic. And in the midst of us all, Takeo swung the sacred sword, breaking a dozen ghostlights into showers of shimmers with a single sweep.

For a moment, I thought we were going to win. I thought it might even be *easy*. Then a ghost near the back of the group turned corporeal with a pistol in his hand and a sharp blast of sound.

The bullet hit Takeo's wrist. His arm flew wide, and his fingers slipped from the sword's hilt. Before he could spring after it, the ghost who'd shot him fired again, catching him in the chest. He staggered backward as his ki worked to dislodge the bullet from his flesh, and the horde of ghosts surged toward us. The kami monkey broke from his ethereal state with a wheeze, a knife stained with dried blood plunged deep into his stomach. The tree fairies scattered as another ghost took aim at them. I tried to hold my ground, but there were too many ghosts around me for me to fend off their blades as I tried to banish them. One sliced across my forearm; another nicked my cheek. I gasped, stumbling backward. They were pressing us farther and farther from the sword that was our salvation.

We'd never reclaim it like this. "To the stream!" I shouted, hoping the others would understand. The running water, thin as it was, should provide us enough protection that the ghosts wouldn't follow. Perhaps we could even draw them to it and dispatch some of them that way.

But the ghosts clearly knew better than to fall for that ploy. As we dashed the last several steps to the streambed and leapt over it, they stopped, hazy lights churning around the few still corporeal forms. The sacred sword lay in the grass in a clear circle in their midst. I stared at it longingly.

Takeo was hunched over, clutching at his chest. Though his breath was ragged, his bleeding appeared to have stopped. He was too tired to heal completely. Before I could speak to him, a tall form emerged from the crowd of ghosts and ambled up to the stream. He raked a hand through his crimson-streaked hair and smirked at us.

"Look at this brave rescue force, cringing behind their piddly stream," Tomoya said.

"Hardly as cowardly as using hundreds of ghosts to attack one teenaged girl," Takeo retorted.

"One very powerful kami girl," Tomoya said. "Who intended to disrupt our plans. You know that even with these new friends of yours, you can't hope to overpower us now that you've lost that pretty sword, don't you? Why don't you take it easy for a few days, and then we'll be done with your mountain, and we can all go on with our lives?"

"You've already had your life," I said. "You have no right to steal another. And can't you see the mountain might not even hold until Obon? It's about to erupt!"

"Then Omori will bring us and your broken kami friends down to the cities, and we'll find the bodies we need there," Tomoya said, as if no other consequences mattered to him. "What isn't *right* is the fact that I died at all."

Before I even noticed him moving, Keiji had jumped back across the stream to the ghosts' side. "And whose fault is that?" he said, his posture rigid. "Who are you blaming?"

"Kei," Tomoya said evenly. "What did they do to you to make them lead you here?"

"They didn't do anything," Keiji said. "I *wanted* to help them. This is wrong. Everything you've been doing— You know why you got killed in the first place? Because you listened to the wrong people, you believed what they told you, even though they were turning you into a criminal."

"I was making money," Tomoya said. "Good money, so we could get out of that crappy house. So you could be happier. Where's the gratitude, little brother?"

"There are other ways of making money," Keiji said. "Ways that wouldn't have gotten you killed, so you would've still been there when Auntie was telling me how useless I was, when Uncle locked me in my room for two days. You're making the same mistake all over again. Omori's just as bad as the people you were hanging out with before. He's worse! Do you really want to be a party to *mass murder,* Tomo? Because that's what this means, really, what you're planning to do to all those 'bodies.' Even I can see that."

His voice was so raw my heart ached, hearing it. Tomoya took a step toward him, and I shifted forward automatically, my hands rising. But Keiji glanced back at me, his gaze worried yet firm, sending a message I could read. *Let me do this myself.* I forced my body to still.

"I have to follow Omori," Tomoya said. "I need my life back. I left responsibilities unfinished. There are things I have to *do*."

"For who?" Keiji demanded. "Not for me—I won't want anything to do with you ever again if you go through with this."

Tomoya blinked. A sort of daze softened his cocky expression. For the first time, I thought to wonder what *he'd* been focused on the moment he died.

"But it's all for you," he said to Keiji. "I knew I couldn't leave you alone. You need me. No matter what I do, Kei, it's always to look after you. I know you know that."

"You really can't believe that I might know it and still think you're totally wrong, can you?" Keiji said quietly. "You can't see anything except what you've already decided."

"I see you," Tomoya said. "I'm your brother. I've always known exactly who you are, Kei."

"Are you sure?" Keiji asked.

Tomoya took another step toward him as if to touch his shoulder, and Keiji jerked back. His feet tangled. He stumbled to the side, toward the stream. A memory flashed behind my eyes: the rabbit startling us, Keiji tripping, my attempt to catch him. But in the glimpse I caught of his face as he fell now, I saw no fear, only resolve.

Tomoya lunged after him, catching his wrist. But Keiji was falling too fast, too hard, for even his taller, stronger brother to stop him. Because he'd meant to fall, and he'd put everything he had into the act. He curled his fingers around his brother's hand and crashed into the shallow water, pulling Tomoya with him.

A few of the watching ghosts solidified, and a voice hollered, "No!" One sprang forward, but there was no time to stop the fall.

Tomoya toppled over Keiji, his red hair streaming like a flame, and his elbow hit the stream. His body burst with a crackle of ki so bright it left dark spots in my vision. A fine mist dispersed around us, but some of the ki shot off through the air in the direction of the mountain. I remembered suddenly what Takeo had said about Tomoya carrying a greater portion of Omori's energy.

And channeling it to the other ghosts. None of them burst, but before our eyes, the crowd shrank back, the ghostlights dwindling, the corporeal forms fading away.

In their confusion, Takeo leapt across the stream and blazed through them to take up the sacred sword. The rest of our allies raced after him. In a matter of seconds, all the ghosts had scattered, fleeing or cut through by the purifying blade. Rin hustled on toward the building where Chiyo was imprisoned.

I knelt at Keiji's side as he pushed himself upright. Mud coated the back of his shirt, and his hair was dripping. His eyes were more watery than I could blame on the stream. I took his hand to help him up. He gripped it, standing, and tugged me forward into a tight embrace.

"I destroyed my brother," he said into my hair.

"I'm sorry," I said, wishing I had better words to give him.

He laughed, a little strangled. "I'm not. Someone had to, and I knew how. He had no idea what he was doing, how he was hurting people, anymore. And he thought he was doing it for *me*."

"I think he really did care about you," I said. "Even if everything else around that feeling had gone wrong."

"Yeah," Keiji said. "I was counting on that. The trick wouldn't have worked if he didn't care. But it wouldn't have worked if he hadn't been so convinced he was right, either." He shook his head. "I guess I'm looking after myself now. That's what I've really been doing the last two years anyway."

Then he drew back just far enough to kiss me, so hard I forgot how to breathe, forgot everything except his cool hand against my face and his body pressed to mine.

He broke away abruptly. "I'm getting you all muddy."

I looked down at the damp patches of stream water and splotches of mud that had soaked from his shirt into mine. As if my clothes hadn't already been ruined a dozen times over. "It doesn't matter," I said. "Come on, let's go get Chiyo."

We hurried across the field to the building hand in hand. Just as we came around the corner to the doorway, two figures swayed outside.

The stench of rotting gore seeped out into the early afternoon air, thick enough to turn my stomach. Chiyo clung to Takeo's side, letting him take most of her weight. Her hair was matted with blood. Cuts she didn't have the ki to heal mottled her face, arms, and chest. She held one leg as if her ankle were broken.

Then she raised her head, and a familiar spark lit in her eyes when they found mine.

"I hear," she said in a halting rasp, "that it's time for me to kick some demon butt."

"Yes," I said quietly. A lump rose in my throat. From Takeo's expression over the top of Chiyo's head, he was feeling much the same as me.

We'd found her. We'd rescued her. Nothing stood between us and the mountain now. But Mt. Fuji's smoke was spreading across the sky, Obon would begin when the sun set tonight, and the girl before us didn't look as if she could defeat a flea, let alone a demon.

TWENTY-FOUR

FOR ALL her bravado, Chiyo fell asleep the second she sank into the back seat of the car. She'd told Takeo that the ghosts had taken Haru to the mountain, but the toll her imprisonment had taken on her ran deeper than even her desire to protect him. As Keiji turned the car around, I wondered if the short time it would take us to reach the mountain would be enough for her to recover. She didn't stir even when the car bounced on the potholed road.

Takeo and Rin fed as much ki as they could spare into Chiyo's wounded body as we drove north. Rin had clasped the necklace with the sacred jewel around her neck. The stones emitted a warm, greenish glow that wrapped around her from head to toe. Slowly, her most obvious cuts healed. But I remembered how weak she'd been after just a few hours imprisoned in that bloody room in the keep. It had been at least a day before she'd regained even close to her full powers.

A growing stream of cars roared past us, heading in the opposite direction—away from the mountain and the destruction it threatened. Smoke smothered the sky ahead of us. Twice the ground shuddered with fresh tremors, so severe Keiji had to pull to the side of the road to wait them out.

But even the mountain's fury wouldn't stop Omori. Tomoya had said so himself. If there were no people on or near Mt. Fuji for him and his vast army of followers to possess come nightfall, he'd take his whole force to wherever the people were. Not even the mountain's obvious anger had been enough to convince him to free enough kami to calm the volcano. He mustn't want to risk them interfering with his plans.

Chiyo was still unconscious when we approached Mt. Fuji's foot. My heart sank.

"Put on the music," I said. I needed something to hold me above despair. Keiji grinned tightly and popped in the CD he knew I meant. The swirling guitars and pounding drums followed us all the way through the evacuated streets of the Nagamotos' town.

"I told those I spoke to around Ise to meet us here with whatever other help they could summon," Takeo said as the road slanted upward. "They should be waiting as close to the palace as they could get."

No ghostlights showed themselves amid the trees. With the volcanic haze choking off the mid-afternoon sun, it was nearly as dark as evening. An ashy, smoky smell penetrated the car. I wondered for a moment if perhaps Omori had evacuated already, taking most of his legions with him. But we weren't even halfway to the tourist stop when a pale figure waved to us from the road's shoulder.

It was Ayame. Despite the horrors she'd faced here, I supposed she'd felt more frantic about staying in Tokyo not knowing what was happening than joining the battle.

Keiji parked, and Takeo immediately leapt out.

"It's an interesting army you've put together," Ayame said to Takeo. Tree fairies, spirit wolves, another dreameater, and even a few foxes lurked in the trees amid the few dozen kami who'd gathered to meet us. "They've scouted all around the mountain. Not far above here, ghosts are patrolling and ogres are watching the road. They'd tip you over in that machine." She wrinkled her nose at the car. Then her gaze fell on Chiyo's slumped body inside. Her hands fluttered. "Is she all right?"

"Her spirit is regaining strength," Rin said. "Soon she wakes."

But what state would she be in then?

While that uncertainty hung over the rest of us, we grabbed every material we could find to write out more ofuda and distributed what remained of our supply of salt. Takeo strode amid our allies, cautioning them about the ghosts' and ogres' preferred tactics. This was a larger group than we'd ever had before, but it was hard for me to imagine them being enough for us to force our way through the massive army that must be smothering the mountain above us.

So much depended on Chiyo. Even weakened, she'd have more power in one hand than I had in my entire body. At least I'd found her. With her on our side we had a chance, however small.

Some twenty minutes after we'd arrived, a squirrel kami who'd been acting as a sentry came scurrying over. It chittered something to Takeo, who straightened up, his face dark.

"The ghosts have become aware of Chiyo's arrival," he said. "They appear to be moving to bring the battle to us."

"Well, then, what are we waiting for?" a thin but bright voice asked from the back of the car. Chiyo had sat up, her lavender ponytails still drooping, the sacred sword clutched between her hands. Her face was pale but determined, her eyes glinting fiercely. She stood slowly, raised the sword with one arm, and tucked the mirror under the other.

"Tonight we take back our mountain!" she said, as if Mt. Fuji had always been hers, as if she'd lived there her whole life instead of me. I wondered if she could feel its call now—if it was already reaching out to her to pull her home. The gathered spirits cheered.

Chiyo glanced at Takeo. "It's Omori who's giving the ghosts most of their power, right?" she said, and he nodded. "Then the most important thing is finding and destroying him. He's probably at the palace, so don't stop climbing until you get there." She tipped her head back to eye the smoke-drenched sky. "I can see we don't have a lot of time."

Her words had barely carried into the air when our allies higher up the mountain gave a shout. A torrent of ghostlights was rushing down through the forest toward us.

Chiyo sprang forward with a battle cry, her sword ready. The kami and the other assembled creatures surged up around her, Takeo and Rin among them. I hurried after them, my tired human feet stumbling through the underbrush in ways theirs did not. Keiji clambered up the slope beside me, his jaw set. Over the anxious beat of my heart, the rhythm of the music from the car echoed inside me, tugging me onward.

Ahead of us, the corporeal kami struck out at and dodged foes I could barely see. A spirit-wolf lunged to meet the charge of a demon dog. A band of tree fairies let loose their tiny arrows into the legs of an ogre lurching toward Chiyo. Keiji and I ducked as a keening flock of flying heads soared by. Several of the ghostlights streaked around the main thrust of our resistance, and we slapped our ofuda out at them.

At the front of the charge, Chiyo was moving slowly but steadily through the glowing mass of ghosts. Light blazed from her sword, arcing along the blade and shattering every ghost it connected with. The mirror emitted a paler gleam that seemed to slow the enemies that drew near her. It lit her skin like moonlight.

My breath caught as I watched her, forming a tiny ache at the base of my throat. I would never have power like that. Not even a fraction of it. But I knew with complete certainty that Chiyo was the girl Rin had seen in her vision. The girl who could save us all. Without her, our meager force would have already fallen.

For a second, the sword's blaze flickered. I saw Chiyo's shoulders tremble as she slammed it into the next wave of enemies. She was fighting hard, but she was far from fully recovered. And we still had so much distance to cover.

More of our enemies poured down, circling Chiyo as she pushed up the slope. A monstrous cat sprang at me and I barely managed to stab out with my sword as it dodged. It fell back, limping, but I didn't like the way my arm wobbled. Chiyo wasn't the only one worn ragged. Exhaustion was starting to dull my senses.

I felt it even more when a group of ogres barged toward us.

Keiji let out a yelp as one's claws slashed across his forearm. I threw myself in the ogre's way, only to be smacked into a tree trunk by its elbow. Head reeling, I shoved myself toward it again, but as I jabbed at its chest, the other two converged on me.

"No!" Keiji cried. He grabbed one's legs, and it staggered into its companions, knocking both of them off balance.

I scrambled out of the way. Facing the five of them, sweat trickling down my back and the scent of smoke searing my lungs, I realized this might be the moment when I died. Keiji had grabbed a branch, but we couldn't fend off this many of them between the two of us with our meager weapons. Our more powerful companions had already pulled too far ahead to notice we needed assistance.

They shouldn't help us anyway, I thought. A cold but calm resolve pierced through my fatigue. I pointed my sword toward the ogres while they righted themselves. Chiyo's other allies should stay with her. At least Keiji and I would be keeping this bunch distracted from her for a little while longer.

As one of the ogres stepped toward us, another snorted. "Leave these weaklings," it said. "It's the girl with the sword we need to catch."

A protest stuck in my throat. I dashed forward as they turned away and sliced at the back of one's thigh. An instant later, another kicked me in the side so hard I felt a rib crack. I hit the ground and wrenched myself around with a gasp. The ogres had already outpaced us, loping on their gangly legs up the mountainside.

A pack of nukekubi shrieked by overhead, ignoring us completely. Apparently they'd gotten the idea to ignore the human "weaklings" too. I couldn't even deny the logic of it.

"Are you okay?" Keiji asked as I swiped my sweat-damp hair back from my face. I glanced at him, and my pulse stuttered at the sight of the blood streaking down his arm.

"Are *you*?" I said, and he pressed his arm against his side.

"It's just a flesh wound," he muttered, and then, sounding more serious, "I'll manage. It didn't get me too deep. But what do we do now?"

I peered up the mountain. I could no longer see Takeo, Rin, or Ayame amid the whirl of ghostlights and wrestling bodies. I could barely make out the flash of Chiyo's sword. Was it slower than before?

"We try to catch up," I said.

My rib ached and my calves throbbed, but I pushed myself on up the slope as fast as my feet would carry me. Keiji kept pace, his breath coming raggedly. Finally we drew closer to the edge of the battle. But only, I realized after a moment, because Chiyo's forward momentum had all but stopped. I paused several feet behind the ghostlights at the thinnest fringe of the fray. Keiji bent over, clutching his branch as he braced it against the ground.

Chiyo's sword was still whipping through the ghosts around her, felling ogres and demon dogs in turn, but for every one she dispatched two more seemed to barrel into the same space. Her form was hidden in the midst of our enemies and allies, but I thought the light of her ki was flickering again. My stomach knotted.

What good would I be doing, really, if I threw myself at the stragglers just to be killed? I needed to find a way to actually *help*.

"We have to get rid of some of the ghosts above her," I said to Keiji. "Let's see if we can circle around the battle—if they're going to treat us like we aren't a threat, we might as well make use of that attitude."

He nodded, and we staggered onward, veering to the right to give the main mass of ghosts a wide berth. As we climbed, others darted past us through the forest, paying us no mind even when I managed to catch one with a quick ofuda. As the veil between the worlds started to thin, perhaps Omori could summon them straight out of the afterworld again, and banishing meant merely a momentary delay now.

A gloom settled over me. If that were true, even if we made it to the front of the battle, what difference could we make there? I might be able to take out an ogre or two before a spirit or beast killed me, but that wouldn't be enough to get Chiyo any closer to Omori.

As I thought his name, a small shape fluttered over us: the feathered form of a sparrow. It dipped from tree to tree, heading up the mountain along the same course. I stared after it as we trudged on.

So Mrs. Omori was with us until the end. Maybe she hadn't completely given up on her husband, even now.

A tremor rattled the ground beneath us, and then another. The smoky smell had coated the inside of my mouth.

"I really hope the mountain doesn't decide to kill us before we can save it," Keiji said with a shaky laugh.

I stared up the slope. "Omori can't know what'll happen if the volcano erupts. Doesn't he care that he could end up buried in the palace? He's never going to get some new life for himself then."

"It's almost Obon," Keiji said. "He might not be able to think about anything else at this point, with all that demonic fury warping his mind. What's a little danger compared to fulfilling his life's—well, his death's wish?"

The image sprang into my mind abruptly of Tomoya walking up to that shrunken stream, the one the rest of his ghostly soldiers had shied back from. The one that had meant his doom. But he hadn't seemed to consider his safety.

Because it wasn't his safety he'd been acting for. He'd been thinking of Keiji, always, in his own warped way. Could it be that Omori wasn't doing all this for his own gain, but for someone else's, and that had blinded him to his own precarious position?

Anything was possible. Every account I'd heard and read of Omori suggested his death had wrenched him far from the principles he'd once held. Would the Omori who'd spearheaded disaster relief efforts approve of provoking another crisis? Would the Omori who'd insisted on a family breakfast every morning not care to acknowledge his wife's spirit? Would the Omori who'd provided amply for the woman who'd cleaned his house believe people who couldn't fight off a ghost's invasion had no right to their own lives?

My calves were cramping. I stopped for a moment, leaning against the trunk of a nearby pine, and realized we'd passed the main thrust of the battle. Chiyo's light was gleaming through the trees slightly below us now. And in the few minutes I stood watching, I didn't see it move forward an inch.

You are the only one of us who has been in Omori's presence, Takeo had pointed out yesterday. Of any of us, other than his speechless wife, I must know him best. I'd seen him hesitate. There might be a part of him, however tiny, that wasn't completely consumed by his fury.

Losing my life taking down one or two ogres might not be worth much, but if I could get Omori's ear and make his faith in this war waver... If I could distract him, even for a second, from channeling all that power to his army, it might give Chiyo the opening she needed.

"I'm going to make for the palace," I said to Keiji. "For Omori. I'm going to try..."

I wasn't totally sure what I was going to do. But blood to blood, heart to heart, or spirit to spirit, I had to find a point of connection that would sing through the demon's rage before Mt. Fuji spilled its own.

Keiji dipped his head. "Where you go, I'll follow."

So we climbed on, over roots and around bushes, into the thickening smoky air. My eyes started to water. The sounds of the fighting faded. My feet dragged over the dry earth, every muscle protesting now, but I forced myself to keep walking.

The landscape was becoming more familiar. When the babbling of the palace spring reached my ears, I turned to tell Keiji we were almost there, and found I was alone in the woods.

The battle raged on down the slope to my left. Sparks of ki leapt. Shrieks and hisses echoed through the air. Evening was falling, but the glow of so many ghostlights lit up the forest like an eerie dawn. I squinted through the dim light. I couldn't make out any movement on the slope below me. Keiji might have stopped to rest two minutes ago, or ten, and simply fallen back without speaking, worried if he'd said something I might have felt I had to stop too.

I swayed on my feet. My hair was sticking to the perspiration on my face; every breath burned in my lungs. But Keiji hadn't wanted me to hang back for his sake. He'd be safer farther behind me.

Gripping branches, I hauled myself onward and upward. After several more steps, something sticky squelched under my feet. A rancid smell clogged my nose, thicker even than the volcanic odor. I gagged as I recognized it.

The tree trunks around me and the pine needles that scattered the ground had been splattered with gore: dark splotches of blood and gristle and I didn't want to know what else. To prevent the kami from reaching the palace, presumably, Omori had drenched the ground around its entrance with his brand of poison.

Our other allies could make their way over this, though—if they had a chance to break through the onslaught.

I picked my way along, careful where I laid my hands. The sounds of the battle dwindled further, and with them the light. But a few seconds later I caught sight of the main entrance to the palace up ahead.

Omori stood at the cave's mouth, watching the fighting, his lips set in a confident smile. The energy within him seeped from his skin in a pulsing glow. A semi-circle of ghostlights hovered around him, but it was a small one.

Creeping from tree to tree, hidden in the dark beyond the ring of ghostlights, I approached the cave. The gore felt nauseatingly slick beneath my shoes, but it muffled the crackle of the pine needles. I palmed more ofuda and touched the gentle weight of the satchel on my back. I still had Omori's possessions, the things Mrs. Kobayashi had given me. Maybe those would help me break through his obsession.

Just before the clearing, I stopped and gathered myself with an indrawn breath. The last controlled breath I might ever take. My fingers clenched around the ofuda. I didn't let myself think of the risk, of the possible consequences. I had to get in there and say everything I could to get Omori's attention, to provoke a response. I sent a brief, silent prayer to the mountain. Then I hurled myself at the nearest ghost.

In the second it took for the ghost to realize that its ethereal form couldn't break the protection of my amulet, I'd banished it and the two on either side, crashing through their circle. Omori turned, but I couldn't face him with the others at my back. With every shred of strength left in my body, I flung myself around the ring, smacking out ofuda as the ghosts charged to stop me. The last one slashed his knife across my shoulder the instant before I banished him. I pressed my now-empty hand to the wound and spun toward Omori, who was striding over to me.

For all the power that buzzed around him, he was no taller than I was. But the hum of his ki radiated over me, humming off-key in a way that made my bones wobble and my words stick in the back of my mouth. I forced them out.

"After the Tohoku earthquake, Kenta Omori initiated a massive aid effort in Sendai," I blurted out. "He dedicated it to his wife, Emiko."

Omori paused a mere two feet away from me. His energy coursed off him so furiously it stung my skin, but I thought I felt the slightest quiver in it. He cocked his head.

"Is that your plan, young lady?" he said conversationally. "Are you trying to cut me down by stating facts?"

I was, I thought over the thumping of my pulse. The sword at my side was useless. My words could be a weapon if I wielded them right.

"Far more people may die *because* of you if you let Fuji erupt with all its kami trapped inside," I said. "Is that the legacy you wanted to leave behind?"

I couldn't even imagine a quaver this time. Omori chuckled, and a fresh sweat broke over my skin. He was playing with me. He could have blasted my human body to bits in an instant if he'd thought I posed any true threat.

"What does it matter to you?" he inquired.

"Why *doesn't* it matter to you?" I said. "Why do you care so much about giving all these ghosts another life, but not about the lives that will be lost?"

"They're already lost," he snapped with a flare of heat. I flinched backward, the sting prickling deeper into my face. Then his voice faltered, just for a moment. "They're all... They're already lost to me."

"Who?" I said quickly. "The people you used to work for? Go haunt *them* if it's revenge you want—they can't stop you. The people who worked for you still remember you. Mrs. Kobayashi told me how grateful she was for all you did for her and her husband."

He didn't seem to hear me. "They were innocent," he said. "They deserved more. They deserved *lives.*"

His rage boiled back to the surface. He stepped toward me, that dissonant ki flaring in his eyes. But my eyes had caught on his hand, on the brief rub of his thumb against his ring finger. Against his wedding band.

Lost. Innocent. Deserved more.

He'd focused on Mrs. Ikeda first in the audience room: the woman closest to the age Mrs. Omori was at her death. He'd stopped when I'd reminded him of a child's connection to her mother. That quiver, earlier—I'd mentioned his wife's name.

"Emiko doesn't want this," I said. "Your children wouldn't want this. Emiko hates what you've become. She wants you to *stop.*"

He halted again, and this time I felt the ripple in his energy for sure. His face grayed.

I saw it clearly then. Of course it was the loss of his family by such horrible, unfair means that had brought him so low, twisted him so monstrously, so much more than simple concern for himself would have. Hadn't Keiji let himself become complicit in a grievous betrayal rather than challenge his brother? Hadn't *I* been willing to give up who and what I truly was in the hopes of staying with the family I'd grown up with, when they weren't even my own? Love was such a powerful thing, but it could bring guilt and desperation. It could obscure everything else that mattered. Maybe I had more in common with Omori than I'd imagined.

Omori shook himself, his energy surging off him to sear my face and arms. "You don't know what you're talking about," he snarled, raising his hands. I stumbled backward, and the second blast he threw at me knocked me off my feet. I rolled away from him, biting back a whimper.

Speaking wasn't enough. He'd gotten so caught up in his desire for power that he didn't remember who he'd wanted that power to save. I needed... I needed...

My sword of words had failed. But I had a sort of mirror, too.

My shoulder hit a tree trunk. I pushed off it, jamming my fingers into my pocket as I pulled myself around. My joints groaned, but I managed to yank out the folded papers I'd been carrying since the first time I'd seen Omori's face. As the demon loomed over me, I tugged open the photo of the man with his family and thrust it up between us like a shield.

Omori froze. His eyes widened, fixed on the picture.

"*Remember,*" I said, my voice shaking. "Your wife. Emiko. Your children. You lost them. You wanted the power to get them back. But you thought you had power before, didn't you, and it only turned your colleagues against you. It's because of that power your family died. Getting more, hurting more people to get it, that can't make anything right."

Omori extended his arm. His fingers grazed the paper that held his family's image. "Emiko," he said. "Jun. Nobuo." His gaze slid up to meet mine and sharpened into a glare. "They shouldn't have died. They didn't deserve any of it. And then the kami left them to wander the afterworld alone, so lost I haven't been able to pull them out. Why shouldn't I make the mountain's spirits fix that mistake? I will never stop fighting for them."

My jaw went slack. Oh. He thought—

She'd tried to show him, but he'd never been able to see.

"That's not true," I said. "Emiko? You're here, aren't you?" I glanced around and spotted the brown shape of the sparrow gliding down onto a branch above me. Omori followed my look. He frowned, his demonic energy coiled around him, swirling and sizzling, restrained but ready to strike.

He couldn't see her even now. How could I clear the haze of rage from his eyes enough to let him recognize the truth?

A sword, a mirror... and a *jewel*. I dropped the papers to fumble with my satchel. Omori's head jerked down toward me. My fingers closed around his wife's ring.

"Emiko," I said. "Show him!"

I thrust my hand upward. The sparrow leapt down, snatching the ring from my fingers. As Omori reached as if to grab my wrist, she landed on his elbow. The emerald gleamed by her beak. Omori stared at it, and the energy blazing around him finally shrank all the way inside his skin.

The air shimmered around the sparrow, and the woman's filmy image appeared above it, her hand held out to her husband.

"Emiko," Omori breathed.

She tapped the sparrow's head, and it chirped. Two butterflies dipped over the top of the cave and swooped to perch beside her. The forms of two ghostly children shuddered into sight. Omori sank to his knees, his arm still held outright, tears streaking down his cheeks.

"I failed you," he said. "I wanted to be strong enough to stop it from happening, to find you, to bring you back... But it wasn't in my power. As before."

His wife laid her hand on his shoulder tenderly. He shivered at her touch. I straightened up against the protests of my legs. All at once I could see exactly how this could end. But I couldn't do it myself. I needed Chiyo.

"You have other kinds of power," I said. "You have the power to save all the people and creatures on and around this mountain from the destruction you've almost wrought, before your rage returns. Accept your death. Release the mountain from the prison of blood you've built, withdraw your support from the dead who are fighting for your cause, and let the sacred sword purify your spirit so you can be absorbed back into the world. Your family will live on without suffering, and you will still be with them no matter where they travel."

Omori looked around him at the gore-splattered forest, and revulsion contorted his mouth. "I... I did this," he said, as if he didn't quite understand. He regarded his wife. "What the girl said—is that what you wish?"

Mrs. Omori pressed her hands to her chest and inclined her head. His expression firmed. As he leapt to his feet, the sparrow and the butterflies fluttered to the side. He strode down the slope, burning a trail through the gore as he went. His family wisped after him, and I limped along behind.

"Stop!" Omori shouted as he approached the fringes of the battle. The nearest ghostlights stilled around him. "This must all stop, now!"

His army parted as he pressed onward, toward the spot where Chiyo was standing. Her face was flushed and her shoulders slumped, but her fingers still held tight around the hilt of the sacred sword. She pulled herself taller as her closest enemies fell back to make way for Omori. He stopped a few feet from her and raised his voice.

"This fighting will end! The pain, the suffering, it is over *now*. There has been too much already. I sacrifice myself to end this war."

He knelt before her, his arms spread wide, his face prepared. Chiyo smiled, weary but brilliant all the same.

"The mountain forgives you," she said, and lowered the sacred sword to his forehead. The second its blade touched his skin, the demon-warped spirit of Kenta Omori dissolved into glittering dust.

All across the forest, the ghostlights dimmed. Hundreds blinked out of existence in the time it took me to draw another breath, as if Omori's power had been the only thing holding them here. Which it quite possibly had. A wail went up as the others scattered. A few, strong enough to keep fighting and apparently unwilling to give up the idea of regaining bodies, rushed at the kami again, but Chiyo dispatched their weakened forms with a few sweeps of her sword. Their monstrous allies hesitated and seemed to decide the tide had turned too far for their liking. Ogres and demon dogs slunk away into the shadows.

My ankles twinged. I sank down onto the warm earth. My head was throbbing and my mouth cottony, but inside I felt light as air.

"Sora!" Keiji crouched beside me. I shifted toward him, resting my face against his chest, feeling the rise and fall of his sigh of relief. He rested his chin on the top of my head as he hugged me.

"Are you okay?" he asked.

I nodded, my throat too raw for speech.

“I saw it,” he said. “I caught up right when you were showing him the picture. You were amazing. And you didn’t even need any treasures.”

That wasn’t true. I’d just had a different sort. Insight. Recognition. Compassion.

Rin had said her vision could have just as easily been of me or Chiyo. Perhaps it had actually meant us both, together, with the strength we each had where the other faltered.

“You know what?” I said. “I’m glad I’m human.”

I heard Keiji’s smile in his voice. “Me too.”

TWENTY-FIVE

WHEN THE last of the ghosts had been dealt with, Takeo took my hand and Rin Keiji's. They helped us across the path Omori had cleared through the brush and blood and pulled us through the palace entrance into the main hall.

The smell of long-dried blood made the kami wince, and I realized my work wasn't done. "Bring in the tree fairies and the wolves and the others," I said.

Takeo nodded. "The rest of us will tend to the mountain's fire at once."

The kami with no training stayed behind to help guide our other allies in. As they joined us, I directed them to buckets, cloths, and water. We trudged in and out of the rooms, scrubbing at the surfaces, untying the ropes and nets that bound the prisoners. Freed, the palace kami stumbled to their feet to embrace us, many touching my face in wonder.

"Sora, you've returned!"

"Sora, I'm so glad you're safe."

“Sora, I hadn’t dared to hope...”

Several rushed off as fast as their tormented bodies could carry them to help soothe the mountain. As we moved on, Fuji’s ki began to tingle up through the floor into the soles of my feet. It felt hot and unsettled, but it calmed more with every moment that passed. Trickling over the walls and floors, it erased the remaining traces of Omori’s gory rule.

Finally we came to a room that held not just kami, but the scattered human prisoners the ghosts had collected as well. Chiyo, who’d been following behind us, squealed and kissed Haru so deeply the fairies twittered. He wobbled a little when he stood, and the scratch along his neck had scabbed, but he appeared mostly unharmed. Tomoya must have thought Omori would like him for a “specimen.”

Farther down the hall, I hurried through an all-too-familiar set of chambers, past the audience room where Omori had conducted his deadly experiment and into the room beyond. At the sight of Mother and Father lying beaten and wounded but alive, my legs locked. Chiyo rushed past me, throwing her arms around her kami mother with a shower of healing ki. I hung back by the doorway as the other kami with us helped their rulers to their feet.

“I heard that Sora is still with you,” Father said hoarsely. I stepped forward tentatively and found myself swept up in one of his massive hugs, then wrapped in Mother’s arms.

“I—” I started to say when they released me, but I couldn’t think of how to continue. My eyes were full of tears, my head spinning with exhaustion and too many emotions I had no words for.

“You,” Mother said, her smooth hand caressing my cheek,

"need to heal as much as we do. You and your friends must stay as our guests, and we can talk more when we've all had time to recover."

I had just enough energy left to nod in agreement.

⁂

Ayame caught me with a stag kami at her side on the way to my old rooms. She looked my bedraggled body over and tutted under her breath. "Kami or no, this is not how anyone sleeps in my palace. Katsu will tend to your injuries, and then I'm seeing you into a bath."

I stood limply as the stag lowered his head, casting cool streams of ki over my burns and bruises with his antlers. The pain in my side melted away as my broken rib knit back together.

"The mountain," I said to Ayame. "The fire—is it—?"

"We reached it just in time," she said, smoothing her hand over my forehead. "It's settled, for now."

When the healer had finished, Ayame drew me into the bathing room. I scrubbed and rinsed myself in a daze, let her drape silky nightclothes over me, and crashed into my bed.

When I woke up hours later, blinking sleep from my eyes as I gazed at the room around me, for a moment I almost believed it was still the night of my seventeenth birthday. I'd taken a nap and gotten lost in the wildest dream. But when I rolled over and felt the aches Katsu's magic hadn't quite reached, tasted the residue of smoke in my mouth, I snapped back to reality.

We'd saved the mountain, the people around it, everyone. I

stretched out on the feathery futon, reveling in that realization. All the fears that had been dogging me, all the catastrophes I'd spent the past days imagining, they were defeated now.

The light filtering in from outside suggested it was mid-morning. As its beams washed over me, it occurred to me that while the war might be over, my life was hardly settled.

Apprehension muted my joy just slightly. I got up and put on the plainest robe I could find in the cedar dresser before Ayame could arrive to fuss over me. Then I hurried down the hall to the rooms of Mt. Fuji's rulers.

Takeo was standing outside the door to their private chambers. The panel the ghosts had shoved the guard through on my birthday had been replaced. Takeo's expression brightened when he saw me, and I remembered the exact wording of my last order to him. *Until Mt. Fuji is safe...*

"Takeo," I said, coming to a halt. What could I say to him—my protector, my teacher, my friend—after everything we'd been through? Our friendship could never be the same as it had been. And his responsibilities lay elsewhere now.

He bowed. "I'm glad I was able to serve you as long as I did," he said. "If you should ever need... anything..."

I touched his arm when he faltered. "I know," I said softly. A lump was rising in my throat. The conversation after this was going to be even harder. "Thank you, so much, for everything."

He tipped his head with a whisper of ki through my fingertips that told me those were the only words he'd needed to hear. That he knew how truly I meant them.

"I'll tell Their Highnesses that you've come," he said. He

ducked inside and returned a moment later to escort me in.

I stepped into the room where once two kami had given their supposed daughter a flute as a birthday gift while she prepared to beg to learn the kami's most precious talents. That evening seemed another lifetime ago. In a way, I supposed it was.

On the other side of the low table, Mother looked as collected and Father as indomitable as ever, but they both had a teary glint in their eyes. Looking at them, I felt just how little remained of the girl who'd sat before them all those days ago. That Sora had never fought ghosts, never kissed, never tiptoed to the edge of death.

That Sora hadn't known she was human.

The pain I'd been braced for flared up, but duller than I'd expected. I'd already taken so many steps away from them.

"My girl," Mother said, and they both rose. "So now you know. I'm sorry we lied to you. It seemed to be the safest way to ensure the secret didn't slip out."

"It's been a pleasure to call you our daughter," Father said gruffly. "I can still remember when you were small enough that I could carry you with one arm..." He folded both arms over his chest awkwardly. "I hope you can forgive us."

What would my life have been like if I'd known from the start? Always aware the ki within me wasn't really mine, that what I thought of as my strength was borrowed? I'd have been spared the shock, but wouldn't my happiness for the seventeen years before have also been less?

"I don't know whether I wish you'd told me or appreciate that you didn't," I said, choking up again. "I loved it here. So much. I know why you did it. I can't be angry about the actions that helped save this place."

"We do love you," Father said. "We've thought of you as ours as much as Chiyo is."

Mother held out her hand. "We'd be so delighted if you stayed here as part of our family, Sora. The mountain won't hesitate to lend you its power again. No one here wishes to say good-bye to you, the two of us least of all."

"It's up to you," Father added. "If you think you'd still be happiest here."

Gratitude swelled inside me, drowning out the rest of the turmoil. But I already knew my answer.

"Thank you," I said. "More than I can say, thank you. But I think I've pretended to be something I'm not for long enough. There's a lot I can offer the world as a human too."

"Of course there is," Mother said, but as she blinked, a few tears slid down her cheek. Father cleared his throat. My own eyes overflowed, and I stepped toward them. They met me, enclosing me in an embrace from both sides. Their ki flowed through me, tinged with love and sadness. And I saw that the family I'd assumed I'd lost was still here after all. For a second, the pain burned deeper, despite my certainty that my decision was right.

"I'll still think of you as my parents," I said. "Even if I have other ones now. I—I don't want to lose you. I'll come to see you whenever I can."

"The palace will always be open to you," Father said as he squeezed me tighter. "And this mountain will welcome you home if you ever change your mind."

❖

When I slipped back into the main hall some time later, cried out but lighter in spirit, Keiji was leaning against the wall nearby. He looked as if he'd been waiting there for a while. His tapping foot stilled when he saw me. His gaze took in my robe, my smile.

"Hi," I said when he didn't speak.

"Hi yourself," he said, a little shyly. He straightened up, but then he just stood there, as if he wasn't sure he should be there at all.

"I think you'd really like it, living in Tokyo," he said in a rush. "There are tons of things kami don't have—at least, I don't think they do—that I haven't had a chance to even tell you about: other kinds of music, and movies, and clubs—and Disneyland, we could go there—I bet there aren't any kami amusement parks. Or malls. Or—"

"Keiji," I broke in. "What are you talking about?"

He lowered his head, his shaggy hair drifting over the top of his glasses and shading his coppery eyes.

"I know you're probably thinking of staying here," he said. "And I know they'd let you. Of course they'd let you. So I thought I should mention all the things you'd be missing."

"I'm not staying," I said.

"Really?" He glanced up so eagerly I almost had to laugh.

"I don't know exactly what I'm going to do," I said. "I have to talk with the Ikedas, get to know them, I guess. And I'm not sure how school will work, since I haven't had a normal human education."

I paused, seeing the twist of his mouth. Why did he seem so out of sorts even now that—

Oh. He was waiting to hear something else entirely. I hadn't thought of that, because it was hard to believe he couldn't hear how loudly my heart sang as I looked at him.

"At least I'll have some help figuring all that out," I said, taking his hand. "I mean, I hope I will."

A grin to match mine spread across Keiji's face. He swept into a low bow, brushing his lips against my fingers. "I would enjoy nothing more than to stay by your side, my lady," he said.

And then I did laugh.

I had to brave a hundred more good-byes before I left. My kami grandparents hugged me in turn, whispering words of encouragement. Ayame took me by the shoulders and kissed my forehead, and then chided me about taking care of my hair. The other familiar figures of the palace came one by one, offering bows and squeezed hands and sometimes more tears.

By the time Chiyo and our kami parents had walked with Keiji, Haru, and me to the palace entrance, I was drained but ready. The midday sun greeted us outside. An early morning thundershower had washed away the smell of smoke and all remaining sign of Omori's bloody defenses. I tipped my face to the hazy blue of the sky, the rain-fresh air rejuvenating me. Then I turned toward the foot of the mountain, where the dark roofs and winding roads of the town lay hidden beyond the trees.

I almost glanced to where Midori would have been hovering by me, ready for adventure, and caught myself with a sharp pang. Not all of us had survived this war who should have.

There were others I might still help. I could go visit Mr. and Mrs. Nagamoto now, properly. The kami rules I'd been committed to following weren't mine anymore. I could let them see me—I could tell them what their family meant to me. If Mr. Nagamoto didn't know yet about the sickness inside him, I could even warn him.

As soon as we got to Keiji's car, I'd ask him if we could make just one stop before we headed to Tokyo.

Mother and Father pulled me into one final embrace, and Chiyo threw her arms around Haru, kissing him soundly. "You'll come visit all the time," she instructed. "At least once a week. And I'll visit you in the city too. Just because I'm kami doesn't mean I'm giving everything up!" She turned to me. "You've got to come hang out sometimes too," she said. "We're like sisters now, don't you think?"

"We are," I said, smiling. "I'll come."

"I wouldn't mind joining you when you do," Keiji said as we started down the path. "I'd like to see more of Mt. Fuji when it's not covered with yakuza ghosts out for our blood."

"I'll second that," Haru said.

I dragged the sweet summer air into my lungs as the breeze tickled over my human skin. I was giving up a life full of magic and music, the only life I'd really known. But I didn't feel a single pinch of regret.

I'd found other sorts of magic. The knowledge that strengths could be weaknesses, and weaknesses strengths. The ability to read my own ever-shifting emotions, to reach through them to imagine life from another person's perspective, and to accept all the ways my many-sided nature allowed me to be. Living as a kami had been glorious, but it was just one kind of music. This new life I'd discovered in the last week, for all the hurt and confusion that had come with it, held more rhythms and harmonies than I'd ever dreamed of.

I couldn't wait to find out where my song would take me next.

ACKNOWLEDGMENTS

THIS BOOK was seven years in the making, and it would not exist without the assistance of a great number of people.

To the guides, museum staff, and all the others who pointed me in the right direction as I followed Sora's path through Japan and who made my travels there an unforgettable experience;

To the Ontario Arts Council, whose Works In Progress grant helped support me and my family as I wrote;

To Deva Fagan, Amanda Coppedge, Robin Prehn, Jackie Dolamore, Jenny Moss, Aprilynne Pike, the members of the Toronto Speculative Fiction Writers Group, and my agent, Josh Adams, whose feedback shaped Sora's story in invaluable ways;

To Izumi Tanaka, Eddy Jones, Misato Soejima, Kimberly Ito, and the others who offered cultural guidance and checked the manuscript for errors (any mistakes remaining are my own);

To Marissa van Uden and Kimberly Ito (again), whose editing skills transformed my manuscript into a fully realized book;

To Carlos Quevedo, whose cover illustration captured Sora exactly as I envisioned her;

To Colleen Sheenan, who created an interior design as gorgeous as that cover;

To all my writer friends and colleagues who've had my back and shared advice when I needed it;

To my family, especially my husband and son, for their patience and love as I worked to bring my vision into being;

And to the readers who've stayed with me across my various books, who've written fan letters and reviews, who've made me feel that what I do is not only appreciated but important;

I offer my immense gratitude and the hope that you find this story worthy of your efforts.

Interested readers can find a more detailed account of my research on Japan and its mythology, as well as recommended media lists, on my website at, www.megancrewe.com/song.

ABOUT THE AUTHOR

LIKE MANY authors, Megan Crewe finds writing about herself much more difficult than making things up. A few definite facts: she lives in Toronto, Canada with her husband and son (and does on occasion say "eh"), she's always planning some new trip around the world, and she's spent the last six years studying kung fu, so you should probably be nice to her. She has been making up stories about magic and spirits and other what ifs since before she knew how to write words on paper. These days the stories are just a lot longer.

Megan's first novel, *Give Up the Ghost,* was shortlisted for the Sunburst Award for Canadian Literature of the Fantastic. Her second, *The Way We Fall,* was nominated for the White Pine Award and made the International Reading Association Young Adults' Choices List. She is also the author of the rest of the Fallen World series (*The Lives We Lost, The Worlds We Make,* and *Those Who Lived*) and the Earth & Sky trilogy (*Earth & Sky, The Clouded Sky,* and *A Sky Unbroken*).